Copyright © 2020 by Lovestruck Romance Publishing, LLC.

All Rights Reserved.
No part of this publication may be reproduced, distributed or transmitted in any form or by any means including photocopying, recording, or other electronic or mechanical methods except in the case of brief quotations embodied in critical reviews and certain other noncommercial uses permitted by copyright law. The unauthorized reproduction or distribution of this copyrighted work is illegal.

This book is a work of fiction. Names, characters, businesses, places, events, and incidents are either the products of the author's imagination or used in a fictitious manner. Any resemblance to actual persons living or dead is purely coincidental.

This book is intended for adult readers only.
Any sexual activity portrayed in these pages occurs between consenting adults over the age of 18 who are not related by blood.

P.O.L.A.R. (Private Ops: League Arctic Rescue) is a specialized, private operations task force—a maritime unit of polar bear shifters. Part of a world-wide, clandestine army comprised of the best of the best shifters, P.O.L.A.R.'s home base is Siberia...until the team pisses somebody off and gets re-assigned to Sunkissed Key, Florida and these arctic shifters suddenly find themselves surrounded by sun, sand, flip-flops and palm trees.

CONTENTS

RESCUE BEAR	1
HERO BEAR	119
COVERT BEAR	233
TACTICAL BEAR	349
ROYAL BEAR	475
Join our group	601
Special Offer	603
Other books from Candace Ayers...	605

P.O.L.A.R.

COMPLETE SERIES

CANDACE AYERS

LOVESTRUCK ROMANCE PUBLISHING, LLC

RESCUE BEAR

P.O.L.A.R. 1

One week.

That's all it took for Megan's world to fall apart.

She lost everything.

Her marriage—shattered.
Her business—demolished.
Her life—ruined.

Enter one hot Rescue Bear to pick up the pieces,
build her back up,
and shower her with the love she's never known and always deserved.

1
MEGAN

I knew before I walked any further into my house that I was about to become a cliché. Wife walks in on husband sleeping with someone else, wife screams and cries and tears at her hair. Husband, wearing a sheet and nothing else, chases angry wife and apologizes profusely as she runs out of the bedroom. There was nothing original about the scene that was about to play out.

I listened to the loud moans, the grunting, the rhythmic knocking of my bedframe into the wall behind it. I couldn't remember the last time I'd been in the room as that bedframe rhythmically knocked into the wall.

I stood at the bottom of the staircase staring at the framed photos that hung on the wall in the hallway just outside our bedroom door. I'd taken each one with care—capturing just the right lighting and angles in each of them. I'd managed to make Dylan look broader and "manlier" while also making myself look smaller and daintier. That hadn't been easy. Then, after selecting the best proofs, I'd obsessed over the perfect matting and frame selection. Weeks of work had gone into the grouping on the wall. A thin layer of dust coated the top of each of the frames.

The third stair always creaked. I skipped it as I climbed. I'd been meaning to fix it. It probably just needed a couple of screws to secure it. I'd refinished the staircase myself last year, but it probably still needed a little work. Just like the railing by the sixth step. The underside could use another sanding and a reapplication of stain. Those things were just a couple of the small projects on my list—a list that kept growing longer and longer. With no time to do anything but work in the shop that Dylan and I owned, the house had been somewhat neglected.

Our bedroom door was ajar. A crumpled shirt on the floor, one that I recognized, had blocked it from fully closing. Or so it appeared. I'd ironed that shirt for Dylan just this morning. Now, crumpled carelessly on the floor with a button missing, it told a story of fevered passion. Said button was next to it, resting face down, possibly in shame of what was occurring on the bed nearby.

Further into the room, were two pairs of pants, entwined. Another shirt, significantly smaller. It'd always bothered me that my shirts weren't much smaller than Dylan's. Really, it was only the cut that made them appear smaller. Beyond the tiny shirt, tiny underwear on the floor next to Dylan's boxers. His socks. Why had he taken his socks off last? It would've made him look so stupid. The nude male body in just a pair of black cotton dress socks looked ridiculous.

Standing outside of my bedroom door like some sort of burglar or peeping Tom, I was too afraid to lift my eyes from the clothing trail to the bed. It was the bed Dylan's mother, Sandy, had gifted us. It was some fancy thing that came with remotes and a built-in heating system. Why we needed that in Florida, I'd never know. The sheets, I'd picked out while visiting my brother in DC. His wife and I had gone on a shopping trip for the perfect bedding for my very first co-owned bed. Something soft, but not too feminine for Dylan's taste.

The sounds grew louder. I felt like a third wheel, the only person in the room not caught in the throes of passion. Why did I feel like the intruder? It was *my* house. I had this weird feeling I'd walked into someone else's home and was witnessing their personal moment. Two lovers, bound together, unaware of the unwanted spectator edging her way in. Why in the world I felt guilty was beyond me.

When I forced my gaze higher, my eyes landed on a petite, shapely back. A small mole dotted her right shoulder and an even tan went all the way down the slim waist with no visible tan lines. Blonde hair bounced wildly from a ponytail, my husband's hand entangled in it as they rocked together. His hand, a part of him that I'd always found so attractive, was a shade darker than her tan, the golden hairs dusting it just so. It was a beautiful hand, strong and well formed. I loved that hand.

My carefully selected sheets were bunched at the end of the bed, the light duvet on the floor by Dylan's socks. From my angle, I could see everything. Dylan's legs, his paler feet digging into the mattress, pumping his hips upward. The owner of the beautiful back had her small feet planted on either side of my husband's thighs, her toes curling. Her tight ass, her perfect curves, their joining, I could see it all.

I could see everything but Dylan's face. His handsome face was obscured by her body, his voice muffled as he grunted a name I didn't recognize. That same face that had smiled at me that midmorning when he told me he had to step out of the shop to run some errands. As it pertained to the business side of the shop we owned, I wouldn't understand it, of course. No need to worry my little brain about it. That face that had kissed my chin, an awkward miss of a kiss that I hadn't thought to laugh at, was buried in the chest of a woman with perfect curves, a beautiful back, and a tight ass. It was calling out another's woman's name as he reached orgasm. It hadn't been so long that I didn't recognize the sound of his orgasm.

Just to the side of their clutched hands, over on the nightstand, was a picture of me and Dylan on our first date. Ten years earlier, at a pizza shop. He'd wanted pepperoni. I'd wanted sausage. We'd gotten pepperoni. A younger, more naive version of my own face stared out from the picture frame and onto what was happening on the bed, her smile appearing strained even then. Maybe she knew deep down. Next to her, Dylan. Dylan, always charming. Dylan, never wrong. Dylan, best boyfriend and worst husband. *My* Dylan.

Groaning and ruffling of the sheets drew my attention back to my bed, and I watched as beautiful back rolled off of my husband and curled into his side. They spoke to each other with the breathiness of an orgasm's afterglow, still unaware of my presence.

I didn't want to be a cliché. I didn't want to be the wife who found her husband in their bed with another woman. I didn't want any of it.

I was never the type to run from problems, though. I squared my shoulders, shoulders much broader than those of the petite woman lying naked next to my husband, and cleared my throat. My voice was steady and clear.

"We should probably talk, huh?"

2

ROMAN

Sunkissed Key was about as hot as the fires of hell. It would've been scorching even if I wasn't a polar bear shifter accustomed to frigid climates. As it was, I was melting into the ground. I couldn't remember a time since we'd arrived that I hadn't been sweat-soaked. My bear absolutely hated this miserable hellhole.

Our P.O.L.A.R. office on Main Street had two window air-conditioning units. The damn things blew a stream of cold air about two feet forward in a straight line, never actually dispersing it throughout the room or cooling much of anything down. Only when I stood directly in front of them did I find any sort of relief. Then, I had to deal with listening to the others bitch about blocking the cool air.

P.O.L.A.R. was our private ops task force, a specialized, clandestine unit within a worldwide army of shifters. Our unit name: League Arctic Rescue. There were six of us in our unit: Serge, Maxim, Dmitry, Alexei, Konstantin, and me. The "Arctic" part of "League Arctic Rescue" meant that we were usually based in a colder climate—Siberia, to be specific—where the daytime temperature didn't plaster our thick fur to our bodies while we drowned in our own perspiration.

Due to a little screwup, we found ourselves abruptly transferred to what could accurately be described as Dante's butthole on Earth—Sunkissed Key, Florida.

A month had passed and none of us had gotten acclimatized. It was mid-September and showing no signs of cooling off. Swimming in the vast expanses of the Atlantic Ocean and the Gulf of Mexico helped, but as soon as we stepped out of the water, the hot sun beat down mercilessly.

I was sitting under one of the AC units in the office when we got the first hurricane warning. It wasn't the biggest surprise. Something had felt off for days, and the way the pressure in the air shifted over our fur had been mentioned a few times. When headquarters sent us the memo, it all made sense. It would be our first hurricane, and I couldn't help but get a little excited.

We were used to doing real private operations work in Siberia—infiltrating organized crime, ensnaring double agents, doing the dirty jobs that government agencies didn't keep paperwork on. The only thing we'd done since arriving in Sunkissed Key was break up bar fights, dissolve domestic squabbles, and drip sweat. The prospect of real danger was almost like an icy cool breeze. Almost.

Serge, the team leader of P.O.L.A.R., stood and walked over to the printer. After a few seconds, the thing spat out a sheet of paper which he snatched up. He scanned it and thumped it, just as excited as the rest of us. "It's about a week out. Looks like its path is going to slam right into us—head on, boys."

Dmitry stood up and nodded. "Okay."

"How do we prepare for a hurricane?" Alexei looked around the office like he was going to find a prep kit at his feet. "I mean, I've watched *Gilligan's Island* and all, but I'm not sure we can tie everyone on this island to a tree."

"They didn't tie themselves to trees." I frowned. "Did they?"

Serge shook his head. "It makes no difference what a bunch of actors did in a zany sixties sitcom. We're getting off track here. Can we focus, please?"

"I'll call headquarters for detailed instructions," I offered. "They hate me slightly less than they hate you bunch."

Maxim snorted. "That's only because your sister works in the main office."

Shrugging, I reached for the phone, but Serge was faster. He pointed the mouthpiece at me and smirked. "Too slow. I love pissing off headquarters. It's what I live for. You useless SOBs scout the island and find out what the locals do in these situations. God knows they've been through this before."

I scowled at Serge, not thrilled about being sent out in the heat. Even though the air conditioners sucked, they were better than the outdoors and straight sunshine. "Should I remind you that we're here, on this flaming head of a matchstick, because of you?"

He just laughed. "Yet, somehow, I'm still the boss and I still outrank you."

My bear didn't like the reminder that someone else outranked him. It was always an issue in our league. We were all dominant brawlers, and our animals tended to be loners. Each one of us knew logically that in order for the unit to work efficiently, we needed to kowtow to an alpha, but knowing it was one thing. Doing it wasn't as easy.

Despite getting us banished to Florida, Serge was a good bear, a great soldier, and an even better man. He had never led us wrong in all the years he'd been our unit leader.

Konstantin stood up from his spot in the corner of the office and stretched. He never said much, and that moment was no exception. He just silently left the office and shut the door behind him just as quietly. He was like a ghost most days.

Alexei groaned. "I'll follow Ghost. He freaks the locals out when he's alone."

Maxim scooted his chair up to his computer. He was the techie of the league. "I've got this. Nothing that Google can't provide answers for."

With nothing left to do in the office, I sighed. Outside, it was. I clapped Dmitry on the shoulder as I passed him and used my best Austrian accent. "I'll be back."

Opening the door and stepping outside, I felt like a casserole stepping into a preheated oven. I shielded my eyes and squinted around at my surroundings.

Our P.O.L.A.R. office was in a rented office space at the southern tip of the island. The last building before the island sloped into a sandy beach leading to the ocean. The view was stunning. Ocean as far as I could see, which, for a polar bear shifter, was far. It was a picturesque place and, if it wasn't so miserably hot, it would've been a nice place for a vacation.

Sunkissed Key was a three-mile stretch of land with one main road splitting it into two halves. Business controlled most of Main Street, from one end to the other, with homes dotting smaller roads that split off it. There was a lot of beach, a lot of beauty, and a lot of vulnerable areas if the hurricane did come at us head on.

It was probably unwise to be excited about the idea of a hurricane coming. Lord knew I didn't want anyone to get hurt or killed, but we were specially trained bears, built to fight and trained to rescue. And, we were slowly dying on this island. If the heat didn't kill us, the boredom surely would. We all could do with a little excitement.

Plus, we would each do everything in our power to ensure the safety of the island's residents. We were the best of the best—highly-trained, adept operatives. If need be, we would protect our charges with our very lives.

3

MEGAN

I sat on the top step of our staircase and waited for Dylan and his mistress to get dressed. Their hushed whispers were a one-eighty from their former passionate cries. I could hear parts of what they were saying. Dylan was shocked that I wasn't at the shop. She was mad at Dylan for putting her in such an awkward situation. He was pissed at me—for coming home. It was great stuff, really.

A few minutes later, she rushed past me on the stairs. She didn't look back. I never even got a good look at her face, although I imagined she was as stunning from the front as she was from the back. Even her voice was attractive.

Dylan was slower to emerge. He even took a shower first. I glanced at my watch a few times, wondering how long he was going to drag this whole thing out. The shop was closed while we were both away. He had to know that. Normally, he had a tantrum if we left the shop closed for longer than fifteen minutes.

I sat there, my elbows resting on my knees and my chin in my hands. I didn't know what I was feeling. My mind was racing with stupid thoughts that made no sense. I couldn't stop thinking about all of the projects I needed to finish around the house and about how much there was on my to-do list.

I expected anger to bubble up at some point—or sadness. My husband had cheated on me. In our own house, in our own bed, while I was off working at *our* business that *he* insisted we open. Yet, instead of being incensed, which would have been the logical response, I sat there picking at my nails wondering when Dylan would emerge from the bedroom. As each minute ticked by, nothing. And I just couldn't stop thinking about all I needed to do.

"Megan..." Dylan's voice had the same edge to it that it always had. Nothing gentle about him, it was like he'd been fighting the world since the day he was born. "Who's at the shop?"

I watched as he skirted around me, descended and stood at the landing at the bottom of the stairs. The entry table beside him needed to be refinished. I'd picked it up at a flea market and it needed some love.

"Megan?"

I looked at my husband and squinted. I recognized the man standing there, but I didn't. Appearance-wise, he was the same. He looked like the man in the photos taken on our wedding day, but he wasn't. There was something in his expression that hadn't been there before. A slight curl to his lip, the wrinkle of his nose, as though he'd smelled something distasteful.

"Come on, Megan. What? Are you really going to give me the silent treatment? Talk to me. You're not a child."

It was me. I was the something distasteful that made his lip curl and his nose wrinkle. I ran my tongue over my teeth, searching my brain for the words that needed to be said, but I drew a blank. I didn't know what to say.

"Jesus. You want me to apologize? Fine. I'm sorry you had to see that. It's not like it's a surprise, though, right? We haven't been intimate in months."

I pulled myself to my feet and made my way down the stairs. "There's no one at the shop. I closed it to go looking for you. You weren't answering your phone, and Hurricane Matilda has altered its course. It's headed this way—expected to slam right into us."

"There's no one at the shop? Fuck, Megan. You're costing us

money that we need. What the hell were you thinking? Let's go. We need to get back."

I didn't want to be near him. I didn't know what to say to him. I wasn't ready to even try to form words from my thoughts or sentences from my words. "You go ahead. I've got stuff I need to do here."

He scowled. "You know you do all the floor stuff. That's your *job*. You can't just skip out on doing your job because we're having a bad day."

An image flashed through my mind—the image of Dylan on the floor, clutching his bloody nose after I bitch slapped the hell out of him. I had to take a step back. The urge to turn that mental image into a reality was so strong it scared me. I took another step back and then another and shook my head. "You go."

"Megan—"

"Dylan, there is nothing I want more in the world right now that to lay you out cold. I want to crack my knuckles on your face and see your nose twist the wrong way and plaster itself on the other side of your face." I balled my fists up at my sides. "The scary thing is that I'm not even angry right now. I just desperately want to see you in pain. So, I suggest you get the hell out of this house for a while. Go, work the job you swore you wanted. Or don't. I don't care. Just get out."

Looking shocked, he grabbed his keys and shook his head. "I don't know what's gotten into you."

I watched him leave and stood there until I heard his car speed away. He always drove through the neighborhood too fast. The neighbors complained to me, and I felt forced to make excuses and apologize for him, but he never felt apologetic about it and he never stopped. He said the car was meant to go fast.

I looked back down at the entry table that needed refinishing and blew out a deep sigh. It would give me something to do until I felt human again. I carefully took everything off it and placed it on the floor before carrying the table to the garage.

I was methodical in pulling out my sander and the sanding sheets. When the sander was ready, I turned it on and went to work on the table. With lots of nooks and crannies, it was a detailed job that eventually calmed my brain.

When I was alone, my solitude helped me arrive at solutions, but this time, I didn't like the solutions I came up with. Reality was staring me straight in the face and handing me some hard truths about my marriage. This truth wasn't easy to handle.

I wasn't a quitter, though. I'd made promises to Dylan and I'd meant them.

I lost all track of time, working and thinking. None of the answers I came up with made me feel any better. And, I still didn't feel sad or angry about Dylan's infidelity. What did that say about our relationship?

4
ROMAN

"This is crazy." Serge looked down the street. Standing next to the road, he posed with his hands on his hips while watching traffic slowly make its way north. "How are they all supposed to get out in time if they creep at a snail's pace?"

I stood beside him, a strange buzz starting inside of me. The energy on the island had picked up. Everyone knew something big was coming. My bear was riled up. Despite the heat, he was eager for the first time since we'd left Siberia. "I guess this is normal."

The northbound lane of Main Street was packed with cars—evacuees heading north to the mainland. Southbound was completely empty. No one dared venture farther south with Hurricane Matilda on its way. She was supposed to be big. According to the weather channel, she would be the biggest storm to hit the Keys in over a century. Unless she changed direction, she would make landfall in just under two days.

"Why didn't they leave when Matilda was first spotted? I don't know what we'll be able to do if there are this many cars still on the road when she hits."

I shrugged. "They'll be gone."

Alexei poked his head out of the office. "Upgraded to a cat five."

"Close the damn door! You're letting all the cold out." Dmitry's irritated voice rang out from inside.

Alexei, never one to follow orders, strode out of the office leaving the door wide open. In low-hanging shorts and an open shirt, he looked like a surfer. He was always laid back and easygoing, even in emergencies.

Dmitry grabbed the door and slammed it shut, grumbling the whole time.

"We should probably go around the island and encourage people to leave. See if they need any help with evacuating." Serge rolled his neck. "It makes my skin crawl to think of weak humans facing a hurricane of this expected magnitude."

I grinned as Serge's mate, Hannah, came out of the office and strolled toward him. Wrapping her very human body around his from behind, she sighed. "They're driving me crazy in there."

I could read the tension in Serge's face. He was very aware of how delicate his human mate was. He also knew she wasn't about to leave the island without him. Unless he nabbed a car and drove north, she was remaining on Sunkissed Key with the rest of us while Matilda battered the island. She was the real reason he was so anxious about the incoming storm.

To avoid hearing them argue about it again, I headed down the street, taking in the scene and trying to mentally calculate how many people were leaving versus how many would be staying. Thankfully, it seemed as though most of the island's residents would be seeking safer ground farther north. Houses were boarded up and garages and driveways were vacant of vehicles. As I scouted, whenever I came upon any of the few people still working, trying to board up their homes, I stopped to help.

The work was a far cry from the often perilous, tactical missions we'd performed while based out of Siberia, but it was something to do. I helped a few more people finish loading their cherished possessions into their cars and helped a few more cut into traffic. The little island was emptying faster by the hour. That was a good thing. People were heeding the threat. Matilda wasn't turning, nor was it growing weaker. She was headed our way with a vengeance.

I cut down Palm Street and then Parrot Cove Road to gain access to West Public Beach. The Bayfront Diner sat just off it, and Susie, who owned the place, was a sweet older woman who happily fed us cinnamon rolls and sweet tea all the time.

The sign in the window read *Closed*, but I could see Susie inside. She waved me in with a warm smile.

"Roman! Come on in, honey. I don't have anything made right now, but I can whip you up some cinnamon rolls in a jiffy." Her tall beehive of hair bobbed precariously on her head. She looked like she'd been caught in the middle of fixing it.

"What are you still doing here?" I sat across from her on a worn barstool and frowned. "You're not planning to stay, are you?"

She looked away. "I'm not planning, no. I *am* staying."

"Susie—"

"Now, Roman. I've lived on this island my entire life. I've been through rougher hurricanes than this one a-coming. I'm not leaving my diner." She reached under the counter and pulled out a coffee cup. "Coffee?"

I shook my head. "I'll watch over the place for you. No sense in you tempting fate."

"And no sense in you trying to convince a hard-headed old woman who has her mind already made up." She poured me a cup of coffee. "You need coffee. I don't care what you say. Everyone needs coffee."

I took a long sip just to be polite. I tried to ignore the fact that I was adding warmth to my already overheated body. "Where will you be bunking down for the storm?"

"Right here. My Sammy helped me build this place. It's all I've got and I ain't leaving it." She looked out through the front windows at the bay and smiled. "Although, I could use some help with boarding up the windows."

I downed the rest of my coffee and stood. "Say no more. Do you have boards, or should I go find some?"

She pointed me to the back and grasped my arm. "You're my favorite of the gang, you know that?"

It would've been a more flattering compliment if I hadn't heard her say the same thing to Alexei just last week. Still, she made me smile. "Flattery will get you everywhere."

5

MEGAN

I dragged the large sheet of plywood out of the rear of the shop and toward the front. The windows were still uncovered. It seemed that while I'd been on a hiatus from reality for the past few days, Dylan hadn't bothered to take care of closing up the shop. Every single business on the island had been boarded up. Every one but ours. Maybe he'd been too busy boning his girlfriend.

I shook my head and huffed as I stopped to take a breather. Balancing the wood against my hip, I looked around the shop dejectedly. Nothing had been put away. Nothing had been taken care of.

Dylan was sitting in the back, in his office, doing god only knew what. He was well aware that I was in the showroom—alone. Working to get the windows boarded up—alone. Did he care? Apparently not.

My anger toward him that was long overdue had been gradually coming to a simmer the last couple days. Suddenly, it threatened to boil over. "Dylan, can you *please* help?"

We hadn't spoken much since the disaster that Monday afternoon. I'd been in the garage pretty much nonstop since then, finishing each and every project on my list. I'd jumped head first into completing all the things I'd put off in exchange for working endless hours in the shop. I'd barely come up for air and, more notably, I'd avoided my husband.

My anger had grown. My sadness had not.

In truth, I didn't even know which one of us I was angrier at. Him, for being a lying, cheating backstabber, or myself for deciding not to throw in the towel.

I wasn't a quitter. I'd made vows. Together we owned a home, a business, and two cars. We'd gone through the ups and downs of life together for over ten years. I wouldn't just walk away from that at the first sign of trouble. There had to be some way to salvage our marriage.

"I'm busy, Megan." Had his voice always been so condescending and I'd just not realized it, or was that a recent development? Maybe he thought less of me for staying, too.

"This is important."

"You're strong. You can handle it." He'd barely stepped foot out of his office before he turned to go back in with a shrug of his shoulders.

"Dylan. I need help. I can't hold this board up and nail it in place, too." My voice sounded like I was forcing it out through gritted teeth. Probably because I was.

"I don't know what to tell you. That's your area. You ought to enjoy it, since that kind of thing is all you've wanted to do lately." He gestured toward the wood in my hand. "You sure have been slacking here at the shop."

"You could've had your girlfriend cover my shifts, I guess." I threw that down like a gauntlet, ready to duel it out with him if he was going to be such an asshole.

"She has a job, Megan. And don't be ridiculous. She's not going to come here and do *your* job."

"Oh, no? She seemed to like doing my job in our bed a few days ago."

"So, you want to do this now?" He nodded and walked toward me. "Granted, Brandi and I shouldn't have been in our bed, Megan, but let's face it, you haven't been meeting my needs. None of this has." He waved his hand around, gesturing to our surroundings.

My head snapped back like he'd slapped me. His indication that our shop was somehow at fault for his behavior was the breaking point. "Oh, this hasn't met your *needs*? The shop that *you* insisted we open? The shop that you begged and pleaded for, the shop you bitched about for months until I gave in? And why was that again? Because no other work around this island fit your *needs*? So, the shop we opened because you couldn't get another job not filling your *needs* either, now?"

"Geeze, you're mad because I criticized the shop? Not that I was screwing someone else in our bed? Doesn't that say it all?"

I opened my mouth to argue and then snapped it shut. Everything that was on the tip of my tongue—all the anger and vitriol that was right there ready to be spewed—was contrary to the decision I'd made. None of it would help solve our issues or heal our marriage. "Dylan, neither of us have had our needs met lately. The answer wasn't to sleep around on me, though. We should've worked it out. Together."

"Yeah, well, that's not how it played out." He turned to walk away. "I need to finish up some paperwork back here."

"No. We need to batten down the shop. It's a two-person job, Dylan. I can't do it alone."

"Stop acting as though you're helpless, Megan. You're a *big girl*."

His words—casual and flippant—tumbled from his mouth so easily, yet they hit me like a brick. The extra pounds I carried were an area of self-deprecation for me. Walking in on my husband and his mistress and seeing her petite figure with a waist the size of a child's hadn't helped my insecurities. Dylan knew all the ways I'd been teased from my teenage years on into college. I was a head taller than most of the rest of the girls and had always had a thick build.

He knew the impact the words "big girl" carried for me. Maybe it was a slip, but it was one he'd never made before.

"Fuck you."

Dylan jerked around and came at me with a furious expression twisting his face. "No, fuck you!"

I let the wood fall to the floor with a loud slap. "Why? For walking in on you? For forcing you to work in the shop alone, the same way you've made me do so many times before, probably so you could sneak off to be with another woman?"

"Oh, poor Megan. You've had it so rough, haven't you?"

I backed away. "You know what? You can close up yourself."

"Fuck that."

"Close up the shop or let everything be ruined by the storm. I don't care. I'm tired of picking up all the slack for you."

"Go to hell, Megan. This! This right here is why I have Brandi. She's not sour and bitter like you." He grabbed my upper arm and yanked me back around to face him. "You think you're so much better than me. I can see it. The way you've been acting the past few days. You think you're suddenly "holier than thou" because you didn't sleep around. But put yourself in my shoes. Married to someone who's cold and dead inside. It's like being married to a big, limp fish. Jesus, Megan, I think I hate you."

His fingers cut into me as he spoke, my arm throbbed under his grip, but I refused to flinch. I wasn't going to let him know how badly he was hurting me—both physically and emotionally. "Let me go."

He immediately released me and shook his head. "I don't know why I even try."

I laughed bitterly while rubbing my arm. "You're trying?"

He just marched back into his office and slammed the door.

I could no longer hold back the tears. Through blurred vision, I let myself out of the shop and drove home. With practically the entire island evacuating north, the southbound lane was vacant. Our home at the end of Beach Street was, appropriately, on the beach. It stood feet from the ocean on pillars. It was a beautiful home, inherited from my grandparents, and I'd nearly completely renovated it myself.

My home. No longer *our* home, if that's what I chose. I could kick Dylan out—send him on his way. There'd been a prenup involved with our marriage, even though we'd gotten married at such a young age. I came from a family with money who'd demanded it. Perhaps they'd been smarter than I was and saw the inevitable future of my marriage to Dylan that I'd been blind to.

Divorcing Dylan was an option. As I looked down at the angry red fingertip marks on my arm that were turning purplish, it didn't seem like the worst option. I hated divorce, though. My family was one with a legacy of divorces. My mother and father were each other's third and fourth spouses, respectively. Their marriage had only lasted three years. And after their divorce, each had subsequently gone through several more spouses.

I didn't want to be another family joke.

In the guest room where I'd been staying, I crawled into bed and pulled the covers over my head. Finally, I allowed the tears that had been choking me on the drive home to flow freely. Once they came, they didn't feel as though they were ever going to stop.

6

MEGAN

Sunday morning. Matilda was still heading straight for us. I'd spent the night crying into my pillow and listening for Dylan to arrive home. He never did. When my alarm went off that morning at six, the same as it did every day, the local news blared warnings about the incoming storm.

Still a category five, it didn't look as though Matilda would go easy on the islands. It took Maverick Maine, the local DJ, sounding out his last broadcast to really light a fire under me. He was leaving the island, and the station would be broadcasting the national weather service alerts until he returned. Matilda was less than eighteen hours away.

I jumped up in a panic. Shit. I hadn't done anything to protect the house. I'd been so lost in the difficulties between Dylan and me that I'd let it completely slip my mind. Ugh, stupid. I didn't take time to change or shower, I just rushed downstairs and raced out onto the beach. The water already looked choppy and agitated. It seemed to know something big was coming. The sky was dark and gray, a harbinger of dangerous weather.

Other than the wind and waves, the surrounding neighborhood was eerily silent. Most people had vacated while I was in my stupor. I ran my hands over my face and then rushed to get to work. I could lose everything if I didn't board up the house.

My fury spurred me on as I worked tirelessly. The windows had shutters that I bolted closed. The first floor of the house was surrounded by a deck so those windows were easy to access. After making sure the shutters were secure, I nailed sheets of plywood over them, ensuring the house would be as protected as possible.

The second-floor windows were more of a challenge. Those had to be accessed by a ladder and each one took entirely too long. I couldn't carry a sheet of plywood up a ladder and then hold it steady over the windows while securing it. Not without help. So I nailed a couple of planks across the shutters on the second floor, in hopes that it would be enough. By the time I finished, I was flushed and sticky with sweat. The strong breeze coming off the ocean did nothing to cool me down.

Time was passing too rapidly. It had taken hours for me to secure the house alone. Before I knew it, it was late afternoon and the sky was darkening faster than it should have been. I was still tuned into the weather broadcast, and I could hear it blasting away in the house. While Matilda had been downgraded to a category four, she was moving in more quickly than first predicted.

In a state of sheer panic, I jumped in my SUV and sped down to the shop. In the back of my mind, I was hoping that Dylan had uncharacteristically stepped up and closed up our shop. I was hoping to maybe pull up and find him still there, finishing up.

Main Street was empty. Everyone had either already evacuated or, if they'd decided to stay put, had retreated indoors. I was the only idiot on the road. It took me less than two minutes to get to the shop and what I found made my heart sink. Nothing was covered. The glass windows that lined the front of our shop were still perfectly naked and I could see right through them to the prints in the shop, still on display. They had also not been packed up or moved to a safer location.

Dylan hadn't done a damn thing. I searched my pockets for my phone but came up empty. It was wherever I'd left it the night before

—probably on the guest bedroom nightstand. I slammed the car door, unlocked the shop, and headed straight to the office to grab the phone. I halted in my tracks when I saw the state of the small back room.

It was completely trashed. Empty file folders littered the floor, the desk drawers ransacked. The computer was gone, the safe under the desk was open—and empty. My hand flew to my open mouth as I sank into the office chair. I hadn't been around to do the deposit drop for a few days, but I knew we'd made several sales. I'd had some thank-you emails from customers saying they loved their new pieces. The register drawer was always placed in the safe. And it was there alright. But it was empty.

My brain reached for possibilities. We could have had a break in —been robbed. I knew the truth, though. My heart was in my toes as I reached for the phone with a shaky hand.

Dialing Dylan's number, I almost hoped he didn't answer. I didn't want to hear the truth. The reality I was facing was ugly and cruel, and I wasn't sure I could handle it while trying to take care of the business we owned together. I was devastated, not so much by the idea of losing him, more by the fact that my life was turning into a joke. I was also so furious with myself for falling into an avoidance/denial trance for the last week. I wasn't usually so lax about protecting the things I owned and cared about. I'd been through hurricanes before. I knew what to do and I'd always handled things capably and responsibly. Not this time. Waiting until last minute was not just stupid, it was dangerous. Hell, I didn't even have a decent evacuation plan.

The line clicked and Dylan's voice came through clear. "Megan."

I sank into the chair and looked up at the ceiling. It was stark white. I noticed a cobweb in a corner. "You took everything, didn't you?"

A heavy sigh. "I didn't have a choice. I needed the money."

"And the business? What? We just let it go?" My voice didn't even sound like my own. It sounded flat and vacant.

"I really don't have an answer. Maybe we should let the hurricane do its thing and collect the insurance money." He spoke to someone in the background and sighed again. "Look, Megan, you and I are over. We both know it wasn't working."

"Okay." I shook my head and sat up, feeling something unexpected pass over me—acceptance. "I guess you evacuated?"

"Yeah, of course."

If I was waiting for him to express an iota of concern for my well-being, I would have died waiting. I just dropped the phone into its cradle and looked back up at the cobweb. Something else I had only just noticed.

I couldn't afford to waste any more time. Even though I wanted to stay in that chair and obsess over how much money Dylan had taken and how he was spending it, most likely on Brandi, I couldn't. I had to take care of the shop. Just because my husband was an asshole, that didn't mean I was going to leave our shop to Matilda's wrath.

The prints hanging around the shop were worth thousands, money I would need to put back into the shop—and whatever damages Matilda wrought. I worked as fast as I could to take them down and layer them between packing blankets in the trunk of my SUV. Then I got all of the other delicate material out of the shop. The cheaper prints that I could redo if necessary, I carted into the office and stored on top of the desk, in case water did come inside.

Screwing plywood over the windows was a task for at least two people, but I managed to do an okay job of it. I had to ignore the strain on my body to get it done. Lifting and using my body to hold the boards in place while I stretched to screw in the bottom was painful and awkward, as was stretching my arms overhead to secure the top of the plywood.

The wind picked up as I went, and the sky grew darker. There were eight windows and a door that needed covering, but I was only halfway done when a gust of wind took the plywood I was holding and tossed it, end over end, down the street. The damn wind ripped it right from my hands, leaving them bloody and splintered from the rough ends of the wood.

My hair whipped around my head wildly. My oversized shirt

billowed out in front of me, and my eyes stung from the salty wind. When the rain started, goosebumps spread over my body. I'd never waited so long to evacuate, nor had I ever stayed on the island through a dangerous hurricane. I was about to experience my first time—with Matilda.

I doubted she'd go easy on me, either.

My brain worked at lightning speed to formulate a plan. I wasn't sure the house would be a safe place to ride out the storm. It was on the east side of the island, facing the Atlantic, and was where Matilda would hit first. I couldn't stay in the shop. Even if I did manage to get the rest of the windows boarded up, it wouldn't be structurally safe. I didn't know where to go. Maybe the medical center on the west side of the island. It was small but made from reinforced concrete. If I could get in, it would be safer than most places.

I turned back to the windows and, with a renewed determination, decided that I had time to finish and still make it to the medical center before the brunt of the storm hit. I went after the board that had flown down the street and got back to work.

My determination faded almost as fast as it had arrived, however, as the wind grew increasingly stronger. I was weak from the physical exertion I'd done all day—boarding up the house and then the shop —and hadn't thought to eat anything. I only got one more window done before I hit a wall. I didn't have enough energy or strength left to finish.

I stepped back from the shop and wiped at a stray tear. I felt as though life was closing a chapter on me that I hadn't planned on closing. No matter the situation, I didn't want to see the building damaged. It had been good to us.

Before I could continue my sentimental journey, a huge wind gust shoved me sideways. I caught myself and then looked east. Horrified, I saw that the shoreline was much closer than normal. The water was already coming in hard and fast. My heart raced.

I did my best to speedily shove everything in the shop higher up and farther away from the windows. When I'd done everything I could, I rushed back out and climbed in my SUV. In just the last ten minutes, the waterline had risen aggressively. I couldn't have made it back to my house, even if I'd wanted to. I floored it down Main Street to the small island medical center and parked in the ER entrance, the only place even remotely shielded from the wind and rain. I went around the back and worked quickly to pull a tarp over the prints, hoping that would offer enough protection if the windows blew out, then I closed and locked the doors.

The medical center had been evacuated early on. Maintenance had boarded the place up, protecting it from the storm and potential looters. I made my way slowly around its perimeter, searching for a way in. When I found none, I retreated to the SUV and sat in it, trying to think. I was soaked. The wind and rain rocked the vehicle; the howling made my stomach clench tightly. I didn't know where else to go. It was pitch dark by that point. The emergency broadcast system was saying that Matilda was arriving soon; a storm surge of ten to fifteen feet was expected.

It was too late to try to drive inland. It was too late to make it anywhere else. I put my head in my hands and cried. It wasn't very helpful, but I was out of options.

7

ROMAN

My bear was unusually unsettled—more so than I ever remember him being. Matilda came in with a raging attitude, beating the little island of Sunkissed Key with unbridled ferocity.

I was an adrenaline junkie—all of us in P.O.L.A.R. were—which was why we chose to do the work we did. Despite the fact that I was no stranger to hazards or risks, and I'd certainly been in more perilous situations, there was something different this time. Exciting, sure, but it also felt like something ominous was lurking just over my shoulder—something that made the hairs on the back of my neck stand on end.

The storm had just started, at a little past ten in the evening, and already, within a half hour, the east side of the island was flooded. Alexei was hanging out on a rooftop somewhere, watching and keeping us up to date. I was jealous, but I didn't want to leave Susie's. I could tell the older woman was nervous, and I wasn't about to let her face Matilda on her own.

For about the thousandth time, I stifled a growl and rolled my neck. My bear was highly agitated. "Having fun so far, Susie?"

She looked up from her find-a-word puzzle book and shrugged. "As long as my place is still standing in the morning, I'm good."

I forced a laugh and paced over to the covered windows. I wanted to see outside. I kept feeling like something was happening out there. Something I should know about, or take care of.

Anything, Alexei? I called to him through our mental link, hungry for any news.

This storm is wild! Even in my head, I could feel the energy radiating off him. *I don't know how much longer I'll stay up here, but it's been worth watching.*

See anyone in need of assistance? My bear growled again, growing even more riled. He kept urging me to go out on a rescue mission, but there was no one out there. No matter how many times I told him, and how much I tried to convince him, he just grew more determined.

No one would be crazy enough to be out in this. I think I'll head your way. Susie have any of those cinnamon rolls?

I looked over at the covered plate—what was left of the cinnamon rolls she'd made for me about twenty minutes ago. *A few. Come on. I'm going to switch positions with you for a bit. I have a weird feeling in my gut.*

Alexei showed up a few minutes later, soaked to the bone and grinning like a madman. He wiped his face and made a beeline for the cinnamon rolls. "Susie, will you marry me?"

She smiled at him. "What would you boys do without an old lady like me to look after you? Why you insist on going out in this is beyond me. It's too dangerous."

I nodded to Alexei and moved toward the door. "We'll be okay, Susie. We're trained for this kind of stuff. Come lock this behind me, Alexei. I'll let you know when I'm on my way back."

I didn't wait for them to reply. My bear was ripping at my flesh to get out and search for whatever it was that had him so worked up. I'd barely gotten ten feet from the diner before he tore free, shredding my clothing and slapping large paws down in the standing water. I lifted my head to the sky and inhaled through my elongated snout. Every one of my senses was heightened in that form, but most of all my sense of smell. I breathed deeply, searching for anything that stood out as unusual.

Salt air, island scents, and something sweet but soiled with the bitter tang of fear. My heart leaped and I ran toward the scent. A faint scream pierced the howling wind and crashing waves. Racing faster, it wasn't long before I was swimming. The surge had hit, and the island was more water than land.

Hear that? Serge came in urgent.

I've got it. Headed toward it now. I'll let you know if I need backup.

I passed the last house and felt a rip current tugging at me. I let it pull me closer to the sound of the scream. It carried me deeper into the ocean, farther south, deeper into the storm. Whoever was out there wouldn't last long. The ocean was a dangerous beast, even when not stirred up.

A flash of lightning lit up the sky, and for a split second, I saw the person. About a hundred yards out, someone was flailing to stay above the rough water. Once spotted, I was able to keep them in my sights, even in the dark. I watched as a wave crashed over them, dragging them under. My heart squeezed painfully and I pushed my muscles through the churning water.

Swimming as fast as I could, it still took me several seconds to get to the spot where I saw the person go down. It was rougher seas than I'd ever attempted to navigate before. I dove under and searched the dark waters.

A white shirt stood out and I was on it—her—in seconds. She was unconscious, and not breathing. She did not look good. My pulse raced. The idea of her not being okay was unacceptable. I had to save her. I clamped my jaw gently over her arm, being careful not to puncture her skin with my sharp teeth, and pulled her to the surface. I had to shift back to resuscitate her. The waves tossed us, and I did the best I could in the situation. One forceful blow of oxygen into her mouth and she was back with me—what a fighter.

Terrified hazel eyes flew open and connected with mine. She was frozen, her body stiff against mine.

"Are you okay?!" I shouted over the raging storm, scared I'd been too late somehow.

She blinked a few times and then looked around. Her nails bit into my skin as her hands locked onto my arms. Her legs started kicking, helping keep us afloat. She shook her head, the panic in her eyes was clear.

"I'll get us back! Just hold on to me."

I didn't give her a chance to think about it. I turned and wrapped her arms around my neck. Then, I swam like I'd never swum before. She was light on my back, but it was an awkward way to swim and I used every ounce of my shifter strength. Her mouth next to my ear was more distracting than it should've been.

She was more distracting than she should have been—especially given the dire circumstance. I was hyperaware of her body against mine. I swam hard, making sure to avoid the rip current, and got us back onto land. The land was more underwater than it had been just minutes before, but I carried her to the closest house. It was a beach house on stilts, so it was safe from the water, if not the wind.

The water level had risen halfway up the staircase. As soon as she could grab the stair railing, she let go of me and pulled herself up until she could climb the top few steps. It was easy to see that she was sluggish and weak, exhausted, and I worried.

At the top of the stairs, the home was boarded up well. I forced the door open and ushered her inside ahead of me. I'd apologize and pay for damages later. As soon as I had the door shut and secured, we were plunged into relative silence. It took a few seconds for the ringing in my ears from the howling wind and crashing waves to subside. I turned to the woman who had almost been a casualty of the storm and looked her over. The hair on the back of my neck stood on end. Tingles shot through my body.

She looked as though she was still in a daze, not quite processing reality, and that concerned me. "Are you okay? Tell me how you feel. Are you dizzy? Any trouble breathing?"

She shook her head and then nodded before shaking her head again. "I...I don't know. I don't know."

I led her over to a barstool and motioned for her to sit. When she did, I looked her over more closely. I couldn't see any damage, anything that would alert me to any injury she'd incurred. Her hazel eyes began to focus, despite everything. A just slightly upturned nose on a heart-shaped face, full lips...kissable lips. Lusciously kissable...

She coughed, her hand going over her chest.

"Do you hurt anywhere?"

"My lungs don't feel the best, but I think that's to be expected... I thought I was dead."

I didn't feel in top form myself. My bear was in a tizzy, consumed by the woman in front of us, torn between panting and growling. I didn't know what the hell was wrong with him, but I needed to gain control over him before he embarrassed me. "Anything else?"

She shook her head and sank back, letting her back rest against the counter behind her. "I'm okay. I know enough about dry drowning to know that this isn't that. I'm just..."

I leaned in closer when she trailed off. She had the most delectable aroma.

"I'm just really glad you came along." When she looked up at me with those beautiful hazel eyes, I was lost in them. But then, she wrapped her arms around my neck in a tight hug.

Shocked, I hugged her in return. The gesture felt way too good—far better than a mere thank-you hug from a rescued victim. I'd had plenty of those since being recruited to the task force. No, this one triggered an immediate arousal, and I realized I'd better cover up because my downstairs was standing at full mast.

"Thank you for saving my life."

8

MEGAN

I pulled away from the man who'd rescued me and tried to ignore the awkward arousal I felt blossoming inside. I shouldn't have hugged him. How was I to know it would start my pulse racing and my body filling with lust? Maybe it was just a strange reaction to nearly dying. I coughed again and looked around the house we'd broken into. "This is Greg Campbell's house."

"A friend of yours?"

I shook my head. "Not since high school. He got this place when his parents moved to Pensacola. I was here a few times when we were kids for parties."

"Greg's really into animal print, huh?"

I looked over at the leopard-patterned pillows on the couch and bit back a laugh. "I think he's married now. Although, those could still be his, I suppose."

We grew quiet again, and I looked anywhere but at the man who'd saved me. I felt strange. When I'd regained consciousness with his mouth on mine, after thinking I was a goner, I'd assumed for a second that I'd died and gone to heaven. There was this beautiful man kissing me, or so I'd thought. I'd been ready to lean in and really kiss him back when I choked up ocean water. It was hard to hold eye contact, knowing that while he'd been trying to save my life, I'd been thinking about making out with him.

"I'm Roman." He held out his hand, and one side of his mouth lifted.

I met his eyes for a second and then slid my hand into his. I couldn't help but notice how much larger his hand was than mine. The guy was huge. "Megan."

"What were you doing out in this storm, Megan?"

I pulled my hand back from his and stood up. On shaky legs, I rounded Greg's kitchen island and occupied myself by getting a glass of water. The salty taste in my mouth was disgusting. "It's a long story."

He followed me closely, without allowing me much personal space, which should have felt creepy, but didn't at all. "I think we've got time."

As if on cue, the lights he'd turned on when we'd stepped foot in the place, flickered and died and the wind shook the house violently. I dropped the glass I'd just taken out of the cupboard and yelped as it hit the ground next to my feet and shattered.

"Don't move." Roman's deep, authoritative command froze me in my tracks until I felt his warm hands grasp my waist.

I squirmed. "What are you doing?"

A rhetorical question. I knew what he was attempting to do. He was actually going to try to pick me up, obviously either overestimating his own abilities or he had no idea how much I weighed. He must not have gotten a good look at me. I was no lightweight, and I was horrified at the idea of him hurting himself by trying to lift me. I pushed at his hands to remove them, but they stayed firmly clasped.

"Stop, before you cut yourself." His voice was stern, and I found myself heeding his command. With seemingly no effort, as though I was a child, he hoisted me in the air and sat me down on the counter behind him. "Where do you think Greg or his wife might keep their broom?"

I sat there, in shock. The guy, Roman he'd said his name was, was big—far bigger than I was—but what he'd done by lifting me without effort shouldn't have been possible. He hadn't even grunted from the strain—nothing. "Uh, the Greg I knew wouldn't own a broom."

Roman chuckled and rested his hand on my knee. "Don't move. There's glass all over."

"What about your feet?"

"I'm tough."

Well, that was proving to be an understatement. I tried to follow Roman's movements through the darkness, perplexed. He'd lifted me like I weighed nothing. He'd swam with me on his back through turbulent waters and torrential rain. Who the hell was this guy? Superman? My heart raced. A wacky idea formed in my mind that maybe I was dead and dreaming. That had to be the case. None of this could be real. I slid off the counter and gasped when pain shot up my leg. Nope, not dreaming.

"What are you doing? I told you to stay up there." Roman was back, his hands on my waist again. Effortlessly, he lifted me back on the counter a second time, tsk-ing like I was an insolent child. This time, he spun me to the right until my foot rested against cold metal. The sink.

I gritted my teeth against the pain that had just started to register. His hands were warm as he held my calf, and I focused on that instead. "This is surreal."

He was close enough that I could feel his breath against my temple as he spoke. "What?"

I laughed. The laugh felt strange forming in my stomach, coming up my throat, tickling my lips. I couldn't remember the last time I'd laughed. "I almost died. I was trying to get out of the floodwaters and back to my house when the rip current caught me. Before I knew it, I was swept out to sea. Yet my worst injury of the day is from stepping on a piece of broken glass."

"Why do I feel like there's more to that story?" His hands were still on my leg. Was he aware that he was absently stroking my calf?

I blew out a frustrated breath at the reminder of my story. "In high school, Greg's parents kept the liquor in the cabinet above the fridge." I motioned with my head to the refrigerator behind me.

"Why don't you check? Maybe we'll get lucky. I think I need some. A lot."

Roman squeezed my thigh. "I can take a hint."

I found myself holding my breath. My heart was racing and there were butterflies in my stomach. I chalked them up to nerves from the storm and from almost dying, but part of me insisted they were from Roman's touch. Either way, I hoped the liquor would help settle them.

Roman pressed a bottle into my hand a second later. "Have at it while I clean up the glass. It'll help dull the pain when I clean up your foot in a minute. And do not get off that counter!"

I twisted off the lid and took a long pull from a bottle that turned out to be cheap vodka. I coughed and sputtered, but forced myself to swallow. A few more healthy swigs and the stuff didn't taste half bad. Before I got drunk, though, I put the lid back on and rested my head on my bent knee.

Roman came back with a lit candle and placed it on the other side of the counter facing me. It was then that I noticed the towel wrapped around his waist. I blinked a few times and replayed the last several minutes in my head. He hadn't been wearing a shirt. That, I remembered. But he'd had pants on. Hadn't he? Shorts, swim trunks, anything? The harder I tried to remember, the more I felt my face heat. He had been full monty and I hadn't even noticed. I guessed that the near-drowning experience affected me more than I'd first realized.

"Okay, let me look at your foot." He was gentle as he cupped my heel and lifted my foot from the sink.

I couldn't stop thinking about the fact that he hadn't been wearing anything. How had I not noticed? As my brain strained to fill in the gaps, against my better judgment, I barely noticed as he prodded my foot.

"This isn't going to feel good." He looked up. "I'm sorry, Megan."

I opened my mouth to ask why he was apologizing, or maybe why he hadn't been wearing clothes, but before the words emerged, a sharp pain ripped up my leg as he pulled a shard of glass out of my foot. At least, that was what I assumed he'd done. I screamed, unprepared for it.

Roman pressed a towel to my foot, but still managed to move close enough to wrap an arm around my shoulders and pull me against his chest in a hug. "I'm sorry. I know that hurt."

I shouldn't have turned my face into him. Or inhaled his warm, masculine aroma. He was a stranger and, despite my current marital situation, I did still have a husband. I kind of couldn't help myself, though. I was too shaken from—just everything—to fight the comfort his embrace brought.

"It's okay. We'll get some more cheap vodka into you and it won't hurt for much longer." His voice was so sure and strong. "I'll get you all fixed up. I promise I'll take care of you."

Those words spoken with such soothing reassurance nearly brought tears to my eyes. After the way I'd been treated by Dylan for the past few days, and far longer than that if I was being honest, having someone—even a complete stranger—say those words to me, "I promise I'll take care of you," and say them with genuine compassion and concern was like a drug to my soul. My heart skipped a beat and butterflies started up in my stomach. But, the side of my face was pressed against the bare chest of a man who wasn't my husband. I needed to stop. It wasn't a dream. It was reality, and the reality was that I was still a married woman.

I forced myself to pull away and blinked back an unexpected wave of emotion. "Um... I wonder if there's a working phone here. I should probably try to call my husband."

Roman visibly tensed and, a heartbeat later, moved away, clearing his throat. "I'll take a look around the place after I bandage your foot."

"Great, thanks." Why did his reaction make me want to crawl back into the ocean and let the storm carry me away?

9

ROMAN

Husband. My bear growled and thrashed as I focused on Megan's foot. A big piece of glass had sliced deep enough that she probably could've used stitches. As it was, several butterfly bandages would have to do. I shut my mind down and focused on the mechanics of the task as I cleaned her wound and dried it off. It was a challenge to focus with her sweet aroma and delicious curves enticing me. I got the smaller bandages on and then wrapped her foot in some gauze and taped it into place.

"There you go." I put some distance between us and focused instead on cleaning up the blood and wrappers from the bandages. "Be careful getting down, but you should sit on the couch and prop it up."

She cleared her throat. "Thanks."

I was tense as she lowered herself from the counter, waiting to catch her if she fell or screamed in pain again. A shiver went down my spine at the reminder of the pain I'd caused her when I'd removed the glass shard. The scream had been like a punch to the gut. Almost as bad as hearing her say she had a husband.

I couldn't help but watch her move away. She was tall for a human female, and her body was thicker than most of the women around the small island. Her hips were wide, her curves soft. I loved the look of her, especially the swell of her ass under the drenched T-shirt. It was as enticing, as the view of her from the front. Before the mention of a husband, I'd been dreaming of running my hands over those curves.

I swore softly and made myself look away. She was taken. She'd made a point of letting me know, too. She'd practically waved a big red flag in my face. It was perplexing, though. Because of the way I was reacting to her, my attraction to her that bordered on a soul connection, I would have guessed that she was my...

"I'm going to get cleaned up in the bathroom. I'm sure Greg, or his wife, has something I could wear for the time being." She limped toward the bedroom as my eyes followed. It made no sense. I let my head fall back and stared up at the ceiling. The way she called out to my bear, to me, was baffling.

I had to check in with the team.

Everything's good here. Local woman got sucked out to sea. Rescue was successful. We've taken shelter in a home on the beach. It's holding up well against the storm.

Serge's voice came back at me right away. *It took you fucking long enough. Did you have to swim to Siberia to pull her from the sea?*

No, asshole, I was administering first aid. She was unconscious and underwater when I reached her. And I'd been busy touching her and ogling her figure. *We'll wait out the storm here. Yell if you need anything.*

I looked around the house. Megan took the candle, but I didn't need it to see. My bear felt like he was ready to crawl out of my skin, the scent of Megan was driving him insane.

While waiting for her to return, I planted myself on the couch and listened to the battering rain of the storm raging outside. The house rocked ever so slightly, just enough to keep me on edge. Still, it was oddly cozy inside the house. And rather quiet. Too quiet. I was hyperaware of every sound coming from the bedroom where Megan had gone.

The steady stream of swearing she was doing would've been enough to shock any sailor. I found myself grinning, listening to her.

"You okay in there?"

"Just peachy."

"You never told me the rest of your story. The long version."

She hesitated for a few moments. "I got swept out to sea during a hurricane. The end."

"There's definitely more to the story than that."

"My car probably got swept out to sea, too."

"Okay, how about all the in-between stuff you're leaving out?"

"I'd just put a few thousand dollars' worth of professional photographs in the back of it to keep them safe from the storm." She grunted. "Lot of good that did."

I whistled. "Why didn't you evacuate?"

Silence. After a while, I figured out she wasn't going to answer me, which made me want to know even more. I resolved to get the whole truth out of her. We had time. The storm wasn't going to let up for hours.

Settling back into the couch, I made myself as comfortable as I could with an angry bear pacing and clawing at my insides. Neither of us was pleased that Megan had a husband. My bear wanted me to go into the other room to be near her, to rub up against her and show her that we wanted her. I gritted my teeth against the urge and rested my forehead in my hand. Never before had I ever felt such a pull to be glued to a woman's side, but I drew the line at attempting to seduce a married woman.

"How long do you think the storm will last?" Her voice was soft as she called from the bedroom.

"It will be several more hours, at least, before it begins to let up. It's supposed to stall over us before moving farther north."

She sighed. "I hope the rest of my worldly possessions make it."

"Besides your car?"

"Besides my car. My house and my business. I didn't get to finish closing them up—not as securely as I would have liked." My guess was that revelation was the beginning of the rest of her story I was waiting to hear.

"No?"

"I found some clothes. I'll be out in a minute."

I heard the bedroom door shut and listened for the sound of a lock turning. *Good, lock me out.* I needed more signs that she wasn't mine. My bear wasn't accepting it, and I was having a hell of a time myself.

10

MEGAN

I stared at myself in the bathroom mirror. The candle Roman had procured was burning brightly, emitting a lavender aroma that was doing nothing to comfort me. I looked like a drowned rat. A giant rat, but still a rat. My hair was in sopping, frizzy curls that stood out in every direction like a perfect rat's nest. I still had slight traces of makeup from two days before, just a bit of mascara flakes and smears hanging out under my eyes. I had bags big enough to fit a couple of designer dogs in. The oversized white shirt I'd been wearing had turned into a see-through dress that was so heavy and cold that even wearing some of Greg's dirty laundry would've been an improvement.

Fortunately, I didn't have to resort to that. I got cleaned up the best I could and, rifling through Greg's dresser, found a pair of boxer shorts and a T-shirt. The shirt wasn't as loose as I would've liked. Greg was a thin guy, like Dylan. Dylan. My husband. Who was not the man on the forefront of my mind. It was the complete stranger in the next room that had monopolized my thoughts and had my mind spinning in circles.

Not just my mind, either. Butterflies seemed to have permanently housed themselves in my stomach. I was facing my reflection in the mirror, obsessing about how I looked and nervous about going back out to the living room with him. I was behaving like a schoolgirl and it was ridiculous. I kept telling myself to knock it off. It was inappropriate. I'd never seen the guy before in my life, and for all I knew, he could be a serial killer. He was probably out there sharpening his knife, getting ready to filet me.

Still, I was concerned about my ratty hair.

"You okay in there? How's the foot?"

I jumped as Roman's voice sounded from right outside the bedroom door. My hands shook slightly, but I forced myself to look away from the mirror and walk over to the door. "Yeah, I'm done."

Sure enough, he was standing just outside the door, and when I opened it, his eyes trailed over me. They stopped at my rat's nest and a smile stretched over lips. "Cute hair."

I ducked my head and limped around him. "I'm just going to prop my foot up."

"You do that. I'll bring you the vodka."

I didn't need vodka. I hadn't had a thing to eat and the last thing I wanted was to get shit-faced with a handsome stranger while huddled together in a beach bungalow as we weathered a tropical storm together. If that wasn't the perfect setting for a romance novel, I didn't know what was. Besides, I had a feeling I couldn't trust myself not to say or do anything stupid around Roman, especially if I was drunk.

He was some kind of magic man, though. When he stepped into the living room, he had the bottle of vodka in one hand, but he also had a bag of chips in the other—family size. The chips were exactly what I needed. He raised his eyebrows when my stomach growled and tossed them onto the couch beside me. "When's the last time you ate?"

I ripped into the bag and shoved a handful into my mouth, suddenly ravenous. "I don't even know. A day or two."

"What?" His scowl of disapproval spoke volumes.

I didn't need his approval, I told myself. I just needed food.

"What's the story, Megan? Are you in danger?" Right on cue, his eyes traveled to my upper arm. When I followed his gaze, I saw the fingertip bruises from Dylan. The longer sleeves on my T-shirt had covered them. Greg's didn't. "Who..."

I shouldn't have been so gratified to see the fury on Roman's face. I didn't know him. Yet, I felt warmed by the angry expression he wore on my behalf.

"Your husband?" His voice sounded a lot like a growl.

"It's not what it looks like." I took the bottle of vodka and downed a swig. "We own a business together and we were arguing... I bruise easily."

"What's his name?"

"Dylan. Dylan Pratt. We own Pratt's Photography on the north side of Main Street."

Roman's eyebrows raised. "I know the place. I walked by a few days ago. I'm guessing it was your husband I saw there. Why didn't he close up the place properly?"

I opened my mouth to lie for Dylan, as I'd done hundreds of times, then stopped. Roman didn't know us. I had no reason to lie to him, and maybe I was just sick of making excuses. "He refused. He doesn't do manual labor. He leaves it to me. I have a bigger build than he does, so he figures it's easier for me."

Roman's eyes looked like they were going to pop out of his skull. He snatched the vodka from my hand angrily and took a long pull himself before nodding to himself like he was making sense of things. "He told you that, did he? That you're bigger than him, so it's easier for you?"

Mortified, I scoffed. "No! No, that's not what I meant." And there I went making excuses again. "It's just, well, I *am* bigger. And stronger, so I do that stuff. He hates physical labor so he handles the office work."

Roman muttered something under his breath. I couldn't quite hear what he said, but it sounded an awful lot like he was calling Dylan a pussy.

Roman focused smoldering eyes on me. "You're not bigger or stronger than I am." Those seven words spoken aloud raised my core temperature to sizzling. The corner of his mouth twitched. "Are you?"

I couldn't look away from him. I needed to look away. Wild, frizzy curls, chip crumbs on my fingertips, vodka on my breath, I was a mess and I knew it. *Look away, Megan.* My eyes didn't cooperate. My voice was barely a whisper. "No, I'm not."

Finally, he shrugged and turned to set the vodka bottle down. Spell broken. Clearing his throat, he ran his hands down his face. The hint of stubble matched the golden blonde of his buzzed hair. "No, you're not."

I swallowed audibly and shoved more chips into my mouth. I had to get away from him. He was doing something to me that made no sense. Maybe I was ovulating or something.

"So, where is your small husband?"

Suddenly, the house shook with a hard wind gust, and I dropped the bag of chips and held onto the couch with both hands, chip crumbs and all. "Are we safe here?"

"I won't let anything happen to you. You're safe."

Why his words relaxed me, I didn't know. A man—even a buff, muscled one like him—who could confidently say he was no match for a hurricane was a little over the top egowise. Deciding it was time to step away from the chips, I glanced down at Greg's couch, covered in greasy crumbs, and winced. "I'll have to pay to have his couch cleaned."

"I doubt they'll notice your crumbs over the animal print."

I reached for the vodka bottle and took another pull. Roman had asked me a question and I could tell from the intensity of his gaze that he wasn't going to just let it drop unanswered. "Dylan evacuated in time. He's inland, somewhere."

Roman's jaw dropped. "He left you?"

I gave a tight little laugh. "Yeah, you could say that. In more ways than one."

"What kind of man leaves his wife to fend for herself in a hurricane?!" Roman began pacing the floor, fists clenching and unclenching at his sides. He looked like he was ready to go out and find Dylan just to beat the shit out of him. He shook his head at me. "You almost drowned. You were underwater when I reached you, not breathing, seconds from the point of no return."

"Yeah, thank you for rescuing me, by the way." I leaned back into the couch, finding it incredibly comfortable. The vodka was hitting me a little harder than I'd meant it to. Still, I was sober enough to know that, now that I'd begun the story of why and how he found me in the water seconds from death, I had to say more. "Yeah, Dylan left. I had to close up the house and the shop myself. By the time I finished securing things, it was too late to get myself to safety."

"So, you tried to go home?"

I nodded. "And the east side of the island was already flooded. It's really my own fault. I should have known better. I should've boarded everything up days ago and given myself time to evacuate. I've never been this irresponsible before. It all just...snuck up on me."

"Dylan better hope Matilda carries *him* out to sea."

11

ROMAN

I was going insane. Megan had leaned over and was peacefully sleeping on the couch. It was as though she wasn't bothered at all by the story she'd just dropped at my feet. Her husband was a dick. Worse than a dick. A cowardly, sniveling, lowlife dick. Maybe it bothered me more than it should have, but I couldn't stop fuming. I wanted to rip out of my skin and find the motherfucker and maul him to shreds.

Her arm had nasty bruises from him. She'd nearly died alone because of him. I was going to make him pay for hurting her. He'd also pay for making her think it was her duty to assume a masculine role as though her size was a good excuse for him to not step up as a man. Her size was quite perfect in my opinion, and she was *all* woman.

I paced around the house, listening to the storm until I was ready to scratch my own eyeballs out. That way, I wouldn't have to be faced with the constant sight of Megan, the thin boxer shorts she wore riding up ever so slightly. Even those boxers were pissing me off. They belonged to Greg. Not me. I wanted to pull them off her and find something of mine to drape her in. Not his. Fuck Greg, the guy from high school. And fuck her dick of a husband—I wanted to rip that asshole to shreds.

The eye of the storm has arrived. It should be calm for about fifteen minutes. Want to make it here while you can? Serge sounded strained, even in my head. It was a tense situation not just for me, apparently.

Maybe. I'll let you know.

I was looking down at Megan. She was stunning. Even with her hair curling in every direction and potato chip crumbs dusting her mouth, she was beautiful. She deserved more than she was getting. I may not have known her well, but I knew that much. She was sweet and loyal, despite her husband not deserving her loyalty.

She groaned and grew restless. Her hands balled into fists on her lap. Her forehead scrunched, her expression was unhappy, and she pursed her lips. Dreaming of something unpleasant, she mumbled in her sleep and then grunted.

I didn't like seeing her unhappy, even in her sleep. It bothered me and it bothered my bear. I was already reaching for her when she mumbled her asshole husband's name and frowned even deeper. My bear growled and I squeezed my eyes shut, needing a second to get him under control, to get myself under control. I didn't know what it was about the woman that had me so agitated, but I was ready to tear up the place in anger over her mistreatment.

"Megan, wake up," I spoke her name gently, not wanting to scare her. Her eyes flew open, and when they focused on me, a light smile lifted her lips, and I fought an intense yearning, wanting so badly to draw her back against my chest that my arms ached.

Husband. What the fuck?

"The eye of the storm is coming. We can safely make it to my office, if you want."

She sat up and rubbed at her eyes. "I want to check on my house."

I nodded. "Okay."

"And the business."

"I don't know if we'll have time for both." I looked at my watch and thought about it. "Maybe, if we're fast and the water allows it.

Otherwise, we'll get to your house and either bunk there or go on to my office. The rest of my team is there, waiting out the storm."

"Your team?"

I shrugged. "I work at the lifeguard station at the southern end of the island."

She nodded, like something made sense to her finally. "That's why you're so good at swimming. Okay. When do we go?"

For whatever reason, I felt uncomfortable lying to her. P.O.L.A.R. was a clandestine league, though. I didn't have the authority to reveal what we did or who we were just because I thought she was pretty and I was inexplicably attracted to her. "Soon. Does Greg or his wife have any shoes you can wear? Tennis shoes or something that lace up tightly?"

"I can look." She arched her back and reached her arms up in the air in a stretch. As she did, the hem of the shirt came up, revealing a sliver of stomach. I swallowed audibly, and she jerked it back in place and stood up. "Sorry."

I had more to say to her, more to ask her, but it wasn't the time. It'd never be the time for what I wanted to say. She was married. I kept my mouth shut and forced myself to look anywhere but at her.

When she returned a few minutes later, her limp was not as severe as before. "His shoe size is a 10. I don't think they'll fit you. And I'm pretty sure his clothes won't."

I looked down at the towel I was wearing and bit back a laugh. "I don't need shoes. Will they be too big for you?"

Her cheeks went so red I could see the blush even in the shadows of the house. "No. You should know I have big feet. You held my foot in your hand."

I frowned. "Size is relative. They aren't big to me."

She looked like she wanted to argue, but instead she just slid her feet into the shoes and laced them up tight. When she was finished, she stood up and looked around. "I'll leave a note for Greg. I'm sure he'll understand that we had no choice but to come in."

I didn't give a fuck about Greg. I didn't want to say that to her and make her think I was an asshole, though. *What's the word on the eye?*

You better hustle. Dmitry paused. *I suggest you avoid the office unless you want a giant fucking headache. Serge and Hannah are bickering because he won't stop freaking out about her safety. You're better off weathering Matilda head on.*

Copy that.

I went to the door and slowly opened it. Sure enough, it was eerily silent outside. No rain, no battering wind. I glanced up and found myself gazing up at a beautiful, starry sky. "We're in the eye. Come on."

"My house is on East Beach." Megan raced up behind me, looking over my shoulder to see what I was staring at. "Wow. That's so strange. But cool."

I didn't disagree. "Come on. We're going to have to swim. I'll go ahead to make sure there aren't rip currents."

"Wait, what if there are?" She grabbed my arm and shook her head. "Maybe we should just stay put. You don't have to do this for me. We can stay here and both be safe."

I looked down at her, the woman who thought she was big, and wanted to kiss her more than I'd ever wanted to do anything in my life. Was she worried about me? "There's no need to worry. I'm an incredibly strong swimmer and well trained. Lifeguard, remember?"

As she stared up at me, I watched her eyes travel to my mouth.

A gust of wind pushed at my back and I snapped back to reality. She cleared her throat and let go of my arm. "Just...be careful."

I wagged my eyebrows at her, wanting to relax her a bit. "We're in the eye of a hurricane, woman. Telling me to be careful is moot at this point."

She grinned at me, I saw just a flash of her true beauty, and then we were off.

12

MEGAN

Traveling in a hurricane was no fun. The trip to my house took so long that by the time we got to my porch, I felt like Matilda was right behind us, ready to strike up again any second. Sunkissed Key had already taken a beating, from what we'd seen, and she wasn't done. My house, fortunately, seemed to be okay. Some damage to the roof was evident, but it wasn't anything I wouldn't be able to fix myself.

As soon as we were in the house, I realized a few things right away. Every gust of wind sent the place rocking as though we were on a boat. More than that, I noticed what I'd somehow failed to notice that morning. Things were missing.

I went from room to room, checking for damage and creating a catalog of the missing items. When I got to the bedroom and looked into the closet, my stomach sank. Dylan's side was empty. All his clothes and shoes were gone.

I sat on the edge of my bed and stared at the empty half of the closet. When had he packed his stuff? How had I not noticed? I'd moved into the guestroom, but shouldn't I have noticed him packing and leaving with his things?

"Megan?"

I glanced up and found Roman staring at the half-empty closet, too. I sighed and tried to quickly bury the feelings that were threatening to surface. I wasn't even sure what they were, but I didn't want to have my emotions explode in front of Roman.

I stood up and wiped my hands on Greg's boxers, like that would wipe away the shock. "Everything seems in order here. Do you think we have time to get to the shop?"

He shook his head. "It's already starting up again."

I turned my back to the closet and nodded. "Okay. That's fine. I'm going to put on dry clothes and…I'll find something for you to wear, too."

Like magic, the towel had stayed around Roman's hips through the trip, but it was soaked and riding so low that I was getting a view of what I was pretty sure was the top of his "down there" hair. And those abs…whew. Danger zone. I turned to the closet and ran my hands through my hair.

"I'll find you something."

Roman chuckled from behind me. "I don't think you'll have anything big enough. Maybe another towel?"

I glanced back at him and shook my head. "I don't think I have towels big enough, either."

He flashed me a cheeky grin and wagged his brows again. "A sheet?"

I looked down at my bed and nodded. "Yeah, a sheet would probably do it. Okay, that'll work."

My door closed, and I glanced back to see he'd gone. In just the glow of a vanilla-scented candle, I stripped and changed into a T-shirt and a pair of yoga pants. I kept my back to Dylan's side as I flipped through clothes, searching for something for Roman.

The man was just…too big. He had to be close to seven feet tall and so broad chested that there was no way anything I had, even my bloat clothes meant for heavy-flow days, would fit him. I pulled an old baseball cap over my hair and went back into the bedroom.

The idea of giving Roman a sheet from our bed made me cringe. Dylan had slept with someone else on those sheets. Washed or not, I didn't want their filth anywhere near Roman. Instead, I went into the guestroom and took the flat sheet off the bed I'd been sleeping in. I told myself that it didn't mean anything, but the idea of a sheet that had touched my body wrapped around his bare skin sent a wicked shiver through me.

Downstairs, Roman was in the kitchen, staring into my darkened fridge. There was nothing in there. Nothing fresh anyway, but he'd managed to find a lone beer. The wet towel hanging around him was even lower and I could see the top of his ass.

"Sheet. I...I brought you a sheet." I turned away from the view and stammered. "It's from my bed."

The sound of the wet towel hitting the ground set my blood on fire. Roman was naked behind me and I could see him, in all his glory, if I just looked over my shoulder. I kept my eyes closed just in case I was tempted to try. He wasn't mine to look at. Why I was feeling so much like a hormonal teenager, I didn't know.

When we were leaving Greg's, I had this feeling that he was going to kiss me. And I wouldn't have minded. Thankfully he didn't actually try. Why I would have been willing to let him kiss me, I had no idea. I was married. Even if Dylan had left me.

That reality helped dampen my mood. My husband left me. He'd also taken things from around the house that weren't his. Artwork, every TV, the home desktop computer. When had he had time to take the TVs off the walls? It made no sense.

Again, I had more anger than sorrow. I had half a mind to find him and rip into him about what he'd done. Rip him apart—that's what I wanted to do if I was being honest with myself. I may have spent several days in denial, avoidance of the mess that was my marriage, but I was ready now to face the reality that my husband was a lying, cheating piece of crap who'd left me and I wanted to repay him for it. I also wanted to not give a shit about what my family would say and not give a shit about what it would feel like to be plunged into divorcehood.

"You want to talk about it?" Roman's deep voice was so close that I felt the vibrations in my chest.

He must have read my expression. I shook my head. I knew that if I opened my mouth, I was going to lose it. Whatever I was feeling was going to fire off like a missile and I didn't trust myself. I needed to think about everything a little more before I put any of my thoughts out into the world.

The house swayed harder and I gasped. "Greg's house didn't sway this much."

Roman put his hand on my shoulder and lightly squeezed, a comforting gesture, or it should've been. Instead, warmth radiated down my arm and chest in ways it had no business doing. "We're okay. Different construction, probably. It stood up to the first half of the storm, it'll stand up to the second half just as well."

Another powerful sway and I wasn't so sure.

"Come on. I found a beer. Drink it. It'll calm you while we ride out the storm on your couch. It's a lot prettier than Greg's animal print monstrosity."

I rounded the kitchen island and went straight to the liquor cabinet. Usually full for the parties that we didn't throw, I just stood there for a second, staring. It was empty. "He had time to pack the liquor."

Roman took my shoulders and gently turned me and pushed me away from the cabinet. "Take the beer."

13

ROMAN

If I expected myself to feel better seeing that Megan's husband had left her, I surprised myself. I was furious. How could he have done that to her? What the hell was wrong with the asshole? I wanted to hunt him down and demand that he beg for her forgiveness. She didn't deserve that type of treatment. I could see the emotion in her eyes, but she was bottling it inside.

I assumed she was heartbroken. No matter how she looked at me, and I was sure I saw heat in her gaze, to her I was some guy she'd just met. He was her husband. As much as it hurt to admit that, it was true. She'd married the asshole. That meant she loved him. She was hurting, and I didn't like it.

I led her to the living room and to the couch, sitting next to her, ready to be a shoulder for her to cry on. Handing her the beer, I bumped her shoulder with mine. "Talk."

Instead of crying, she started laughing. She popped right back off the couch and started pacing in front of me. The swaying of the house would throw her off a bit, here or there, but she was focused on wearing a hole through the rug.

"Sonofabitch. He took the liquor. Who does that? I mean, the

TVs? Okay, fine. He loves TV, so I get that, kind of. The liquor, though? He doesn't even drink the stuff. He likes wine. What the hell is that? Maybe *Brandi* likes liquor."

I just watched as she went on.

"We've been married for over ten years. This December would be twelve years, actually. Twelve years of marriage and he fucks someone named Brandi—in our bed!" She nodded to the sheet around my waist and crinkled her nose. "Not on that sheet. Don't worry. I gave you my bedding."

I knew that. It carried her scent so strongly that I had to mouth breathe to keep from getting aroused. "Thanks for that."

She paused. "And that. You say thank you. I can't remember the last time Dylan thanked me for anything. He just expects me to bend over backward for him, and the only time he acknowledges it is if I don't do it. Then, he has plenty to say."

"The shop? I do everything. It was my money that financed the business and I'm the photographer. I shoot the photos, edit them, do all the matting and framing myself, and I run the floor while he sits in the back office doing *the important part.* What important part? What else is there to do? I literally do everything, and when I finally get home, I have no time to do anything but eat and sleep. How did he have time to sleep around?"

"I think you answered that."

She stopped and made a face. 'True. I'm so angry. I want to rip his goddamn head off."

"I can arrange something like that."

"I caught them sleeping together, you know. I walked in on them. In our bed. He didn't even apologize. He just basically made me feel like I was at fault for not seeing it coming." She took off the baseball cap she'd been wearing and twisted her hair up on the top of her head. After securing it with some band she had on her wrist, she pressed her palms against her eye sockets. "He stole all the money from the shop. The shop that's probably getting torn apart right now because he took no responsibility for securing it against the storm. I tried to do it myself, but I'm only one person."

I remained calm on the outside, but her pain had me raging internally. My bear was ripping at me, desperate to get out and kill the stupid shit that would treat Megan so horribly.

"I can't believe he took the liquor. I mean, that's just low."

I opened the beer and handed it to her. "I can't believe he thought he could find someone better than you."

She stopped pacing and faced me. Then, she snorted a laugh through her nose as if in disbelief. "You don't have to say that. I know that I have flaws, too. Plenty of them. Just...not the ones *Brandi* has, apparently."

"I'm not telling you anything that isn't true. Even a stranger can see that you're loyal and kind, even to a man who doesn't deserve it. It's not hard to imagine how well you'd treat a good man. A better man." *A man like me.* I cocked my head and looked at her harder. "And that's saying nothing of your beauty."

"Which I lack." She shook her head, and the ball of hair on top of it wobbled. "I still deserve better, though."

"Worlds better. And your beauty is hardly lacking. Megan, you're gorgeous. I'm not going to make you uncomfortable by telling you just how attractive I find you, but I'm not exaggerating when I say I think your husband is the biggest fucking idiot on the planet."

Her cheeks were rosy, and she looked away before taking a long pull from the beer and then passing it back to me. Our fingers brushed when I took it, and I felt the connection down to my toes. Her slight gasp told me she felt it, too.

"Do you love him?"

"No." She covered her mouth with her hand, shocked that she'd answered so quickly, or maybe it was the answer itself that shocked her. "I mean...well...no. We've grown apart. Maybe I should've known something like this was coming. I can't remember the last time I felt a connection to him. More than that, I don't know if I even like him. But we made vows to each other. We promised..."

"You wish you could have remained with him?"

She met and held my gaze, pain and confusion evident in her eyes. She was clearly hurt by everything that was happening to her and felt she had little control. "I...don't know. No, I guess not. I guess I was living a fantasy. Pretending he was someone else, a different kind of man, and that *we* were something else. Before I was rudely shaken back to reality. I don't what to be with someone who could do this."

"Someone who could take the liquor?"

She laughed lightly and rolled her eyes before taking the beer bottle back from me. "Yeah, someone who could take the liquor."

I smiled at her and shrugged. "So, you don't love him and you don't want to be with him."

She shook her head. "I guess not, no. I'm thirty-two, though. I can't just start over. I don't want to be like the rest of my family going through marriages the way normal people go through mascara."

"Mascara?"

"Makeup. You're supposed to throw it away after six months. It's dangerous to use it... Not the point. The point is, I don't want to start over."

"So, you'd be happy if he returned?"

"No."

"I don't think you're making much sense right now."

She sank onto the couch next to me and turned her head so she was looking at me. "I want him to magically be someone else entirely." She let out a long, slow sigh. "I don't want to be alone."

I raised an eyebrow. "Let him go. I promise you won't be alone."

Megan's eyes rolled and she scoffed. "Yeah, okay."

I caught her chin in my hand and lifted her face so she was looking at me. She thought so little of herself. I didn't understand how it was possible. She was beautiful, and sexy. To me she was more beautiful than any woman I'd ever seen before. My heart raced when I looked at her, and I desperately had to be closer to her. I wanted her. As I thought it, I realized that I wanted more than be closer to her. I wanted every part of her. I wanted her to have every part of me.

Megan blinked and bit her lip. "Why are you looking at me like that?"

There was no more denying it. This woman was my mate. My stomach tightened and my bear roared, confirming my suspicion.

She was the one—ours. Before I had time to consider the revelation more fully, Maxim's voice broke through my thoughts.

Tornado incoming, brother.

14

MEGAN

My entire body was tense. Roman was staring at me like he wanted to kiss me again, and damned if I didn't want him to. I had no business wanting him the way I did, but I couldn't stop the feeling.

"Fuck." Roman was on his feet in a split second and had me up and in his arms just as fast. "Tornado."

I was still in romantic la-la land. "What?"

He picked me up in a bear hug and literally ran us toward the bathroom. "Tornado."

The word clicked into place in my brain just as the house swayed harder and a sickening howl sounded. "Oh, fuck."

Roman shoved me into the bathroom and vanished, only to reappear a few seconds later with half the couch cushions in his arms. "In the tub. Get in the tub, Megan!"

I no sooner did as he said, then he was on top of me, the cushions on top of him. Flattened on the bottom of the tub, the weight of Roman plastered to me, I felt fear for all of two seconds before my body switched back into hormonal-teenager mode. A tangle of limbs and cushions, Roman was twisted to fit over me, but our faces had somehow ended up inches apart.

I could hear a shutter come loose upstairs. The banging that followed probably should've worried me more. The house was being damaged. With Roman on top of me, though, his face was hovering just above mine, his breath mingling with mine, and his bedroom eyes focused on me, I kind of didn't care about anything else.

"Am I too heavy?"

I shook my head the slightest bit. "Nope."

His arms were planted on either side of my head and he shifted slightly. "I don't believe you."

"I like it." I realized what I'd said and stuttered. "I mean, it's, um, fine—nice. Like a weighted blanket."

"You like it?" His breathing shallowed and his eyes flicked down to my lips.

I told myself to change the subject or to say no. I couldn't, though. I just watched him. I looked at his mouth, the fuller top lip enticing, then at his eyes. Those thick lashes lowered. "Yes."

"Megan?" He looked down at my mouth again, and the gap between us became even smaller.

"Yes." I didn't even know the question, but my answer was still yes. I felt like my blood was on fire. I could feel him pressed against me and I wanted more. My body had woken up for what felt like the first time.

Roman's lips were a breath away from mine, and I felt pulled into his magnetic field. His lips rested against mine, and I felt him shudder before pulling back just enough to speak. "I'm going to kiss you."

He already had, but I didn't argue. I nodded, bumping our noses together. "Yes."

He kissed me again, and I realized that he meant he was *really* going to kiss me that time. His mouth was warm and passionate against mine, his beard rough against my skin. His forearm wedged between my head and the tub to provide support and then he licked the seam of my lips, demanding entrance.

"Yes." I gripped his sides, the only thing my hands could reach, and held on while he stroked his tongue over my lips. Electric currents had nothing on his kisses.

Pulling back and then kissing just my bottom lip, his mouth made love to mine. When his tongue slipped into my mouth, it tangled seductively with mine. His fingers pressed into my scalp and I could tell he wanted more. Unable to be still, I tried to maneuver so I could feel more of his body pressed against mine. I got one leg free and twisted my hips just the right way. Roman's body lined up with mine just right, and I could feel his hard length pressing between my thighs.

I cursed my yoga pants and wrapped my leg around his hip. Stroking his tongue back and then sucking his top lip, I heard myself moan, but couldn't care. Roman deserved to know what he was doing to me. His other hand worked down and gripped my ass, pulling into his body.

Tired of being confined, Roman sat up, knocking the cushions all around. Still kissing me, he pulled me to my feet and then into his arms. Locking my legs around his waist, I moaned into his mouth at the feeling of his body between my legs.

The sounds of the storm raged on outside of the bathroom, but it didn't faze us. I felt the counter under my ass and then Roman's hands under my shirt, stroking the skin of my back. I ran my hands over his skin, finding ridges and dips of muscles. He was smooth and soft, the light dusting of hair rougher. I opened my legs wider and cursed the sheet between us.

Roman tugged at the hem of my shirt. Up and off, it was lost to the darkness of the bathroom. He slid his hands into my leggings and growled.

"Too fast?" His voice was like gravel. It shook with an audible need.

I shook my head and ran my hand down his arm. Catching his hand, I delighted at the size of it before pulling it out of my leggings. I lifted myself and pushed them down. Roman caught them and yanked them the rest of the way.

I tried to pull him back between my thighs, but he resisted. "Roman?"

He kissed me. "Let me taste you. Please."

I hesitated. "What?"

His hand stroked up my bare thigh and then cupped my sex. "I need to taste you. Here. I need you in my mouth, Megan."

I swallowed. That was…a lot. Dylan didn't do that. It'd been…years.

"Say yes." He kissed me and then went down to his knees. Kissing my inner knee, then my inner thigh, he moaned. "Fuck, Megan, say yes for me."

"Yes."

He growled and raked his teeth over my thigh. "You're stunning. I want to taste and lick every part of you."

I gripped the edge of the sink as he pulled me forward. His face was right in front of my sex, and I was torn between wanting him to do it and wanting to cover myself and run out of the room to avoid having him see me. What the hell was wrong with me? Dylan had really made me that insecure about my sexuality?

His tongue stroked my inner thigh and then he nipped me there. When I jerked, he growled and pulled my thighs onto his shoulders.

I tried to hold myself off him, knowing I was heavy.

He just pulled me farther so I had no choice. Resting my weight on his shoulders, I gripped the countertop and let my head fall back. Roman made a delighted moan and nipped closer to my sex. "That's it. I want all of you."

I squirmed at the first flick of his tongue across my folds. The second went deeper and I gasped. When he stroked his tongue deeper, I clamped my teeth down over my lip to keep the sounds from escaping.

"Let me hear you. I want to know what I do to you, Megan. I want to hear you." When Roman stroked his tongue over my most sensitive spot, I squeaked. That made him growl against it and flick his tongue harder.

Helpless to his assault, I panted, I moaned, I cried out. He rewarded me with harder and faster flicks of his tongue and then by sucking me into his mouth. Where had he read the book on exactly what my body liked? Within seconds, I was on the edge, fighting to keep an orgasm at bay. Roman would have none of it, though. He licked and sucked me right over that edge and kept going.

15

ROMAN

My mate. I knew for sure now. I didn't want our first intimate encounter to have any negative feelings attached for her, so I didn't go past tasting her. When I finally finished and she'd come on my tongue a few more times, I pulled her shirt back over her head and helped her get her pants back on. She was quiet as I dressed her and then settled us back in the tub with her curled between my legs, the sheet back in place.

I was rock hard and desperate to take her and mark her as mine, but I knew that she had unfinished business to attend to first. But she was going to be mine and that was that. I wasn't going to share her with anyone once I marked her. Already, the possessiveness I felt over her was overwhelming.

"I can do that for you, too..." Her voice was quiet, shy.

I tilted her head up to look at me and found that she wouldn't meet my eyes. Growling lightly, I nipped at her shoulder through her shirt. "Don't clam up on me."

Meeting my heated gaze, she lifted her chin and licked her lips. "I can return the favor. I'm not... I'm not greedy. I don't want to be greedy, I mean."

My dick throbbed, but I ignored it. "I'd love that, but another time. That was about you. About me showing you what I think of you. How attractive and sexy and magnetic I find you."

She didn't breathe. "Later?"

I leaned forward and caught her mouth in a kiss. "Later."

Heat burned in her eyes, but she just nodded and settled against my chest again. "Later."

I wrapped my arms around her waist and sighed, content with where I was. For the first time since landing in Florida, I wasn't focused on the stifling heat, or the fact that I missed the steady action of our missions in Siberia. I felt like I'd just come home and it was time to relax.

"I don't know anything about you." Her fingers stroked over my arms. "And, god, what does that say about me?"

I held her tighter. "It doesn't say anything about you, but that you want me and I want you."

"What about you, though?"

"What about me?"

"Tell me something about yourself. You've heard all about my recent melodrama. I wanna know about you."

I wrapped my legs around her as the storm raged on outside. Cradling her, ready to save her with my life, I pressed my lips against her hair. "My team and I moved here just a little while back. A month ago. We were in Siberia. Now, we're here."

"*Siberia?*"

"Yeah. We all grew up there."

"What? That's so unexpected. You sound like you could've grown up down the street." She rested her head on my shoulder and smiled. "What kind of lifeguarding does one do in Siberia?"

I chuckled. My mate was sharp. "The lifesaving kind. And where we grew up is kind of an area of expats. I can speak perfect Russian for you, if you'd like.

I dropped my voice and spoke to her in my native tongue. "вы прекрасны."

She giggled. "I like it."

"I like you."

"No, we're talking about you. Tell me more."

"What do you want to know?"

With a little shrug, she sighed. "I don't know. Have you ever been married?"

"No."

"Girlfriend?"

"Of course not."

"Children?"

"No. Do you have children?"

"No. I would've mentioned them by now." She looked up at me. "What's your favorite food?"

"All of it." I smiled. "Do you cook?"

Megan nodded. "I'm a good cook. I learned from my nana growing up. She was a stereotypical Italian grandmother who lived to feed her family homemade meals. She taught me everything."

"I can make sandwiches."

"That's not cooking."

"Well, it's better than most of the guys on the team can do. That's got to count for something."

"Are your parents still living?"

"Yes. They're still together, living happily in Siberia." I smiled to myself. "They still act like kids."

"That must've been nice growing up."

"It was. How was your life growing up?"

Her hands went still and she curled into herself more. "Fine, I guess. We had money and I never wanted for anything."

"But?"

"But my parents were only married for three years, and I don't even know how many stepsiblings I have. I have several half-siblings that I don't see. Typical rich-kid sob story. My nanny raised me. Mommy and Daddy didn't spend enough time with me. Blah, blah, blah."

"We don't have those stories where I come from. You'll have to tell it to me some time."

With a light laugh, she began stroking my arms again and settled back into me. "Are you really this nice?"

I frowned. "I guess?"

"You don't know?"

"I'm not sure what you mean. I haven't really done anything especially nice."

She sat up and turned to face me. I missed her in my arms instantly. "You saved my life. You are very kind and generous in the things you say and the way you say them. You did...that...*you know* to me without demanding anything in return. You're nice."

I scowled. "Wow, your standards are low. I saved you because you needed help and it's what I do. The things I say are completely true. And what I did to you was just as much for me as it was for you. I wanted the taste of you on my lips."

She blushed and turned back into me. "Okay."

"You deserve more than what he has given you." I pulled her back against my chest and breathed in the scent of her hair. "I can show you."

She stayed quiet. If she thought for a minute I just meant sexually, though, she had another thing coming. I didn't care if I ever went back to Siberia anymore. She was my mate, and she was going to learn through my actions what to expect from a mate. I was going to make sure she knew how she deserved to be treated. And what *nice* really meant.

16

MEGAN

Spending the rest of the night in the tub with Roman should've been uncomfortable. Somehow, I'd dozed against his chest and got the best sleep I could remember having in years. When I came awake the next morning, I was still in his arms and he was stroking my hair. I didn't want to read too much into it. What would a man like Roman see in a woman like me? The whole night was probably just a coping mechanism—human contact as a way to deal with an intense situation. Yet, the way he looked at me promised so much more. Or maybe I was being overly hopeful since I wanted more.

"Storm's over."

I climbed to my feet and smiled down at him. "I need to brush my teeth and then look around the house. You probably need to go check on your team."

Shaking his head, he stood up and out of the tub, right into my space. Cupping my face, he kissed me tenderly and grinned against my mouth. "Trying to get rid of me?"

Not a chance. I'd given up on ignoring the sexual attraction I felt when next to him. I wanted him to stay and keep doing really amazing things to me. "Nope."

"Good."

I found him a spare toothbrush and we brushed our teeth together, our eyes meeting in the mirror, a tense game of awareness. His chest was still bare and I could still feel his beard between my thighs. When we were finished and I put the toothpaste away, Roman picked me up and sat me on the counter, kissing me deeply. He gripped my ass and rocked his erection into me.

"Good morning."

I bit my lip when he pulled away and sighed. He was so hot. "Good morning."

"I need to get myself some clothes."

Did he really? I trailed my eyes over his back as he walked out of the bathroom and fought the urge to drag him back inside. "Okay."

"I'll be back in just a few minutes, okay? Stay here until I get back? We can go check on your shop together."

I arched an eyebrow and shrugged. "I guess."

He pulled me into his arms and nipped my lip. "Please?"

Melting against him, I nodded.

Laughing, he backed away. "I'll be back as fast as I can."

I didn't want to see him leave, for some reason, so I climbed the stairs to investigate the crash I'd heard the night before. I wondered how much damage had been done.

I had to laugh. The master bedroom window had shattered. It'd rained into the room and the bed was soaked—ruined, without a doubt. Nothing else was severely damaged inside the house. I'd gotten lucky.

I took a fast shower and got dressed in another pair of yoga pants and a T-shirt. By the time I got back downstairs, Roman had returned. Seeing him standing in the doorway, in a pair of board shorts and a T-shirt, I realized I'd missed him. I was happy to see him back, and something inside of me breathed a sigh of relief. It should've scared me that I was getting attached to a man so far out of my league. And, even though my husband left me for another woman, I was technically still married. It was a recipe for disaster, but when he smiled at me, I felt like he'd missed me, too.

I stepped into his open embrace and wrapped my arms around his waist. He smelled like cedar and citrus and was so warm. I wanted to stay curled in his arms all day. "Hi."

He wagged his brows at me. "You look beautiful."

I looked down at my bare feet and ignored the compliment. "How is it out there?"

"Rough." He took my hand and led the way out to the porch. Part of it was missing. "It looks like the porch and the upstairs window are the only things that suffered significant damage. A few shingles on the roof, but I can fix that easily."

I grinned. "I can, too."

"Touché."

The water had receded and left behind seaweed and lots of debris. The streets were littered with bricks and boards and bits from damaged homes—and probably my porch. Most of the houses I could see weren't damaged beyond repair, though. With some hard, steady work, we could get the island back in good shape in a month or so.

"You stayed behind, Megan?!" My neighbor, Cameron Patrick, stood in her driveway with her hands on her hips. "I thought you left with Dylan. I saw him loading stuff up in his sports car."

I dropped Roman's hand, instantly ashamed of myself. I'd forgotten that I was on the island that Dylan and I had made our home. People knew we were married. I couldn't be out with Roman as though it was completely normal. I winced and rubbed at my head, a headache forming already.

"You okay, honey?"

I blinked a few times and then nodded at Cameron. "Sorry, yeah. I was just... The storm really freaked me out. I usually evac, but I got caught up in it. Did you stay?"

"No way. Bobby and I left days ago. We had a little vacation at his mom's. I had to come back first thing this morning, though. You know how I love this little house."

I looked over her house and forced a smile. "Looks like you faired pretty well."

"Yeah, we did." As her gaze fell on Roman, she looked like she was about to jump out of her skin. "Who's your friend, honey?"

Roman stepped forward and shook her hand. "Roman. I'm newer to the island. Megan and I ended up stranded together last night."

Cameron sighed happily. "How romantic."

I blushed and didn't know what to say, so I just stared at her.

She rolled her eyes and waved me off. "You deserve a night of being stranded with a man like Roman, honey. Dylan mentioned to Bobby that you caught him cheating last week. I didn't know about any of it, I swear. I'm still mad at Bobby for not telling me. I would have come to you immediately. Before you had to find out like you did, I mean."

I had no words, so I just nodded.

Thankfully, Roman was there to save me again. "Well, it was nice meeting you, but we've got to run."

He didn't take my hand for the rest of the walk to the shop. He just walked by my side and shared the silence with me. I was floored to know that my neighbors knew about Dylan cheating on me. If Bobby Patrick knew, everyone knew. I was a joke. The laughingstock of the neighborhood. Not that I had a right to feel self-righteous or anything. Not after what I'd done with Roman. I didn't feel like I had much of a leg to stand on.

When we got to the shop, I just stood there in complete shock. Where the building used to be, there was now only a frame of a building. The whole place had been wiped out—reduced to a pile of rubble.

I waited for tears or even sorrow to hit, but I just kept staring, feeling more and more relieved as the minutes passed. Then, I laughed. The whole damn shop was gone. Matilda had wiped me clean out of the business I shared with Dylan. I still had my house, but my SUV was gone, the shop was gone, and my husband was gone. It was like fate had snipped all of the ties I had with the life I was living a week ago.

"You okay?"

I wiped my eyes, tears forming from laughing, and then took Roman's hand. "Yeah. I'm...uh...I'm good, actually. Really good."

17

ROMAN

I didn't know what was going on inside of Megan's head, but she'd taken my hand again. When her fingers intertwined with mine, I felt like the luckiest guy on the island. She'd just found her business destroyed, yet she was laughing. Why was she happy? I didn't want to chance upsetting her, so I just walked with her. To the other end of town we went, taking in the extent of the damage along the way.

I was sweating, but I felt like the heat wasn't as miserable with Megan next to me. I couldn't focus on it as much when she was there. "Want to meet my team?"

She nodded. "I'd like that. Your lifeguarding team from Siberia."

I nodded. It was obvious she didn't buy the lifeguarding story, but she didn't push either. She just accepted it.

The P.O.L.A.R. office was standing unharmed. There didn't appear to be any damage done to it at all. The door was wide open and gripes and complaints could be heard coming from inside. With the power out, there was no AC. The rest of the guys were probably roasting.

"I'm coming in with a guest. Are you all decent?"

Serge came to the door and grunted. "Are they ever?"

"Serge, this is Megan. Megan, my alph—*boss*, Serge." I kept my hand on her back, my bear was bristling, not at all appreciating that I was leading her into an office full of other unmated males.

Hannah stepped out from under Serge's arm and smiled at Megan. "Another woman. Thank god."

I introduced everyone. Megan smiled politely and said hello to everyone, but she remained close to my side, her back pressed against my hand harder, like she needed the connection, too.

"The generator isn't working. I can't take this torture." Alexei wiped his face and growled. "A couple more degrees and I'm going to spontaneously combust."

Megan snorted but tried to hide it behind a cough. "Sorry. I could take a look at it. I'm good at fixing things."

Serge raised his brows. "Yeah, sure. Have at it."

"If you fix it, I'm going to plant the biggest kiss on you, Megan." Alexei winked at her and blew her a kiss.

I surprised everyone by curling my lip, baring my teeth, and growling at him. Staring him down, I pulled Megan into my side and shook my head at him. "No."

Megan just giggled and pointed to the back of the building. "The generator around there?"

Serge nodded, his mouth slightly ajar. "Roman?"

"Later." I followed Megan like a lost bear cub, happy to trail behind her for the view, if nothing else.

"Did you just growl at your friend?" Megan found the generator on the ground by the back door and sank to her knees in front of it.

I didn't want to talk about it. I didn't want her to think I was scary. Or weird. She didn't know my nature. Until she did, she wouldn't understand. "How'd you learn to fix things?"

She looked back at me over her shoulder, those hazel eyes crinkled at the corners like she was enjoying herself. "Okay, we won't talk about how you growled like a zoo animal back there. I learned how to fix stuff by just doing it. When I first moved into my house, it was quite a fixer-upper. I watched hours and hours of YouTube videos. That got me pretty far. Trial and error took me the rest of the way."

I knelt beside her and watched as she did her thing. Without any tools, she was limited, but within five minutes, the generator roared to life. I laughed as a loud cheer rang out from inside. "Looks like you're the real hero here."

I loved the smile that spread across her face—and the confidence. "What can I say?"

Her genuine smile was so beautiful that my chest ached looking at her. "Should we head back to your house, now?" I had to admit, I had an ulterior motive for getting her alone again.

Her eyes went to my mouth and darkened. With a nod, she stood up and dusted off her hands on her pants. "Yeah, I guess I better get started with those repairs. The sooner the better."

"Stop by and see Susie, Roman. She was climbing the walls worried about you last night." Alexei stuck his head out of the back door and winked at Megan again. "And you, sweets, you're welcome to stay here. You miracle worker you."

I gritted my teeth and barely held my bear from bursting forth and attacking the hell out of Alexei. "Go!"

He just grinned cockily. He'd been intentionally trying to get my goat. "Don't forget Susie."

I sighed. I wanted nothing more than for the two of us to head straight back to Megan's, but Alexei was right. I should stop by Susie's. "Quick stop on the way?"

Megan nodded. "As long as you're talking about the Susie Davies at the Bayfront Diner, I'm more than happy to accompany you. Especially if her shop sustained little damage and she's back up and running. I could use a cinnamon roll."

When she grinned, I pulled her into me and kissed her, unable to stop myself. "I guess I should feed you."

"I think I can feed myself."

"We could feed each other?"

Blushing, she pulled away and looked out at the ocean. "It's crazy how much it can change so quickly."

"The ocean?" I watched the sea with her, my hands itching to touch her again.

"Life."

"My people put a lot of significance in change. We're always changing, shifting. Change is good."

When she looked back at me, she was blinking away tears. "Maybe you're right."

"Come here."

She wiped her eyes and let me pull her into my side. My need to claim her transformed into a need to take care of her, and I wanted to hold her until she realized how much good her change in marital status would bring both of us.

"I don't know what I'm doing, Roman."

I stroked her hair and pressed my lips to her forehead. I wanted her to be mine and all mine right this minute, to be as devoted to me from here on out as I was to her, but I couldn't expect that. She did have feelings for me, of that I was sure, but she probably couldn't comprehend why she was feeling them so intensely or so quickly. "I know. You'll catch up."

She looked up at me and her brows wrinkled. "There's something you're not telling me."

I stared into her eyes, desperate to lay all my cards on the table. Knowing the turmoil she'd been through in the past couple days, though, I wasn't sure she was in the right frame of mind to have another life-changing bomb dropped at her feet.

She wasn't ready to hear the whole fated-mates concept quite yet. "Not right now. Later."

She made a face. "It's always later with you."

"It'll be worth the wait."

She walked a few steps away and looked at me over her shoulder. "I'll be the judge of that."

18

MEGAN

Dropping in for breakfast at Susie's turned out to be an hours-long endeavor. As we strolled Main Street, we ended up stopping to help several different people along the way. Someone needed help removing a tree that had fallen across their driveway. Someone else needed help getting debris cleared away from the front door and into a pile. Roman was never reluctant to pitch in and lend a hand, even to perfect strangers—so different from Dylan. And he seemed to have the strength of ten men! They sure made them tough in Siberia. When people saw him coming, smiles lit their faces. He'd said he'd just arrived on the island a month before, but it was obvious that he'd made an impression in a month's time, and it was easy to see why. He was friendly and generous to everyone.

Dylan wasn't very friendly, and I'd never seen him be generous to anyone but himself. How had I been in denial about him for so long? No one smiled when he walked into a room or when he passed them in the street. No one was excited to see him. And it wasn't hard to figure out why. He either acted as though he was superior to people, or he outright ignored them. I'd even had customers complain about him to me, not knowing that he was my husband. And, of course, I'd made lame excuses for him.

My mind kept going in circles comparing Dylan to Roman, but there wasn't much time to dwell on the comparisons or formulate any conclusions. We stumbled into people that could use our help, and every time, Roman would shoot me a look as if to ask if I minded before he rushed to their aid. He was considerate and thoughtful, two things that I found so refreshing.

We worked until my body ached, and I wasn't sure I could propel myself up the stairs to my house, much less clear away another pile of rubble. Roman didn't seem to have the same problem. He was so strong that he made everything look easy. Next to him, I actually felt small and feminine for the first time in my life. I found myself thinking about what it would be like to slip on one of his T-shirts. It would be large on me, maybe even fit like a dress. I loved that thought.

As tired as I was, my libido still reacted when I looked at him, remembering the way his body felt against mine. But I was exhausted. My bones ached, and the lack of proper sleep, not just last night, but for the past week, was catching up to me.

I watched Roman, still hauling trash and piling it out of people's way. The man had probably cleared a quarter of the island himself. As if he sensed my gaze on him, he looked back at me. His gaze instantly turned heated. Self-consciously, I ran my hands over my hair and then crossed my arms over my chest. I was sweaty, dirty, and I knew my hair was a wreck.

"You are so beautiful." Roman straightened and walked over to me. Mr. Barnes was watching. His wife, Luanne was watching, too.

I forced a smile. "Yeah."

He caught my face in his hands and tipped my head up so I had to look him in the eyes. "I should've taken you straight back to your house this morning. I'm sorry."

Luanne smacked Mr. Barnes on the arm, and they both looked away from us. I knew my cheeks were red and I was so tired that tears filled my eyes. It was embarrassing.

Roman wrapped his arms around me and held me. "Tired?"

I nodded into his chest and sighed. "Sorry. It was a long night, I guess."

"I'll swing back by tomorrow morning to help, John." Roman scooped me into his arms and smiled down at me. "I have to get my girl home."

"Put me down, Roman. I'm too heavy." I squirmed. I wasn't about to let him carry me home. Besides the fact that I really was too heavy, people would see us.

"Do I look like I'm struggling?"

I stopped and looked up at him. He didn't. Not even an inkling of strain anywhere on his face. "What are you, Superman?"

He shot me a panty-melting grin and shrugged. "I'll tell you someday."

"This is insane. You're going to break your back."

"By carrying you? Hardly." He bounced me and laughed when I gasped and locked my arms around his neck. "I'm carrying you. Deal with it."

I stopped fighting since we were so close to my house. I figured he'd put me down when he needed to, and I might as well just enjoy it. His neck was damp under my hands and he was drenched in sweat, but instead of finding the smell of him a turn off, it had the exact opposite effect. He smelled warm and cedary and citrusy and I wanted to rub against him and trap that smell in my brain forever.

I remained in his arms as he carried me to my house, up the stairs, inside, and all the way to the guestroom. He dropped me on the bed and reached over his shoulder to grab his shirt and pull it over his head. In low-slung shorts and a whole lot of glistening abs, he looked down at me and licked his lips. "I'm hungry, Megan."

I stuttered. His smoldering facial expression had sent my brain out to the stratosphere, so his words caught me off guard. "I... I could fix something. There's probably something in the—"

He ran his hand up my calf and didn't stop until his fingers were playing with the hem of my leggings. "Not for that."

I stupidly giggled when I realized what he meant. My heart sped up and my body hummed. When he tugged at my yoga pants, I lifted my hips and let him pull them off of me. The mean little voice at the back of my head screamed that it wasn't a good idea to let him see me in that light. My thighs jiggled too much, my stomach was too soft, my hips too wide, my breasts too small. Not to mention I'd been sweating and I could use a shower.

Roman tossed my yoga pants across the room, pressed his lips to my ankle, and as though he'd read my mind, said, "You smell delicious. Absolutely delicious."

I rolled my eyes, despite my heart racing in my chest. "Sure."

He licked up to my calf. "Like sunshine and cool spring water. I want to devour you."

My mouth went dry. I shivered.

"Roman..." My voice was unrecognizable, breathy and full of desire. It was full-on sex kitten, come-hithering my man to me.

One knee on the bed, Roman moved closer to me.

"Megan? Are you here?"

Roman's head snapped up, the look in his eyes ferocious.

I jerked out of the bed, in a full-on panic, and grabbed for my yoga pants. "Oh, shit. Oh, no."

"Megan?!" My husband's voice called up the stairs, his footsteps following.

Roman pushed the door closed and looked back at me. "I wasn't finished."

I wanted to laugh at the poutiness to his voice, but my husband had just about walked in on us doing...that. I fell into the wall trying to jump into my pants and grunted. Turning my back to Roman so I didn't have to know that he'd seen that, I finished tugging them on and ran my fingers through my hair.

"Megan? Is that you?"

I turned, but Roman was already opening the door. I couldn't see around Roman, but judging by the startled yelp, Dylan had just come face to face with him. *Fuck.*

19

MEGAN

"Who the hell are you and what are you doing in my house?" Dylan demanded to Roman, like he wasn't an entire head and a half shorter than the man.

I stuck my head under Roman's arm and held out my hands, not wanting the weirdness to escalate to something worse. "What are you doing back in *my* house, Dylan?"

Dylan acted as though he'd been slapped. His head jerked back when he saw me, and his face pinched as though he'd been sucking on a lemon. "You... What were you doing in there, Megan?"

"Something private that you interrupted." Roman's voice was a pure growl, the heat that always radiated off him growing stronger.

"Excuse me?" Dylan gathered himself quickly. "That's my *wife* you're talking about."

I squeezed out of the door, planting myself in front of a very angry Roman. "Maybe we should take this downstairs?"

"Fine." Dylan stomped down the stairs, shooting dark glances back at us periodically.

I looked back at Roman and winced. He was not happy. "I don't know what he's doing back here."

He looked over my face, like he was searching for something, and sighed. "I know."

"This is so awkward. I didn't think I'd have to face off with him in front of you." I looked up at the ceiling and groaned.

"You would prefer me to leave?"

The hurt in his voice surprised me, almost as much as the alarm I felt at the thought of him leaving. "No! No. I'm not saying that."

He rolled his shoulders and blew out a breath. "Good."

"Okay." I nodded and turned to the stairs. "I guess we just go down there and see what he wants?"

With a hand on the center of my back, Roman led me down the stairs and into the kitchen. Dylan was looking through the liquor cabinets, slamming doors when he couldn't find anything.

"Yeah, empty. But you should know. You cleaned it out completely." I crossed my arms over my chest and prayed for strength.

Dylan scowled and pointed at Roman. "What is he still doing here?"

Roman growled, something I realized he was prone to doing, and actually curled his lip and bared his teeth at Dylan. It should've been weird, but it actually looked rather natural on him. It was, however, scary as hell. Probably more so when it was directed your way.

"Dylan, what are *you* doing here?"

"I live here, Megan."

I scoffed. "No, actually you don't. You literally don't. All of your stuff—and some of mine, I might add—has been removed."

He glared at Roman but didn't say anything else to him. "That wasn't me. It was Brandi. She told me I should take everything and I fell for it, Megan. I can't tell you how sorry I am."

I scrunched up my face in confusion, suddenly feeling as though I'd been teleported to an alternate reality. "What are you talking about?"

"*She* took everything. Apparently, it was her way of paying me back for not telling her about you." He looked away. "I don't know what came over me. I just had a hankering for something different, or so I thought. She wasn't it, though. I want you back, Megan. You're my wife. We've been together for twelve years. We shouldn't let anyone else get between us."

My brain reeled. "She took everything?"

"The money, the stuff, all of it. I woke up this morning to a rude note. She split—took it all. I came back here immediately when I realized the mistake I'd made. I knew right away I'd messed up."

"You knew 'right away'—after you woke up and she'd cleaned you out and dumped you?"

"Well, I knew yesterday."

I shook my head and sat down on one of the barstools. "Dylan, you stole from the business, left me to board up this home and the shop myself, took things from this house that didn't belong to you, and that's not even the worst! You've also been cheating on me for who knows how long, and when you left me to pick up your slack, I was nearly killed."

"Yeah, you stupid sonofabitch. I found her half-drowned in the ocean." Roman shook, his big hands balled up on the counter next to me. "The only reason I haven't snapped your scrawny ass in half yet is out of respect for Megan."

"Who the hell are you?!" Dylan tempted fate. "And why are you still here?"

"Stop. Dylan, you need to leave. You don't live here anymore. That was your choice, and I am not taking you back."

"Oh, I should have known. Just like your parents, huh? Give up on marriage at the first sign of trouble, is that it, Megan? You won't even honor our marriage by giving me another chance?"

I froze. Dylan was playing his trump card, and it felt like a gut punch. As if that wasn't enough, the icing on the cake was when he pulled out his wallet and slid across a picture of the two of us on our first date.

"I still carry this. I still love you. I don't care if you slept with him. I don't care. We can get past all of this. We can rebuild the shop. I'll do my part. I'll do more than my part. You deserve more."

I closed my eyes and shook my head harder.

"Megan, please. We can make it work. I *know* you don't want to follow in your mom's shoes. You give up on me, how long until you give up on the next guy? And the next? How many more men will you go through, just like her? It's easy to walk away, but anything worth having is worth fighting for."

I opened my eyes and the first thing I saw was Roman's hands. Still balled up, still tight, the veins strained. He was clearly holding himself back. He wanted to punch Dylan, I knew. Yet, he didn't. He was just waiting—giving me the chance to be in control.

My heart pounded. Dylan was right about one thing. I was willing to throw everything I'd worked at for the past twelve years away for a chance with Roman. Looking at him, touching him, was such an uplifting experience, it was like magic. Yes, I felt like there was magic happening when I was next to him. He was everything I admired. He behaved honorably to others, and to me as well. He said kind words to me, and his actions backed those words up. I'd never been treated so well by anyone before.

Could it be real, though? How long could it last? How was it possible that a man like Roman wanted to enter into a long-term relationship with me? It wasn't that I lacked self-esteem entirely, but I wasn't blind, either. He was stunning. I was...average.

He suddenly swore from beside me. Looking down at his watch, he swore again and then shot a deadly glare at Dylan. "I have to leave. I will be back."

"Don't bother."

Roman eased me off the stool and, with an arm around my waist, pulled me to the door with him. "Something's going down at the office. It's urgent or I wouldn't dream of leaving right now. Don't make any decisions while I'm gone. Please. I can see the wheels in your head turning and I know he's getting to you, but what he's saying is complete bullshit. He's trying to play you. You don't belong with him, Megan. You deserve so much better."

I felt like crying. I stared at my feet until Roman slid a finger under my chin and raised my head.

"Look at me. This I will promise you right now. If you chose me, there will not be another man after me. I'm not a twelve-year kind of guy. I'm a forever kind of guy. Just, please, wait for me to return."

I wanted to hold onto him, but he pressed a kiss to my forehead and was gone that fast, leaving me there with Dylan, who had no qualms about hitting below the belt to get me back.

There I was, the same large-stature woman with small breasts and big hips, who'd walked in on her husband as he went to town screwing his slender, beautiful mistress in our bed. A week later, I was still the same woman with a flabby belly and cellulite thighs, but now there were two men fighting over me. Life made zero sense.

20

ROMAN

I ripped the roof off the house without a strain. Throwing a slew of trashed shingles behind me, I growled and tugged at a beam that blocked my way in.

Roman! Calm yourself before you bring the entire house down on them!

I let out a wild roar in Serge's direction, unable to heed his command at that moment. I knew, deep down, that he was right. The family trapped in their bathroom could easily be crushed to death if I didn't handle the extraction delicately, but I was riled to the core.

Konstantin moved in next to me and grabbed a beam that was starting to slip. "Go!"

I lowered myself into the house and cleared a path headed in the direction of their screams. Dmitry and Alexei were right behind me, both offering support when the house shook. Serge grabbed me and yanked me backward just as I was about to pull the bathroom door open.

"Stop!" He jerked his chin up and gestured to the beam over the door. It was balancing precariously and would have undoubtedly cracked my skull if I'd followed through and opened the door.

The realization should have sobered me. It should have forced me to stop and pay closer attention to what I was doing. It didn't. I couldn't focus on anything other than the fact that I'd left my mate alone with a man who didn't deserve her but had a claim to her anyway. A man who was talking out his ass a mile a minute. It had been so obvious to me that he was saying whatever he thought would get the reaction he wanted from her, with no regard for the truth.

"You go and help Konstantin support the structure until we can get them out!"

I growled but did as I was told. My bear ripped at me, demanding to be let out. I knew exactly what he'd do—run back to Megan's house and tear her weasel of a husband to shreds. Unable to maintain control, I felt claws begin to extend from my fingertips.

"What the fuck happened, brother?"

I shook. I didn't know how much longer I could hold myself together.

Seconds later, the team emerged with the family—all injury-free. Good. We could get the hell out of there. The house didn't stand on its own for much longer, and as it collapsed in front of us, the family cried. The parents hugged their two children close and thanked us profusely for rescuing them and getting them all out safely.

My mind was elsewhere. I kept seeing Megan with that slimy little asshole. Would she buy into his manipulative bullshit? I knew he was only looking for someone to sponge off of and Megan had a heart of gold. He had nowhere to sleep and no money, but it was what he deserved. A taste of his own medicine. He'd had done to him exactly what he'd done to Megan. Karma. It pissed me off how he thought he could just waltz right back in and pick up where he left off.

I would dedicate myself to caring for Megan and respecting her needs and feelings. He never would. She didn't necessarily know that, though.

"You and me need to have a talk, Roman." Serge glared at me and pointed to the team's van. "Now."

The rest of the guys climbed into the back, as though that would give Serge and I any privacy. Not from shifter hearing, it wouldn't. I sat fuming, terrified that I might be losing my mate. I needed to get back there as soon as possible and fight for her.

"What the fuck is going on with you?"

"You know damn good and well what."

Serge nodded. He knew because he'd acted the same way when he met his mate. We'd been on a mission and he'd nearly blown the whole thing to hell after meeting Hannah. "I have a feeling. Mate?"

"Yeah."

The guys in the back cheered, but Serge growled. "What's the problem, then? And there is a problem, isn't there, Roman?"

I growled. "There is. She has...a husband. He left her, and she almost died because of his lack of concern." I released a slow breath. "He just came back. Says he's sorry. Says he loves her."

"Well, that explains why you almost got an entire family crushed to death."

"She's *my* mate. Mine. The fucker walks back in acting as though nothing ever happened. He's trying to trick her into thinking he cares and that she needs him."

Serge sighed. "Man, she's yours. No matter what the asshole says or does."

"What if she picks him?"

"She won't. It's not going to happen. If she's truly your mate, she's going to feel the same for you as you feel for her. She just won't understand it the same way. Non-shifters don't really listen to or trust their instincts the way we do. They also lie and deceive, so..." He shrugged. "I wish I'd have explained everything to Hannah earlier. It would've made things easier."

"Yeah, might I suggest you not give her your claiming mark until she understands why you do that?" Alexei called through the back glass.

Serge stepped on the brakes hard enough to nearly slam Alexei's face into the glass. "Shut the fuck up."

I looked out the front window, thinking. "Should I tell her? Everything?"

"Are you sure she's your mate?"

Scowling at him, I debated throttling him. "Are you sure Hannah is your mate?"

He snarled back at me. "Point taken."

I sat there and tried to think it through. If she understood what was happening between us, maybe it would help her make her decision with more confidence. Maybe she would understand that we were meant to be together.

"Explain it to her. Just do it as gently as possible. It's a lot for a human to take in."

I nodded. "Let me out near Latte Love coffee shop."

"Do I look like a chauffeur?"

"Serge."

"Fine."

I was nervous about revealing my shifter nature to Megan. She was my mate, though. That had to make it easier for her to understand everything. She was made for me, a shifter. That had to mean something.

When he stopped outside of Lotte Love, Serge clapped me on the shoulder. "Good luck, brother."

"Give her your cub eyes if you have to." Alexei grinned. "It works for me."

"Shut up." Dmitry punched him and shook his head. "She's all yours, brother."

I rolled my shoulders and walked toward her house. With each step, I felt more tense. I didn't want to lose my mate before I even got the chance to show her what a life together would be like. Growling at myself, I broke into a run. This had to work.

21

MEGAN

I'd left Dylan in the kitchen while I started the generator and took a long, hot shower. I figured, what else could he steal? I emerged, to find that he'd lit candles and produced a bottle of wine from somewhere. When I came back to face him, he was in the shadows of candlelight. I flipped on the lights, willing to suck power from other things in the house to avoid sitting in the dark with him.

"Oh, okay. I just thought the candles added a nice ambiance." He crossed his ankle over his knee and stretched his arms out along the back of the couch, cockily sure of himself, which pissed me off.

"You can stay."

He grinned. "You're making the best choice, Megan. I—"

"ONLY until you find somewhere else to live." I balled my hands into fists to help me contain my emotions. "You'll need to figure something out with the bed in your room if you decide that staying here for the moment is best for you. It was damaged in the storm."

Sitting up, he shook his head. "Megan, let's talk about this."

"Okay."

"I apologized." He waited.

"And?"

"Well, I meant it. I am sorry. I shouldn't have gone the route that I did. I should've come to you when I felt dissatisfied."

I nodded and stared over his shoulder. "You should have. You didn't have to blindside me, Dylan. You didn't have to cheat, you didn't have to steal, and you didn't have to evacuate the island without the slightest concern for my safety or wellbeing."

"What do you want me to say here?"

"Nothing. There's nothing you can say. It's just as much my fault that it's come to this. I don't think I ever really saw you until this past week—not really. Every glance has been through rose-colored glasses. I've been in complete denial about the person I'd been living with—married to." I scrubbed my palms down my face. "We don't love each other. Maybe we used to, I'm not even sure. Did we just stop at some point? If we did, it was long before Brandi or Roman. If you loved me, you wouldn't have treated me so cruelly. If I loved you, it would've crushed me when you...well, you know. Honestly, though, Dylan, I feel relieved."

He leaned back on the couch, his kind expression replaced with one of disgust. "You feel *relieved*?"

"Yes. Relieved. Free. Like maybe I have a chance to actually be happy." I met his eyes. "I spent most of our marriage feeling inadequate and doing everything you wanted because I felt like I had to...to earn your love. I didn't think there was any other way because I wasn't pretty enough to keep you, or thin enough, so I figured I'd just bend over backward doing what you wanted for the rest of my life and that would ensure a long, happy marriage. You *let* me do that. You let me feel those things. And I wasn't happy at all."

"I didn't make you feel ugly."

"You never once told me I was beautiful—or attractive, even. You didn't call me pretty or tell me that you liked the way I looked. You wouldn't even touch my stomach."

He scowled and sat forward again. "So, it's all my fault?"

"No. It's not. But you pulled some massive shit this last week, Dylan, and that really opened my eyes. Even if I wanted to forgive you, I'd never be able to, not fully. I'd never stop looking over my shoulder to see if you were fucking someone else, or stealing from me, or setting me up to pull the rug out from under me again."

"This is bullshit, Megan."

"What did you think was going to happen? Honestly."

"You don't have to be a bitch."

I raised my eyebrows. "I'm being serious. Tell me what you honestly thought was going to happen when you walked back in here today. Talk me through it."

"I thought you'd fucking be glad that your husband came back. Instead, you were already spreading your legs for the first guy who wandered by. Didn't take you long."

"For the sake of argument, I'm going to ignore the fact that you're being a condescending ass, and ask you why you thought I'd be glad you were back. After what you did." I shook my head. "I was seconds from drowning. You left with zero regard for me. Instead of helping me and the two of us both getting out of here safely, you cleaned me out and ran off with your mistress. I nearly died trying to secure the house and the business. Is any of this sinking in?"

"Come on. You're not serious."

"Yes, I am. I got caught in a rip current and swept out to sea. I couldn't stay afloat. The last thing I remember was panicking when I realized I was going to die. Do you want to know what went through my head in those final moments?"

For a change, he looked slightly shaken. "What?"

"I was thinking about how easy it would be for you. If I died. No messy divorce, no prenup, no embarrassment. You'd just get a nice lump sum of life insurance money and get to run off with your Brandi."

"That's not... I... Megan, I wouldn't prefer you dead."

"I was so angry, thinking that I'd made it easier for you. You don't deserve anything else from me. You've taken more than you deserve already. Still, I feel like it's only right to be decent." I blew out a rough breath. "And that's the only reason I'm going to let you stay under my roof until you get your life together. I'll call the lawyers in the morning and get them started on the divorce papers. If you do decide to stay here, you're going to need to stay out of my way and don't bother me. We should probably talk about a timeline, too. My hospitality does not extend indefinitely. I suggest you find a job as soon as possible and then look for a place of your own."

"Megan, don't do this. I have nothing else." For once, there was emotion in his eyes. "I'm sorry I did all of this to you. I'm sorry about Brandi. I'm really sorry. I'll change. I'll do whatever you want. Just, please, don't make me start over."

"You did it to yourself. Don't make me out to be the bad guy. I'm going to go out and get some fresh air." I steeled myself against his hang-dog expression and walked away.

I pulled the door shut behind me and leaned against it. My heart was hammering in my chest and I felt nauseous. Why? Why did I feel like the villain? I wasn't being mean to Dylan. I was standing up for myself for a change. My patterning told me that I should comfort him, placate him, please him even if that meant being unfair to myself. It was hell to get out of that old way of thinking. The truth was that I wasn't leaving Dylan. I wasn't walking out on *him*. He had already walked out and left *me*. The only reason he'd come back with his lame attempt at groveling was that it hadn't worked out with his mistress and he had nowhere else to go for the moment. It had nothing to do with his feelings for me. He was a user, and I had been an enabler.

I walked down to the beach and sat in the sand just inches from the water's reach. I was still mad at it for trying to kill me. I figured it would be a while longer before I could wade back out into it without my mind reliving its force as it dragged me under.

Wasn't that just life, though? It knocked you down, and you had to take a moment before you had the strength to get back up and have another go at it. Was it crazy to even be thinking of starting something new with Roman when I was still reeling from Dylan's betrayal? If it was too soon, would I just get sucked back underwater?

22

MEGAN

"Hey."

I glanced over my shoulder at Roman and forced a smile. "Hey, yourself."

He sat next to me in the sand and stared out at the Atlantic, too. "Crazy to think that it's the same ocean that tried to take you away from me last night."

I looked away, afraid to let him see the tears well in my eyes. I buried my fingers in the sand and rested my cheek on my knee.

"I have something I need to tell you." He sighed. "You're probably going to think I'm crazy, but please hear me out."

My stomach twisted. "What?"

"I want to be with you. I want it so desperately that I can't think of anything else. I know it probably sounds insane to you. We met less than twenty-four hours ago, but I know that you are the woman I was meant to be with." He turned to face me full on. "My people...they just know when they meet 'the one.' Our soulmate."

My stomach twisted tighter. "Your people? Russians?"

"No. I'm not...normal, Megan. I'm sorry if it all sounds ridiculous and I'm just blurting it all out like this, but I need you to know. I need you to know about me before you make a decision."

"What are you talking about, Roman?"

"Shapeshifters. My people are shapeshifters. We have the ability to shift—to transform—into bears. Polar bears, to be specific." He paused. "I'm a polar bear shifter from Siberia, and you're my soulmate."

My heart sank, plummeted right to my feet. "Shapeshifters. Polar bears."

"Yeah. I know it probably sounds crazy to you, but we're real. I'm real. And so are soulmates. I am one hundred percent sure that you and I are made for each other. We're meant to be together."

I blinked a few times, unsure of how to react to everything he was laying at my feet. "Um... You're a polar bear shifter, and I was made for you."

"I know it's a lot to digest. You might even think I'm off my rocker right now. I can show you, though. I'll shift into my bear if it'll help, Megan. Let me prove it to you. Let me fight for you the way you deserve to be fought for."

I was going to cry. I just felt physically ill. "Can I think about it?"

Roman sat back, his face crestfallen. "You already chose him."

I shook my head. "No. He's leaving. It's definitely over between us."

"But you haven't chosen me, either."

I bit my lip hard and shook my head again. "I just need time to think."

"This was too much, huh?" He looked crushed, and the contrast between the true devastation on his face and the irritation that had shone on Dylan's made this all that much harder. But he was obviously insane.

I nodded and squeezed my eyes shut.

"Fuck. I'm sorry. Come here." His voice sounded heavy with emotion as he pulled me into his arms and held me against his chest. "I'm thinking of myself, and you're going through the end of your marriage. I'm sorry, Megan. I won't pressure you. I promise."

I dug my fingers into his shirt and held on, desperate for things to be different. He clearly had serious mental issues. I couldn't pursue anything with him. I wasn't going to drown again. Yet, it hurt. Walking away, saying goodbye to him was harder than walking away from my twelve-year marriage.

He held me as I cried, his arms wrapped tightly around me. He murmured softly into my hair and cradled me through my tears. Damn, I felt so safe in his arms. Why did I have to fall for someone with such huge issues?

He apologized again and again, but he didn't beg me to change my mind. When I'd finished crying and pulled back, he let go. He didn't hide the sorrow in his own eyes, but he forced a smile for me. We stood up, and he pressed one last kiss to my forehead before standing rooted to the spot as he watched me walk away.

I couldn't go back to the house. I was in no mood to face Dylan. Instead, I walked past the house and through the sand dunes that separated Main Street from the residential area. On Main Street, I headed toward the shop, keeping my head down until I got there.

Not knowing what else to do, I plopped down on the concrete in front and stared at the crumpled wreckage. My whole life had been completely upended this week.

I was all cried out, so I just sat there relatively numb. The sun had set, the island was in darkness, and I wasn't sure where to go. Sunkissed Key suddenly felt suffocating.

I needed to scram. My mom had a place in Miami. It wouldn't take me long to get there, provided Matilda hadn't wrought too much damage along the way. It was a perfect plan, a chance to get away and to get my head on straight again.

As I headed back home, I saw Cameron Patrick lying in her hammock, her cat in her lap, and let myself in through her open patio door. "Cameron?"

She jumped, sending her cat skittering away. "Megan! You scared the living tar right out of me!"

"Sorry."

"What's up?"

"I can't stay here on the island. Dylan's back and I need to put some distance between us. I lost my SUV to the storm. Any chance I could borrow your car for a few days?"

She sat up gracefully and came over to me. "Oh, honey, yes."

"I wouldn't ask if it wasn't an emergency."

"Stop. It's fine. You know I walk everywhere anyway. Take the car for as long as you need. I'm not going anywhere unless another hurricane happens along." She hugged me tightly and then pulled me into her house. "Where are you going? Somewhere safe, I hope?"

"My mom's."

She patted her chest. "Good. Just be good to yourself, honey. You deserve some pampering, you really do."

I nodded and took the keys she handed me. "Thank you, Cameron. I'll repay you when I get back."

"Nonsense. Go on, now. Get out of here. I've got plans with that hammock tonight and they don't involve you." She pushed me toward the garage door and flashed me a smile. "Be safe."

I settled into her car and backed out after hitting the garage button. Minutes later, I was on the highway, heading north to the mainland and some breathing room.

23

ROMAN

"I understand what you're going through, Roman, but I need you to drag your mopey ass somewhere else. Kerrigan has been trying to get into that drawer behind you for the last hour."

I looked up at Serge and blinked. "Huh?"

"Move, brother." He gestured toward Kerrigan and shook his head. "You're in her way, but she's not going to be bold enough to ask you to move."

"I would've asked...eventually."

I scooted out of the way and looked around. What was I supposed to be doing? "Any jobs for me?"

Kerrigan, P.O.L.A.R.'s new dispatcher shook her head and gestured to Serge.

I looked at Serge. "You're still not giving me anything?"

"No can do. You're not in the right headspace. Until you're able to focus on a task, sending you out will make you a liability to yourself and others."

Kerrigan smiled at me, a gentle smile that someone might give to a feeble grandparent or a sick child. "Maybe there are smaller tasks that need doing? If you're feeling up to it."

Serge shook his head. "Nope."

"Fuck, man. What do you want me to do?" I stood up, sending my chair flying into the cabinet behind me. "I'm going crazy."

"Outside. Take it outside." Dmitry stood up and pointed at the door.

Serge gave him a weird look and shook his head. "He's right. Come on, brother. Outside with me."

I stomped out the door and looked around, the same way I did every time I stepped outside. I was hoping to see Megan. It'd been over a month since I'd last seen her that day on the beach and it was killing me. Even if she didn't choose me, I just wanted to see her and make sure that she was okay and happy.

"Go after your mate, Roman. This isn't going to resolve itself until you do."

I growled and shoved him, my anger boiling to the surface. "You think this is my choice? You think I don't want to go to her every second of every day?!"

He shoved me back. "I don't know! All you're doing is sitting around, mopey-assed and bitchy about it."

I drew back my fist and slammed it into his jaw before I even thought twice about it. It felt so good, I almost did it again, until Serge ducked and hit me with an uppercut that sent me flying backward into the side of the building. That felt good, too. After feeling nothing but deep sorrow for a month, I was ready to trade it some good old anger.

I went for him again and he was there, ready for me. He took my punches and gave back just as good as he got. Rolling around on the ground, we tussled until we were too tired to keep going.

Flat on my back on the sandy ground, I looked up at the sky and swore. "I don't know why I just blurted it all out to her like that."

Serge sat up. "We told you to. Sure, maybe you could've had a little more finesse about it, but we all thought it was the right way to go, man."

"This is killing me. Literally."

"I was there. When I couldn't get Hannah to talk to me, I thought

I was dying, and that was only for a couple of days. I feel for you. I really do. You can't just give up, though."

"I haven't." I sat up and looked out at the ocean. "I go by her house every night to see if she's back. She's not. Her jackass of a husband—"

"Ex-husband, from what I hear."

"Yeah. Ex-husband. He's still there. The fucker hasn't done a thing to the place. It still has damage from the storm. You'd think he'd at least make the repairs since he's staying there. I'd really like to tear him to pieces and feed him to the sharks. Hell, maybe if I did, she'd come home."

"No hurting humans—if you can help it. Just remember that."

I dug my fingers into the sand and scowled. "She's got to come back. She has to."

"She will. And then things will work themselves out. You're mates. That means something." He stood up. "If you hit me again, I'm going to have the rest of the guys beat your ass, though."

I waved him off and sighed. Looking back out at the water, I wondered for the millionth time where she was. I wanted to believe Serge was right, but I wasn't so sure. I'd somehow managed to fuck things up so royally. I shouldn't have told her. I should've just waited until she trusted me more. I hadn't been thinking, though. I was so afraid of losing her to that asshole's manipulation that I'd jumped the gun and scared her.

Everything in me felt like it was closing down—dying. Now that I'd met her, I found living without her pointless. I wanted to come home to her smiling face, and taste the sweetness of her lips. I wanted to be the one to comfort her when she was upset and build her back up when she was feeling down. I wanted her to be the one I shared my day with. I wanted to indulge in simple things that I hadn't thought mattered before her.

The kicker was that the heat didn't bother me anymore. While the other guys still sweated in front of the crappy AC unit, I couldn't care less. What did it matter that I was a little physically uncomfortable when the real pain was lodged deep in my heart?

I swore and dragged myself to my feet. I had to do something, anything. I was slowly going insane. Without anything better to do, I decided that it was time to take out her trash.

I couldn't hurt her fuckface ex-husband, but Serge hadn't said anything about scaring the shit out of him.

24

MEGAN

"Hello?" I let myself into the house and prepared myself for coming face to face with my now ex-husband. "Dylan?"

I hadn't talked to him since the lawyers fast-tracked the divorce for me. I wasn't looking forward to it.

But all that met me was silence and an empty house. I looked around before breathing a huge sigh of relief. It appeared that Dylan was gone. There was nothing of his anywhere in the house and the entire place had been cleaned and put in order. The window in the bedroom was fixed, and even the destroyed mattress had been hauled away.

Back downstairs, I sank into the couch. That was a big weight off my shoulders. I closed my eyes, letting the silence envelop me.

My mother's house was never quiet. Mom had been living in Miami lately since her newest husband, Jerry, wanted to be closer to his middle-school-aged daughter, especially after the hurricane scare. Mom was always yelling at the poor hired help. Jerry was always yelling at his daughter, and the daughter was always just yelling.

Then, there were the parties. Mom was a social butterfly when it came to parties. She even threw one for my divorce, much to my dismay. She invited all of her socialite friends, and I saw way more than my fair share of drug use and weird sex that night. Apparently, divorce parties made the jet set frisky.

I should've left and gotten myself a nice, quiet hotel room after the first night, but it had still been hard to be alone with my thoughts. I'd even become good friends with one of her gardeners, a middle-aged guy named Emmett. We snuck into the shed during my divorce party and played gin rummy all night long. Anything to avoid being alone.

Being alone meant I would be obsessing over Roman. I still had dreams about him every night. I woke up hot and bothered and tangled in sweaty sheets. And it was only getting worse! There wasn't anything that didn't make me think of Roman. I had to make up some phony excuse for my middle-school-aged stepsister as to why the documentary we were watching about polar bears made me cry.

The only reason I'd finally decided to return home was that the divorce was finalized and it was time to stand up to Dylan and take my life back. I couldn't hide forever.

Sitting on my couch, I now wondered if I'd returned too soon. The silence already felt heavy. I needed to face things, though, like an adult.

I headed up to the guestroom to shower and get ready for bed. Wearing a new nightgown that Mom had bought me, I slipped between the sheets and tried to think of anything other than the last night I'd been in the same bed, and the handsome man who'd been showering me with attention.

It was too early to sleep, just after sunset, but I really didn't know what else to do, and now that I'd returned, the thoughts of Roman were becoming even more overwhelming. A month should've been enough time to work the guy out of my system. I'd blinked and been over Dylan. Why couldn't I do the same with Roman, who I had only known for a day?

My phone rang from my pants pocket on the floor and I ignored it. When the ringing started up again, I leaned over and fished it out. "Hello?"

"Hey, baby girl! Did you get home okay?" My mom sounded tipsy already.

"Yeah, Mom. I'm home."

"Is that asshole still there?"

"No, actually. He's gone. The house is clean, too, which was completely unexpected. I thought I'd find it destroyed." I settled back against my pillow and stared up at the ceiling. "Everything okay there?"

"Well, yes. We're just missing you." She paused. "Sweetie?"

"Yeah, Mom?"

"The best way to get over Dylan is to just jump back into the dating pool. Go out on a date and have some fun. You're beautiful and there's no reason you should sit around moping and wasting your best years."

I just rolled my eyes. "Okay, Mom."

"I'm serious. Put on your best Spanx and one of those little dresses I got you."

"The nightgowns?"

"Yes! Aren't they just the cutest?"

"You want me to go out in a nightie to get a date?"

"Why not? You're young and free, Megan. Oh, to be single and in my early thirties again…"

"Okay, Mom. I need to go." Before she could scar me permanently, I hung up and turned my ringer off. I didn't need any more unsolicited advice from my mother.

I closed my eyes and played the counting sheep game, which actually worked. It didn't keep me asleep for long, though. I awoke with a start a few hours later and realized I'd been dreaming about Roman again.

I got up and stretched, knowing that I'd had about all the sleep I was going to get that night. My mind was spinning. I wondered what Roman was doing. Had he moved on? Had he just told me that stuff about being a polar bear to scare me off because he wanted to get away from me, or did he really believe that he was a shapeshifter?

They were the same questions I'd asked myself over and over

again, but they were always freshest on my mind after a dream. The dreams were usually of a massive snow-white bear walking beside me, but I was never scared of it. It was my protector. It was Roman.

I walked downstairs and had just passed the windows that looked out over the ocean when I froze. "You're absolutely losing it, Megan."

Slowly, I backed up. I looked out the window again and felt my heart skip a beat. Something was in the water. Something large and white and much bigger than a person. My stomach fluttered, and I gasped when I got a really good look at it. It was a bear. A huge, fucking polar bear.

Before I could even think through what I was doing, I was racing out of my house, down the stairs, across the sand, and plunging into the water. "Stop! Come back!"

Up to my hips, I moved harder, desperate. I had to know. The butterflies in my stomach swore that it was Roman. Had I lost my mind, too? There could not really be a polar bear swimming off the Florida Keys. "Roman!"

And then it was just a few feet away from me. Standing on its back feet in the water, it towered over me.

Its eyes. Those were the giveaway. A sob tore from my throat and I covered my mouth with my hands. It was definitely him.

A bear one second, Roman the next, he stood in the waves with me, just staring back at me. His face looked pained and hesitant. I don't know which one of us moved first, but a second later I was wrapped around him like a burrito.

If this was a dream, I didn't want to wake up.

25

MEGAN

I kissed him, desperate for the taste of him on my lips. I grasped his face and then his head and neck as I deepened the kiss. His hair was longer under my fingers, his beard thicker against my face. I'd missed him so much. I locked my legs around his waist and cried. "You aren't crazy!"

We were moving through the water, the waves hitting me lower and lower until we were out of them. Roman gripped me with one hand under my ass and the other braced around my back. "Why would you run into the ocean toward a bear?"

I might have taken offense to the tone of his question if he wasn't kissing me back in between words. I tilted my head back when his lips moved to my throat. "I knew it was you. Why didn't you show me? All this time, I thought you had mental problems. Why didn't you make me believe you?"

We stumbled up a few steps and paused for a second. Roman's hands never stopped moving. "Stupid. I was so stupid."

I gasped as he bounced me higher and carried me the rest of the way up the stairs in his arms. He kicked the door closed behind us and sat me down on the kitchen island. The granite was cold under my ass, but Roman was there, stroking my throat with his tongue, pushing the nightgown straps down my shoulders.

"Tell me you're okay with this, Megan. Tell me you want me, too."

"I want you." I gasped as his mouth moved across my shoulder. "I'm more than okay with it. As long as you don't stop."

He growled and nipped my shoulder before pulling back and staring into my eyes. "I have to tell you a few more things before we do this. I want to make sure you know what you're getting into."

I bit my lip, needier than I'd ever felt. "Talk fast."

"I'm going to bite you."

I moaned and dropped my head back. "As in foreplay? I don't need it, Roman."

"I'm going to mark you. If you'll let me. My bear...he recognizes you, too, as our mate. I want to claim you as mine. Forever." He growled as my foot stroked up the back of his thigh. "Do you understand that? Forever, Megan."

I met his heated gaze and clarity washed over me. It was a clarity that ran deeper than his words. How it could be the easiest decision I'd ever made, I didn't know. It should've been harder, especially after Dylan, but it wasn't. "Forever."

He stepped back into me and kissed me fiercely. His hands worked my nightgown lower, exposing my bare breasts and stomach. As he kissed me, his fingertips traced up my sides and then down my back before lowering me back on the island.

I gasped at the cold granite, but it faded when I saw the way Roman was staring down at me. Heat—pure, unfiltered heat and need washed over me as I saw the same reflected back from him. He growled low in his throat and cupped my breasts. I arched my back and offered them up to him.

"Fuck, you're beautiful." He closed his mouth over one nipple and then the other, slowly torturing both of them until I writhed. He only pulled back to kiss down my stomach, dipping his tongue into my navel before ripping my nightgown down the middle, exposing my panties.

He pressed his mouth to me over the panties, his tongue hot and wet enough to drive me wild. His hair had grown long enough to grip, so I did. Pulling his face into me, I rolled my hips under his mouth. Roman yanked my panties down and quickly devoured me.

I screamed out an orgasm in seconds—faster than I wanted, but then he was lifting me into his arms and carrying me up the stairs. In my bedroom, he gently put me on the bed and then climbed over me.

"You're the one for me, Megan. The only woman for me." He kissed me slowly while lowering his body to mine.

"I haven't stopped thinking about you while I was gone. I missed you. I missed you as if I'd known you my whole life." I wrapped my arms and legs around him and gasped when his shaft rested against my core. "Roman."

He gripped my hips as he lifted himself and lined our bodies up. Then one of his hands grasped the hair at the back of my head as he slowly sank into me, inch by inch.

Clutching his shoulders, I let out a soft moan as he filled me completely. White hot pleasure tingled through me instantly and I rode out that wave until Roman pulled out and then sank back in. His mouth next to mine, our breath mingled. His eyes burned into me as he watched my reactions. Stroke by stroke, he drove us both higher.

His hands gripped me tighter, the one on my hip had moved to my thigh, and he reached between us to stroke that little bundle of nerves. My neck was stretched back and to the side by his hand in my hair and then his warm breath was fanning over my neck.

I felt him hesitate and knew that he was waiting for a signal from me that it was okay. It was more than okay. I needed it. I felt like I was going to snap into a million pieces if he didn't do it. I pulled his mouth down to my neck and moaned his name.

Roman sank his teeth into my neck—sharp pain that lasted for less than a second. Then a wave of immense pleasure rolled over me. Going under, I knew there would be no coming back up from what was consuming me. My body tightened painfully around him as I felt him swelling even larger inside me, exploding my world.

I came with a scream and a violent shudder. Everything I thought I knew about love was shattered by Roman. He growled against my neck as he came, and something powerful snapped into place between us as he did. Wild, desperate, we sought out each other's mouths and kissed as we both trembled from what had just happened.

I could feel a part of him, so deep within me that nothing would ever be able to remove it. Soul deep.

That quickly, I knew that everything he'd told me was true and that we *were* bound by fate, or whatever it was that drew us together. I could feel the bond between us like it was a real, tangible thread running between us.

It should've been embarrassing that I cried, but Roman just rolled us over and held me against his chest. Stroking my hair and whispering soothing words, he spoke to me with a hint of an accent that rarely came out, and I knew he was feeling emotional, too.

Roman had come into my life and rescued me with a force and speed that rivaled Matilda, and I would forever be his. And he would forever be mine.

26

ROMAN

"Your house isn't meant to hold me in my bear form, Megan." Standing in my mate's bathroom, I stood with my hands on my hips, staring at her with raised eyebrows. "It's not a good idea."

Megan, who'd come into her confidence after spending the last few days naked with me, stretched with her arms over her head, showing me every inch of her sexy feminine form. Her bottom lip poked out, and she batted her eyelashes at me. "Please?"

I swore. "Fine. It's your floor."

"Yeah, floors that I put in. They'll hold you." She pulled herself onto the counter and watched me with wide eyes. She really wanted to see my other form again.

Unwilling to fight her on it any longer, I shifted. The floor creaked under my weight, but she was right, it held. I filled every available space in the bathroom and then some. Looking down at Megan, I cocked my head to the side and sniffed at her.

Her eyes were wider than I'd ever seen them. She lowered herself to the floor and was instantly lost in my fur. "Ahh! Oh, my god!"

I shifted back, afraid I'd accidentally hurt her, but I found her giggling wildly. "You scared the shit out of me! Why'd you scream like that?"

She was laughing so hard, I thought she was crying. "I'm so sorry. I just got excited. You're so cuddly and soft."

"I'm not cuddly! I'm an apex predator, woman. Top of the food chain."

"Yeah, okay." Laughing again, she wiped at her eyes. "I'm sorry. I really am. I just... I can't stop thinking about how my mom had a dog when I was young who would pee on this fur rug she had."

I gave her a deadpan stare, unamused.

"I'm so sorry! I just..." She laughed harder, holding her side. "I want to take naps in your fur."

I tried to keep scowling, but her laughter and amusement were pleasing. I easily picked her up and threw her over my shoulder, slapping her ass as I did. "You're not very respectful of my deadly predator status."

She laughed wildly when I dropped her onto the bed and came down on top of her. I buried my face in her neck and growled. She instantly arched her back and rubbed her soft body against mine.

"I love you, Megan."

She froze and blinked up at me.

I just smiled, knowing that she loved me, too, whether she was ready to say it aloud or not. I could see it in the way she looked at me, and in the little things she did for me. I could feel it radiating off of her through our bond. Her feelings for me were as real as mine were for her. "I love you and I'm going to spend the rest of my life giving you everything you want. Naps in my fur, babies, anything."

Her eyes filled with tears, and she grabbed my neck to pull me down for a kiss. "I love you, too."

I rolled us over so she was on top of me. I felt my own wave of emotion at hearing the words. She wasn't holding anything back. She was giving every part of herself to me. "Yeah?"

She stroked her hands down my chest and bit her lip. "It's later, Roman."

For a second I didn't know what she meant, but then I remembered that first night we spent together in the bathtub. The promise that she could return the favor later. "It's later?"

She grinned. "It's later."

"Thank god for Florida." I gritted my teeth as my sexy little mate slid down my body seductively, licking her lips with her own eagerness to make later happen.

THE END

HERO BEAR

P.O.L.A.R. 2

Substandard job performance,
Indebted to a sleazy loan shark,
Crushing on a shifter who's out of her league,

Kerrigan is in a heck of a pickle.

Dmitry's not gentle.
He's not the nurturing type.
He's a cold-blooded killer—a P.O.L.A.R. assassin

But, when he steps in to protect her, Kerrigan doesn't see a killer, she sees a Hero Bear.

1

KERRIGAN

If I'd ever needed an intervention, it would have been at the moment I decided that moving into the house with all six of the guys from P.O.L.A.R. would be better than living out of my car. I'd chosen to live under the same roof with the guys I spent all day working for. There was such a thing as too much togetherness.

When Serge, the Alpha of the team, found out I'd been living out of my Honda, he made a big stink about it. And, since Roman had recently moved out to live with his new mate, Megan, there was a room vacant. That meant either I stand up to Serge and say no, or I go along with his wishes. I was terrible when it came to confrontation. Especially with an Alpha. So, I guess it wasn't totally my choice to move in. I just didn't decline the request. Still, an intervention would've been nice.

The large, two story bungalow that housed P.O.L.A.R. was prime beach front real estate. Located on the west side of Sunkissed Key, only a short walk from the P.O.L.A.R. office, it was a beautiful, old house on a beautiful white, sandy beach. Rumor was, it had been an old bed and breakfast at one time and, with a little renovating, had been transformed into the house for the team. It was certainly large enough to fit a whole gang comfortably. At least, it should've been. If the guys were normal sized men. They weren't. They were shifters, and the shifters of P.O.L.A.R. made the hallways feel narrow, and the kitchen and dining room laughably miniscule.

Roman had moved out just the day before and I was lugging in the two bags containing all my worldly possessions. I struggled with the garbage bags while Serge and Konstantin watched me. When I paused to take a breath, they both offered to help. I didn't want their help, though. It was embarrassing, especially since I sucked at my job. I could at least carry in my own bag and prove that I actually could do something without screwing it up.

Alexei stepped out of the bathroom and into the middle of the hall grinning at me and shaking his head before disappearing back into his room. I appreciated his hands off approach as I continued to drag the bags up the stairs toward the corridor.

I'd already gotten the suckers up two flights of stairs. The heaviest bag held a collection of books hidden in a blanket at the bottom. I was almost to the door of my new bedroom. Unfortunately, like most things in my life, the move didn't go as planned. The bag advertised as a "heavy-duty steel-sack" tore like tissue paper. The force I'd been applying to pull the weighty bag up the stairs set me off like a rocket and I went flying backwards until I landed on the hardwood floor with a *thud*.

Flat on my back, I stared at the ceiling and groaned. Heavy-duty my ass! Actually, most of the impact had been absorbed by my ass and it stung. Not nearly as much as my ego, though. I couldn't seem to catch a break.

"Damn. You okay?" Serge's face appeared staring down at me wearing what he tried to present as a concerned expression. But I could see him struggling to keep the corners of his mouth down. He was laughing inside.

I gritted my teeth and nodded. "Perfectly fine."

"Why are you carting around an entire library? Did you have all this crap in your car?" He lifted a book to read the title and then cleared his throat before putting it back down. "Well, I'm going back to work."

I flew up, realizing my books were on display, and made quick work of gathering them together to get them into my room asap. That was how Dmitry found me when he opened his bedroom door—on my hands and knees kicking, shoveling and brushing books out of the hallway and into the privacy of my new room as quickly as I could.

His room was across the hall from mine and I'm sure I looked lovely, ass out, on all fours, surrounded by erotic novels and wearing the red-faced shame only a way-too-old-to-be-a-virgin could possess when her guilty pleasure was on full display before a house full of men.

My thick glasses were sliding down my nose, and I felt Dmitry standing behind me. I looked over my shoulder to see if I was right. Of course I was right. I could always sense Dmitry.

The little squeak I let out was embarrassing enough by itself. The position I realized I'd frozen in—on elbows and knees, ass in the air, was mortifying. I was suddenly reminded of the time I saw an ape at the zoo offering herself...never mind.

Dmitry said nothing. He just stepped back into his room and shut the door.

Konstantin let out an awkward *oof*, adding to my horror by letting me know that I'd had quite an audience for the whole Kerrigan Tran shit-show.

Struggling to my feet, I kicked the rest of my things into my room, ducked in behind them, and shut the door—a little too hard—behind me. Maybe I could stay in there and never come out.

I leaned against the door and focused on normalizing my breathing.

"Well, that could have gone better," I mumbled aloud.

The guys already thought I was a complete incompetent moron at my job. Because I was. They also thought I was small, scrawny and weak. Because, again, I was. They'd just learned I was a major klutz as well.

And Dmitry had to be home to witness that. I'd had the biggest crush on Dmitry since the moment I'd laid eyes on him—through my Coke bottle lenses.

It was so childish and stupid. A crush was a silly thing to have as an adult especially since I was too chicken shit to let him know how I felt. My grandmother, may she rest in peace, would've tactfully told me to shit or get off the pot. Approach the man, speak your mind, and get your answer or move it along. I had absolutely zero intention of doing any of that. Dmitry was a real life hero and I was a clumsy nerd who broke my glasses a couple times a year and either walked around with my arms out in front of me feeling my way around or held them together with electrical tape until I was able to afford a new pair.

Even though I had no intention of taking my crush on Dmitry to any level other than admiring him from afar, the damned crush remained. Instant and ever-present, my attraction hadn't faded one iota since I began working at P.O.L.A.R. If anything, it'd grown increasingly stronger. For some reason, I couldn't stop making an idiot out of myself in front of him, either. It was degrading. And the real reason I would have preferred living in my car.

With him across the hall from me, I was bound to see him even more often than I already did. I didn't need that. It was only a matter of time before I said or did the next incredibly stupid or appallingly embarrassing thing. At least living in my car, I had the chance to recover from job related screwups at night—alone in my own plastic and faux leather sanctuary.

I shoved a book away from me and thumped my head against the door. "Idiot."

The sound of rolling waves drew me away from the door and across the room to the large window I'd opened earlier. One thing that the house had that my car didn't, was an absolutely spectacular view. Beyond the beach, for as far as I could see, was the beautiful turquoise waters of the Atlantic and bright blue expanse of Florida sky. Breathtaking.

It also was a reminder of how lucky I was. Of all the places to be assigned a job, I had the good fortune to be sent to Sunkissed Key. Sand, sun, a constant bevy of shirtless men, and umbrella drinks at beach bars that a girl who lived out of her Honda Civic couldn't often afford. It was heaven.

I just had to get my head out of the metaphorical sand and get my toes in the literal sand. I could go down to the beach and get ideas for my next book as I watched all the men run around. Maybe it'd be just what the doctor ordered to get my mind off Dmitry.

I pushed my glasses up and studied the inside of my new bedroom door. To get to the beach, I'd have to travel through the house and possibly run into some of the team. They might even joke about my latest clumsy maneuver or my trashy book collection. Was it worth it?

Out the window, down on the beach, a male volleyball game was starting up. Well, that made up my mind for me. I grabbed my notebook and a pen before darting out of my room and down the stairs as fast as I could.

"Where's the fire?" Serge called out from the kitchen.

"Volleyball!" *And getting away from your hot bear brother!* I groaned and let the door slam behind me.

Slipping my shoes off, I left them near the back door as I sank my toes into the sand and started the short trudge to find a good spot to plant myself and watch the game.

2

DMITRY

I stepped out of my bedroom glaring at the closed door across the hall. That door had been ajar until quite late the night before. The room's new occupant, Kerrigan, had stayed down at the beach all evening. She sat in the sand watching some locals play at tossing a ball over a net for hours while scribbling in a notebook. She always had a notebook with her. Not always the same one, either. Then, as if that wasn't bad enough, she'd fallen asleep right there on the beach.

She was small and vulnerable. There was no way I could take my eyes off her. I'd had to stay at the window for hours looking after her and making sure nothing happened to her until she woke up—way past eleven—and decided to head back in. I'd lost sleep watching her from the window.

Downstairs in the kitchen, I yawned as I made myself some oatmeal and honey. Bears needed their sleep. Sleep was very important and I didn't like to miss it for anything. Grumbling, I poured myself a second cup of coffee and tossed it back on one swallow.

"Who pissed in your Wheaties?" Serge strolled in, looking refreshed and well rested. Bastard.

I was only half listening to Serge because just then, I heard Kerrigan's bedroom door open upstairs and her soft, light footsteps pad down the stairs and toward us. Her jet black hair was pulled back in its normal ponytail, and she entered the kitchen with a beaming smile on her face. Fake, but almost convincing. "Good morning."

Serge smiled back at her and nodded to the cabinet with the coffee cups. "Morning. Get yourself some coffee."

"Oh, no, it makes me jittery. I'll just grab a banana or something."

I ran my eyes over her lithe figure and readjusted myself in my seat. She was sexy as hell. But, would a banana be enough? I had half a mind to make her some oatmeal. She needed a real meal.

"How'd you sleep?" Serge leaned against the counter and folded his arms over his chest. "It had to be better than sleeping in that little car of yours."

Her eyes darted to me and then back to Serge. "I didn't mind the car, but I have to admit, it was nice to be able to fully stretch out."

"I'm sure."

"Well, I'm going to go for a quick swim before work." She backed away. "Bye."

I winced as she tripped over a chair and bumped into the wall. She giggled and her face flushed pink before she turned and hurried away. I gritted my teeth and shook my head. Maybe I needed to follow her—for protection. She was a bit of a hazard to herself.

"How did you sleep, Dmitry? Better, I would think." Serge smirked at me knowingly before walking out of the kitchen.

I growled. His remark told me that he knew I hadn't been sleeping at home lately. What choice did I have, though? Kerrigan seemed to have no regard for her personal safety. She'd been sleeping in her car with the windows open a crack. I had no choice but to watch over her every night. Why no one else thought it was necessary to look out for her was beyond me.

She made me nervous as hell. I never knew what she was going to do next and I felt like I was watching her with baited breath, waiting to derail her next near-catastrophe.

I thought I'd find relief with her moving into the P.O.L.A.R. house, but so far it had gotten worse. When she finally did come in from the beach last night, I'd been hyper-aware the entire night that she was just across the hall. So close I could almost reach out and touch her.

Touching her was a concept I'd been fighting since the moment I'd met her. The very second I first laid eyes on her, I'd wondered what it would be like...

I set my coffee down a little too hard and shattered the mug. As I cleaned up the mess, I focused on clearing my head. I had work to do. I needed to concentrate. Thankfully, we hadn't had any big cases since Kerrigan had started working for us. I didn't think I'd be any good to the team until I figured out how to sort out what was happening in my brain. And body.

"Hey, brother." Konstantin raised his brows. He was standing propped against the doorway. "You look like shit."

I finished throwing away the pieces of shattered mug. "Thanks."

"It wouldn't have anything to do with our newest roomie, would it?"

I glared at him before tossing the dirty towel down the laundry chute and walking out the back door. I ignored his question.

Unable to resist, I followed Kerrigan's sweet scent down to the beach and watched as she swam in the ocean. She was too far out to be able to see me. Too far out for my comfort. I had half a mind to swim out there and drag her closer to shore.

She was a good swimmer, though. I watched as she glided through the water, cutting a strong path under waves and coming back up on the other side of them. She seemed to be a different person out there. She was far more clumsy on land.

Still, my heart was in my throat the entire time I kept watch. No one had ever gotten me wound so tightly before. Kerrigan had me genuinely scared that she was going to trip and land on an open switchblade, or something equally as freaky. And, I felt it my obligation to keep her safe.

Her clothes were piled up nearby and I saw the notebook she was never without peeking out from under them. Curiosity niggled at me, but I ignored both the curiosity and my bear. He was itching to get out and go for a swim with Kerrigan. He wanted to brush against her, feel her silky skin, and roll through the crashing waves with her. He loved swimming anyway, but the thought of swimming with Kerrigan took the pastime to a whole new level.

Even though Kerrigan knew all about shifters, she'd never actually seen my bear. Most humans never came face to face with a polar bear. They might see one from afar in a zoo once or twice in their lifetime, but the size of a shifter animal was massive compared to a non-shifter animal.

When I noticed Kerrigan start to swim in, I climbed to my feet and headed back toward the house. She didn't need to know I was watching her.

3

KERRIGAN

To say that I wasn't qualified to work for P.O.L.A.R. would be a gross understatement. I was trained to work as an office assistant, but I'd never worked in an office where every call that came in could literally mean life or death. What if I screwed up? The stuff mattered. I had to take calls from the main office and send the guys out on location to wherever they were needed. Sounded easy, but when the office called, it was hectic. Messages were loud and rushed and I panicked.

Knowing that I was responsible for fielding calls containing critical instructions left me wound tighter than a winch pulling a two ton truck. I was a wreck. People's lives depended on my accuracy and I wasn't reliable enough for that.

Every workday, I bounced back and forth from one side of the office to the other, organizing everything I could and making myself as busy as possible. I wanted to be useful, but I also wanted to mask the fact that I'd scored the job because my mother was mated to a higher up in the organization.

It didn't help my nerves any that most of the guys in the unit hung out in the office when they weren't out on a job. They sat around, talking or horsing around, or doing whatever else they did. They kept the air conditioning set so low that I had to wear a winter jacket and they were always in the way. Not that I had any right to complain. They were the heroes, the ones actually making a difference in this world. I felt honored to be in their presence.

The enormous pressure, though! At any moment a life or death call could come in and they were all going to be there watching me, judging me. It tied my stomach in knots. I would've quit and let them find a more qualified dispatcher if I didn't desperately need the job. Of course, there was a very real possibility I'd be fired.

Dmitry was my biggest problem. He was always somewhere nearby. He stayed in a back office, but it didn't make a difference. Knowing he was so close was giving me a perpetual tremor. It was only a matter of time before I was revealed as a bumbling buffoon and it would no doubt happen right in front of him. He'd never understand. Already I was a bundle of nerves compared to his calm stoicism. I could never tell what he was thinking, but when his attention turned to me, I had a strong feeling it wasn't anything good. Whenever our eyes met, there was something strained about his expression, like I gave him heartburn.

The guys were sitting around discussing M4 versus M4A1 carbine weapons, whatever those were, when the phone rang. All eyes turned to me. My heart rate skyrocketed and I took a deep breath before answering. "P.O.L.A.R."

"Police scanner 411. 560 at 348 Second Street." The line clicked off in my ear.

Scribbling on my notepad, I stared at the numbers I'd written down for a second and then up at the guys. Even Dmitry had stepped out of the office to look at me expectantly.

"Um... Code 548 at 360 Second Street." That was right. Wasn't it? I looked at my notepad and nodded. "Yeah. 360 Second Street."

Serge appeared, slipping a handgun into his side holster. "548. Strap up. Let's go."

I watched as they all slipped guns onto holsters, horror filling my gut. I wanted to shout at them to stop—wait—let me call back and double check to make sure I'd gotten it right, but it was too late. They were already out of the door.

I ran my hands down my face and blew out a huge sigh. I didn't have a good feeling about this. What was a code 548 anyway, and why did it require guns?

"Shit."

The back door to the office opened a few seconds later, and Hannah appeared. She took one look at me and frowned. "What's wrong, Kerrigan?"

I must have looked like I felt. I'd already been fighting the urge to cry, but there was something about having someone ask you that question that made the tears inevitable. Still, I fought them. "Nothing. I'm okay."

She shook her head. "No you're not. Spill."

"I suck at this job. I know it; the guys know it. I think I may have just sent them to the wrong address, but I can't remember. It's too stressful for me, but I can't quit. I tried for weeks to find another job before this one and I only got hired here because my mom's mate pulled strings." The tears were flowing now. I reached for the box of tissues and blew my nose. "I spent so many years in school and I'm useless."

She came over to me and wrapped me in a hug. "Oh, sweetie. It's okay. Let it out."

As if I had a choice. There was no keeping it in. "The guys hate me. I know it. I'm so bad at this. I'm going to get someone killed."

"No, you're not. You'll learn. You're going to get better at it and things will be fine. It's not an easy job, taking calls from the main office. I filled in a few times. It's hard to keep up with them. You'll be a pro in no time, Kerrigan."

I didn't buy it. I was going to be fired before I ever got the chance to improve. Then, I'd hear about it from my mom—how embarrassing it was to have a daughter who was virtually incompetent and how her mate had gone through all the trouble of getting me the job in the first place. Talk about feeling like a complete failure at life.

"Maybe you should take the day off. You know, a mental health day. I could come with you? We could do a girl's day. We'll get a couple frozen margaritas and get our 'girl talk' on."

"It's ten in the morning."

She laughed. "It's never too early for frozen margaritas and girl talk with a friend."

I slid a tissue under my glasses and wiped at my eyes. I hadn't heard her call me a friend before, and at that moment, I really needed a friend. "Maybe we could go after work? I can't afford to be docked any hours right now."

"Okay. Tonight. I'm buying. I'll see if I can get Megan to come, too. If I can pry her away from Roman for a few hours. It'll be so fun!"

I pictured Dmitry rushing to possibly the wrong address with a gun drawn. "I hope I still have a job by then." Or did I? I wasn't so sure. Half of me would feel relieved to be fired.

She laughed and gave me a knowing look. "Okay. Just don't drive yourself crazy in here, Kerrigan. What you're doing is important work, yes, but not as important as your sanity."

"That's implying that I have any sanity."

She laughed. "Do you?"

Fighting a grin, I shook my head. "Not really."

4

DMITRY

We entered the home, guns drawn. A 548 was code for an armed home invasion. 360 Second Street was a lovely little cottage owned by a sweet, elderly, retired couple. When we kicked in the front door and rushed the place dressed in full tactical gear, they had been seated at the breakfast table staring calmly at the morning waves while enjoying their Earl Grey and soft-boiled eggs.

The couple, Mr. and Mrs. Fuller, were so shocked that Mrs. Fuller fainted dead away. Mr. Fuller tried to fight us off using his tea cup and cane. Serge suffered a minor burn and a good whack to the side of the head.

In the end, we'd stayed to repair the door and apologize profusely. The real crime had been a simple B&E at 348 Second Street. Fortunately, the local police officers had handled the situation just fine without us.

I was torn. Part of me wanted to strangle Kerrigan. We were highly trained specialists. A fuck up like that made us look like first rate idiots. Since she'd started working at the office, we looked like idiots more and more often. The other part of me was itching to get back to her to make sure she was safe and hadn't burned down the office, with herself inside.

The guys weren't torn. They were one hundred percent pissed off at Kerrigan. Well, not Alexei. He thought the whole thing was hilarious.

Serge was fuming. "This can't happen again. The office said we had to have her, but if this keeps happening, I'm going to be forced to request a replacement. That girl's a liability."

I balled my hands at my sides and took a deep breath. He wasn't wrong. He had a job to do, too, and if a link in our chain wasn't holding its weight, someone could get hurt—or killed. It was Serge's job to make sure all links functioned. Still, I didn't like him talking about Kerrigan like that.

"How many times are we going to screw up because of her? What's going to happen when someone get injured because she can't take a simple phone message and dispatch us to the correct location?"

I growled. "Enough. We're all upset. We get it."

"I'm not. I just got to see Serge get his ass kicked by a geriatric." Alexei laughed. "Today is the best day I've had since we arrived. I think we should give the woman a raise."

Maxim snorted a laugh through his nose, but his words rang true. "It's not fucking funny, though. Mrs. Fuller could've had a heart attack and died."

I gritted my teeth and stared out the front window. "Yeah, well, she didn't."

Serge pointed a finger at me. "Teach your girlfriend how to do her job or she's gone, Dmitry."

I growled again at Serge and glared. "She is not my girlfriend, and last I checked, you're the boss. Shouldn't you have trained her better?"

Gauntlets thrown down, we drove the rest of the way back to the office in a tense silence. When we parked the van outside of the building, everyone dispersed. Roman headed toward Megan's, Serge headed towards the house, probably in search of his mate, Hannah. Konstantin, Alexei, Maxim and I went back into the office.

The silence inside was painful. Kerrigan sat at her desk with her eyes down. She already knew she'd sent us to the wrong place. I could feel the tension and humiliation rolling off of her. I sat down at the desk next to hers and sighed. She had to do better at taking down the calls from the main office. Someone had to show her.

"When the main office calls, you need to be fast. They're abrupt because they're dispatching hundreds of calls every hour to all parts of the world. You can't take your time."

Her shoulders were tense, her eyes still down. "I know."

"It's not hard. Not once you get the hang of it."

She nodded. "Okay."

Feeling frustrated, I growled. "They're going to fire you if you keep sending us to the wrong place, Kerrigan."

She stood up abruptly and looked over my shoulder. She never made eye contact if she could help it. Not with me, anyway. "I need to take care of this filing."

I stood up, towering over her, and shrugged. I wasn't sure what else to say to her. I locked myself in the back office, to get away from her. I didn't know what it was, but she drove me fucking crazy in every way. I wanted to shake her and comfort her and argue with her and kiss her.

Her feelings seemed to be so delicate and I was terrible at subtlety and tact. She probably needed some kindness and encouragement—two things I was unable to provide to anyone. I sensed that something else might be wrong with her. Something underlying that was eating away at her and keeping her mind preoccupied. I really wanted to ask her about it.

That wasn't my place, though. She was shy and sensitive and her cry reflex was near the surface. I wasn't good with crying women. I was a cold-blooded killer, not a priest. I didn't comfort people. The way I solved problems was by killing bad guys. My soul was too dark to pretend that I could make someone as gentle as Kerrigan feel better about whatever was troubling her.

None of it mattered. I was only on Sunkissed Key to do my job. Once the main office decided we'd served our penance in this blazing inferno, we'd get to go back home and I'd put Florida behind me. I'd never have to think about it again and the only thing I'd leave behind in this hell hole is perspiration.

Still, I found my mind straying to Kerrigan. It was impossible not to, her scent, her little sounds, they all permeated the walls that separated us and jumbled my senses. She kept sniffling. She was crying.

I wasn't capable of remedying a situation like that so, instead, I made myself remain in the back office. I wasn't her hero. I was no one to her.

5

KERRIGAN

Sharing a bathroom with any man could be a challenge, but sharing a bathroom with a handful of men who regularly shifted into massive polar bears was truly an experience. I had to clean the place before I showered. The thought of Alexei using the shower before I did made me cringe. Like the rest of the guys in the unit, he was all male and I tried not to let my mind wander to the pastimes he might have indulged in while enjoying his bathroom time. And allowing myself to think about Dmitry and I sharing the same shower stall, albeit at different times, was a definite no-go.

I went straight home as soon as my shift ended. No one else was home, so I was able to snag the bathroom for myself. After scrubbing it, I set my stuff up inside and then took a nice, long shower. I took my time washing my hair and shaving, using the shower as therapy to wash the day away. When I was finished, I moisturized and brushed my teeth before wrapping a towel around me tightly and opening the door.

Dmitry stood in the hall just outside the bathroom, his mouth slightly ajar. He looked as though he was in a trance as his eyes traveled down my body and back up to my face.

I felt myself blush from head to toe and wasted no time side stepping him to get away from him. Besides still feeling humiliated about the earlier work incident, I was in a towel in front of the man I couldn't stop crushing on. I wanted to crawl in a hole and never come out. I hurried into my room, slamming the door behind me, then leaned against it and blew out a rough breath.

Barely a second passed before someone knocked at my door. "Sorry. I, uh, just needed the bathroom."

I squeezed my eyes shut and covered my face with my hands. "No problem."

"Yeah, okay."

I groaned and pushed away from the door. Why was it impossible to get Dmitry off my mind? I tried as I looked through my clothes deciding what to wear, but the effort was futile. It wasn't the gentle scolding he'd given me at the office that kept playing through my head, either. It was the sizzling look he'd given me just then as his eyes had devoured me in the hallway.

Did he find me attractive? Maybe a little? As hot as he was, he could have any supermodel in the world. He probably had. There was no way he was attracted to a skinny four-eyed woman with no hips and itty bitty titties.

I chose an emerald green maxi dress that fell to my ankles and sported a halter top with a lowcut back. I hadn't worn it for a few years, but it was the sexiest dress I owned and it complimented my black hair and the slight yellowish undertones of my complexion.

Once I had it on, I ran my hands over the lines of my panties. Eww, that wouldn't do. Thinking of the heroines in my stories, and feeling a little wild and uninhibited, I slipped off my panties. I pretended Dmitry did find me attractive, that when his eyes had raked over me out in the hall, he'd been memorizing how I looked—fresh from the shower wearing nothing but a towel—to use as fodder for his spank bank. My thoughts easily escalated from there into erotica land, dreaming up and plotting out ten different scenarios.

Not wanting to waste the creative juices, I sat down and my pen flew over the paper as started quickly jotting the ideas down. Before I knew it, the sun had set and someone was knocking on my door.

I sat back. The notebook in front of me was filled with scenes that should've made me blush. Instead, I was all hot and bothered. Light beads of sweat had formed between my breasts and I felt almost dizzy with arousal. It was insane, but Dmitry was a helluva muse.

When I opened the door, Hannah stood on the other side with a friendly grin. She took one look at me and whistled. "Well, look at you."

I fanned myself with my hands and smiled back at her, the stress from the early part of my day pretty much forgotten. "Ready?"

She nodded. "What were you doing in there? You look dewy. Normally, as a non-shifter I'm practically frostbitten in this house. More blue than dew, you know?"

I laughed. I did know. "I was just doing a little writing. So, where are we going tonight?"

She gave me an inquisitive look, but let it go. "Mimi's Cabana. It's a little tiki bar on the east side of the island. Mimi makes the best margaritas in Florida, I swear."

The door across the hall opened and Dmitry stepped out. When he gazed over at me, his eyes did that smoldery thing again. I looked away quickly, instantly aware of the fact that I was pantiless, and it was too late to run back into my room and change.

"Hey, Dmitry. We're heading over to Mimi's Cabana for a girl's night out. Doesn't Kerrigan look stunning?"

I didn't wait to hear his answer, instead racing down the stairs to the first floor as fast as I could and stumbling down the last two. Before I fell flat on my face, I was caught by a rough grip on my upper arms. My head snapped around. Dmitry, quick as lightning, had slipped past Hannah to catch me.

He was closer to me than he'd ever been—touching me for Christ's sake—and my body responded in the extreme. His eyes were almost completely black, pupils dilated. His nostrils flared and his grip on my arms tightened.

"Whoa! Way to be fast on your feet, D." Hannah moved past us and blew out a sharp breath. "She almost snapped her neck there."

I was suddenly aware of the moisture pooling between my thighs, my heaving chest, and my tightening nipples. I was in a heightened state of arousal and wanted to climb Dmitry like he was a tree. My throat was dry so I licked my lips and raised my eyes to his.

He just set me on my feet and stepped away, though. "Careful."

I deflated. I was a mess.

Hannah rested her hand on my shoulder and grunted. "You've got it bad, sister."

Was I that obvious? I dropped my face into my hands and groaned. "I need a drink."

6

DMITRY

"Fucking hell." I walked straight out of the house and down to the ocean, stripping out of my clothes along the way. I waded into the water and, once I was far enough out, shifted.

I continued swimming farther out, letting the cool water sooth my raging bear. He dove under and swam a lap before coming back up to bob in place. Kerrigan's scent was still clinging, burned into our brains. The sweet aroma of her arousal had been wafting out of her room for hours, but getting smacked in the face with it while being inches away from her was something completely different.

My bear wanted to drag her into our room and devour her, savor every morsel of her sweetness, pleasure her in every way imaginable. He wanted to make her ours.

And, it wasn't just my bear wanting those things. I had the same thoughts. After the physical contact of catching her from falling, they intensified. Touching her bare skin had been an electric shock of awareness. She'd felt it, too. I'd seen her skin flush, heard her heartrate increase and scented her arousal. I'd watched in fascination as her tongue flick out over her pink lips.

And now she was headed to a bar. Where people would see her.

In a dress that exposed her bare back and accentuated her slender, waiflike figure. The slight swell of her breasts were there, for any man to see.

My bear tossed his head back and let out a wild roar. He didn't want anyone else looking at her silky skin.

Still, I stayed in the water. I was in control of my desires, mostly, and I wouldn't just cave to them when it came to Kerrigan. She was innocent. I was sure of that. I could feel it, her purity, her naivete. She was untouched and, and I damned sure wasn't the man to waste herself on.

On the other hand, someone could touch her. A man. The thought of another man touching her was enough to spike my blood pressure to a boiling rage. So much for being in control. Before I could stop myself, I was racing back to the shore. I shifted and dressed, still dripping wet.

Mimi's Cabana wasn't too far. Running, I made it there in under five minutes. I barely managed to refrain from bursting in and letting a roar rip from my throat as a warning to every swinging richard in the place to stay the fuck away from my Kerrigan. But I did manage to refrain. Instead, I paused at the front door and took a few deep breaths before calmly opening the door and glancing around.

Kerrigan was at the bar with Hannah and Megan on either side of her, sipping a frozen margarita. She reached up and tucked her long, black, silky hair behind her ears. It was the first time I'd seen it down. Like she could sense me, her eyes moved directly to me and her mouth formed a little O of surprise.

Time seemed to stand still as we stared at one another. What now? I didn't want to interrupt her girl's night, and I certainly didn't want to start something with Kerrigan that I couldn't finish. Fuck, I needed to leave her alone. I stepped backwards, back out of the bar, and headed to the house. I had no business thinking of her, let alone acting on any of those thoughts. She didn't belong to me, and a good thing, too. I'd ruin her.

I made myself go back to my room and stay there. It wasn't easy, but I had to. I was neither a good man nor a safe man—not for a woman like Kerrigan. There was nothing about me that suited a gentle woman like Kerrigan.

I stripped and climbed into bed. I wasn't tired. I figured I'd lie there and listen to the ocean until Kerrigan got close enough to the house that I could tune into her.

A few hours passed before she came back home. She went straight to her bedroom and I listened as her dress hit the floor and her mattress springs squeaked faintly as she crawled into bed. Within minutes, she was asleep.

It soothed me to know she was so close and no longer sleeping in her car, but it didn't stop me from being concerned about her safety. I listened to her steady breathing and found myself nodding off a little bit later. I woke a few hours later to the sound of Kerrigan talking in her sleep. It was the whisper of my name on her lips that had me sit up straight in bed. In her dreams she was murmuring my name—breathless and strained. I pictured her neck muscles stretched taut, her head thrown back and her spine arched as the dream took her. My name.

Sweet Kerrigan was having a dream about me. From the sound of it, it was a good dream. I paced the room, fists balled at my sides. I wanted to go to her, but that was a bad idea. A very bad idea. Terrible.

I had to cool off. The sounds were louder to my sensitive ears in the hallway, but I made it down the stairs and outside in less than a minute. Jogging down the beach and into the water, I swam far out into the sea hoping to cool off and calm down enough to get a few more hours sleep.

It took forever to regain control and by the time the sun rose, I was exhausted. I felt like I'd been whipped and beaten then drawn and quartered. It was all I could do to make it to work. Fortunately, it was Saturday and Kerrigan was off. I was hoping I could hide out in the back office and catch up on some Z's. No such luck.

A call came in about a hostage situation involving a shifter in Miami. A little out of our way, but right up our alley. Despite each and every man on our team being a deadly and highly trained operative, we each had our own unique skill set. Terminations were mine. I was a crack shot and skilled at virtually any weapon, but I was best at hand to hand. I was the assassin.

So, when a particularly out of control alligator shifter was rampaging and threatening the lives of a woman and her children, I did what I had to do. I didn't love it. But it was a necessary evil. Taking out shifters who were threatening and posing a deadly risk to humans sometimes included an odd twist. After the fact, the victims sometimes looked at you as though *you* were the villain.

The alligator shifter had been seconds from snapping her young son's neck, but she was screaming mad that I'd killed the fucker. It didn't take much to deduce that mom was high on something and that, whatever it was, he had been her supplier. Hell, maybe she did love him. What did I know about love? I just knew my job. And I'd done it. I'd neutralized the threat and saved the kid's life.

It didn't matter to Mom, though. She screamed and wailed and called me a heartless monster. According to her, there was a special place in hell for me. I didn't doubt that.

Her screeching could be heard over her child's sobs and continued on even after the police arrived to clean up the messy scene.

The ride back to the island was quiet. No one wanted to talk about what had just gone down. None of us had the stomach for small talk.

Kerrigan was on my mind more than ever. I kept seeing her shy features transposed onto that woman's screaming face. Surely, Kerrigan would have been appalled if she knew what I'd just done. I pictured Kerrigan with a horrified expression—crying and screaming. Telling me to get away from her, telling me there was a special place in hell for me. There was an ugly side to our job that none of us loved, or wanted to rehash. We did what had to be done.

Feeling like the weight of the world was on my shoulders, I chose not to go back to the office. I was in no mood to plaster a fake smile on and hang with the guys. Despite knowing it probably wasn't the best choice, I went home. Not to see Kerrigan, or so I told myself. She probably wouldn't even be home. I'd just close myself in my room and forget everything.

In truth, deep down, I hoped she was home.

7
KERRIGAN

I'd quickly decided that Saturdays in the P.O.L.A.R. house were my favorite. I was off on Saturdays but the guys usually went in to the office, and Hannah along with them. So, I could just hang out and spend lazy alone time without worrying about bumping into anyone who was ticked at me or disappointed in my job performance. I spent the morning at the dining room table, writing until my hand cramped. Then, I watched an episode of Iron Chef in the living room before making a bologna sandwich for lunch and retreating to my room. I was just finishing my sandwich and thinking about going out for a swim when I heard the door slam downstairs.

I knew who it was because the hair on the back of my neck instantly stood on end. Dmitry. I hadn't seen him since the night before when he'd appeared in the bar, took one long look at me, and then turned and fled. Probably didn't like what he saw, and decided to drink elsewhere.

I left my bedroom door open and was standing just inside, waiting for him to come up the stairs. Maybe I should have closed the door and minded my own business, but something in the air felt different.

Dmitry hurried up the stairs and slammed his bedroom door shut behind him. Just that quick glimpse of him made my pulse race. His face had been drawn and his expression even darker than usual. It wasn't my business. I should have just closed my door and let it go.

The image of his haunted face was too much, though. It touched me to the core. My feet felt like lead as I dragged myself across the hallway pausing just outside of his door. I was being an idiot. He didn't need to be comforted by me, no matter what was bothering him. He probably wanted to be left alone.

Still, I lifted my arm and gently tapped on his door. When it swung open a few seconds later, I gasped. He stood tall but something about him looked...broken. "Dmitry? Are you okay?"

I'd been expecting him to slam the door in my face or ignore me or give me a dirty look and tell me to get lost. I was no one to him. Just the incompetent, nerdy dispatcher who was a living anti-nepotism argument. I couldn't blame him for not liking me. Instead, he shocked the hell out of me when he reached out and snatched me into his arms.

He hugged me against his chest and in the split second before his mouth claimed mine, I took every sensation in—his muscled abs against my worn t-shirt, his smoky, fresh scent seducing me with every inhale, his blonde hair begging for my fingers to comb through it.

With my hands and arms trapped between us, palms flat against his rock hard chest, and my thighs pressed against the thick canvas of his cargo pants, it was enough to fill pages and pages in my notebook.

Then, his kiss was on my lips. Hard and urgent, Dmitry devoured me like we were on a sinking ship and this kiss was the only lifeline. He kissed me with a fierceness that was almost rough. His hands on my waist were hard and punishing, his fingertips digging into my flesh, the shadow of his beard leaving a friction burn. I loved it!

His actions had caught me so off guard that it had taken me a second to realize he was kissing me. Before I could really get into it and kiss him back, he lifted me and spun us so my back was pressed against his door. His hands caught my ass and squeezed as he kissed me harder. I gasped and my libido kicked into overdrive. Yes! Forget the rules—all of them.

I held on to his shoulders as his tongue explored my mouth. He tasted like sunshine. I moaned into his mouth as our tongues tangled. He was demanding, controlling, and almost panicked in his intensity. There was no hiding how much he wanted me. He rocked the proof into my core.

He tilted his head and kissed me deeper, stroking his tongue against mine, creating a dance that fueled every nerve ending of desire I possessed. My head was flooded with the feeling of him against me. My dreams had barely scratched the surface of what this really felt like. His body was hard and hot against mine. The smell, the taste of him, I was reeling with pleasure.

I didn't realize we'd moved until I felt his fingers at the top of my waistband. We were on his bed, with me straddling him. My knees rested on the plaid blanket of his perfectly made bed, and he was nipping and sucking kisses down my throat. It never crossed my mind that we should slow down. Or stop to think. We were both consenting adults. As far as I was concerned, full speed ahead.

I ran my fingers through his short blonde hair and held onto his head while he sucked on my collar bone. His teeth were rough, but they felt like they were nibbling away the tension I'd been holding. Like a drug, I wanted more.

Dmitry slid his hand into my panties and his long, thick finger stroked over my folds. He growled before he captured my mouth again, kissing, devouring, reddening my face with the faint stubble of his beard. Both of us were breathing raggedly as I held myself up on my knees and locked my arms around his neck.

His finger continued to stroke me, parting my folds. I was in heaven. With his other arm bracing me behind my back, he slid his finger into me, filling me. He swallowed my moans and held me tighter as I trembled against him, the sensation so amazing that I couldn't hold off an orgasm if I wanted to. My body felt as though I'd collapse at any second but he didn't stop. Holding me, peppering kisses all over my face and neck and chest, he pumped his finger in and out of me, drawing another orgasm from me before I could even recover from the first.

I couldn't hold on. I'd never felt someone else's anything inside of me and Dmitry was hitting me in all the right places. His fingers were thick and long and rough. He was not gentle and something about that pushed me straight over the edge. He pinched my nipples with his teeth as my hips worked against his hand, his palm grinding against my clit.

The third orgasm started fast and hit me like a tidal wave. I held tightly to Dmitry and bit down on his lip while his fingers continued to piston within my tightening walls. Shaking, hips bucking, the only thing that kept me from flying off of his lap was his arm locked firmly around me.

My head snapped back and I screamed out his name as my climax hit. I tasted his blood on my tongue and I should've been more concerned about that, but I was flying high. Dmitry's lips were on my throat, still. His fingers still filled me, his palm still rested against my sweet spot.

I had never felt so amazing in all my life. I wanted to tell him, but I couldn't get my mouth to work just yet. My heart slammed against my rib cage, my pulse fluttered at the base of my throat, near Dmitry's mouth. Everything felt surreal, like I'd floated into another dimension—someplace where everything was a party with rainbows and unicorns.

Reality always had a way of crashing the party, though.

Dmitry pulled his hand away suddenly and set me on unsteady feet, a foot away from him. Not meeting my eyes, he gestured towards his door. "Go on."

I didn't understand, so I just stood there like an idiot.

He turned away from me and fiddled with something on top of his dresser. "Go on back to your room, Kerrigan. I'm so sorry."

My stupid, fluttering heart that had been soaring the stratosphere suddenly crash landed at my feet. I think I kicked it as I turned and rushed out of his room. By the time I was safely shut away behind my bedroom door, I was crying big, fat tears. They rolled down my cheeks and dripped off my chin. I sat on my bed staring at the door hoping he'd been joking and was going to come rushing in at any second, sweep me into his arms, and carry me back to his bed. Instead, his door shut with a loud slam. I flopped back onto the bed and stared at the ceiling.

I had no clue what had just happened. Had I done something wrong? My body was still floating on air from the first and only orgasm given to me by someone other than myself. My body clearly hadn't gotten the memo that shortly thereafter, I'd been curtly dismissed. Not even dismissed. Kicked out. With an apology too, as though the whole thing was an accident.

I choked back a sob and dragged a pillow over my face. I felt devastated. Humiliated.

The more I racked my brain, the more confused I felt. I knew anger would come eventually and I welcomed it. It was far easier to deal with than humiliation.

8

DMITRY

I'd behaved unforgivably. After kicking Kerrigan out of my room, I spent the rest of the weekend locked inside, berating myself, ashamed of what I'd done to her and how I'd done it. Well, I was sorry for how rough I'd been. I couldn't deny that every time I closed my eyes, I pictured her lithe body and her soft moans of pleasure. It was torture. The memories of her crying out my name at the height of ecstasy played through my head like a porno on a loop. I knew it had been wrong, though—all wrong.

She deserved better. She was high-strung and fragile, easily reduced to tears. I'd been rough and then kicked her out. Worse, I'd heard her crying and smelled her tears. I knew she was upset and I wanted to go to her and comfort her, but anything I might do or say would only make the situation worse. I didn't know how to comfort someone—anyone. For someone like Kerrigan, I was a problem not a solution.

There was another reason for staying away from her—the main reason. She called to my bear like no other person on the planet. I wasn't convinced I could control myself around her and not grab her and do it all over again if the opportunity presented.

My bear had nearly ripped me to shreds trying to claim her the first time, the woman he was referring to as his mate. I supposed she was. She had to be based on the feelings I was having for her. But it wasn't fair to her to act on such things. Fate was cruel to pair me with Kerrigan. She deserved so much better. So, while my bear demanded his mate, I refused to allow it.

Instead, I avoided her. It was hell, but it was necessary. I waited until she was asleep and I had no chance of an accidental encounter before I snuck out to eat and swim. Like a complete coward, I even climbed out of my window to go to the office and to use the bathroom. I wasn't proud but it had to be done. I kept picturing her sorrowful, tear-stained face and that gave me impetus to continue to avoid her.

It was almost laughable that I, a polar bear—the largest, fiercest, most dangerous bear in existence, was spinelessly shaking in his fur at the thought of facing a tiny, 100-lb woman.

By sheer coincidence, I'd also ended up avoiding the rest of the P.O.L.A.R. unit. When Monday morning finally rolled around, I wondered if the team would know what a monster I'd been. Maybe Kerrigan had spilled to Hannah and Hannah in turn to Serge who told the rest of the unit. Maybe Kerrigan hated me. It would make everything easier if she hated me.

As I stepped into the office that morning, and the guys treated me as always, no questioning looks or smartass remarks, though, I knew she hadn't told a soul. But Kerrigan's desk was empty. I stared at it for a few seconds too long, when Serge came in and caught me.

"She's sick, I guess. She called this morning to let me know she couldn't make it in today."

"She *called* you?"

He frowned. "Yeah, she hasn't been out of her room all weekend. I guess she's been sick the whole time. I don't know. Hannah's taking her soup, or something. Looks like we get a day free from looking like completely incompetent idiots."

I growled under my breath at Serge's insult to Kerrigan, but there was nothing I could say. What I'd done to her was worse than Serge's implied insult. I sauntered to the back and sank into an office chair.

"You look bright and chipper today." Alexei followed me and sat across from me. "This wouldn't have anything to do with our missing dispatcher, would it?"

I scowled at him. "Don't start with me, Alexei. I'm in no mood."

"No? Whyever not? A lover's quarrel with everyone's favorite Disney Princess Mulan, perhaps?"

I knew he was attempting to push my buttons, and I should have ignored him, yet I didn't. "Mulan is Chinese not Vietnamese, dumbass. And furthermore, fuck you."

"Me? Fuck me? Please, we all know it's not me you want to fuck."

I was up and dragging him across the room before either of us could blink. I slammed him into the wall so hard we both went through it and fell into the front offices where the rest of the team was holed up. I shoved off of Alexei and stalked angrily toward the door.

"Um, excuse me? You two want to explain why the fuck you just remodeled the place?" Serge gestured towards the chalky mess that had been a wall seconds earlier. Alexei was on top of the pile of drywall pieces, a stupid grin on his face. "And why are you grinning? What did you do? You're fucking with him, aren't you? Shit, what am I saying? Of course you're fucking with him."

I ignored them all and left. I needed some air and to calm the fuck down.

I worked through every trick I'd ever learned about how to calm the animal inside as I headed toward the beach, including counting slowly to a hundred. Nothing was working. My bear was pushing to get out.

It took me a few seconds to realize that Kerrigan's scent was what was riling him so much. Her naturally delicious aroma was mixed with the acrid scent of fear and I also scented another male near her. I growled low in my throat and charged forward, teetering on the verge of a shift, more bear than man.

Down the beach, I spotted Kerrigan, her sandals in her hand, staring up at a fully dressed man, dress slacks and collared shirt, whose back was to me. Her face was contorted in worry and I could feel the anxiety rolling off of her.

Instinct told me to charge the man. He was threat and needed to be taken down. But before I could implement the maneuver, Kerrigan hung her head and stepped around him. Eyes downcast, she strode quickly toward the house, not even noticing me.

"Don't cross me, Kerrigan." The man's warning carried to me due only to the direction of the breeze and my shifter hearing. "You hand over more or you'll be paying in other ways."

Kerrigan's shoulders stiffened and she froze for a moment without looking back, before running into the house. I watched until she slipped inside and shut the door behind her.

Back down the beach, the man was already walking briskly away, whistling the theme from Jeopardy. The picture of ease and contentment, I was pretty sure I'd just overheard a threat of some sort—possibly a blackmail attempt.

My already agitated bear eating me alive trying to get me to shift right then and there and end the fucker. Fortunately, I still had some rational brain power—enough to put two and two together. Kerrigan was in some kind of trouble. The man may have thought he had the upper hand, but what he didn't know was that Kerrigan had a small army of highly trained, lethal polar bear shifters at her back. Or that it would require only one of us to neutralize him. Me.

9

KERRIGAN

Back in my room, I emptied the contents of my purse on my bed and gathered all the loose change that had fallen to the bottom. Then, I emptied the shoebox under my bed. I didn't have much. Everything went toward my student loan payments. One loan in particular. I gathered the small stack of bills in my trembling hands. It wasn't enough.

I wouldn't get my paycheck from P.O.L.A.R. until Friday. Once I did, I would have just enough to settle with Knuckles for the next month. The problem was that I didn't know how to convince him to hold off until I cashed my paycheck. But, there was no other way. I couldn't ask Serge for an advance. I hadn't even worked there long enough. Plus, I was pretty sure he hated me. They all did.

I was praying my miniscule savings would hold Nicky over until payday. I shoved the cash into an envelope and sat on the edge of my bed wondering if I was just prolonging the inevitable. How long could I hold the man off? He was getting pushier and pushier—demanding double the normal payment amount. Why? Because he could. I had no recourse. Private loans weren't governed by any laws, so he could do whatever he wanted. It hadn't taken me long to realize he was a loan shark. A greedy, evil loan shark named Nicky "Knuckles" Palermo who was known on the street as Nicky Knuckles. Unfortunately, I'd learned of his street reputation too late, after I'd already borrowed a hefty chunk of change. Now I was drowning in my biggest mistake.

I rested my head in my hands and tried to steady my erratic breathing. It wasn't easy. I was terrified and rightly so. Knuckles was getting nastier. He'd threatened me with horrible things. Breaking my kneecaps had been an early threat. Selling me into sex slavery was the latest. The threat worked because I was pretty sure he actually had the power to do it. So, with my personal safety on the line, I was willing to do whatever I could to procure and hand over double my normal payment.

The trouble was, whenever I met one of his demands, he had another, more difficult stipulation and I had no recourse. I was between a rock and a hard place. I knew I needed help, but I didn't feel right involving anyone else in my mess. Besides, I didn't have anyone else to involve.

My mom was off in Northern Russia somewhere with her mate. My father had been dead for years. I had no siblings or any other family. I'd been too busy in college, with my nose always in a textbook, to make friends or engage in social activities. After college, I'd hustled my butt off working two jobs—nightshift at a convenience store, and days writing for a small magazine. No time for social pursuits. When the magazine shut down, I lost my tiny apartment and lived out of my Honda Civic. I was lucky to have Mom's mate find me the job with P.O.L.A.R. even though it meant moving an hour away and losing the second job at the convenience store.

I was alone. Worse than alone, lonely. Oddly, before meeting Dmitry, alone and lonely weren't synonymous. Now, the loneliness was a slow burning ache.

I rubbed my tired eyes and stood up. I couldn't be bellyaching about Dmitry. Not when I had real problems to deal with. Knuckles was back to his highly effective intimidation tactics. He was a legit danger.

Whatever had happened with Dmitry was a mistake, anyway. A

dumb, stupid mistake. If anyone found out, I would lose my job and right now, that was the only thing keeping Nicky Knuckles from selling me into sex slavery. I'd had to sign a strict non-fraternizing contract. After some incident that caused a big tadoo and got the team in trouble, the main office wasn't taking any chances. If I was caught dating or otherwise sharing intimate relations with any of the guys in the P.O.L.A.R. unit, I was out. And not even my mom's mate could stop it. It was bad enough that I sucked majorly at my job, I couldn't afford to be a rebellious rule-breaker, too.

My silly crush and my raging hormones had allowed me to jeopardize the house of cards that was my life. If I was out of a job and Nicky Knuckles found out, I'm pretty sure his reaction would be swift and brutal. I damned sure couldn't afford to let thoughts of Dmitry allow this precarious balance to crumble.

And I had! I'd called off sick because of what had happened with Dmitry even though I couldn't afford to be shorted a day's pay. Not only that, but I had to do better and work harder, so P.O.L.A.R. wouldn't fire me.

I pulled my hair up in a ponytail and headed back out in the direction of the team office.

Like a cruel joke from life, Dmitry was opening the front door just as I was about to. I didn't meet his eyes as I sidestepped him and rushed away. Part self-preservation, part hurt, I didn't want to see him. I never wanted to see him again. Already, as it was, I couldn't stop thinking about him.

"Kerrigan..."

I tossed a wave in his direction. "Can't talk. On my way to work."

I picked up my pace until I was running, and made it to the office in minutes. Shocking everyone, I burst into the frigidly cold building sweaty and out of breath. Serge stood up from my desk and frowned. "What are you doing here, Kerrigan?"

"Miraculously, I'm healed. And reporting for duty."

"There's no problem with you taking a sick day. We'll manage just fine. You should take the day to rest up so you're at 100% tomorrow."

I didn't meet his eyes, and simply plopped into my desk chair. "No, thanks."

He looked like he had more to say but the phone rang.

I yanked it up and brought it to my ear. "P.O.L.A.R.."

Listening while a harried woman shouted numbers at me, I yelled them out to the room just as she'd yelled them to me. Slamming the phone down, I turned to the men who were all staring at me and widened my eyes. "Well?"

Alexi sported a half-grin. "That works."

Maxim nodded. "Got it."

Serge patted my shoulder with his heavy hand. "Good job, Kerrigan. Keep it up."

I stared down at my desk as they did their thing and geared up for the job. I didn't want to see if the call involved weapons or not. I just wanted to do my job and pay my debts. If I could avoid getting sold into slavery, that would be great, too.

Alexei stopped at my desk and ruffled my ponytail. "The yelling technique. I like it. Serge likes to be yelled at—keeps him in line."

Serge slapped the back of Alexei's head and shoved him towards the door. "Hannah is stopping by. Do me a favor and lock the door while the two of you are here alone."

"But not when I'm here alone?" The question was out before I could stop it.

He hesitated and frowned. "Yeah, you should lock the door when you're alone, too."

I nodded. "Sure."

It was just another reminder that I meant nothing to them. He wanted his mate safe, but it hadn't crossed anyone's mind to care about me.

I waved them off and left the door unlocked. What did it matter? The most dangerous man to me was already on the island and had my number. The second most dangerous man slept across the hall from me. I was screwed, no matter what.

10

KERRIGAN

I needed a drink, and not just one. Most of my money was going to Nicky Knuckles, but I'd seen a flyer posted at Mimi's Cabana when Hannah, Megan and I had been there on our girls' night outing that advertised dollar beers for Monday night happy hour. It was Monday and I was planning to hit those dollar drafts hard.

I headed to Mimi's straight after work. Alone. I didn't care that it might look weird to be sitting on a barstool sucking back cheap beers all by my lonesome before it was even dinnertime for the senior crowd. I truly didn't care.

The interior of Mimi's Cabana was all Polynesian themed with tiki masks, palm trees and coconuts. I was surprised Mimi hadn't carted in sand for the flooring. Mimi herself was a larger woman who wore a coconut bra and grass skirt to work daily. She had curves on top of curves, but she actually made it work. I liked her. She was all smiles and sunshine.

The dollar beers were served from 4pm to 6pm. It was a little after four thirty, so I had to get right to drowning my sorrows. I started out strong by ordering two beers from Mimi. I sat at the bar so it would be easy to get my refills when those were gone.

Dollar beer tasted a little like flat sour ginger ale without the ginger, but it was ice cold and after the first, the next went down easily. I found the more I drank, the lighter my problems became. The alcohol was numbing my weighty emotions for the moment and I was all for it. It was just the respite I needed. Beer number two had gotten warm, but I didn't care about that. When Mimi came back, I ordered two more.

"Honey, what's going on with you? I only gave you two beers to start out with because I thought you had a friend coming." Mimi poured me another but held it back. "A little slip of a thing like you shouldn't be downing so much so fast. What's got you chugalugging?"

"Men." I shook my head. "Two men, to be exact."

She pouted her thick lips and poured a fourth beer for me. "That I understand. If I wasn't working, I might join you in guzzling these things myself."

I saluted her with my Beer number three and burped. "Excuse me."

She just laughed and patted my shoulder as she wandered off to serve her other patrons. "Hold it together, honey."

Hold it together. Didn't that sound easy? I was intelligent, compassionate, well-educated. I could write a novel in under two months and be proud of it. Yet, there I was chugging back dollar beers and wondering how much longer I could balance on the tightrope I was walking.

The fourth beer was the best of all. I saw some fruity drink with a fancy umbrella served in a coconut go by and almost fell out of my chair drooling over it. Mimi noticed and grinned. "Stick to beer, honey, or you'll hate yourself in the morning."

So, I did. I had a fifth before the happy hour deadline arrived. I was wasted, anyway. I wasn't much of a drinker, but I usually held my alcohol fairly well for a woman who was a hair over five foot tall and weighed about 100 pounds soaking wet. Or, I could at least pretend to hold my alcohol. That night was different. I felt every ounce of cheap draft sloshing around in my gut, taunting me with the knowledge that it wasn't actually going to solve any of my dilemmas.

The numbed emotions were still there, just under the surface, but now I felt out of control. I swayed on my stool, which had nothing to do with the song playing in the background.

When someone sat down on the stool beside me, I paid them no mind. I was in my own world, wondering how long it would be before I could safely stand up without embarrassing the hell out of myself. Mimi had brought me a glass of water, but I needed to pee again and not another drop of was going to fit inside of me until I did.

"You drinking away all of my money, Kerrigan?"

I steadied myself by grasping the lip of the bar and digging my fingernails in. My eyes remained on the bar top. Nicky Knuckles. What the hell was he doing here? I'd already texted him that he could have my meager savings and that I'd give him the balance when I got paid. Why was he stalking me?

"Don't ignore me, sweetheart. That's not very nice."

"What do you want, Nicky?"

He wrapped his arm around my waist and leaned into me, his stale breath on my face was like a warm breeze rolling off a trash heap. "You know what I want."

I shuddered, the feeling of him so close was worse than having a slithering snake crawl over my skin. "I-I already told you when I'd have your money."

He *tsk*-ed and lightly tugged at the end of my ponytail. "I'm an impatient man. If you want me to wait until Friday, I'll need to be entertained in the meantime—in other ways."

I tried to pull away, but he was strong. "Leave me alone."

He grasped my chin between his thumb and forefinger and forced my face to turn his way. His grin was bone chilling. "Let's dance."

I tried to hold onto the bar, but it was useless. Nicky was a big man and he easily picked me up merely by scooping his arm around my waist. He put me down out of reach of the stool and bar. When I tried to pull away, I felt the room spin and he simply wrapped his arms around me and held me against his chest. My face pressed into his shirt, his sickly sweet smelling cologne made me gag and the gold chain he wore dug into the side of my cheek.

"There we go. Isn't this nice?" He ran his hands up and down my back, his grip firm. "Just a nice dance between old friends—or maybe a little more than friends."

The threat was clear. He was letting me know how easily he could overpower me and that, unless I wanted everyone to know my shameful secret, there was nothing I could do about it. I wanted to scream, to beg someone to help me get away from him, but I knew it would only make things worse for me. Even filled to the brim with liquid courage, I knew better than to try to cross Nicky. The punishment would be too severe.

His strong cologne was mixed with cigarette smoke. I could feel the prickliness of his chest hair through the silk shirt he wore. My heart hammered in my chest and I had twin death grips on each side of his shirt, fighting to stay upright. I felt like I was going to vomit.

There were other couples dancing around us to the piped in calypso music and I knew that we didn't stand out. A bar full of people around and Nicky could maul me in plain sight without anyone noticing.

"There's something you should know about me, Kerrigan. I always get what I want. Always."

"Just let me pay you on Friday. Please."

He dug his fingers into my back suddenly and then pulled away with a big smile on his face. "Thanks for the dance."

"Honey, you okay?" Mimi was right behind me, undoubtedly the real reason Nicky had let me go. "Let's get you to a chair. You can barely stand on your own, child."

I wanted to kiss Mimi I was so thankful for her. I didn't notice whether or not Nicky left. I didn't see anything else. I was too focused on putting one foot in front of the other on a relatively straight path back to the barstool. That, and trying to keep the room from spinning.

"Okay, here we go." Mimi tried to help me, but I was already wobbling like a newborn colt.

Trying to get onto the stool was a joke. I lifted one leg and the other one buckled beneath me. Before I could help it, I was going down.

11

DMITRY

The job we were on—a stakeout of a suspected arsonist—had run long and I didn't make it back to the house until after six. I had a slight gnawing in my gut all due to Kerrigan. My mind kept straying to her, the strange man who'd threatened her and what kind of trouble she might be in. Planning to confront her, I went straight to her bedroom and found the door cracked. The room was empty.

I walked over to the office to see if she was still there, but she wasn't. I tried the beach and scanned the waves to see if maybe she'd gone out for a swim. She was nowhere to be seen. The gnawing in my gut was worse than ever.

Anyone seen Kerrigan?

Immediately Serge's thoughts filled my head. *Nope. Hannah said she wasn't looking too good when she saw her at the office today.*

Shit. Something was wrong. She was in some kind of trouble. But what kind, exactly?

Megan says to check Mimi's. They all talked about the happy hour deal when they were there the other night. Maybe she stopped for a drink. Everything okay? Roman's voice was laden with concern which merely served to amp my fear up even more.

I don't know yet.

I took off at a sprint towards Mimi's Cabana. I had to cross Main Street and cut down Flamingo Lane, but as soon as I got close, I could smell her. Her natural aroma was mixed with the sour scent of fear and the pickling of alcohol.

Found her.

I all but ripped Mimi's door off to get inside and what I saw incensed me and enraged my bear to the point I had to fight him to keep from an uncontrolled shift in a barroom packed with people. Kerrigan was there. So was the dickweed who'd been threatening her earlier—and he was touching her. His back was to me, but he was easy to distinguish from his clothes and stature. He had his arms around her so tightly that it looked as though he was trying to suffocate her.

Mimi, a concerned look on her face, was behind Kerrigan and while I concentrated on counting to ten before I did something stupid like rip that fucker's head off and sully Mimi's Caribbean décor with spatters of blood and chunks of flesh, he stepped back. When he did, I saw the state Kerrigan was in. So much for counting to ten. She could barely stand on her own. The fucker had to have been holding her up. Had he been trying to take advantage of her in her intoxicated state?

I was seconds from a gruesome kill when I was distracted by Mimi supporting Kerrigan and guiding her to a barstool. Kerrigan was falling backwards. Even with my shifter strength and speed, I was too far away to catch her before she hit the ground. The *thump* was painful to hear, but Kerrigan didn't seem any worse for the wear. She just hiccuped and grinned, an embarrassed pink tinge to her face.

Mimi spotted me coming and whispered to Kerrigan, "You didn't hold it together honey."

"I really tried." Kerrigan's voice was watery and I was concerned I was going to see tears.

I didn't want to *see* the tears. I heard them on occasion. Smelled them, too, but that was different. I could almost pretend they weren't real. I had a feeling I was about to be hit with a motherlode of tears. "You okay, Kerrigan?"

Her head snapped to me and, the tears I'd been expecting vanished. Her brown eyes focused on me and she groaned as though seeing me was the thing she'd expected or wanted. "Oh."

I frowned. "Come on. Let's get you home."

She took Mimi's hand over mine and when she was on two feet again, she took a moment to steady herself. Blowing out a deep breath that smelled like beer, she nodded to herself and squared her shoulders. It would've been more convincing if she hadn't also been chewing her lower lip.

I ran my hand down my face and looked around, trying to spot the asshole who'd been touching her. He'd already slipped out. Fuck. I'd let him get away.

Kerrigan stumbled when she took her first step, but still recoiled when I held my arm out to help her. That's how it went. Getting out of the bar took forever. She took a few steps and then stumbled, but refused to accept my help. I let her go it on her own while we were in the crowd of people because I didn't want to make a scene—or any more of a scene.

As soon as we cleared the doorway, though, I swept her into my arms and carried her home. She weighed next to nothing, even while wriggling in an attempt to get down.

"You need to put me down. Right now." She hiccupped and burped at the same time, something that clearly embarrassed her. She groaned and buried her face in her hands.

"You're too drunk to walk a straight line. It'd take you until next week to get home at this rate." I cut through someone's side yard to make it home faster.

"I can walk just fine. I don't want you to carry me."

"Too bad."

"Put me down." She hiccupped again. "You...you...overgrown teddy bear."

I cocked my head at her and looked up and down Main Street before crossing it. "Excuse me?"

She sighed. "Oh, I'm sorry. I shouldn't call you names."

She was apologizing to me. She'd done nothing wrong. I was the asshole, or the overgrown teddy bear, as she'd put it.

"Kerrigan..."

She shook her head and hiccupped again. "I don't want to conversate with you. *Hiccup.*"

I walked the rest of the way in silence, arriving at the house faster than I wanted to. I put her down on the front steps of the house to have a few words with her privately. "I think we—"

She bent over, stumbled, hiccupped, took her shoes off, and then started weaving her way down to the beach. I watched her go, stumbling and falling two, three, times, before she settled into the sand at the edge of the water and let the tide roll over her feet. Following behind her, I was fully intent on taking advantage of her inebriated state to get her to open up and talk to me—to tell me what was wrong and why that asshat had been all over her earlier. I thought we'd finally get a chance to talk and the fact that her inhibitions were reduced by alcohol was a benefit in my mind. Okay, maybe it wasn't the most honorable plan, but I really needed to find out who the man was that had been hanging around and what the hell was going on with her. I also wanted to apologize for treating her so poorly.

My plan didn't work, though. Kerrigan had nothing to say to me.

12

KERRIGAN

I didn't want to hear a word Dmitry said. Not a word. I was still too drunk to trust myself with rational conversation. Who knew what might come out of my mouth? Besides, whatever he wanted to talk about was probably going to sting like hell. Something along the lines of, "I never should have put my hands on you. Please don't tell anyone, blah, blah."

When he sank down next to me in the sand, I didn't look over at him. I'd already spent too much time dying inside over the way he'd carried me back from Mimi's. I kicked off my sandals and then leaned back to get to my pants button.

"What are you doing?"

I stood back up and walked to the water. "Going for a swim."

I kicked out of my pants and then threw my shirt onto the small pile before wading out in the water. It was cold against my overheated skin, the sand rough under my toes. Still plenty of daylight left. I should've been embarrassed to be swimming in my bra and panties in the late afternoon on a public beach. I wasn't.

Up to my hips, up to my breasts, up to my chin. When I couldn't touch the sandy bottom of the ocean floor, I breaststroked out deeper. I'd swim across the ocean if that's what it took to get far away from

Nicky Knuckles and his slime ball threats. I even wanted to get away from Dmitry.

I swam out farther and farther until I could look back at the beach and not see him through my water-spotted glasses. Floating on my back, I stared up at the bright blue sky until my eyes burned and I had to squeeze them shut.

The alcohol was still flowing through my system, making my problems just a bit out of reach. I felt like my fingertips could just graze them, but not pull them close. They loomed, just out there on the horizon, reminding me that they would still be there when I sobered up, tomorrow, next week, maybe forever.

I was pitiful. My life was pitiful.

I held my breath and let myself sink under the water. Blowing out my breath, I sank even lower. My eyes closed, my lungs tight, I paddled my arms to keep myself under. I felt free there—cloaked. I pretended no one would be able to find me and I could float under the water and never have to worry about a thing.

No rent or mortgage, no exorbitant student loans, I'd just float in the ocean, under the waves. It wouldn't matter if I sucked at my job and no one liked me, or if the only man I'd been intimate with wanted to pretend it never happened. It wouldn't matter because the fish didn't care.

My lungs burned, but I stayed under. I didn't want to die. I just didn't want to be up top, up above the waterline. The world was too hard.

Something brushed against my leg and I felt something massive wrap around me, dragging me upwards. I didn't have to open my eyes to know what it was, who it was. Dmitry. More specifically, Dmitry's bear.

We crested the surface and I sucked in a huge breath of air and coughed.

Next to me was the largest animal I'd ever seen face to face. Snow white with a black nose and Dmitry's dark blue eyes, the bear was awesome—as in awe-inspiring. It opened its mouth and roared, revealing huge, razor-sharp teeth and a black tongue. Still, I felt no fear.

I bobbed in the water next to it and found myself smiling. I was clearly still drunk. Running my hand over its head, I felt something melt inside of me. There was pain and heartache in the real world, above water, but there were also amazing, extraordinary, incredible things. I was stroking the head of a polar bear shifter. The most beautiful polar bear I'd ever seen. He was growling while I did it, but still, he was letting me.

Then, a split-second later, the bear was gone and Dmitry was in front of me again. My hand was still stroking over his head and face.

I should probably stop petting him. Yeah.

He stared at me with a furious scowl and shook his head. "Out of the water."

I sighed. The beer buzz was still with me, strongly, but not enough to keep me from feeling down that he looked at me like that, like he hated me.

Dmitry wasted no time in wrapping his arm around my waist, and all but dragging me back to shore. When we got close enough to stand, he let me go, stepping ahead of me, but grabbed my hand to pull me after him. Wow, he had a tightly formed ass—and no tan lines. When I giggled, he glared at me over his shoulder.

His shirt and pants were in a pile next to mine and he stepped into his pants with his back still to me. He seemed to be waiting for me to do the same, but I wasn't putting my clothes back on. I wasn't ready to go back to real life just yet.

That just seemed to deepen his scowl. Especially when he turned around and saw me sitting in the sand in just my bra and panties. He threw his hands up. "What the fuck was that?"

I furrowed my brows. "What was what?"

"That! Were you trying to drown yourself?" He put his hands on his hips and glared down at me. "You went under and you didn't come back up. You about gave me a heart attack."

"You're a shifter. You'll be fine." I waved him off. "Do shifters even have heart attacks?"

It was the wrong thing to say. "Kerrigan, you can't... I forbid you to drown yourself! Jesus Christ. I can't believe I have to say that to you. You can't just swim out and go under like that!"

"I wasn't drowning myself. I just wanted to be under the water for a while."

"Why?"

I shrugged. "It's nice under there."

He threw his hands up. "It's nice under there. Great. I'm glad. I'm glad that you had a *nice* time enjoying your near-drowning. You're drunk, clumsy, and accident prone as hell. You can't be taking risks with your life like that. You could've gotten caught on something. Then what? What would you have done then, huh?"

I met his angry stare and hiccupped. "P.O.L.A.R. would've gotten a better, more competent replacement."

"Not fucking funny. I'm not fucking laughing right now, Kerrigan. See my face. Serious as shit." He pointed his finger at his chin. "You're a fucking menace to yourself."

13

KERRIGAN

"You think I don't know that?" My calm demeanor seemed to throw Dmitry for a loop. I just kept staring at him, accepting that we were going to have whatever conversation he wanted. That's how things seemed to work—everything on his terms.

He paced in front of me, his bare feet leaving a trench in the sand. "What's wrong with you?"

I laughed. "I don't think you have the time."

"Try me." He came to a stop in front of me and stared at me. "Tell me what's going on."

I hiccupped again and pulled my knees into my chest, locking my arms around them. "I owe someone money."

"The guy who's been hanging around you?"

I didn't even need to ask how he known about Nicky Knuckles showing up. The bears seemed to know everything. "Yeah. I borrowed a lot of money from him and I've been paying it back, but he wants more."

"You borrowed money from a loan shark?" He sounded incredulous.

"Yes. Well, no...but, yes."

"Well, which is it?"

"I didn't know that's what he was at the time. Not really. I needed money and I heard his name mentioned around campus a few times. So, I went to him."

"How much did you borrow?"

"Ten thousand."

Dmitry swore and started his pacing again. "Why, Kerrigan? What would possibly make you do that? Ten thousand dollars from a loan shark? Jesus."

"He was my last resort and I just did it."

"What'd you need it for?"

I looked past him, out at the ocean. It was calling me back. "School. I was a year away from finishing my master's. I did everything else. I took out student loans, applied for grants and scholarships, worked two part time jobs. Still, I needed more."

"For school?" It was obvious he thought I was an idiot.

"Yes, for school. I didn't know…anything. I didn't know who he was or how he would be." I shrugged. "But, I've made the payments. I haven't missed a month since I took the loan, but he keeps leaning on me for more."

"And now he's threatening you?"

I met Dmitry's eyes and nodded before looking away. "He wants double."

"Or what?"

"It doesn't matter."

"Or what, Kerrigan?"

"Or the usual. What do men always threaten women with? He's a typical sleazeball and certainly not original." I rested my chin on my knees and sighed. I'd quickly lost pretty much all my buzz. It was probably for the best.

"Fuck."

"It's fine. I'll handle it. I'm just trying to hold him off until I get paid on Friday. I'll sign over my paycheck, and he'll go away for another month."

"You won't have anything to live off of. And that won't put a stop to it. You jump through that hoop and he'll demand triple next month." Dmitry squatted in front of me and met my gaze. "What exactly do you mean by 'the usual'? What is he threatening you with? Be specific and spell it out for me. I have to be sure."

I blinked away sudden tears. "He has girls in Miami, apparently. He wants me to...you know...work off some of my debt by servicing his clients." I didn't know what I was going to do. Drinking had been so temporary it had hardly been worth it. And in the end, even that had landed me right in the arms of Nicky Knuckles.

"You're saying he runs a prostitution ring in Miami and he's threatening to pimp you out if you don't increase the payments?"

I swallowed a lump in my throat and stood up. My life sucked. I scooped up my clothes and turned to walk away.

Dmitry growled and stopped me with a hand on my waist. "You've got bruises."

I looked over my shoulder at what I could see of my lower back. Sure enough, there were bruises from Nicky's fingers. I was so drunk at the time, I hadn't even felt them. "They're not gonna kill me."

I pushed Dmitry's hand away and started towards the house. There was no point in explaining anything else to Dmitry. He just wanted to judge me and point out what a lonely idiot I was.

"Kerrigan, stop."

I kept walking. I still swayed a bit, but I walked with enough determination that I made it to the house and up the first flight of stairs to the front door without a problem.

"He can't do that." Dmitry caught my arm and pulled me to a stop. He didn't let go and when he looked at me, I wondered if he was remembering the same thing I was remembering. He just shook his head and frowned, though. "I will not let him do that."

I looked down at my feet and wondered where I'd left my shoes. "People like him do what they want. Don't worry about it, though. It's not your problem."

"It *is* my problem."

My heart skipped a beat and I looked up at him, a sliver of hope daring to emerge. "Why?"

"You work for P.O.L.A.R." He let go of me and stepped back. "You're part of us. Part of the team."

Right. Part of the team. Hardly. I was the weakest link. In fact, my job with the team was skating on such thin ice I was about to drown in the pond. I sighed and pushed open the door. "Ha! That's a laugh."

Hannah was coming out of the kitchen and spotted me. "Kerrigan! What happened to you?"

I looked down at my underwear and sandy clothes clutched to my stomach. "Um... Nothing. Nothing happened. I'm going to take a shower and then head to bed. It's been a long day."

She looked behind me at Dmitry, and frowned. "I'll walk you up."

"You don't have to do that."

"I want to." She smiled and linked her arm through mine. "That's what friends are for."

14

DMITRY

I watched her climb the stairs on shaky legs and waited until Hannah escorted her into her bedroom before I looked away. My heartrate was finally starting to return to a normal pace after the scare she gave me. Seeing Kerrigan go under and not come back up had convinced me of two things. One, she needed me to protect her. Two, I needed her to be safe.

Fury like I'd never felt ignited within me. Every dark thought and every torture technique I'd ever heard of were begging to be unleashed on the man who was threatening her. My bear didn't need the darkness to help. He was bloodthirsty. He wanted to tear the man apart with his teeth and make it a slow, painful death.

I needed more information. When Kerrigan was sober, I was going to get it all out of her. I needed his name and where he was from. I was going to make it right for her. No matter what I had to do. She couldn't survive the way she was going and I wasn't going to let her go under the water again. Not on my watch.

"What's up? Was everything okay with Kerrigan earlier?" Serge put down his sandwich and looked at me expectantly.

I hesitated. If it did come to me having to eliminate the asshole threatening Kerrigan, the less Serge knew, the better. "Yeah, I just needed her input on something and I couldn't find her. Problem solved."

"Yeah, okay. I completely buy that."

I shrugged. "Buy it or don't. Are there more sandwiches where that one came from?"

He scowled. "Make it yourself. If there's anything I need to know about Kerrigan, I expect you to tell me, Dmitry."

"What could you possibly need to know about Kerrigan?"

"That's what I'm asking you."

Hannah walked back into the kitchen and stepped against her mate's side. "What are you two arguing about?"

Serge fed some of his sandwich to his mate. "Is there anything going on with Kerrigan?"

Hannah smiled. "Is there a woman on this earth that doesn't have something going on?"

"Anything that I need to know? As her boss?"

"Not that I know of. I think she's just torn up about a guy."

Serge groaned. "Never mind. Forget I asked."

My appetite was suddenly ruined. I nodded a goodbye to them and went up to my room. I could hear the shower running and sat on the edge of my bed, waiting for the water to shut off.

It was pure torture. Since I'd held Kerrigan in the very spot I was sitting at that moment, my mind had been going in circles. I'd been beside myself. Seeing her, hearing her voice, thinking about her, all of it was painful.

Knowing she was naked in the next room over was bad enough, but knowing that she was hurting made me ache. I knew why. My bear knew what it was. She was ours and I couldn't stand her pain. She was under my skin bigtime.

When the water cut off, I waited a few minutes and then went across to Kerrigan's room. I lightly knocked on the door and waited for her to answer.

"Hang on." Her voice sounded tired. "Just a sec."

I leaned against the doorframe waiting for her to let me in. After a few seconds, I could sense her hovering by the door, thinking about whether or not she should open it. She was angry and hurt, both of which were justifiable. I needed to be in that room with her, though. "Let me in, Kerrigan."

She sighed and pulled the door open. Blocking me from coming in, she stared down at the floor. "What do you want?"

My bear grumbled low in my chest, but I cut him off. It didn't matter what the fuck he wanted. I needed to make sure Kerrigan was safe. That took priority over everything. "I want to finish talking."

She groaned and shook her head, but I took advantage of my size and leaned into the room and into her personal space until she reflexively stepped aside. Dirty trick, but I needed to be in the room with her. I needed to make sure she was safe.

"You can't just—"

"I can and I am." I walked over to the window, pushed it closed, and latched it. Then, I slid her curtains closed and turned to face her. She'd been hiding herself behind the door, so it was my first full look at her since I'd entered. She took my breath away.

The oversized t-shirt she wore stopped mid-thigh and fell off her right shoulder. Her hair was damp and piled on the top of her head in a loose, spiky bun with a few stray strands hanging in her face. Her eyes looked even larger than normal behind her thick glasses. Her perfectly shaped lips were puckered out in displeasure as she watched me, slim arms crossed over her chest.

I'd just seen her in her underwear, but something about her bare shoulder and bare stretch of leg from toe to thigh was killing me. That exposed shoulder should've been illegal.

I took a deep breath and inhaled her fresh, clean scent. Okay, that didn't help, so I turned back to the window and took a minute to compose myself. "We have to come up with a plan to keep you safe."

Bare feet padded across the floor. The bed let out a light squeak as she sat on it. It was the ruffling of the bedding that caused me to turn around. She was getting under the covers.

"What are you doing?"

"I'm tired. I don't want to talk." She looked over at me and, in a rare moment of steady eye contact, she held my gaze while she pulled the blanket up to her chin. "You should leave. It doesn't look right."

Frowning, I shrugged. "It's fine. We're just talking, Kerrigan."

She popped up like a jack in a box, her face flushing as red as her lips. "It's not fine. It's the farthest thing from fine. After what happened...between us... You haven't said two words to me about that."

I grunted. "I'm sorry."

"Oh, my gosh. Don't apologize! Do you think that's what I want to hear?" She clutched the blanket in a death grip and stared at it. "*That* happened between us and then you kicked me out and apologized. You don't want me? Fine. I'm a big girl. I can accept rejection and I can move past it. What I can't accept is you coming in here and talking to me like it's not weird that we're both this close to my bed and I'm not wearing any underwear."

I guess I had a funny bone somewhere deep inside that I hadn't known existed because I wanted to laugh. Not at her, but just... because. She was cute. More than cute, she was beautiful and intelligent and irritating, and perfect.

"Why are you looking at me like that?"

I straightened my face and shrugged. "Like what?"

"Like you want to laugh at me. Is it funny that I thought you might have actually wanted to be with me? It probably is, isn't it? You're this hot looking hero guy and I'm this mousy little four-eyed virgin. Literally, the last thing on your mind is someone like me. I guess the other day was just scratching an itch with whomever was available? I just happened to be in the right place at the right time? Lucky me. It's terrible to laugh at someone because they have a crush on you." She gasped a big breath and turned a heated stare on me. Her bottom lip began to wobble. "Please go. I'm not drunk anymore, but I still might cry about this."

15

KERRIGAN

"I'm not going anywhere." To prove his point, Dmitry pulled out my desk chair and sat in it, his long legs spread out in front of him. "And I'm not laughing at you."

I felt disoriented. I'd worked up a big anger and he'd just deflated my anger balloon. "What?"

"I'm not going anywhere." He crossed his arms over his chest and rolled his neck. "And I'm not laughing at you. Got it?"

I turned to face him and shook my head. "No, I don't 'got it'."

He watched my finger quotes with another one of those little smirks on his face. "I'm going to make sure you're safe. I don't like the idea of you being in here by yourself, so far away from help."

"Across the hall is far away?"

Ignoring me, he continued. "This way, I can make sure you're safe and no one is trying to sneak in through your window."

My stomach twisted at the idea of Nicky Knuckles climbing in through my bedroom window. I turned and stared at it like it was a four-headed monster with drool on its fangs.

"No one is coming in, Kerrigan. I'm staying right here to make sure of that."

"Why?"

He shifted. "Because."

"That's not an answer."

"It's the only one you're getting."

I kicked the covers off my legs and sat on the edge of the bed. My feet were just inches from his. Oddly, I wanted to rub my feet against his so some part of us touched. I wasn't a martyr, though. I could only take so much rejection.

"Did it feel to you like I didn't care who I was with, Kerrigan?" The husky tone of Dmitry's voice surprised me and when I glanced up at him, it was clear by his expression he was expecting an answer.

I bit my lip and played with the hem of my T-shirt. I was afraid to lay all my cards out in front of him. It was so obvious to me that he had all the power in our exchanges. I needed to keep something close to my vest. "I don't know."

"I'll tell you, then. I knew absolutely who I was with and you were exactly who I wanted. It was how rough I was with you that I am sorry about, but not for touching you or tasting you. That I'm not sorry for."

My stomach fluttered. "Oh."

"It's pretty obvious that the desire was there long before that night."

South of my stomach fluttered, too. I found a worn spot on the hem of my shirt and tugged at a thread. "It wasn't. Pretty obvious, I mean."

As if he realized that he was saying too much, he grew quiet, but I could feel his eyes on me. They burned like a thousand suns over my skin.

I licked my suddenly dry lips and scooted back into bed. "None of it matters, anyway. Even if there was desire, or whatever, I signed a contract. If anyone found out about what happened, I'd lose my job. And, as you know, I can't afford to lose this job."

"What? What contract?"

I made a big deal of fluffing my pillows. "To work here, I had to sign a non-fraternization contract. Dating or otherwise engaging in romantic or sexual relations with team members is grounds for my immediate dismissal."

"You're not serious."

I looked up and found that he'd sat forward, his eyes, more smoky gray than dark blue right then, locked onto me. Nodding, I shrugged. "Yeah, I signed it before coming here. I just figured it was normal. Although, I guess I can see why they didn't make any of you sign it. None of you seem to want to date each other."

He cocked his head to the side.

Realizing what I'd said, I sped ahead, into oncoming word traffic. "I mean, it's fine if you do. I'm not judging or anything. I was talking about us, anyway. *Me*. Not you. I don't want to imply that you wanted to sleep with me. I mean, it's obvious that you don't. Don't feel the need to make that any clearer, okay? Or say anything at all. No comment necessary."

Still, Dmitry said nothing. His eyes were so still and focused on me, his head was cocked slightly to the side as he listened.

"Well, anyway. I should get some sleep."

"It's not even dark out yet."

"And still, somehow, I've managed to tire myself out." I sank back under the covers, needing the protection of a blanket to hide myself.

"Kerrigan..."

I held up my hand to stop him. "I do not want to hear anything you feel you need to say in reply to my verbal diarrhea. In fact, I'd really appreciate if we could both pretend I didn't say any of it. So, I'm going to go to sleep. You should go back to your room. I don't need a babysitter."

Dmitry was nice enough to be silent after that. He stayed where he was, though, which was torture enough. My body was so overtly aware that he was in the room and only a few feet from my bed, that I couldn't think of anything else. All I could do was lie there and squeeze my eyes shut, hoping I'd fall asleep as fast as possible.

Miraculously, having Dmitry that close seemed to also settle a restlessness deeper within me. Under the sexual tension, I realized all of my other fears had faded enough that I wasn't worrying about them. It allowed me to fall asleep and I slept like the dead. The only thing stirring me throughout the night were dreams of Dmitry.

16

DMITRY

My heartrate didn't return to normal until Kerrigan had been asleep for several hours. I pondered what she'd said—and what she hadn't said. I was all but sitting on my hands to keep them away from her, but no way was I going to touch her. I couldn't. The contract. Her confirmed virginity. I was bad news for her. I just sat as she slept.

I watched over her, with heavy lids tracing her outline, memorizing the details that made up Kerrigan. Her bare shoulder peeked out from under the blanket. Her skin was smooth and looked like silk. Without her thick glasses on, her face was fine-featured. Flat, delicate nose. Fringe of short, dark lashes brushing her cheeks. When she turned, I noticed a dark birthmark on the back of her shoulder that looked like one of the astral constellations. I couldn't remember which one.

My mother had been into the stars. She would give readings and map astrological charts for clients, telling all sorts of stories based on the position of the stars. It'd been so long since she'd passed. I couldn't remember any astrology. That whimsical kind of thing had never mattered to me when I was young. The stars, the moon and sun, all of them were just...out there. I do remember one particular story, though. I remember her talking about how the stars had aligned just right for her and my father, and that the same would happen for me one day.

What would my mother think of me now? Seeing that constellation shaped birthmark on Kerrigan's shoulder touched me deeply. I wished my mother could have met Kerrigan. For the first time in quite a while, in the darkness of the room, I found myself mourning the loss of my mother.

With the sorrow of loss came a mighty dose of reality. Life was fragile. Even a shifter's life. Things happened. People died. Everything about Kerrigan was fragile, small and virtually defenseless.

I knew she was my mate. I'd known it the moment I'd first set eyes on her. She'd walked into the P.O.L.A.R. office with Serge and my jaw had dropped clear to the floor. When her eyes drifted to mine, even hidden behind thick glasses, I thought I saw recognition in them as well. She'd looked away quickly, but not before I noticed the way her cheeks had flushed.

How the stars could have aligned to send me someone as pure and delicate and perfect as Kerrigan, I would never know. I was undoubtedly damned, my soul as dark as the deepest depths of the ocean. My story was set, my deeds committed. Nothing I could ever do would make up for the acts I'd already wrought. Why fate would give me Kerrigan was a mystery. I wasn't right for her. Christ, my fantasies alone, the things I wanted to do to her were dirtier than a woman like her ever deserved.

None of it made sense to me, but I'd at least accepted the truth. We were mates, but we needed to refrain from consummating the mating or going through with the claiming.

Even if it weren't for the fact that I didn't deserve her, the contract she'd signed would've made things too difficult for her. The main office would fire her, without a doubt. If they'd gone as far as to make her sign something so fucking asinine, they would surely stand by it.

I didn't want to cost her the job she needed, although I would handle her debt myself, and I should've been grateful for the excuse to stay away from her. I didn't feel grateful. I felt pissed off that the company I worked for would dare to think they could dictate something so personal to Kerrigan. They had no right to control what she did on her own time and with whom.

I knew it was a direct response to Serge and Hannah mating while he was on the job. It had led to the team breaking protocol and disobeying direct orders. The contract was their way of showing us that we didn't get to pull a stunt like that again. Actually, the more I thought about it, the more it pissed me off. If Kerrigan did "fraternize" with one of us, she would lose her job and we would, what? Get a slap on the wrist? A high five? Way to go, bro? Men will be men and all that? Fuck that.

As soon as I handled things with Kerrigan's loan shark, I was going to have plenty to say to the main office. They'd get an earful from me. I was already ticked that they'd jerked the team around by sending us here from Siberia. They'd punished us and were continuing to do so by keeping us on the island, where we weren't doing any real work. To think they could keep our mates away from us, if and when we found them, was overreaching.

We were trained operatives but, especially when it came to mates, we were shifters, too. Looking at Kerrigan's sleeping form, I felt like a man first, operative second, shifter third. Maybe that's what the main office was trying to stop from happening—an operative valuing a mate over the job.

I knew that I would fight twice as hard as I'd ever fought if I was fighting to keep her safe. Just like Serge and Roman with their mates.

Kerrigan rolled over and softly spoke my name in her sleep. She did that almost every night. Maybe I was an asshole for keeping my ears peeled and prying into her private moments, but I didn't know how to stop.

I stood up and paced over to the window, pulling just the edge of the curtain back so I could stare out into the night. Nothing but the expanse of ocean and sky stared back at me.

Her loan shark wasn't coming for her, yet. But when he did, he wasn't going to like what he found. Twice, he'd gotten to her. He'd left bruises on her body. Never again. He was either going to go away peacefully, or he was going to wish he'd never set eyes on Kerrigan Tran. I'd make sure of that.

17

KERRIGAN

What had I been thinking getting wasted on a Monday night? I felt like a Mack truck had run over my head and my stomach wasn't much better. Worse than either was my pride. That was so wounded that I couldn't meet anyone's eyes at work the next morning. I felt like everyone knew all of my dirty secrets. I *knew* Dmitry knew them.

I was horrified at how I'd behaved in front of him. Flashbacks of the verbal onslaught alone were enough to send me scrambling for the bathroom that morning in a wave of nausea. At least in the bathroom I could avoid having to look at him or see him laughing. Even if he said he hadn't been laughing at me, I didn't believe him. How could he not? I'd made a complete ass of myself.

My head throbbed and my stomach cramped. I sat at my desk with my head down and tried to pretend like I was a braver woman, someone who would've seduced Dmitry into her bed instead of awkwardly flapping my gums and revealing way too much.

Dmitry seemed fine, though. He brought me a cup of coffee, with one sugar the way I liked it, and handed me a small bottle of Tylenol. He turned the air conditioners down, too. Their normal humming had been lowered to something tolerable, despite the rest of the team grumbling and giving him shit about how hot it was. He was hot, too. When I dared look up, I could see the sweat bloom on the back of his shirt. Still, he kept the AC down.

I didn't know why he was being nice. Why hadn't he gone running for the hills after last night.

The guys were all in the office, suffocating me. They were loud and, no matter where I needed to go, in my way. Getting them to move was always a project. I just wanted the office to myself for the morning to be able to readjust, but it was impossible.

When the phone rang, I was so eager for them to leave, that I answered it faster than I ever had before. As I listened, I hastily repeated what I heard, calling out the address and code to the men, ready for them to leave and give me a break.

"998?" Serge hesitated and gave me a stern look. "Are you sure?"

I nodded. "That's what they said."

After the guys came out a few minutes later with a huge cage and a gun bigger than me, I started to second guess myself. My stomach somersaulted and I pressed my hand to it. The person on the phone had said 998, I was pretty sure. That was a big gun, though.

"You're sure?" Serge had a protective mask in his hand and kept giving me that hard stare.

It was too late to take it back. I nodded and looked down at my paperwork, wanting the interaction to be over.

Dmitry stopped next to my desk and tapped his finger on it twice. "Lock the door behind us, Kerrigan."

My heart fluttered, the stupid thing, and I nodded awkwardly. "Okay."

I did like he said and locked the door. I hoped I hadn't just told them to go somewhere dangerous, but most of all I hoped I hadn't gotten the message wrong. I didn't think Serge was going to give me another chance. He didn't even like me.

To add to my headache and heartache, my mom called right when I sat back down at my desk. While I would've normally screened her call, she called on the office line and I didn't know it was her until too late.

"Mom, this is an emergency line."

"I won't talk long. I just wanted to see how things were going." Her voice seemed far away.

I squeezed my eyes shut and dug my nails into my palm to keep from crying. I was a grown woman. I had no business crying to my mom. "Things are fine."

"I heard you're having some trouble adjusting." She hesitated. "If they let you go, I don't have anything else, honey."

I bit my lip and made a sound of acknowledgement.

"Just try your hardest." Laughter sounded in the background and her voice lifted in joy. "Sorry, Kerrigan, I have to let you go. We're on the ski slopes. Just do your best, honey."

I put the phone back down in its cradle and blew out a big breath. Talks with my mom always went like that. Disappointment with me and eagerness get off the line. It had been that way since she'd met her mate when I was in my second year of college. I was a problem and the rest of her life was amazing.

I took another Tylenol and swallowed it with cold coffee. I was just getting up to file more paperwork when the locked front door burst open, both the lock and the doorknob flying across the room. I screamed and shielded my face with the files in my hand.

"Kerrigan! How fucking hard is it to listen to a phone message and repeat it?!" Serge was suddenly in front of me, his face bright red, a vein in his forehead pulsing. "Do you have any idea what you just had us do?"

Cringing away from him, I prayed for the floor to open up and swallow me whole.

"You sent us on a run to capture a rabid shifter. At the home of a nice young *human* computer programmer." He seethed. "We had him in the cage wetting himself before realizing we'd just tranquilized a human!"

I covered my mouth with my hand and backed away from him. "I didn't mean…"

"I should fire your ass right now. I should send you back to your car and let you go on to ruin someone else's business."

I was going to cry. I tried hard to fight it, but—his shouting...and my horror. I'd messed up again.

"We're stuck in this sweatbox because of fuckups. With you working here, we're never going to get our asses back home. Tell me why I shouldn't fucking fire you on the spot!"

I didn't have a reason that wasn't purely self-motivated. I stuttered out an apology, but I was choking on tears and I couldn't get it out very clearly. It just seemed to make Serge angrier.

"Cry all you want. It doesn't make me any less furious with you."

I wiped at my eyes and hurried over to my desk. Time to go. He was so angry that there was no way I wasn't fired. What the hell was I still standing there for? I'd just scram and save him the trouble.

"Where are you going?"

I hurried for the door, but Dmitry stepped into my way, his eyes on Serge behind me. I watched as a fine layer of white fur rippled across his face and his eyes glowed. He reached out and pulled me towards him and then behind him. "Wait outside."

18

DMITRY

Kerrigan didn't need to see what was about to happen. Moving farther into the office, I growled low in my throat at Serge. I didn't give a fuck who he was, Alpha or not, he wasn't going to treat my mate like that.

"Don't start with me right now, Dmitry."

I curled my lip and bared my teeth, showing him how serious I was. "You want to scream at someone, scream at me. Pick on someone your own size."

"Fuck off. I'm not picking on her. You were there. You know how bad that was. You really want to let that shit happen again?"

"You don't scream at her." I rolled my neck from side to side and sneered at him. "You scream at Hannah like that?"

That did the trick. Serge was instantly as ready to brawl as I was. "Don't fucking bring my mate into this."

"You started it." I took advantage of his shock. Charging at him, I slammed into his stomach with my shoulder and sent us flying backwards.

The fight was on. I forgot that Serge was my boss and a friend. I was strung out so tightly and so angry that I just needed to brawl. Serge was pissed, too, though, and he gave just as good as he got.

Desks and chairs that were innocently caught in our path were flattened, the front door was left hanging off of its hinges, file cabinets were upended. We beat the shit out of each other.

Serge shifted and pinned me down with one giant paw on my chest. Growling in my face, drool dripping from his canines, he let out a mighty roar that shook the walls of the office.

It did the job of breaking through haze of fury I'd been in. I blinked a few times and looked up at him, instantly regretting that I'd gone after him so hard. I let my head hit the floor under me and groaned.

He shifted back and landed one last painful punch to my ribs—a cheap shot. "I'm fucking sick of you assholes fighting me."

I grunted and sat up. "You deserved this one."

He stared at me hard for a full minute before shaking his head. "Maybe you're right. I shouldn't have yelled at her."

My fists balled up at my sides. "Don't ever do it again."

He grunted that time. "She can't keep working here if it keeps happening."

I shrugged. "We'll see."

"I'm serious, Dmitry. We look like clowns. No way are we ever going to get back to Siberia like this. They're going to send us to the fucking Sahara at this rate."

I looked over my shoulder and tried to spot Kerrigan. "I'll help her."

"Do something." He stood up and offered me a hand. When I tried to take it, he let go and watched me fall back. "Don't fucking pull that shit again. Tell her I'm sorry."

"Tell her your fucking self." I climbed to my feet and went out to find her and see that she was okay.

Alexei grinned at me when he saw me. "Nice one. You really picked a fight with Serge, huh?"

I ignored him. "Where's Kerrigan?"

Konstantin looked up from studying his shoes. "She headed toward the house. She looked pretty freaked out."

Fuck. I'd scared her. I hurried towards the house, needing to see her and convince her that everything was okay, despite also wondering if it wasn't better to just let her continue to think I was a monster. I couldn't, though. The idea of her scared of me was intolerable.

I heard her crying as soon as I entered the house. Not that she was crying loudly, but I was tuned into her. She was in her room sitting on her bed, her face buried in her hands. Her door was ajar, just a hair, so I pushed it open, stepped in, and squatted in front of her.

"I'm sorry, Kerrigan."

She jerked upright and turned away from me. Sniffing and wiping at her face, she cleared her throat. "Um, I'm just... I'm fine."

I sat on the bed next to her, but she was turned so her back was to me. Close enough to touch, I still didn't. "I didn't mean to scare you."

She swayed, her back coming closer to me. "You didn't."

I inched closer. "It's okay if you were freaked out, Kerrigan. I shouldn't have shown my anger in front of you like that. I should've remained calm and just talked to Serge about the way he treated you."

Her neck was bare, her hair pulled up. I could see the tail end of that constellation shaped birthmark. "*He* scared me. You didn't. But, I didn't like that you were fighting for me. You... You shouldn't have to fight for me."

Giving in, I closed the gap, pressing my stomach against her back, feeling her shiver against me. Still, I kept my hands to myself. "I want to fight for you."

She let out a little sigh, more exhale than anything. "I deserved his anger. I do suck at the job. I keep messing up. If I wasn't so hard up for money, I'd quit so he could hire someone worthwhile."

"You are worthwhile." I slowly lifted my hands and hovered just above her shoulders. My heart thudded in my chest and I barely stifled a possessive growl. "You're more than worthwhile."

She pressed herself back into my chest. "I don't know what's going to happen now."

I dropped my hands back to my side. "Nothing's going to happen.

Everything's fine. Serge shouldn't have yelled at you. He's sorry. You'll get better at the job."

I heard her sniffle again as she scooted forward a few inches, away from me. She'd sensed my mood change that fast. It was like we were already bonded. Her arms crossed over her chest and she glanced over her shoulder at me with a fake smile. "I'm fine, Dmitry. Go back to work."

I didn't want to leave her. I could hear the pain in her voice. She was not fine. She deserved better.

Backing out of the room, I pulled her door closed and stood there for a moment, wrestling with the urge to go back in. It was painful to walk away, but it was for the best.

19

KERRIGAN

I turned to watch the door close and let out the breath I'd been holding. I bit my fingernail and stared, like I was going to be able to see him through the door. I didn't know what was happening, but what I did know was that Dmitry had fought for me. The feeling of his body pressed against mine was seared onto my skin. The way he'd stared at me, his eyes so intense, all signs that he was interested in me. Yet, he withdrew every time.

My emotions were all over the place. I was getting neurotic about Dmitry and whether he wanted me or not. My entire mood seemed to depend on how interactions between us played out. I'd never been that way. I'd never been all that concerned with how men felt about me. Dmitry was the first—in so many ways. My feelings for him were different—deeper. I couldn't break through his walls, though. He kept me at an arm's length. Which, now that I thought about it, was probably was a pretty solid sign.

I grabbed my notebook; I needed to write. The feelings he inspired—his chest pressed against my back—bounced around my brain until it was all I could think about. I let myself have time to get everything out on paper and then changed into a nice sundress and sandals.

Getting my thoughts out on paper was often an exercise in clearing my mind, gaining greater insight, and a perhaps developing a new perspective. And, in this instance, it had worked. Another idea began to solidify in my brain. I had to find another job. Not only was working at P.O.L.A.R. killing what little confidence I had, but I couldn't figure out what was going on with Dmitry until I had a job to fall back on. If I didn't have to depend on P.O.L.A.R., I could, as Grandma, may she rest in peace, would have said, shit or get off the pot.

I hadn't had any luck before Mom helped me get the dispatcher job, but now that I'd relocated to Sunkissed Key, maybe there was something on the island. I could at least try. I'd go back to living in my car until I could afford a place of my own.

I made my way out of the house and to Main Street on a mission. I headed north, away from P.O.L.A.R., and looked in at all the different businesses. I put in applications at Clotilde's Creamery, a lovely old fashioned ice cream shop, Latte Love, the coffee shop, as well as the grocery store. I stopped in at Rise and Shine Bed and Breakfast. They weren't hiring, but a purple haired woman with tattoos asked me to sign her petition—something about endangered rabbits on the island.

I tried Mimi's Cabana, and another bar called Cap'n Jim's. No go. It wasn't looking good. At the far end of the island was Sunkissed Key Wildlife Sanctuary, not hiring.

After exhausting all my options on Main Street, I tried side streets. They were mostly lined with residential homes, but at the very end of Parrot Cove Road, off of West Public Beach, I found the Bayfront Diner. I figured it was worth a shot. Plus, I was getting hungry. I ordered a cinnamon roll and sweet tea and spoke with the owner, a sweet woman named Susie.

Susie was older, with a beehive of steel-gray hair, and reminded me of Alice from the Brady Bunch. Her full figure was covered in a bright blue apron, and her smile was as warm as the Florida sunshine.

Her eyes had lit up when I told her I was job hunting. She'd made me fill out an application and then told me that I needed sunscreen if I was going to be walking up and down the island.

After leaving Susie's, I hit a lull. I didn't want to apply anywhere else. I wanted to work for her. She was like happiness in a bottle, pouring little bits out with every stroke of her pen on her order pad. I meandered around the island for a bit more, remaining alert, quite aware that Nicky Knuckles was possibly still around and could pop out from a dark alley or from around a corner at any moment.

I ended up at the beach on the east side of the island, hoping to avoid any and all of the team members. I sat in the sand and watched the ocean gently lap the shore. Wrapping my arms around myself, I stayed there as the sun moved across the sky, determined to pretend I didn't exist for a while. I felt the sun heat my skin and remembered what Susie had warned about using sunscreen, but I didn't want to move.

"Kerrigan?"

I jumped, shocked out of my trance. Looking over my shoulder, I was shocked to see Megan. "Hey. What are you doing here?"

She pointed to the house behind me. "I live there."

I suddenly felt as though I was intruding on her space, and quickly got to my feet dusting sand off. "Oh, I really had no idea. I just ended up on this side of the island and decided to sit on the beach and watch the water."

She smiled and nodded behind her to her house. "Come on inside. I need to put these groceries down."

I started to shake my head, but she looked hopeful and I didn't want to offend her by refusing. "Sure."

She led the way, talking to me over her shoulder. "How have you been? I've been meaning to organize another get together with you and Hannah, but I've been busy trying to remodel this porch. I decided that I wanted a little something extra special, but it's turned into a pain in the ass."

"You're doing it yourself?"

She pushed open the door and led me into a beautifully decorated home. Amongst the decor were tools of all sizes, discarded clothes, and a few boxes of take out. "Ignore the mess. Roman and I have been kind of...busy."

I trailed behind her into the kitchen, knowing perfectly well what she meant by *busy*. She and Roman were newly mated. I forced out thoughts of Dmitry that tried to surface. "Your house is beautiful."

"Yeah, well. I lost some things when my ex left. It's going to take me time to get everything back to the way it's supposed to be." She started putting groceries away and sighed. "Life, you know?"

Perched on the edge of a stool, I wrung my hands together and let out a slow exhale. "Um, yeah."

Megan paused with her hand halfway up to a cabinet, a jar of sauce frozen in the air. "What's wrong, Kerrigan? You look shaken."

I ran my hands down my dress and fought with a brittle smile. "I'm okay."

"No, I don't believe that. Come on. The rest of these groceries can wait. Let's sit on my couch and talk. You look like you need some girl talk."

"No, really. I'm okay. It's just been a long day."

"I'm not taking no for an answer. And I have wine." She waggled her eyebrows. "Just talk to me about today. Nothing else, if you don't want to."

I studied her for a second, everything about her seemed together and as though her life was in order. I turned and looked out of the window. "How do you keep everything in your life so together? How does everyone around me have their shit so together? We're around the same age. Why am I so far behind everyone else?"

She frowned. "Behind everyone else? What do you mean?"

"My mom got me my job. I suck at it and I'm one minor screw up away from being fired. I lived in my car until Serge insisted I move into the house with the team. I'm still a virgin and lusting after a man who doesn't seem to be very interested in me most of the time. I have no pets. I cry all the time. My credit score is crap. Literally, I feel like I'm a failure at adulting." I turned back to face her and blinked faster in an attempt to keep the tears at bay. "I spent so much time in school, working hard to earn a degree in English and creative writing, but for what? I write all the time but I can't get a novel published. I have so many loans and nothing to really show for them. I put my life on hold to get through school and pay for it myself and now, I'm trying to live and I have no clue what I'm doing."

Megan scooted closer to me and gently wrapped her arm around my shoulder. "Oh, sweetie. None of us know what we're doing. And it's not a race."

I sank into her side and wiped at my eyes. "I'm sorry. I didn't mean to cry on you. I just... I'm feeling so lost."

She hugged me harder and rested her head against mine. "It's okay. We're friends, right?"

I laughed. "Are we? You might want to rethink that. I'm not kidding you when I say that I'm a mess."

"Well, dry your eyes, sunshine. You and I are friends. Hannah, too. And this is what friends are for. To hug you and comfort you, but also to tell you to stop being so hard on yourself. You're not doing any worse than any of the rest of us. I just watched my entire life crumble to dust and had to restart from scratch. Hannah had her life upended and relocated here because of being mated to Serge. None of us really have it that together. We're all just trying to do the best we can."

I blew out breath and smiled shakily. "I'm glad you and Hannah are my friends. I could really use a couple of friends right now."

20

DMITRY

After leaving Kerrigan's room, I went back to work and tapped into all the techniques in my arsenal trying to remain calm and levelheaded. By the end of the workday, I was so tense I felt like I was going to snap in half at any moment. I hurried back to the house feeling lighter from knowing I'd find Kerrigan inside. But, she wasn't there.

My bear demanded to be let out so he could comb the island until he found her, but I had a different agenda. *I'm looking for someone.*

I sent out all of the details I knew about Kerrigan's loan shark and searched the beach while waiting to see if the rest of the guys found anything. If Kerrigan needed space, I wouldn't intrude. But, I needed to make sure she was safe and her absence had nothing to do with a certain slimy loan shark.

Not even ten minutes later, Maxim came through. *At Mimi's now. I think your man is here.*

Make sure he doesn't leave. I raced across Main Street and through a neighborhood to get to Mimi's, eager to nab that asshole. The fucker had to go.

Sure enough, the sleazeball was sitting at the bar, smiling at one of Mimi's female bartenders when I walked in. Maxim was at the back of the bar and tipped his head to me when I walked in.

I went straight to the little weasel and sat down on the stool next to him. When the bartender approached me, I shook my head. She must have read my expression because she backed off with hands raised. "You and I have a problem."

The man put his beer down and turned to me with a nasty scowl on his face. "You talking to me?"

I held his gaze and took a deep breath in an attempt to calm myself and rein my bear in. "Yeah, I am."

He smiled, more a sneer than a smile. "Let's hear it. Why do we have a problem?"

I pulled out my phone and pulled up the app I used to move money. "Kerrigan Tran. You're not going to bother her anymore."

"Oh, that's where I've seen you. You're the sorry sonofabitch who's been trailing along behind her like a lost puppy." He chuckled. "I get it. She's got a nerdy librarian thing going on. You wanna tap that ass, huh?" He leaned forward and lowered his voice. "I could arrange it for a small finder's fee."

I growled and counted to ten. Slowly. "I'm going to pay you what she owes you. Then, you're going to get the fuck off of this island and never return."

His eyes widened. "You're going to pay me?"

"Yeah, I am. Then, you're done with her." I held out my phone for him to enter his information to complete the transfer. "Ten thousand. On top of what she's already paid you."

"Oh, my man. No can do. She owes more than that in interest."

I inched closer to him. "Let me tell you something. You're going to take the money and get the fuck out of here. It's a very generous offer; take my word on that. I'm inches from snapping and you're not going to like what happens if I do. Take the money and go. That's your one and only option."

"There's always a second option."

I bared my teeth. "You're right. The second option includes your remains and a body bag."

Finally, he stopped seeing the humor in the situation. "You asshole."

I shrugged and slid the phone under his nose. "Take the more-than-generous offer. Door number two means having your flesh shredded to ribbons by razor sharp claws longer than your fingers. Let me be clear what that will be like. It will take a few seconds for your brain to process what happened. You'll feel everything. You'll watch yourself fall apart."

He yanked the phone away from me and jabbed at the screen. Finally, he gave it back to me. "I need a couple thousand more for traveling expenses. I had to come all the way out here to the Keys to collect."

"Maybe you didn't hear me. Not a penny more. You chose to fuck with the wrong woman."

Nicholas Palermo, I learned from the info on my phone, stood up and scowled at me. "Fuck you and that bitch."

I stood up, fighting down my anger. Fortunately for him, he was already scurrying for the door. I sat back down and rested my fists on the bar top. It wasn't easy to let him leave, but I didn't just kill in anger. It was always for a reason. He was leaving, holding up his end of the deal, which meant he was safe.

Maxim slid onto the stool beside me and gave a low whistle. "That sounded interesting."

"Asshole has been threatening Kerrigan."

He raised a brow. "You're fighting for her a lot lately."

"She's a nice girl."

He laughed. "Girl? Are we talking about the same Kerrigan? Kerrigan is shy at times, maybe a bit inexperienced, but she's no girl. She's definitely a grown woman. You might want to remember that."

Cutting my eyes to him, I shook my head. "Be careful what you say right now, brother. I'm holding on by a thread."

He held his hands up in front of him. "She's all yours. I was just giving advice. Me? I've got my eye on that sweet little blonde over in the corner, Sheila...or Shelly. Maybe Sharon." He stood up and slapped me on the shoulder. "Shannon. Yeah, it's Shannon. I think."

I looked down at my phone and completed the transaction to Nicholas Palermo, ready to be over and done with him. He'd receive the money, untraceable, and he'd leave Kerrigan alone. If he wanted to live. She'd have one less thing to worry about and I wouldn't have to be afraid of her getting hurt.

"Your friend left you with his bill, Dmitry." Mimi nodded at the door, letting me know she meant sleezeball. "Nice guy, huh?"

I pulled out a couple of bills and dropped them on the bar. "That cover it?"

She nodded. "More than. Is he going to be around a lot?"

I shook my head. "Matter of fact, if he shows up again, call us."

She nodded, handing the money to her bartender, and grinned. "I saw you with my favorite Asian yesterday. She's a sweetie pie, isn't she?"

Standing, I slipped my phone and wallet back into my pocket and held her gaze. "Keep an eye on her if she comes back in. For me."

Mimi laughed. "You men and your demands. Like I told Serge, if you want someone to keep an eye on your ladies, I suggest you do it yourselves. I'm here to help them have a good time."

I growled, frustrated, and headed out. With Nicky taken care of, I wanted to get a handle on where Kerrigan was. Just to check up on her.

21

KERRIGAN

I fell asleep on Megan's couch and woke up to find that it was morning and I'd slept the entire night through. There was a blanket over me and a cup of steaming coffee on the table next to me. I sat up and rubbed at my eyes, feeling sluggish.

"Good morning! I made coffee."

I looked over to see Megan aiming a camera at me. She snapped a photo and then grinned. I winced and ran my hands over my hair. "Sorry I fell asleep."

"No, it's fine. I would have woken you but I figured you needed the sleep. Living in the P.O.L.A.R. house with all that testosterone—and fur—can't be very restful." She made a face. "And I hear that Maxim has a revolving door of female guests."

I shrugged. "I guess I haven't been there long enough to notice."

"Lucky you. Now, smile. These photos are going to be amazing. You're very photogenic." She aimed the camera at me again and snapped a few pictures. "Drink your coffee, too."

I took a huge gulp, managing to burn my tongue, and caught a glimpse of the clock behind her. "Oh, crap. I have to go."

"Wait! One more!" She moved around, the camera still clicking.

"I'm working on a new project and I think these are going to be perfect."

I shoved my feet into my shoes and hurried towards her door. "Thank you for last night, Megan."

"That's what friends are for. Don't forget, drinks tonight!"

I stopped for a second and wrapped her in a hug. "Bye, friend."

I quickly left Megan's and headed toward the P.O.L.A.R. house. I walked across the beach, to Shipwreck Way, and then cut through someone's yard to get to Main Street. Avoiding the office, I went straight to the house, up to my room, and stripped quickly wrapping a towel around my body for the traipse to the shower.

I didn't have time to clean the shower before using it, so I tried not to let my imagination get hung up on what might have gone on in there. I scrubbed up as fast as I could and then hurriedly wrapped the towel back around myself. My glasses were steamed up, but I couldn't see without them and when I opened the door to dart across the hall, still dripping wet…I almost ran smack into Alexei.

As it was, I just bumped him lightly and clutched my towel tighter. "Sorry."

He just smiled. "You okay?"

I met his eyes and nodded. "Just late for work. What are you still doing here?"

"I had a late night. I don't function at my prime with less than nine hours of sleep."

I giggled. "Cause you're a bear."

A loud growl came from the bottom of the stairs and we both looked down to see Dmitry wearing an angry scowl. Alexei held up his hands and scooted around me to get into the bathroom.

I scurried across the hall and was about to close my door when Dmitry caught it and stepped in after me. I gaped at him. "What are you doing, Dmitry?"

"You didn't come home last night."

"I spent the night at Megan's."

"I was worried."

"Why?"

"Because!" He faltered. "Because...someone was threatening you."

I sighed and walked over to my closet. I picked out clothes, aware of his eyes on my back, and tried to remember that I was okay and his opinion of me didn't matter.

"Where'd you go yesterday? Before Megan's?"

Turning to face him, I held his stare and frowned. "I was applying for jobs. Is that okay?"

He took a step back. "What? Why?"

"You know why." I puffed my cheeks and released the air slowly. "I don't want to work for P.O.L.A.R." I didn't need to add that I sucked at the job and Serge was a hair away from firing me anyway. I especially didn't add that I wanted to find another job so I could get up the nerve to demand that Dmitry and I finally engage in the "fraternizing convo". All of the questions and the demanding way he spoke to me, it wasn't normal behavior. I couldn't tell if he liked me or he just felt protective of me—as though I was incapable of taking care of myself.

He turned away from me and gripped the edge of my dresser. "You want to leave?"

I clutched my towel tighter very aware that it was the only thing keeping me for baring it all to him. "Yeah, I do. I want a job that I'm capable at, where I'm not hated."

"No one hates you." He stared at me with intense eyes. "What makes you think that?"

"Well, I don't want to keep walking on eggshells afraid I'm going to screw up and at any second be fired on the spot—lose both my home and my job."

I grabbed my clothes and held them to my chest. "I think we both know that this isn't the job for me. Why do you care anyway? If it's because you think I'm the trouble-bound, worrisome team member, then this works best for both of us. You won't have to worry anymore."

He just shook his head and left, slamming my door behind him.

I huffed out a breath, angry that he hadn't picked up on what I was throwing down. I'd given him a chance to tell me that he didn't want me to go, but he'd just left. I supposed I should take that as an answer. I got dressed and walked to the office, kicking sand and muttering to myself the whole way.

I didn't even look at Serge when I walked in and sat at my desk. I was mad at him, too. I was mad at everyone. At least I didn't feel like crying, though.

When the phone rang, I was too angry to be nervous. Instead of the main office, however, it was Susie. She invited me to the diner for lunch to discuss the job. I'd had to force myself to not scream with joy. That meant she was considering me—maybe she'd even offer me the job. I might be getting away from P.O.L.A.R. Hopefully.

I hung up and realized that all the men in the room were staring at me. Of course, as shifters, they'd heard the entire conversation. I felt a twinge of shame, but I met Serge's questioning gaze head on and raised my eyebrows. I wanted to crumble under his stare, but I didn't allow myself to.

He just nodded. "Good for you."

I let out a breath I hadn't known I was holding and smiled. Maybe I'd manage to get my life together after all.

22

DMITRY

Kerrigan must have finally realized that I wasn't any good for her. She'd left. After a job interview with Susie at the Bayfront Diner, she packed her things and took off the same night.

I'd thoroughly vetted Susie. The woman had grown up on the island, and her husband Sammy, now deceased, had been from Pensacola. They'd met when he'd vacationed on the island over forty years ago. According to the locals, Sam had dreamed of opening a diner on the west coast, but Susie hadn't wanted to leave Sunkissed Key. They'd compromised and opened their place on the Gulf of Mexico, but named it after the San Francisco Bay.

I was glad that Kerrigan was still on the island, but I could take a hint. She didn't want to be around any of us.

Two days had passed since I'd last seen her hauling her bags down the stairs on Wednesday night. She hadn't asked for help, she hadn't said goodbye, she'd just left.

Kerrigan had probably felt the connection between us, but wanted nothing to do with it. I understood. I had nothing to offer her that she needed. She knew that. I had no idea how to be kind or nurturing or caring. She was sweet, light, gentle. I was dark, ominous, dangerous. And not fun to be around. I was a speedbump on her road to bigger and better things.

It wasn't hard to imagine her meeting and marrying a nice, regular guy, settling down and having a couple of kids. They'd have a quiet life—family movie nights, a dog or a cat or both, barbecues in the backyard, and the zoo on weekends. Yeah, they'd get to the zoo and look at animals like me in their cages. Maybe take pictures. She'd be happy. She'd be safe.

I had no excuse to complain about any of it. I'd tried to keep Kerrigan at arm's length, and when I had let her closer, I'd been rough and mean. She was smart to run away from me.

Still. I hurt.

I kept reminding myself of why I was no good for Kerrigan. Why I had to stay away. I visited every ghost from my past—every kill, every assassination. I thought about the questionable acts I'd committed. I saw every drop of blood that I'd ever spilled.

My bear mourned her. When he wasn't moping, he was fighting to make me go after her. When I refused, he went into mourning again. It was a vicious cycle.

Work sucked. I finally understood what Roman had gone through when he thought he had lost Megan. He'd been careless. He'd almost been responsible for a roof caving in on his head, and he hadn't much cared. I understood that now.

What was the point? Of *anything* anymore.

"Brother, you look like someone kicked your dog." Alexei strolled into the kitchen, his hair tousled all around his head from the wind outside.

"I don't have a dog."

He stopped. "Okay. What's going on?"

I shook my head and pushed my dinner plate away from me. "Nothing."

He cupped his hand behind his ear as though he was hard of hearing and trying to capture sound. "What's that? Kerrigan, you say? You're fucked up because she left?" He smirked at my shocked look. "Everyone knows, man. Duh. You've been drooling over her since she got here. You attacked Serge because he raised his voice to her. What none of us can understand is why you haven't gone after her."

I scowled. "You think you know so much. You have no idea."

"Is she your mate?"

I opened my mouth and then snapped it shut. Saying it out loud would make it too real, too painful, but I couldn't deny it. I wouldn't deny it. "Yes."

"Then why the fuck are you hanging around here? Go, get her." He rolled his eyes. "You dumb fucks and your mates. You make everything so much harder than it has to be. It's literally as simple as one plus one equals two. You're her mate. She's your mate. Bam."

"It's more complicated than that, smartass."

"Why?"

I stammered. "It just is."

He shook his head. "Or you're making it more complicated. But, hey, if you want a great big mess, fine. I would say it's just on you, but it's not. It's on Kerrigan, too. If you think she's not suffering just as much as you are, you're wrong. She's been waiting on you to make a move since the moment she saw you."

"Shut the fuck up, Alexei. I'm not in the mood."

He held up his hands and backed away. "Okay, okay, I can take a hint. None of my business anyway."

I swore and stood up. "*She* left."

"Yeah, because she was miserable here. Anyone with eyes could've seen that. She didn't like the job and she didn't like being told constantly how she'd fucked things up. She probably also didn't like how the man she was into semi-hooked up with her and then kicked her out of his room."

I snarled. "How do you know that?"

"These walls are paper thin, bro. And you're a fucking idiot."

Anger surged and I wanted to smash his face in. "I have my reasons."

"I'd love to hear them. Matter of fact, I'm sure Kerrigan would love to hear them, too."

"You of all people know what I do, Alexei. Who I am. My unique contribution to this league." I walked to the window and looked out at the ocean. Without even realizing it, my eyes scanned the beach for Kerrigan.

"Save lives?" He came up behind me and rested his hand on my shoulder. "What you do is for a reason, brother. You save more lives than any of us with your 'unique contribution' as you call it. Not a one of us are without blood on our hands, but we do what we do for the common good."

Shaking my head, I stepped away from him. "Do you really believe that?"

He laughed easily, drawing my eyes back to him. "Yes, I do. How do you think I remain so carefree? What we do isn't always pretty, but our job is to save lives and protect the innocent. That's what we do. If there are necessary evils along that path, then so be it. Some of us have to do the dirty work so others can live in peace and freedom. It doesn't change anything, though, Dmitry. You're a good man. And, although I have my occasional doubts about Maxim, the rest of the team is good, too."

"You're serious?"

He nodded. "As a heart attack. So, do whatever you need to do to get over this shit, brother, because you have a mate waiting on you."

I couldn't believe as easily as he did that I was a good man. Even if I was, did I deserve Kerrigan? I didn't think so.

"You think you're doing her a favor, but you didn't see her face when she walked out of here. She's in pain."

I turned away from him again and continued watching the ocean, thinking.

"Don't fuck up."

23

KERRIGAN

"Any plans for the night, pumpkin?" Susie grinned at me, knowing I found her new nickname for me charmingly ridiculous.

"Not much. I have to meet someone to pay a bill. I'm quite the wild weekend partier, you know." I frowned, thinking about it. Nicky Knuckles was the last person I wanted to see, but I had to. He'd been oddly silent, yet when I'd texted him earlier, he'd agreed to meet me.

"A bill? On a Friday night?"

I sighed and finished filling the salt and pepper shakers on the tables. "You don't want to know."

"Is everything okay?"

"Yeah, of course. Things are fine." I looked out at the water and barely stifled a heavy sigh.

"Uh huh." She flipped the open sign to closed and started tallying receipts. "I haven't known you for long, but I know when you're full of it. Things aren't okay. I suspect it's man troubles, but that's only because with a young woman your age it's almost always man troubles, isn't it?"

I gave her a genuine smile as I walked into the kitchen untying my apron. "I wouldn't know."

She laughed and then paused. "Wait, what?"

I leaned against the walk-in cooler. "I've never really been in a relationship. So, while I don't disagree with you that it's almost always man troubles, I don't have personal experience. Except…"

"Except?"

I forced myself to remain calm—not to allow the hurt and anger to get the better of me. "I thought there might be something with a guy. I don't know. I hoped leaving my last job would clear things up between us. It did, I guess, just not in the way I wanted. He hasn't contacted me since I left."

"Since you left—two days ago?" She laughed when I nodded. "Pumpkin, you're giving up mighty fast. He's a man. Two days isn't enough time for him to get his head out of his backside. And why haven't you gone to see him?"

"I don't know."

"Maybe *you* need to get our head out of *your* backside?" She raised her eyebrows questioningly.

I hesitated. "You think I should approach him?"

"You have to decide that for yourself. But if you want my advice, I wouldn't be sitting around waiting on a man to call. If you like him, give it a shot. If you crash and burn, at least you know. Shit or get off the pot."

Wow, exactly what my grandmother would have said, may she rest in peace. I blew out a shaky breath and shook out my hands. "I'm terrified of a crash and burn."

"Well, if it does come to that, Mr. Bryan, one of the breakfast regulars, has had his eye on you."

Mr. Bryan was a stooped, white-haired, wrinkled ninety-something who shuffled around the island with a walker. "Not funny." I waved her off and headed out.

One of the amazing things about my new job at Susie's Bayfront Diner was that it came with a small studio apartment over the diner that Susie allowed me to stay in rent free for as long as I worked for her.

Just behind the bed and breakfast, I climbed the stairs to the apartment and paused for a moment on the staircase to appreciate the sun lowering over the water. Bright pink and orange clouds dotted the sky. Susie's advice had given me a sliver of hope, like maybe things could work out with Dmitry.

Already my life was looking up. It turned out that I was pretty good at waiting tables and I was also adept at lending a hand in the kitchen. I'd always loved to cook. Susie had also encouraged me to take breaks between busy times to sit in the corner and use her laptop to work on my writing.

The only things in my life that were still problematic were Nicky and Dmitry. Nicky Knuckles was going to be around for a long time. I was making less at Susie's than I had been at P.O.L.A.R., but the tips weren't bad. I accepted that I'd be paying him off for the rest of my life. I just hoped he'd stop pressuring me for more.

Dmitry…just thinking of him made my heart ache yet I couldn't stop thinking of him. I'd had this naïve fantasy that he might come after me. He hadn't. Susie was right, though. If I ever wanted to have the conversation with him about what was going on between us, I needed to just do it. If he didn't want anything to do with me, at least I'd know.

Something in my heart held fast to the hope that it wouldn't go that way. I felt a bond with Dmitry and I wanted to believe that he felt it too and that it meant something big. I wanted to believe that we were mates.

I was being incredibly starry-eyed. Dmitry had walked away from me so many times. That was probably a strong sign that I wasn't his mate.

I'd still try. I dressed in my emerald green dress and let my hair fall and fan out around my shoulders. I took extra care with my makeup and even ditched my thick glasses for contacts—something I only did on very special occasions. I wanted to do everything in my power to make it hard for Dmitry to walk away from me.

I had to meet Nicky first, but as soon as that was over, I was going to find Dmitry and demand that we have a talk.

I was supposed to meet up with Nicky Knuckles at a place called

Cap'n Jim's Bar and Grill, but as I strolled down the beach, headed in that direction, I practically ran smack dab into Nicky. I had the payment all ready for him since I certainly didn't want to draw out our interaction any longer than absolutely necessary. As I reached into my purse to pull out the money, he reached into his pocket and pulled out a knife.

My stomach dropped and I worried that I was actually going to lose control of my bladder. I knew the threat in front of me was real. Nicky Knuckles didn't play around.

"I take it you and your boyfriend aren't in communication?"

I frowned. "What are you talking about?"

For every step I took backward, Nicky Knuckles took a step forward. "Your boyfriend paid off your debt days ago. Ten G's. I was debating how to collect the interest when, lo and behold, I got your text. Talk about a stroke of luck!"

I thrust the money at him, my brain struggling to keep up with both what he was saying and the flashing blade in front of me. Dmitry had paid off my debt? What the hell? "Please take the money. Just take it."

He grinned and moved in closer. "That measly stack of bills isn't gonna cut it. Sorry, sweetheart, but I need to make an example outta you. I can't have others thinking I've gone soft."

I had only one way out and it was a longshot. I prayed that the suspicions I had about Dmitry and I being mates were real and that, if so, that we had enough of a bond that this would work. Then, instead of screaming out loud, I closed my eyes and screamed inside, as loud and as powerfully as I could. If there was a chance that we had bonded in some way, maybe he'd sense me. Then, just to be sure, I opened my eyes, met Nicky's sinister gaze, and screamed with every ounce of lung power in my chest.

My scream was cut short when Nicky's fist connected with my face.

24

DMITRY

I sat straight up in bed and let out a violent roar—a verbal decree of the rage and fury suddenly coursing through me. I could sense Kerrigan's fear and desperation in my head as though she'd shouted it into my ear. Seconds later, I heard an actual scream. I was already running down the stairs when it ceased abruptly.

My heart ached. She had to be okay.

Alexei was right behind me. "I heard it, too. What's going on?"

I didn't take the time to answer. I sprinted out into the sand and pushed my body to get to her faster. Down the beach, I saw her on the ground, her hands covering her face.

That fucking loan shark was standing over, a flash of silver in his hand. Knife. He was holding a knife on her.

"No one's coming for you, bitch. It's just you and me."

My bear was halfway out already, my body stuck in mid-shift, a visual that was one hundred percent monster. It made me faster, made me more vicious. Bloodthirst like I'd never felt demanded his life and this time, I was going to give in to the beast.

Nicholas Palermo had no idea what was coming until it was too late. By the time he heard us and his head snapped around to see us rushing him, he was already a dead man. I slammed into his body, hard, and sent him flying away from Kerrigan. I threw myself on top of him, snarling down at him with every ounce of vengeance I had for him in that moment.

The fear in his eyes just heightened my need to kill. I bared my teeth and raised my arm, claws fully formed and out.

He screamed.

I sank my claws into his chest, cutting off his scream and ending him.

The night was filled with the sound of my panting, the fury I felt still blinding me, demanding retribution, for extorting extra money from Kerrigan, for threatening to sell her into sex slavery, for the other women he'd threatened. Who knew how many of those threats he'd actually followed through on? Kerrigan had said something about him having girls in Miami who serviced clients. Death wasn't good enough for this creep. I finally let my bear fully take over. He had none of the hesitation I had about taking a human life. He fully embraced the cycle of life and death.

The life had already drained out of the asshole, but my bear was still consumed with the desire to make it right. He ripped and tore and shredded until he started to calm down.

When we turned, the entire unit had encircled Kerrigan, guarding her. They were too close to my mate, though. I was too far gone. I snarled a menacing growl, a warning to get away from her— or else.

Serge stepped out in front, his arms raised. "She's safe, brother. She's safe. You need to calm down before you go near her, though. You could hurt her."

I roared out my anger at him. I would never hurt her. She was mine to protect. I moved closer, my growls echoing through the night. They needed to get the fuck away from her.

"Dmitry, stop!" When that didn't work, Serge balled his fists up at his side and let out a heavy exhale, preparing to shift and fight.

Kerrigan squeeze between them, and dodged their attempts to keep her away from me. In a calmer state, I would've thanked them for trying to protect her from my animal who was still showing signs of being bloodthirsty.

She held out her hands, palms up. They were trembling, but she still closed the gap between us and stared at me with tear-filled eyes. "Are you okay?"

I sniffed her hands and snorted. The scent of her was soothing to my bear who was starting to come down and see things more clearly. I rubbed my face against her and huffed out a breath. *Mate.* I pushed even farther into her space, needing more.

Her arms locked around my neck as I almost knocked her over. She choked back a sob and stroked my fur.

I could smell her tears and see the bloody smudges I was leaving on her skin and clothing. Needing to comfort her more than I was able to as a bear, I shifted back and caught her in my arms when she stumbled forward.

"Get cleaned up and take care of her. We'll take care of this, Dmitry." Serge stepped forward and nodded to me. "You did the right thing, protecting her."

Alexei nodded and stepped closer. "You saved her."

I couldn't think past making sure she was okay. I was still feeling slightly crazed, though, and I needed to get her away from them. I pulled back enough to look into her eyes. What I saw there made my heart squeeze painfully. "I'm not going to hurt you."

She nodded, but if the roundness of her eyes was any indication, she was still terrified. Then I realized I still had blood all over me and it probably didn't help relieve her fear any.

"The ocean. I'm going to walk us down to the water, okay?"

She nodded again, her hands starting to come lose from around me, but I couldn't let her go. I needed to maintain contact. I easily lifted her into my arms and carried her away from the gruesome remains. I didn't put her down until I was hip deep in the water.

"I'm sorry."

She blinked a few times and shook her head. "Sorry? You saved me. You came."

"I heard you."

"You heard me scream?"

"I heard you here." I gently tapped her temple. "I'm sorry, Kerrigan. That should never have happened. I should've done a better job of keeping you safe."

"Are you my mate?" She phrased the question as a statement, anger coloring her tone. "That's what that means, right? We're mates."

I nodded.

"Why didn't…? Why did you stay away from me?"

I couldn't tell her what I was feeling while we were both covered in her enemy's blood. "Can we talk after?"

She held my gaze and nodded. "Okay."

I set her on her feet and ran my hands over myself, scrubbing all the blood off me. Kerrigan watched and then held her breath when I moved closer and poured handfuls of water over her skin. The blood rinsed free and left goosebumps behind.

"I don't want to go back to P.O.L.A.R." She looked off in the distance behind me. "I have my own place now. Can we talk there?"

I knew about the tiny apartment over the diner. I nodded and as we left the water, I found that not only had the team made quick work of disposing of the body as though it had never been there, but someone had also left a towel and pair of shorts for me.

As I let Kerrigan lead the way, my heart pounded painfully in my chest. She was too quiet. I was terrified of what she was thinking. I knew she was mad and she'd been scared, but I had passed the point of no return. I could no longer live without her.

25

KERRIGAN

I had thoughts banging around in my head like ping pong balls as I led Dmitry back to my efficiency apartment. The walk up the stairs and into the small space that made up the kitchen, living room and bedroom, held tension in in every step. I motioned for him to follow me into the bathroom where I turned on the shower.

Testing the water temperature, I hesitated before stepping back. I knew Dmitry was right behind me, watching and waiting. I didn't know quite what to say, though. He'd saved my life. He'd shown up and fought for me—been my hero.

"You should clean up better." I forced my legs to move backward, and stepped out of the shower. I edged around Dmitry and motioned for him to get in as I turned my back to him. "I'll get you a clean towel."

There was still blood on the towel he'd been carrying as well as on him. There had been blood everywhere. Even down the back of his head and neck. His broad shoulders were still streaked in it. He'd killed. For me! I'd seen the truth in his eyes in those moments afterwards. He'd do it again. And again. He would've attacked his friends if they'd been any closer to me. The animal in him had been unleashed and I finally got a good look at it. I supposed it had always been there, at the back of his eyes, something hungry and dangerous.

I wasn't afraid of his bear, though, even if I should've been. He'd ripped Nicky to shreds with eight inch claws that were sharper than any knife I'd ever seen. He'd snarled and growled, wildly, viciously, ferociously. Yet...I wasn't afraid of him.

Dmitry was darker and more dangerous than I'd realized, but that shouldn't have surprised me. The things the team did, their job, it wasn't easy. He'd probably had to use deadly force more than a few times. Yet, I knew instinctually that he'd never hurt me. Just as I knew my own reflection in the mirror, I knew it. I wasn't afraid of him.

I heard him step into the shower, heard the water hitting his body. My temperature climbed higher. There was so much that needed to be said. We had to talk and I needed to know why he'd been avoiding me when it was clear that we were mates. But, before any of that, I needed to touch him and feel him next to me.

I didn't give myself time to stress about it. I didn't stop to worry about how it might or might not be perceived. I stopped being scared for once in my life.

Shit or get off the pot.

I turned to face the shower and found him watching me, the water hitting the back of his shoulders and running down his back. My heart skipped a beat, a little stumble, but it didn't change my mind. I swallowed and took the first step towards him.

Sliding my dress of one shoulder and then the other, I took another step closer. The steam from the shower filled the bathroom and fogged the mirror, and I was so glad I'd decided to wear contacts. My already wet dress clung to me, and I peeled it off of my chest and pushed it over my hips to drop at my feet.

Completely naked, I moved closer.

Dmitry's breath caught in his throat. I could sense his desire.

My chest rose and fell faster, my hand shook. My mind was steady, though. I needed him right then.

Dmitry stayed still, his eyes smoldering. They locked with mine until I was right in front of him. Drops of water splashed over his shoulders and onto me. His eyes followed the droplets. Still, he didn't touch me. His erection jutted out between us, proving his arousal, but he kept his hands at his sides. They balled into tightly clenched fists when I reached behind him for the soap and my stomach just barely grazed his erection.

I lathered my hands and focused on the sound of his breathing. Ragged and strained, I could feel how much control he was exerting. I could feel his need to touch me. Yet, he let me take control.

What I wanted was to touch and explore every part of him. I didn't feel like an unsophisticated virgin. I felt like a passionate, sensual woman who was wild about the man in front of her. I wanted to learn every single inch of his body and what he liked and didn't like. Right then, I'd start by running my soapy hands over him and, who knew, maybe then I'd run a little more over them.

I held his gaze as I placed my hands on his chest. I could see that darker part of him there, too, in the depths of his eyes, watching me almost like I was prey. Now that I'd met the darkness, seen it first hand, I knew that it was his bear I was witnessing. He may look at me as though I'm prey, but I was who and what he'd protect with his life and fight to the death for.

I washed Dmitry's chest and his stomach, my soapy hand dipping low enough to have his stomach tensing and his breath hiking. Still, I didn't go where he needed. I lathered my hands again and stepped in closer, trapping his shaft between us while I ran my hands over his sides and then up his arms. Skirting around behind him, I sighed at the sight of his back. Beautiful and so strong, I took extra care washing it. Stretching to reach his shoulders and neck, I then washed down and over his ass.

Dmitry's fists clenched and unclenched and I knew he was struggling to let me continue rather than taking the lead, but he let me clean him. I squatted behind him to clean the back of his legs and moved around to run my hands up the front of his knees and thighs. Looking up at him, I saw the glow of his animal in his gaze, but still, he held strong. I let the tip of his cock drag over my body as I slowly stood, and then reached up to cup his chin. Pulling lightly, I ran my hands over his face, taking care to trail my fingertips over his lips.

My body pulsed, every part of me readying itself for him. I shook with desire, but I wasn't finished. I rinsed his face before lathering my hands again and stepped in closer.

Holding his gaze, I cupped his erection and bit my lip as a low growl escaped the back of his throat, but he still remained perfectly still. His pupils dilated as I stroked his length, rubbing both of my hands back and forth, slowly up and down every inch of him. I dropped one hand lower to clean him there, too.

Instead of feeling self-conscious about never having done it before, I felt powerful because of his reaction. The man and animal both watched me, radiating lust and hunger, but still, I was in command of both of them.

I stroked him until all pretense of cleaning him was gone. I watched his face change, his jaw clench harder. I wanted him to come apart in my hands, wanted to see him tumble over the precipice of that control he was clinging to.

When it happened and I felt his seed splash against my stomach, I only wanted more. I knelt in front of him and slid him into my mouth, finishing him that way.

Dmitry's hands locked in my hair and before I'd finished stroking him with my tongue, he pulled me up to my feet and backed me against the cold shower wall behind me. His eyes blazed and I found myself surrendering—to anything he wanted to do to me. Anything.

26

DMITRY

I'd held back for as long as I could, letting Kerrigan slowly torture me. I'd stayed still while she took control, did what she wanted, and I enjoyed every second of her delicious exploration. But I couldn't hold back any longer. She'd been teasing more than just me. She'd been teasing the bear who'd been itching to mark and claim her. The sultry little looks that she kept casting had nearly brought me to my knees. After orgasming, I was still rock hard and ready for more of her—all of her.

I spun her under the water and made quick work of rinsing us both off before scooping her into my arms. I stepped out of the shower and carried her to the bed which was in the corner of the one-room apartment, leaving a trail of dripping water to her bed.

Her breathing was as labored as mine and her arousal perfumed the room and drove me insane, like the most exquisite torture. I tossed her onto the bed, getting an excited squeal from her.

I wanted to seduce her slowly, take my time, show her just how much I adored every part of her, but I couldn't wait. I needed to be in her, needed to make her mine, and be hers in every way. I knelt on the bed and kissed her ankle before moving up. I kissed her hip and then the valley between her breasts before capturing to her mouth. Tasting her mouth, I rested my weight on one forearm while reaching between us and running my fingers through her wet folds. She was ready for me.

I rolled my fingertip over her clit before moving lower and sliding one finger into her. Her hips tried to buck, but I was on her, keeping her steady. She bit my lip in her eagerness and I slid a second finger in, stretching her for me. Her nails dug in and scratched my back, a welcome sting. I pumped my fingers relishing in the way her body clung to them tightly. As I slid in a third finger, she broke our kiss to beg for more.

I could've listened to her sweet, breathy pleas for hours, for the rest of my life even, but I needed to be in her. I slid my fingers out and lined our bodies up. I held her gaze and released a low growl. She was mine. She was always going to be mine. No one else was ever going to threaten her or harm her again.

Her arousal had called more of my bear forward and I fought for control as I sank into her wet heat inch by inch. Her body gripped and squeezed me, pulsing around my length. More sweet torture.

Kerrigan dug into my back and her head pushed into the mattress under her while I entered her. Her exposed throat was an invitation I couldn't refuse and as I thrust the rest of my length into her, I sank my teeth into her delicate flesh, marking her as mine.

She screamed, her body clamping down on my shaft as an orgasm rocked through her. I continued to pump through it, thrusting in and out of her as the claiming mark bound us together for the rest of our lives. The bear was more in control than he should've been, but I was there, too, losing myself in her.

She lifted her legs and gripped my hips with her thighs, her hands rising from my back to my head. Holding tightly to me, she cried out my name and begged me to never stop.

I licked her neck clean to seal the ragged wound and kissed up her throat and chin. Claiming her lips again, I poured every ounce of emotion into the kiss and prayed she'd understand.

Trailing my hands down to her ass to grip her silky flesh, pulling her against me to be even deeper in her, I thrust slow and hard. The burning need to empty myself into her was growing stronger. I wanted to mark her with my seed as well—mark her in every way possible.

Kerrigan arched her back as another orgasm bloomed in her. The new angle had the tip of my shaft hitting her deeper, making her cry out louder. Her walls tightened around me until I couldn't hold back.

I pressed my forehead to hers and looked at her. "Open your eyes, mate."

Those deep brown, beautiful eyes met mine and I felt my world come together in completeness. She sank her teeth into that full lower lip and moaned. "Dmitry, please."

Another stroke and my release burst forth. Kerrigan was right there with me, milking me as we both came together. Her eyes fluttered shut and I lowered my face to her neck once more.

Everything heightened until we both collapsed together on the bed. I eased my weight off of her and held her in my arms. Holding her against me, I marveled at how everything in me—all of me—felt like it'd been taken out and shaken up. The woman pressed against my side had just turned my entire world upside down.

I drifted in and out of consciousness, still holding her. I hadn't been sleeping well since she'd left the P.O.L.A.R. house and I'd felt the need to trek to her apartment and patrol the perimeter of the place several times a night.

Having her tucked in next to me gave me allowed me to relax for the first time since I met her. Until I woke up in the middle of the night and she wasn't there.

I groggily got to my feet. I knew she was safe and nearby; I could sense her. I needed to be near her, though. My bear was still in a heightened state after feeling as though he'd almost lost her.

She was just outside the door, sitting on the landing at the top of the stairs, a blanket wrapped around her still unclothed body. She looked over her shoulder when I stepped out and raised her eyebrows at me when she noticed my shaft rising.

I ignored it and sat next to her. "What are you doing out here?"

She looked out at the ocean and smiled. It was a sad smile that tightened my stomach. "Thinking."

"About?"

"You. Me." She met my eyes and her smile faded. "Why didn't you want me? You knew we were mates…"

My chest tightened and I shook my head. I reached out for her hand, needing the physical connection. "Kerrigan, I wanted you."

Her bottom lip jutted out. "But, you didn't."

"I did from the second I saw you. It's not so simple, though…" I dragged my hand down my face and sighed. "What you saw earlier… that monster is who I am. I know I scared you, but that's not just what I do, it's who I am. I am a monster—a killer. You…you're so pure and untainted. I'm not."

She turned to stare back out at the ocean and took a deep breath. "You want to know what I thought when I saw you and Nicky Knuckles fighting?"

I frowned. "What?"

She looked back at me, her eyes intense. "I saw his knife and I thought that if he hurt you, I would find a way to kill him."

I didn't know what to say to that.

"I don't think things are as simple as good and bad, Dmitry. They can't be. What you do isn't bad. You save people." She stroked her finger down my cheek. "I'm pretty much a loser. Until Wednesday, I had a job my mom got me, no home to speak of, nothing of my own. Still a virgin, unable to hold eye contact with most people, I was ashamed of myself. Good and bad are too finite to describe people. We're all so much more complicated than a single label."

I slid my arm around her shoulder. "You're not a loser."

"And you're not a monster."

I swallowed a lump of emotion. "I don't deserve you."

"And I don't deserve you." She narrowed her eyes. "So, should we just run away from each other and act like this never happened?"

"No!" I hesitated. "Was that a jab?"

"Yeah, it was. Cause if you're going to leave and pretend like we're nothing to each other again, I need to know now."

"I'm sorry, Kerrigan. I'm sorry I made you feel like that's even a remote possibility." I sighed and gently kissed her temple. "I'm not going anywhere. You're my mate. You're stuck with me for life."

She scooted over and slid onto my lap. "Good, because your bear won't let you leave, anyway. He loooves me."

I made a confused face. "What do you mean? I mean, yes, he does, but how do you know?"

She suddenly grinned. "You talk in your sleep. Didn't you know that?"

"What? No."

"Or maybe your bear talks in your sleep. Either way, he *really* likes me."

I snorted a laugh. I felt the same way.

She laughed, the sound so beautiful and sweet, I gave her a squeeze. "And you, Dmitry?"

I stilled and looked down at her suddenly realizing what she was getting at. "You were worried I didn't feel the same way? Is that why you were out here?"

She nodded. "I was worried that you might disagree with him."

"I don't."

"Good."

"Kerrigan?"

"Yeah?"

"We're the same being, my bear and me. What he says and feels about you? It's from me, too."

She rested her cheek against my chest. "You don't even know what he said."

"Kerrigan?"

She giggled. "Yeah?"

"I love you."

She turned and flashed me the happiest smile before kissing me deeply and passionately. When she finally broke off the kiss, we were both breathing hard. "Show me."

With her wearing my fresh claiming mark, I was able to take my time this time and really show her just how much I loved her. Lost in pleasuring her, I almost missed when she whispered the words into her palm while coming apart under me.

"I love you, too."

THE END

COVERT BEAR

P.O.L.A.R. 3

Vilified by strangers,
Friendships aren't Heidi's forte.
Unless it happens to be with a displaced polar bear.

Hey, he's a great listener!

Alexei knows she's his mate.
But she refuses to date him.
All he wants is a chance.

And, as far as he can tell, there's only one way to get it—as a Covert Bear.

1

HEIDI

Jayden and Jonas Perez stared up at me with wide, blue puppy dog eyes and pouty little mouths that were turned down just the slightest bit at the corners. Skillfully, they'd perfected that hard-to-deny look before they'd even reached their third birthday and they used it for everything. It didn't matter how ridiculous their request was, when they shot me that look, my heart melted and I had a hard time denying either of them anything. Once, they'd almost convinced me to let them play in the street. I'd been scouting around looking for items to use as roadblocks before realizing I'd been played by two little masters. Those two had definitely figured out their superpower.

At that moment, they wanted the cup of coffee I was drinking. It took one stern *no* from me to have them both in tears. I knew the drill, though. Crocodile tears. Even so, my stomach knotted at their pitiful howls. The little con artists.

"What if I did give you coffee and it made you climb the walls? What would your momma say when she came home and found you on the ceiling?" I wagged my finger at them and drained my cup. "I don't think she'd be very happy with me if her precious baby boys were on the ceiling."

Jayden, the gigglier twin, broke protocol and laughed. Forgetting about my coffee, or more likely, seeing that it was gone and deciding to surrender the fight, he shoved his fingers in his mouth and turned to play with the blocks precariously stacked behind him. Jonas, the serious brother, had laser focus. He grabbed for my mug and scrunched up his face in a scowl when I slid it out of reach. He fell back on his diapered butt and let loose a full out wail. Jayden looked at him for all of two seconds before joining in.

I'd been watching them since they were days old, but I'd never grown a thicker skin against their cries. I scooped them both up—one in each arm—and carried them out to the porch. The warm sunshine and the sounds of the waves crashing always soothed them when they were tired and cranky. I sank into one of the deck chairs and held both boys against my chest until they stopped crying and fell asleep. Under the shade of a large porch umbrella, my feet kicked up, I let the beautiful sun and sea of Sunkissed Key relax me, too.

Maria Perez found us there when she arrived home from work a half an hour later. She took one look at her boys and smiled a bright, glowing smile. "You're the best. They don't nap for me."

I shifted and handed Jayden off to her. "Do you think the terrible twos will be over soon?"

Maria grinned wider. "Nope. Jake's parents tell me all the time about how Jake and Kyle were terrors from birth on. I'm geared up and ready for them to remain in their terrible twos until they turn eighteen and go off to college."

I shuddered. "Let's not talk about that. I don't like the idea of them ever being that old. Besides, it makes me think about how old I'll be when they reach adulthood."

"How old *you'll* be? Yeah, okay." Shifting Jayden to her right hip, she reached out and gently took Jonas from me, too. "I've got seven years on you. Do you know how much living happens in seven years? You'll still be young. I'll be practically be an old hag."

Rolling my eyes, I stood up and opened the door for her so we could all go back inside. "How was work?"

Maria worked at Mann Family Dentistry as a hygienist. Roger

Mann, the owner and main dentist at the clinic was a misogynist and usually made work difficult for Maria. Her face said it all. "He approached me about cutting my hours again this morning. Before our first patient. Told me that he'd understand if I needed to be at home with my kids more often. After all, kids need their mothers."

Scowling, I shook my head. "You've already cut back to half days. What does he expect from you?"

"I think he wants me out completely. I heard a rumor that there's a younger hygienist on the island. Cheaper and hotter." She sighed and rested the boys both on the couch. Looking up at me from her stooped over position, she said, "It's getting ridiculous."

I sighed, feeling for her. She'd been my best friend for over a decade and I loved her like a sister. I hated that she was having a hard time. More than that, her life had been a challenge for years. That much we had in common. "Have you thought any more about opening your own practice? You could do it. Just hire your own dentist. People love you and you have loyal patients who would follow you."

She shook her head and looked back at her boys. "Maybe when they're older."

I let it drop and headed into the kitchen. As part of my day job caring for the boys, I snuck in some extra TLC for Maria too. When she needed it, anyways. I had the time during the day and, honestly, I was glad to do it.

I'd just picked up some deli meat and freshly baked bread from Mann Grocery, owned by Roger Mann's brother, Ramsey. Ramsey was a lot nicer than Roger and didn't have a negative bone in his body. His wife, Martha, baked fresh breads and desserts daily and kept the island supplied. Their grocery store smelled like heaven on earth, every single day. I sliced a few pieces of bread and put together a sandwich with the deli meat, a slice of cheese, and some veggies.

"That looks so delicious." Maria sat down at the kitchen island and groaned when I pushed the plate over to her. "You're more treasured than gold, Heidi. I'm starved. Mayo?"

"Of course. On the top and bottom slice, just the way you like."

She took a hefty bite and moaned. "I love you."

I just rolled my eyes and put everything away. "Unless you need anything else, I'm going to head out. I need to clean my house before work tonight."

She waved me away. "Go. Thank you for this. And everything."

"Uh huh. I'll see you in the morning."

I left the house and took the beach path down to my house. Maria and the boys lived on Bluefin Boulevard and I could take the beach to avoid Coral Road and most of Gulfstream Lane. My house was at the end of Gulfstream Lane, on the beach. West Public Beach wasn't as populated as East Public Beach for whatever reason, but there were still a handful of people enjoying the sun and sand.

My house was a one story little beach bungalow on stilts. It'd weathered many hurricanes, including the most recent Hurricane Matilda. It looked almost like something the crew on Gilligan's Island would've built to live in, but it was quaint and beautiful to me. It needed a new coat of the dusty blue paint I'd chosen for it years earlier. The porch needed sealing against the ocean weathering, the roof was probably ready for an update, and the front door screeched like a banshee when you opened it. To me, it was home.

I had to jiggle the doorknob and use a hip thrust to get it to open, but the welcoming screech was so familiar that I usually replied to it. "Hello to you, too."

With a sigh, I looked around and got started cleaning.

2

ALEXEI

The ocean was cool against my large, furry body. Even with the sun beating down on me, I wasn't miserable. I dove under and swam down several feet, twisting and spinning until my lungs tightened and I had to come up for air. I loved the water... cool, freeing, and it did wonders toward making a 900 pound bear feel weightless.

I'd never liked being anywhere more than in the water. While the rest of the team was busy feeling tortured by our move to Sunkissed Key, I was just as happy as I'd been in Siberia. Well, maybe not when I was being forced to sit in the office, sucking up everyone's funk with the weird, "conditioned" oxygen. In the ocean, though, I was happy.

I'd taken the move better than everyone else. The ocean, bikini clad women, tacos... Things could've been so much worse. The only real downgrade was the work. Instead of conducting insertions and extractions, accomplishing covert, special ops missions, or capturing high-value enemy personnel, we were chasing down shop lifters and petty criminals and making sure locals and tourists didn't get drunk and punch each other out.

I felt like a babysitter. Worse, I felt like a useless babysitter. I missed stopping coups and assassination attempts, infiltrating terrorist cells, and protecting world leaders. Mostly. As I ducked under the water and swam down to the sandy bottom of the ocean floor, though, I felt like maybe babysitting wasn't all that bad of a career change.

My bear spotted a fish while we were down there and set off chasing it. He loved fishing. And eating. And, he especially loved filling his belly with fresh fish he'd caught himself. He was a simple bear. Hunt, eat, sleep, repeat. The stifling heat didn't even bother him all that much, as long as I took him for regular dips in the water.

Got an assignment. Rendezvous at the office. Serge's voice broke through my tranquility like a loudspeaker and interrupted fishing time. Serge was the task force Alpha.

The lucky fish were free to swim another day and my stomach grumbled. Oh, well. I'd eat later. Even though I swam in what was usually a secluded section of the island, I swam as far in as I could without being spotted by the locals before shifting. I kept a pair of swim trunks hooked to the side of the pier and easily slipped into them before emerging from the water and jogging along the sand down to the office.

Dripping wet with my lower body coated in a layer of sand by the time I got there, I made quick work of rinsing off with the outside shower head before going in to see what was up.

Serge stood in front of one of the window AC units, talking to the rest of the team. His eyes cut to me and he frowned. "About time you showed up."

I shrugged, not minding the reprimand.

"A woman was assaulted last week in Key West. A few days later, another woman was assaulted a few miles north. A couple of days after that, another one another few miles north of that one. If the timeline remains the same, whoever attacked these women could possibly be in our area either today or tomorrow."

Dmitry growled. "And you let me leave my mate at home, alone?"

"He's only attacked sex workers so far. Still, I hear you. I'm not any happier leaving Hannah by herself right now." Serge sighed. "I'd like to send Hannah, Kerrigan, and Megan on a trip for a couple of days, but I seriously doubt—"

Roman laughed. "Not going to happen. Megan's way too stubborn to be 'sent away'."

I shrugged into a t-shirt and watched as the three mated members of the team fretted over their mates' safety. I was lucky that I didn't have to worry. Of course, I wanted a mate, but at least without one I was spared going into freak-out mode every time the slightest hint of danger arose. Having a mate appeared to turn an otherwise level-headed bear into a crackpot. Going solo, at least I didn't have to worry about my blood pressure.

As the conversation turned into a discussion about how to protect one's mate without her detection, I looked over at Maxim. "Are we needed here?"

He snorted. "Not for this part."

Konstantin looked over at us and frowned. "Mate or not, we should all be concerned about the women on the island."

I sighed. "If you don't lighten up, you're headed for a stroke, Kon. You're way too high strung."

He just frowned deeper and turned back to Serge.

"Keep an ear out today, and your eyes open. Report anything out of the ordinary, asap." Serge sighed. "No one has been able to provide a description, so we're flying blind in that regard."

I got up and nodded to Serge. "Will do."

I left the office and headed down Main Street, using my keen shifter senses to astutely case the surrounding neighborhoods. I tended to be light-hearted, a jokester, but I took the job seriously. If there was someone on Sunkissed Key that was out to hurt women, I'd take him out and have absolutely no qualms about it. I may not have had a mate of my own, but I was fond of my team members' mates and I'd be damned if I'd let anything happen to them.

I wasn't halfway down Dolphin Avenue when I saw a man leading a woman away from the street. Something wasn't right about the scene. She looked as though she was with him willingly, but I scented an eagerness from him—and eagerness tinged with an evil, deranged enthusiasm. I followed. By the time I got to the rear of the house he'd led her behind, he'd already slipped a cloth over the woman's face and she was slumped against his body. Chloroform.

Beady eyes looked up at me from a hard face, and he bared his teeth. "What the fuck are you looking at?"

I tipped my head from side to side, popping my neck. "A dead man."

I reached out to the P.O.L.A.R. unit:

If you want this asshole to live, you'd better get here quick. I smiled outwardly. *Feel free to take your time.*

3

HEIDI

"Four Buds and six tequila shots!" Sarah hung half her body over the bar to call out the order to me. "In a rush!"

I popped the top of four ice cold bottles and slid them down to her. Making quick work of the shots, I slid them down, too, before tending to my customers seated at the bar. A handful of orders later and I finally got to slow down a bit. I took orders from the bar and doled out drinks as fast as I could. I was a damn good bartender. I'd done it for fun when I was barely old enough to see over the bar top and I hadn't really ever stopped.

My Uncle Joey owned a bar up in my hometown of Rocky Gorge, Colorado, and I'd ended up there every day after school from kindergarten through my senior year of high school. My parents, both high-powered career people, had been busy at work so Uncle Joey was the only one who could keep me. He'd taught me everything he knew, and by the time I was eleven, I could sling drinks like the finest Manhattan mixologists and put on a darn good show while doing it.

I put myself through a few years of college by bartending and when everything else in my life went to shit, bartending put a roof over my head and paid the bills. So, there I was, at the age of thirty, with nothing to show for my years of existence but a bunch of trick pours and head full of fancy cocktail recipes. Almost thirty, anyway. That next birthday was coming up faster than I liked.

"Heidi! I've got a big party that just got seated. You going to be ready for it, or should I tell Mimi to come out front and give you a hand?" My boss, and the owner of Mimi's Cabana, Mimi Tuatagaloa, was a plus sized Samoan woman who wore a coconut bra and grass skirt to work daily. Fortunately, she didn't make her employees do the same. Everyone loved Mimi, who was almost never without a smile. And, although she had curves on top of curves, she actually rocked the coconut bra thingy.

"No, I'm ready."

She looked at me and made a face.

I walked down to her. "What's up?"

"That table of fifteen. It's a table full of women on the island for a bachelorette party. You know that they're going to get hammered, fuck up their table, and forget to tip."

I winced. Bachelorette parties were notorious for being nothing but trouble for the waitresses. I felt for Sarah. "I'll share tips with you. Don't worry about that part."

She pouted. "You're the best, but you don't have to do that."

"It's not a problem. Come on. We'll start them off with a complimentary jello shot and maybe they'll be warmed up to you enough to remember to tip." I reached under the bar for the shots I'd made earlier in the day. Pulling a stack from the fridge, I slipped them onto Sarah's tray and winked. "No one needs to know that they're mostly jello."

She laughed and squeezed my hand before scooting away. I heard their rambunctious cheers just a few moments later. I hoped that they'd be a good group for her if they felt like she was being really cool to them.

When she came back a few minutes later with their drink orders, I just put my head down and got to work. Fifteen mojitos later, I was annoyed with muddling fresh mint and starting to get behind on the orders of the customers sitting at the bar, but I worked hard to get caught up.

Not even two minutes later, Sarah came back with one of the mojitos, frowning. "One of them doesn't like it."

I stiffened, but made another. When she came back right away, I frowned. "What is her deal? It's a mojito. What exactly is she looking for?"

Sarah looked worried. "She said she'd prefer it wasn't you who made her drink."

I felt my eyebrows try to crawl off of my forehead. "Excuse me?"

"I'm sorry, Heidi. I think we're going to need to get Mimi out here. She's causing a fuss...because of you know what."

My stomach sank and embarrassment rose. I kept my face expressionless, though. I wasn't going to show that it got to me. "Think I should just go talk to her?"

Sarah shook her head. "No, I don't think this is one of those situations that can be made better. I think she was a huge Callie super fan."

I tipped my head back and stared up at the ceiling of the bar. Toothpicks with little ribbons of color had been shot into the tiles up there over the years and it was hard to find a spot of ceiling that wasn't dotted with color. My past was colorful as well, to say the least. The fact that it'd been almost eight years and I was still getting negative reactions was insane, though. The whole thing should have been long forgotten by now. It certainly wasn't, though. Not by some people.

"Okay. Call Mimi up front. Have her make the damned mojito. I'll take care of the rest of them, if that's okay."

"I'm sorry, Heidi."

I shrugged and focused on the patrons at the bar. I poured drinks and took care of them as fast as I could while still plastering a smile on my face. It wasn't easy.

Hours passed and as the bar thinned out, the bachelorette party remained. They'd had plenty to drink and eat, but didn't look as though they planned to move their party elsewhere. Mimi was still interrupting her paper work in the back office to come up front and make the brat's drinks, since the woman was adamant that I not taint anything of hers with my unholy touch. Mimi should've been able to leave earlier in the night, and let Sarah and me close, but she stayed because of the brat.

I was discouraged and angry, but there was nothing I could do about it. I just had to take it. I wasn't going to chance making Mimi or her bar look bad. Mimi's Cabana was a Polynesian themed tiki bar that Mimi herself had opened almost twenty years ago. I was going to smile and carry on like nothing bothered me. Just ignore the hater.

That had been the plan, anyway, except the brat got emboldened by her Mimi-made mojitos and approached the bar. My smile was brittle and I wanted to excuse myself, but that never shut people up. The best thing, or so I'd discovered, was to face the hate head on and simply smile through it.

Brat floated over to me immersed in a cloud of Chanel, alcohol, and cigarette smoke. Her blonde hair was spiral curled and her eyes were smoked out perfectly. She was beautiful, all except the dark scowl on her face. "I know who you are."

I winced at the way she said it. It wasn't just a statement; it was an accusation. I held my smile firmly in place and rested my hands on the bar. I noticed that my nails were chipped beyond belief and pulled them back to my sides. "Heidi Garcia."

She scowled harder, her lip tucked up into a sneer Elvis would've been proud of. "Homewrecking Heidi. The Cuban slut of the decade, Heidi."

I shrugged it off. "If you're dead set on believing everything you see on TV, that's your problem. The bar is closing in half an hour. Do you need anything before it does?"

"Not from the likes of you. Who knows where your hands have been?" She flipped her hair over her shoulder and shook her head. "How you even show your face in public is beyond me."

4
ALEXEI

The sun was just breaching the horizon when I slipped into the ocean that morning. It was earlier than I normally went for a swim, but I'd had a restless night after disposing of the asshole who'd been preying on women around the Keys. My animal never felt guilty for what the job sometimes entailed. To him, it was clear cut. But it just sat a little heavier with my human side.

The water was cooler than normal and I took my time gliding through it, letting it wash my cares away. I swam out farther than I normally had time to and watched as a cruise ship powered by. Cruise ships didn't make a lot of sense to me. I didn't get the idea of locking yourself away in a small room, or set of rooms and calling it a vacation. Why go out onto the ocean for that? You could do that on land. I'd rather just swim in the water, like I was.

When the sun was cresting over the houses on the east side of the island, I swam closer to shore and floated on my back. The waves rocked me soothingly and I considered taking a nap. My bear loved naps. As I was contemplating it, a scent wafted through the air around me and captured my attention fully.

I looked around for the source and spotted an unfamiliar woman on the pier. She was too far for me to make out much about her, but I could smell her just fine. The wind was carrying her delicious aroma directly to me. She scented of vanilla and something sweet and sugary that reminded me of freshly glazed donuts, my absolute weakness. Completely entranced, I swam closer.

The woman sat on the end of the pier, facing the ocean, a fishing pole in one hand, a cup of coffee in the other. Her tall, statuesque body, from what I could tell, was a work of art, curving out and dipping in and so many fun places. In short cut off denim shorts and a cut off t-shirt, she was incredible. Her bare toes were painted a bright blue and my tongue lolled out, wanting to lick every part of her.

The face of an angel, she stared out at the ocean pensively, her eyes narrowed in concentration. I wondered what she was thinking.

Her line caught and she jumped into action, reeling in whatever was tugging on the end of it. She fought hard but after about a minute of wrestling with it, the line snapped and she fell back on her ass. Instead of cursing or getting angry, she knelt and patiently repaired her broken line and then cast it again. Her face remained serene the entire time, like she couldn't possibly have been doing anything more relaxing.

I wanted to sit on the pier with her. I swam closer, my bear drawn magnetically to her. There was something about her that just called to the both of us.

When I was close enough to see the bright green of her eyes, I bobbed in the water under the pier, wondering what I should do next. I wanted to interact with her. My bear wanted to play. I contemplated for a few more minutes and then swam out from under the pier. Looking up at her, waiting for her to see me, I chuffed in annoyance when she didn't.

She was so focused on whatever thoughts were buzzing around her head, she didn't notice me. I chuffed again and splashed a little water at her feet. Still nothing. I was a huge fucking polar bear in a tropical setting and she wasn't noticing me. What the hell?

Feeling more determined, I splashed a little harder. When that didn't work, I grabbed her fishing line and yanked on it.

She snapped to attention and looked down, her hand already reeling in the line. Her eyes moved right past me at first. I was about to become highly offended when they snapped back to me with a laser focus, and she let out a squeal that just about popped my eardrums. Stumbling backwards, she fell on her ass again and crab walked nearly halfway back up the pier, towards land.

I took her forgotten pole into my mouth and swam towards her. I hadn't meant to scare her. My bad. I should've thought through how anyone might react to seeing a big ass polar bear in the water next to them. We didn't exactly have a reputation for being gentle and cuddly.

I pawed at the water and tried to grin at her, but it must've looked more like a snarl because she blanched and yanked herself up by the wooden post between us. She stared down at me, those green eyes wide with fear. Her mouth worked up and down. Her pink tongue slipped out to wet her lips, and then vanished into her mouth again.

Just that flash of tongue sent a rocket of heat pulsing through me that rivaled even the hottest Florida sunshine. I wanted to climb the pier and beg her to do it again. As a man. The bear would have to kick rocks for a while.

She leaned over the railing and blinked. "You can't be real."

I chuffed and splashed her with a swipe of my paw. Her shorts grew darker and I watched droplets of water roll down her long, tan legs. I was real, alright.

Her hands went to her hips and she narrowed her eyes at me. "Okay, so maybe you are real."

I chuffed louder and splashed her again. I was having fun. I also selfishly wanted the t-shirt she was wearing to cling a little more tightly to her curves.

She slowly moved towards the beach a few steps and paused when I followed her. "Please don't eat me," she whispered. "I promise I won't taste good."

I flashed her my teeth again because I was pretty sure she'd taste delicious—better than anything I'd ever tasted before in my life.

She walked a little faster towards the beach and then broke into an outright run when she saw I was still following her. She was fast, but I was much faster. I got to the beach before her and tore across the sand so I could meet her at the mouth of the pier.

Panting, she froze when she saw that I was blocking her path. She looked scared, but the set of her jaw spoke of a stubborn resolve. I worried about that, because it looked like she was willing to go head to head with a polar bear. This particular situation aside, that would be very unwise. "You are *not* going to eat me, big fella. Do you hear me? I've got shit to do today."

I didn't want to scare her. My bear balked at the idea. He flopped down in front of her, rolled onto his back, and looked up at her like some docile puppy. I was nearly a thousand pound animal, but it seemed that I was putty in her hands. I spit her pole out at her feet and gave her my best "sweet and innocent" look.

"What the hell was my coffee spiked with?" She rubbed at her eyes and shook her head. When she looked at me again, she took a deep breath and reached a shaking hand out to touch me. Her fingers brushed my fur and she yelped again.

I sat up and gave her a look that I hoped implied that I didn't love her screaming at me, but that I wouldn't hurt her.

She held up her hands and let out a shaky laugh. "Sorry, sorry. I wasn't sure you were real. You are, though. You're very much real. Jesus H Christ. What is a polar bear doing in the waters off the Florida Keys? What are you doing here, big guy?"

She smelled better up close. I couldn't stop myself from leaning into her and nuzzling my head into her chest. She was silky soft. My nose ended up caught in the heavenly valley between her breasts. I sniffed her again and again, trying to imprint that delicious aroma on my brain.

She stood frozen, her hands held out to the sides of me in obvious fear. When I moved and rubbed my head against her hand, she let out another squeak and jostled backwards. I was desperate for her to touch me at that point, so I followed and rubbed against her again.

"Please don't eat me. Please." She muttered the words before turning her hand over and lightly resting it on my head.

Heaven.

5

HEIDI

I was touching a polar bear. There was a real, live polar bear right here in Sunkissed Key and I was touching it and I was probably going to die a gruesome death as its morning snack. My fear subsided ever so slightly as the giant animal blinked and rubbed its muzzle against me. It was heavy and the weight of it knocked me back a step. Every time I moved, it followed, though. I wasn't sure if I wanted to cry or laugh. I had to be dreaming.

It buried its nose between my breasts again and huffed. It seemed to like putting its nose there, but I was terrified it was going to bite off something that I couldn't easily replace.

"Please be careful. I want to keep both of those."

The giant bear chuffed at me, a noise that sounded oddly like a chuckle, and then lifted its head and ran its large, black tongue over my face. I stepped back, shocked by the gesture.

It sat back on its haunches again and seemed to smile at me. It even lifted its hand in what looked to be a wave. I just stared. I couldn't be seeing what I thought I was seeing. No way.

When it waved again, it smiled even larger and then chuffed again. If I didn't know better, I would've thought it was laughing at me.

I looked around, waiting on someone to pop out and yell, "Surprise," or, "You just got punked," or "You're on Candid Camera." Only, no one did. It was early in the morning, the sun had barely risen, and the beach was deserted. The sound of seagulls was the only thing that could be heard, other than my heavy breathing and the polar bear's, uh, laughter...?

"What the actual fuck?" I rubbed at my eyes, but quickly had to drop my hands again to keep from falling over as the giant animal bumped its nose into my stomach. "This isn't real. This *can't* be real. Polar bears don't live on Sunkissed Key. Polar bears don't swim up to the beach and rub up against people."

He sat up again and, I swear to god, blew me a kiss.

"Okay, now I know my coffee was spiked with a hallucinogen." I moved in closer, feeling emboldened by the idea that it was probably just a big dog—a Great Pyrenees, maybe. Or, it was a wealthy woman in a white fur coat. Although, why wouldn't someone wear a fur coat on the beach? *Wait, no, don't ask that. No trying to make rationalizations while your brain is on LSD, Heidi.*

I ran my fingers over its chest, and they got lost in its thick fur. I surreptitiously searched for a seam because maybe it was a costume, and—

"Eek!" I was suddenly plastered against the bear's stomach as it wrapped its massive paws around me.

Holy shit! Struggling to get my footing back, I ran my hands up to its face, assuming I'd be able to remove the mask. What I found instead were the sharpest set of teeth I'd ever felt. A wet mouth, sharp teeth, and a wide tongue that was rough as it stroked itself over my hand. The tip of one of those teeth pricked my finger and I gasped before yanking my hand away.

Real polar bear. I was in the arms of a real fucking polar bear. I froze in fear, thinking I was about to die. No matter what happened next, I was a dead woman. I could feel the massive paws of the thing trapping me against it, its body heat scalding me, and the weight of it as it rested its chin on the top of my head. I wanted to scream, but I didn't think it would help anything, besides, it might rile the creature and hasten my demise.

It was too late for me.

I was a goner.

"D-do you think you can make it quick?" I buried my fingers in its fur and turned my head so I wasn't being suffocated. My cheek was pressed against its chest, its growling vibrating me. "Please, kill me fast. I don't want it to be like those nature shows, where you eat my leg and I live for another two days until you come back to gnaw on my arms. Just...go for the head first, okay?"

The thing chuffed again and then released me. It looked down at me and I swear it rolled its eyes. Then, it went down on all fours and started rubbing against me again.

"So...does this mean you're not gonna eat me, then?"

Its tongue came out and stroked over my stomach. Then, the tip of its nose dug under my shirt and I had to step away and push my shirt down to keep from being exposed.

If I didn't know better, I would've said that bear had been around too many human men in its life. It seemed...tame, though. It didn't seem to want to hurt me. The whole thing just got weirder and weirder.

Like a lightbulb, I suddenly remembered the animal sanctuary on the island. The Sunkissed Wildlife Sanctuary was a tourist attraction for the island. The man who ran the place took in animals that had been retired from Hollywood, or traveling circuses. I'd never been, because the idea of it made me sad for the poor animals, but evidently my polar bear was from there. Mr. (Leon) Zoo, a surname legalized through a "Florida Petition for Change of Name" form and a filing fee, ran the place. I'd bet money he was probably frantically searching one large, displaced polar bear.

"You're from the animal sanctuary, aren't you, big fella?" Knowing the animal was probably retired from some weird circus made me feel slightly better. He was probably old and lost, but used to humans. That was why he hadn't eaten me. Yet. "You want to go back home? I'm sure Mr. Zoo is missing you right now. He probably hates the thought of having to send out a missing polar bear alert to the local authorities."

The bear licked my stomach again and then my face. Then, he rested his chin on my shoulder and made a happy, almost purring sound.

"You're not so scary." I swallowed. "Well, okay, that's a lie. You are scary, but you're sweet, too."

I looked up him and wondered how I could lead a bear back to the sanctuary. It wasn't as though I had a leash or anything. The back entrance to the place wasn't all that far. Maybe I could actually cut behind my house and across Pelican Drive to get him back home. I didn't know how to get a bear to follow me, though. Too bad I hadn't caught my fish of the day or I'd use that to lure him. Not that I especially wanted to dangle a snack in my hand and tease a half-ton apex predator with it.

"If I lead the way, will you follow me?" I edged away from him and moved back to the beach. He'd pushed me back onto the pier, slowly but surely, and I was starting to worry about it being on the old wooden structure with such a large animal. "Come on. I bet Mr. Zoo is really worried that you're out here, getting yourself into trouble."

Miraculously, he just followed me. Without hesitation, he walked along right behind me as I headed toward the sanctuary. It was crazy, but then again, not crazier than anything else that had happened in the past ten minutes. All the way past my house and in between two houses on Pelican Drive, we went. I crossed my fingers that no one came out and had a stroke over the sight. Then, when we reached the back entrance of the wildlife sanctuary, Mr. Zoo seemed to have anticipated our arrival.

I was about to knock on the wooden gate when it swung open. He took one look at my polar bear and sighed loudly. I smiled, as best as I could in my still slightly apprehensive state. "Did you lose something?"

He reached out and patted the bear on the nose and nodded. "Thanks for bringing him back. He's a major troublemaker, but harmless as a pussycat."

I shrugged, like it was no big deal and I hadn't been so terrified a few minutes ago that I'd begged the polar bear to eat my head first. "He's really cuddly."

"Oh, I'm sure he is that." He maneuvered around the bear and shifted his weight into pushing the ass end of the bear inside the gate. "Thanks, again."

I watched as he led the creature away and felt oddly sad when the gate closed and I was separated from my bear. *The* bear, not *my* bear. Why did I think of him as mine?

6

ALEXEI

I shifted back to my human self and glared at the zookeeper, who was a shifter himself. Some sort of buffalo, if my sense of smell wasn't mistaken. Leon Zoo, a man the team had lectured a few times regarding the way he kept his animals, was a jackass. "I should bite your head right off your shoulders for prodding me in the ass like that."

"Oh, excuse me. I'm not really up on the normal protocol for herding a *shifter* into my compound. Not to mention having to pretend that I just *lost* an animal—a polar bear no less! I have a reputation, you know."

I rolled my eyes. "Not a very good one."

"You can leave now, sunshine."

I left, naked, and snuck back to the pier to find my shorts. Then, after looking around and having no luck spotting my human, went back to the house. My bear was damn near giddy with excitement at the morning's events. I thought of the way he'd rubbed himself all over her and laughed. Maybe that hadn't been all him.

I should've felt bad for the way I'd touched her and tasted her skin, but she was utterly irresistible. I was aroused just thinking about the way she'd felt as her fingers stroked my fur. I wanted to feel her against my human body. I wanted more than to feel her.

I let myself into the house and went straight to the kitchen. I was famished. If I couldn't have her right then, I was going to need to satisfy myself in other ways. Luckily for me, Serge was there, cooking.

"Thank god. I was afraid I was going to have to cook for myself."

Serge looked me over and raised his eyebrows. "You look keyed up. What's up?"

I couldn't tell him the truth. We weren't supposed to interact with humans in our animal form the way I just had. Not without a good enough reason. Serge wouldn't consider just wanting to be close to her a good enough reason. "Just had a refreshing swim."

He made a face. "Uh huh."

I watched and as soon as he put the first stack of pancakes on the island, I grabbed them. He complained, but I didn't care. I poured a half a bottle of syrup over them and dove in head first. I didn't come up until the ache in my stomach eased up some and I felt the beginnings of a sugar coma. It was easier in that state to not be so focused on my new human obsession.

"What the hell, Alexei?"

I grinned and pushed away from the counter. "Thanks. I'm heading up to get ready for work."

"Asshole."

I waved Serge off and took the stairs up to my room, three at a time. I grabbed a towel and a change of clothes before stepping into the bathroom. What started out as an innocent shower soon became my hand wrapped around my cock, the woman from the pier's tall, sexy body playing across my mind until I came with a low growl.

I had to see her again. I didn't know what it was about her, but I was smitten. I not only wanted to see her and touch her more, I *needed* to, as crazy as that was.

The rest of the day passed in a blur. We had a steady stream of asinine jobs, with Halloween right around the corner. It seemed everyone got a little wilder around that time—shifter and human alike. All day, I went through the motions, but I was distracted as hell.

It was early when I fell into bed, and I laid there counting down the hours until I could go back to that pier. I hoped she'd come back there. She *had* to. I'd never seen her around the island before, but surely she wasn't a tourist. She was out fishing, and by herself. That wasn't touristy activity.

By the time morning came, I was climbing out of my skin, eager to find her again. It was still dark when I left the house and sank into the ocean. Hooking my shorts where I always left them, I shifted and swam out to sea, using the time to swim hard and really push my bear. He needed to work on releasing some energy before seeing our little human. It would be too easy to get overly excited and accidentally hurt her.

Again, as the sun was coming up on the east side of the island, turning the horizon a deep purple color, I swam up closer to the pier and watched as she appeared. Strolling down the beach then stepping onto the pier, the slight sway of her hips was hypnotizing. She was all long legs and perfect curves and her bare feet made the softest of sounds as she stepped. She stopped at the end of the pier and pulled her fishing pole out before hesitating and scanning the water.

If I wasn't mistaken...hmm...was there hope in her eyes as she looked around? Then she spotted me. The corners of her lips lifted as she braced herself on the railing and leaned forward.

"What are you doing out, again?" She watched me swim closer and giggled when I splashed water at her again. "You're a naughty boy, aren't you?"

Naughty? She had no clue. I swam closer and then ducked under the water right in front of her. Swimming as deep as I could and then shooting back up, I did my version of a bear grin when she squeaked and pursed her lips. I belly flopped back into the water and my large splash soaked her.

Her caramel colored hair clung to her head and face and the tie-dye shirt she wore suctioned to her breasts. "You're a ham. Come on. Let's get you back to Mr. Zoo. As rude as he may be, that's where you belong."

I growled and splashed her again. I wasn't done hanging out with her. I went under again and found a large fish. I easily caught it and came up with it between my teeth. Getting as close to her as I could, I spit it out next to her feet on the pier and tried to grin again. Damn, I wanted to be in my human form.

She squatted, giving me a glorious view of her inner thighs, and picked it up. "Is this for me?"

I nodded my head and then swam alongside the pier, needing to be closer to her. She grabbed her things and followed me, the fish tucked into the bucket she'd carried up. She hurried along with an excited expression. It seemed that she was as eager as I was.

When we both got to the beach, I made myself slow down so I didn't hurt her. Her fear from yesterday seemed to have vanished. She came right up to me and stroked my head. When I purred like a fucking kitten, she leaned into me and scratched me with both hands.

"You're a real charmer, aren't you?"

I ran my tongue over her neck and let out a low growl. That spot... I wanted to bury my face there and taste her for weeks. Or months. I wasn't sure which.

She shivered against me and I eased up my affections. I let her touch me more, let her stroke my fur and scratch me behind the ears like I was a dog. It should've been embarrassing, but it wasn't. I was in heaven and wanting more of her touch.

I wanted to shift and show her how much I really liked what she was doing. I wanted to strip her naked and worship at the temple of her body. I wasn't fool enough to think that she wouldn't run screaming if I suddenly shifted and became a man in her arms, though.

7

HEIDI

"You know that this is crazy, right? You're a polar bear. You're not supposed to be out just roaming a Florida beach by yourself. You know? Mr. Zoo should really keep better tabs on you." I hugged my new favorite animal again and then pulled away. "You're such a snuggle bear. I can't stop hugging you."

He used a big paw to draw me back closer to him and made a happy little noise when I fell against him. He'd seemed as excited to see me as I'd been to see him and I hadn't felt an ounce of fear that morning. I'd *wanted* to find him. It made no sense, but there it was. I supposed that after the first encounter, my sixth sense kicked in and now I viewed him as completely harmless which was really stupid considering the fact that no matter how tamed he'd been by the circus or trainer or whoever had him before Mr. Zoo, he was a wild and potentially deadly animal. Still, I'd never even known a dog that was as lovable and cuddly as he was.

"Come on. As much as I'd love to take you home and let you live with me, I'm sure that would violate about fifty local ordinances. You have to go back to Mr. Zoo." I sighed. "Maybe this time he'll do a better job at containing you so you can't get out again."

Again, same as yesterday, I led him back to the sanctuary and knocked on the gate. I looked back at him and sighed again. He kept staring at me with his eyes all big and pleading, like he wanted something from me. He seemed to be attracted to me and I wanted to spend the rest of the day hanging out with him. That wasn't the adult in me speaking, though. No way should a polar bear be on this island unless it was in a cage or reinforced enclosure of some sort. I couldn't keep him out in public, where something could set him off. At the end of the day, he was a wild animal.

It was hard to believe he was a wild animal when I looked at him, though. "You're too darn cute, you know that?"

Mr. Zoo opened the gate when my bear chuffed out what I thought of as a laugh. He took one look at us and rolled his eyes—not the reaction I was anticipating—before gesturing the bear inside. The bear was obviously well trained in non-verbal commands because Mr. Zoo didn't say a word the whole time. The bear just lumbered in and Mr. Zoo closed the gate after him.

I stood there, feeling angry and lonely, all of a sudden. I wanted to go in with my bear and make sure he was being cared for. I didn't get the impression that that would be a welcome intrusion, though. So, instead, I forced myself to walk back to the beach.

It made no sense to feel sad and lonely after returning a stray animal to his proper home. So why, I pondered as I gathered my fishing supplies, did I suddenly feel hollow inside? It was the strangest thing. I almost felt as though I'd had to give away a pet dog that had been my loyal companion for years.

It was also foreign for me to feel lonely. I'd gotten used to the solitary life that I'd built for myself. I hadn't felt lonely in years. Yet, the hollow pit inside begged to differ.

At home, I put my supplies away and carried my fish—the gift from my polar bear—inside. It was a nice looking fish and larger than the fish I usually caught. I put it on ice. It would make a delicious dinner later. A fish caught by a polar bear. I shook my head at the very thought and went to shower and get ready to head over to Maria's to watch the boys.

My morning with Jayden and Jonas was spent fending off their cuteness attacks and taking them out to play on the beach. By the time Maria got home from work, I had lunch prepared for her. I said my goodbyes and see ya' tomorrows and left to slip back home and take care of some errands before heading to work at the bar that night.

I was in the middle of my errands when I ran into *him*. At the grocery store, heading up the canned good aisle, *he* stepped into the aisle and walked towards me.

Tall, broad, sexier than hell. He was a muscled god in a tight-fitting t-shirt and camo pants. Army camo, I noticed right away. His blonde hair was sun-bleached and kind of went everywhere all at once, a little too long. I had the strangest urge to run my hands through that hair.

I'd never felt such an instant attraction before. It was like someone had suddenly turned the heat up in the canned goods aisle. I was instantly aware that I hadn't changed out of the thin tank top I'd worn to play with the boys earlier. I felt on display and the way *his* eyes raked over my body told me very clearly that I was.

I'd never seen him before, but I instantly had an idea of who he was. I'd heard plenty of talk at the bar about the group of military looking guys who'd moved onto the island several months back. A few of them had even stopped into Mimi's on occasion—not this one, though. Apparently, they all lived in a large house that used to be a B&B, and rented office space on Main Street. No one knew what exactly they did or why they were here, but looks-wise, they had the locals in a tizzy. The women, anyway. Some men, too. Seeing *him*, I now understood why.

His cart was empty when he parked it next to me. I averted my eyes and pretended to be highly interested in a can of beets. I went as far as to twist the can so I could read the label. Yep, still beets.

As he reached over me to grab a can of sauerkraut, his arm just barely grazed my shoulder when he pulled back. "Oh, sorry."

My skin burned and tingled where he'd touched me and I had to work to make my mouth form words to respond. "No problem."

He dropped the can in his cart and stepped back just slightly. "I'm Alexei. I don't think I've seen you around the island before."

I looked up at him and took a deep breath. He was so tall—6'4" or 6'5". At 5'11", I wasn't a short woman by any means, taller than average, but he was a giant. His eyes...they were crystal blue like tropical waters. His eyelashes, long and thick, made those eyes look bedroom ready.

"Um... Heidi."

The corner of his lips raised in a sexy half-smile for a split second before repeating my name. He said it with his deep voice and just the slightest bit of an accent. "Are you new to the island?

I realized I still had my hand lifted in mid-air, halfway to the can of beets, and immediately dropped it. "No, actually. I've lived here for a number of years."

He reached up to grab another can from behind me, and his chest came even closer to me. He smelled...familiar. I couldn't place it, but it was a scent that made me happy, like ocean and sun. I wanted to breathe him in deeper, maybe even bury my face in that broad chest to get more of it. I almost asked what kind of cologne he used.

When he pulled back, his jaw muscles worked. "Has anyone ever told you that you smell like fresh glazed donuts?"

I laughed. "Like donuts? No, nope. I can't say I've heard that before."

He dropped another can into his cart and smiled down at me. His teeth were perfect, of course, and when he exposed them, I felt like he was more animal than man. That smile held a hint of a warning and an overwhelming sex appeal. Until he spoke again. "You know, if you asked me out, I wouldn't say no."

Hold the brakes! Cute, sexy, but cocky and arrogant as hell. Dangerous, too. I wasn't going to take that warning lightly. He was too much man, too much heat and promise. My body wanted to adhere to him like a suction cup. My stomach was a flutter of butterflies, all beating wings toward him. I wasn't stupid, though. I knew trouble when I saw it.

"Enjoy your sauerkraut." I forced myself to grab my cart and step away from him.

Walking away from him felt like trudging through quick dry concrete. My body begged for a chance to rub against that big, delicious hunk of a man. I'd been so long since I'd been with anyone, but Alexei wasn't a man to fan some flames with. He was all inferno and I already had metaphorical burn scars. I'd vowed never again. So, as hard as it was to fight the pull, I kept walking, headed to the checkout, unwilling to run into him again. I wasn't sure I'd be as strong a second time.

8

ALEXEI

I showed up the next morning with a wounded ego and a desperation to see Heidi. I'd spent the previous night at Cap'n Jim's Bar and Grill, drinking and licking my wounds. I had felt a wild attraction to Heidi as soon as I saw her, but seeing her while not in bear form, while I could talk to her and get skin to skin with her was an entirely different thing.

As soon as I'd seen her in that tiny tank top, her long, flat torso exposed, I'd wanted to rip it off of her, while simultaneously needing to cover her from anyone else looking her way. She was tall and slender but curvy in the right places and had the most exotically beautiful coloring—skin and hair the color of caramel and light green eyes with a darker green ring around the iris.

I'd been so sure that she'd felt the same attraction. I'd seen the way she looked at me. Yet, maybe I'd been mistaken.

The memory of how easily she'd brushed me off compounded the discomfort of my melancholy and my hangover that morning. Still, I floated next to the pier, waiting for her to show up. And she did! The moment I saw her, a desperate neediness and longing arose in me and I knew I looked like one of those fucking animal rescue commercials.

Heidi didn't saunter her way down the pier like she normally did. She stopped on the beach and slid her little jean shorts down her hips. Her tank top followed and then she waded into the water in a small yellow bikini that left me drooling.

I swam closer to her, ready to rub all over her, but she beat me to it. When she was close enough, she wrapped her arms around my neck and hugged me.

"You big devil. How the heck did you get out again? If I didn't think you were completely harmless and didn't love to see you so much, I'd report Mr. Zoo to the authorities. Or, are you some kind of Houdini of the animal kingdom?" She moved back and scratched the top of my nose. "Come on. Let's have a swim before I have to take you back to that sorry excuse for a zookeeper."

I wanted to stay distant, but my bear wasn't having it. He was overjoyed at having her next to him, splashing us back. She swam beautifully, in long strokes that cut through the water easily. When she was far enough, I nudged her with my nose, worried about her going too far out. I wouldn't let anything happen to her, but still, I worried.

As she swam in place, she chatted away. Her mood was bright that morning, her eyes glittering as she looked at me. She spoke to me like I was a pet. Or a friend, not just some random animal, and I found myself listening to everything she said with apt attention. I wanted to know more. Maybe she wanted nothing to do with me as a man, but I could still spend time with her.

After a few more minutes of swimming, she moved closer to the beach and stood in waist deep water, looking around. "This place is so beautiful. And you're displaced in this setting but I think that makes the fact that you're here even more extraordinary. I wish I had a camera right now."

When I grunted, she laughed.

"I swear you can understand me. It's amazing that I just went for a swim with a polar bear, but I feel like you're my buddy. And I should probably be checking myself into a mental health facility." She stroked my face and sighed. "If not for talking to polar bear like he's my long lost pet pooch, then for walking away from that hot guy in the grocery store yesterday."

I perked right up. I was afraid to move for fear of her changing the subject.

"*He* was beautiful. Sexy, muscled, he had literally everything going for him. He even smelled good. Too bad he was cocky as hell, although he had good reason to be, I'm sure." She tilted her head back to dip her hair into the water, giving me a full view of her chest. "I know I should be over an interaction that lasted all of two or three minutes, but I had a dream about him last night. I woke up in a hell of a state, all hot and sweaty. I still haven't been able to get him off my mind."

Unable to resist, I ran my tongue up her stomach. When she squealed and splashed me with water, I just grinned at her.

"Keep your tongue to yourself." She wagged her finger at me. "You have nothing to worry about. You're still the most interesting guy in my life. I walked away from Hottie McHotterson. I can spot trouble when I see it and he had trouble written all over him."

I wanted to tell her that I wasn't trouble. I was a good time.

"Although, you're trouble, too. You keep breaking out of the Wildlife Sanctuary and Mr. Zoo's going to find some other refuge to take you. You'll be too much of a risk." She frowned. "Does he treat you well?"

I desperately wanted to shift and talk to her. I wanted to tell her who I was and how I felt like we were buddies too and that I wouldn't be trouble. I'd take her out and I'd listen to her talk about whatever she wanted, like I was listening now.

She sighed and twisted her hair into a knot on top of her head. "I'm conversing with a polar bear like it's not utterly bizarre."

I grunted. It wasn't bizarre. She liked me. I liked her. She would like human me, too, if she'd give me a chance.

"Okay, my big snuggle bear, it's time to get you back to Mr. Zoo's." She held my head in her hands and brushed a kiss over my nose. "He told me I smelled like fresh doughnuts. Ugh! I'm thinking of him again! Okay, I'm stopping right now."

Following her back to Zoo's place was no fun. I didn't want our time to end and I especially didn't want to have to wait another day to see her again. I was hooked.

She stopped before she knocked on the door of the sanctuary and I mentally called out to Leon Zoo telling him not come to the gate yet. "I wish I could bring the boys to see you. Jayden and Jonas would flip out. Maria would have a heart attack. Rightfully so. I'm not ready to share our time together yet, though. Although, this will probably be the last time. Mr. Zoo's got to do something about you wandering around the island. I know you're a sweetheart, but still."

I pushed against her and nuzzled my face into her chest. I wanted to remain with her. For a second, I was starting to feel like I actually was an animal being dropped off at the zoo. I didn't want to be left behind. My bear was miserable, too. We were both desperate to stay with her.

She knocked on the gate and smiled at me, though. "Is it weird that I'll miss you? Yeah, it's weird. I probably need a lobotomy."

I grunted at her and then growled at Leon Zoo as he opened the gate and waved me in. Once again, I left Heidi's side and stepped into the sanctuary reluctantly. The gate shut and she was left on the other side.

I was spurred with a determination to see more of her, though. A few minutes in the mornings with her just wasn't enough.

9
HEIDI

That night at work, Hottie McHotterson, a.k.a. Alexei, showed up. He was with another guy, both of them in similar outfits of tight, black t-shirts and some type of canvas military pants. Heads turned and jaws dropped as the two of them walked in. Alexei had combed his hair back from his face and it looked like he'd been running his hands through it over and over again. It had the effect of making me want to run *my* hands through it.

I'd been mid-pour on a whiskey double when I spotted him. He wasn't reserved about his intention. He was staring right at me as though his eyes were laser pointers boring holes in me. His slow smirk heated my blood and he nodded to his friend before heading over to me. I wasn't able to take my eyes off of him until I felt liquid splashing on my hand and looked down to find I was still pouring the whiskey into an overflowing glass.

Cursing, I put my bottle down and slid the glass towards the customer, not caring that I'd given him more than he was paying for. I leaned towards Alexei and raised a brow. "Coincidence?"

He flashed those pearly whites and shook his head. "Not even close."

"Just stubborn then?"

He bit his lower lip and grunted. "You could say that."

I rested my hands on the bar in front of him. "What would you like to drink?"

"Whatever's on tap." He watched as I poured him a beer and brought it over to him. "You're a hard woman to track down."

My stomach fluttered and I was about to answer when Sarah called out an order. I held up a finger to Alexei and went to fill the drinks. I worked fast, but my hands were shaky. I could feel his eyes on me, taking in everything I did.

When I passed the drinks to Sarah, she grinned. "Looks like you've got an admirer."

I glanced back at Alexei and released a breathy little sigh. "So, I do."

"Well? Why are you still over here? Go, girl, get him."

I wanted to drag her back and use her as an excuse to keep my distance from Alexei. The man still spelled out trouble with a capital T. Sarah vanished on me, though, and I had no choice but to scoot back over to him. The bar wasn't busy enough that I couldn't stand and talk to him for a bit.

"Hi." Alexei leaned towards me, his dark eyes focused on mine. He gave me a slow smile that sent heat coursing through my body. "I should apologize."

I found myself leaning into him and braced myself on the bar top. "For?"

"For not being able to take a brush off when I get one." He took a long pull from his beer. "I should've gone to Capt'n Jim's where I usually drink and left you alone, but I was craving glazed donuts."

I laughed suddenly, unable to help myself. "Are you always so full of shit?"

He grinned and shrugged. "Pretty much. Are you still denying me the pleasure of taking you out?"

"I don't remember denying you that. I remember you telling me that I could take you out."

"You're right. May I have the pleasure of taking you out?"

I heard someone call out an order but held his gaze. "No."

He laughed and the sound sent warmth pooling in my lower belly. His eyes practically twinkled and he bit his lower lip. "You're busy. I'll ask again when you're free."

"The answer will still be no."

"We'll see."

I shook my head as I moved away to fill more orders. When I got back to him, he was still watching me, his eyes hyper-focused. I just leaned against the bar and raised a brow. I was playing with fire, but I felt like there was something drawing me to his side, like a crazy strong magnet.

"Change your mind yet?"

I ducked my head to hide a smile. "You're stubborn."

"I like to think of it as determined." He glanced over his shoulder and his face grew serious as his friend came up beside him. His friend said something quietly to him and then he stood up. Leaning over the bar, he slipped a couple of bills into my hand. The brush of his skin over mine was electric, but he just moved back and forced a smile. "Duty calls."

I wanted to tell him to come back. It was insane. I wanted to slip him my number and tell him to call me, visit me, *whatever* me. Instead, I shrugged. "Saved yourself the embarrassment of another denial."

He winked at me and then was gone.

I sagged against the bar, not exactly sure what to do with myself after being so amped up while Alexei was there. Fortunately, my duty called, too. People came and went at the bar and I kept busy until the closing.

I slept fitfully that night, dreams of Alexei taunting me the entire night through. In the dreams, I was with him and my polar bear, swimming in the ocean. I could feel the brush of his legs against mine under the water, the way he wrapped his big arms around me, and the way his fingers trailed over my face. Some of the dreams had been sweet, while others had been enough to leave me blushing when I remembered them the next morning. Dream Heidi was a kinky woman.

I was wired. Wired and tired. It was a vicious combination that made me cranky. It was almost enough to keep me in bed and persuade me to skip my morning fishing routine. Almost. I couldn't resist going out to the pier on the off chance that maybe my polar bear had outwitted Mr. Zoo again and found a way to get out. I just skipped bringing my fishing gear and went straight there.

Only, when I arrived, he wasn't there. I waited around for a while, a part of me hopeful, but he never showed. Which was a good thing, or so I tried to tell myself. it wasn't safe for a polar bear to be freely roaming an inhabited island. Still, my mood sank lower and lower with each passing moment. I didn't understand why I was so tied to seeing the damn bear, but I was. When the sun had fully risen and one by one, joggers and sunbathers showed up on the beach, I headed to the animal sanctuary. I knocked on the back gate for what felt like eternity before Mr. Zoo opened it.

"What?"

I frowned. "I guess the polar bear didn't escape today."

"No."

"Could I see him?"

"No."

I stammered. "What?"

He shook his head. "No. Not today."

I stepped back and stared in shock as he slammed the gate in my face. What the hell? I crossed my arms over my chest and walked away muttering to myself about how he should be a little more grateful to me for saving his ass and returning one of his runaway animals to him—not once, not twice but three times. I had half a mind to go back and tell him what I thought about that but I had to get to work and, really, what was the point?

I wondered how he managed to contain my bear. Maybe he'd reinforced whatever home the bear was living in. I'd definitely have to go by and check on him.

10

ALEXEI

I showed back up at Mimi's Cabana the next night, unable to stay away from Heidi. I hadn't been able to see her that morning and I was jonesing for some time with her. The job from the night before had run over. Two hundred miles north of the island, we'd ended up chasing a rogue shifter through swampland. By the time we got back home, it was late morning—too late to show up at the pier where Heidi fished.

I half worried that she wouldn't be at Mimi's. I needed to know the other places on the island she frequented so I could plan to "accidentally" run into her. I'd spent the day searching for her, but I'd had no luck. As soon as I got close to the bar, though, I could smell her. She was there.

When I entered the place, I spotted her and knew right away that something was off. She had a frown on her face as she spoke to someone at the bar. She turned away from them before I could zone in and hear what she was saying. There were dark circles under her eyes and she looked tired. I wanted to fix whatever was making her frown like that.

That thought struck me, the truth of it settling into my bones. I wanted to take care of her, to hold her and to do whatever I could to make her feel better. No matter what was wrong, or what it took to fix it.

She glanced up from the bar at that moment and spotted me. Something passed over her face and then the corners of her mouth tipped up slightly. Her smile made my heart melt. Surely, she knew what it did to me.

I crossed to the bar and slid onto a stool. I didn't pretend that I wasn't watching her as she moved around, waiting on other customers who'd been there before me. Her body swayed, the short dress she wore flitted around her thighs as she moved. It was tantalizing, wondering if I'd catch a glimpse of one more inch of thigh when she grabbed a bottle of liquor from the top shelf or bent to grab a bottle of beer from the cooler under the bar. The curves of her breasts had me leaning forward and holding my breath as she leaned across the bar to hand someone a drink.

Then, there was the way her eyes kept landing back on me. Every few seconds, she glanced my way, her head down, looking through her lashes. I could see the pulse at the base of her throat work, smell her sweet, sugary scent strengthening. As she danced around behind the bar, working fast and efficiently, I felt like I was back in the wild, honing in on prey. When she turned her back to me, I could see the way her body tightened, like she was aware of the precarious position she'd put herself. Her body recognized the apex predator in mine, and maybe even felt the desire I had to leap over the bar, drag her off with me and make her mine.

When Heidi did make her way over to me, her eyes seemed brighter. The frown from earlier was gone. "Should I be worried that you're stalking me?"

I nodded. "Very."

"At least you're honest." She pushed her hair behind her ears. "Beer?"

"I can't stay." No matter how much I wanted to. "I just figured I'd try again. I'm hoping I can wear you down eventually with my masculine good looks and endearing charm."

Someone called for a drink but her eyes were locked on mine.

The bright green looked almost glowing in the lighting over the bar. "How long can you hear 'no' before it just breaks that endearingly charming heart?"

I stood up and leaned across the bar. Not touching her, I spoke with my lips only a hair away from her ear. "More times than either of us want to count. Save yourself the trouble."

Her blood pumped faster, her heartrate sped. A barely audible little intake of breath was followed by the scent of her sexual arousal filling my senses. "I don't think there's anything about you that isn't trouble, Alexei."

Hearing my name on her lips just about killed me. I just barely brushed my mouth over her ear before pulling away and leaving her in her own space. I ran my hand through my hair, the interaction shaking me probably more than it did her. I clamped my teeth down on my lip to keep from begging her.

Another call came for more drinks, but Heidi just held my gaze and shivered. "Like I said. Trouble."

I watched the guy who'd been talking to her earlier snap his fingers to get her attention. She frowned. He was clearly a fucking asshole. Just when I had decided to not rip his fingers off, I heard him lean over to his friend and snort.

"Maybe they need to replace bimbo over there with someone who can actually tend bar."

I knew Heidi had heard it. Her eyes dimmed again and she shook her head. "Sorry, I've got to get back to work."

I forced a smile and casually stepped over to the guy. I rested my arm along his shoulder and applied just the slightest bit of pressure. My anger was like a living, breathing entity. "Hello, friend."

The guy looked up, and up, at me, his smirk dying. "Hey."

I squeezed his shoulder tighter. "So, I got the impression that you don't know this lovely woman's name. It's Heidi. I'm sure you didn't mean to actually call her something other than Heidi."

He shifted, uncomfortable with my clear aggression, but not wanting to lose face in front of his friends. "Dude, fuck off."

I growled and he jumped. "I've had a long day and you're starting to piss me off. Not good. I'd hate to lose control and snap your head off your scrawny little neck."

He winced at the pressure I was putting on his shoulder. "Whatever, man."

"What's her name?"

His friends were leaning away from him, leaving him to face the big, bad bear alone. "Heidi."

"Good!" I patted his shoulder harshly and stepped back. "There we go. That wasn't so hard."

His hand went to his shoulder and he scowled at me. "I didn't mean anything by it."

I pulled out my wallet and threw several bills on the counter. "Of course you didn't. Have another beer on me."

I walked back to the end of the bar, grinned and nodded a goodbye to Heidi before heading out. I really didn't want to leave, but I had to get back to work.

"Alexei."

I stopped and turned.

Heidi made a face at me. "It doesn't mean I'm going out with you, but thanks."

I laughed. "You're welcome."

Her mouth worked like she was fighting back a grin and then she lost. Her lips stretched wide and she rolled her eyes before turning away. "My answer's still no."

"Uh huh."

11

HEIDI

"He's beautiful." I ran my hand over my bear's head and sighed. "He's this perfect specimen of maleness and he's hitting on me. And he gives me this feeling... I can't even describe it. It's like I *want* to throw caution to the wind and just go crazy all over him."

Bear rested his head on my knee and grunted.

"I can't, though. That's just not my life. And he doesn't know the truth about me." I looked out at the ocean and watched as the waves rolled onto the shore. It was a red flag sort of day, dangerous water to swim in but still beautiful to look at. Clouds hung heavily in the sky, but it wasn't supposed to rain until later in the day.

The gloomy, overcast skies should've had me feeling moody, but I was on a high from being pursued by Alexei. He made me laugh and something about him was intoxicating.

"I'm lonely. I hate to admit it, and I really didn't realize it until just a day or two ago, but I am." Maybe I was moodier than I realized. "My life is so full. I have the boys and Maria. I have other friends... I have..."

He adjusted his head and growled.

"Yes, I have you. Kind of. As much as one can have a polar bear with escape artist tendencies." I scratched behind his ears and kissed the top of his head. "I don't want to feel lonely. I was fine before he came along."

I *had* been fine. It had been easy to accept the life I'd chosen for myself when there hadn't been anything working against it. Alexei was working against that life. It was hard to be okay with being alone when there was someone as magnetic as Alexei showering me with attention.

"I came here to be alone. Almost a decade ago. I came with the expectation that I'd find solitude. Not counting Maria and the boys. I was okay with it. More than okay, I was happy with it. It was better than the other options, honestly."

The sound of a car door shutting somewhere in the distance pulled me from my reverie. I shook my head and patted my bear on the head. Houdini, as I was calling him, understood. He stood up with a growl and butted into me with his nose before backing up and letting me stand.

"I hate having to take you back to that jerk. I hope he's nicer to you than he is to me." We walked down the beach and took the path we always did to get to the sanctuary. "Maybe I'll bring the kids to the wildlife sanctuary today. No, not today. I promised them I'd take them to Clotilde's for ice cream today, and it's supposed to rain. But soon. I'll bring them soon."

I knocked on the gate and as we waited, Houdini rubbed against me and snorted, his big dark eyes seeming to smile at me.

"I bet you'd like ice cream. You probably like anything having to do with ice. I'm not sure anyone could afford to keep you fed with ice cream, though. I've seen the way you eat fish."

Abruptly, Mr. Zoo opened the door and ushered Houdini in. Without a word, the gate slammed shut and I stood there, frowning at it.

I couldn't dwell on the rudeness for long, though. I had to get to the boys and so Maria wasn't late for work. I stopped by my house to change quickly and then ran to Maria's. When I walked in, she had a twin hanging from each arm, both of them crying.

"Thank god you're here. Take them, please." She passed Jonas to me and then Jayden. "I've got to stop and get gas. I'm going to be late."

The boys cried harder. I bounced them on my hips and made soothing noises. "Sorry I'm late, Maria. I got caught up."

"Doing whatever it is that's making your face light up lately but you won't tell me about?"

I snorted. "You'd better go."

She winked at me and hurried to the door. "Good luck with them today. Sorry to dump them on you in their condition and run."

"Well, they'd better be good if they think I'm taking them to Clotilde's for ice cream. Naughty little boys don't get ice cream." I laughed when both boys stopped crying instantly. I mouthed the word "Magic" to Maria.

Maria rushed back and planted a kiss on each of her boys' heads. "Love you all!"

She left and while the boys had stopped crying, they were still cranky and whiny. They fell asleep on the couch while I made them breakfast. The sound of the cartoons on the TV kept me company while my thoughts faded back to Alexei.

I did my best to suppress those thoughts, though. I wouldn't be wise to act on them with him. No matter how forceful he was, I couldn't trust whatever it was Alexei thought he wanted from me. It was always the same with men. They initially swore they could handle the snickers and the stares and the open contempt, but eventually it always ended the same way. A man could only hear the same bullshit so many times before he couldn't help but start to believe it.

After everything that happened in the period of my life I liked to refer to as LBSK (Life Before Sunkissed Key), I had attempted to enter into a few different relationships. I'd learned the hard way that it was impossible for a man to truly trust a woman when he was told over and over again that she was a vicious, backstabbing whore.

Then, there was the added stress of strangers who looked at them with pity. One of my exes had left me because he couldn't handle constantly feeling like a fool.

At the end of the day, for most of the people, I wasn't worth the trouble. My own family had had to distance themselves from me after the show. They were relieved when I'd moved out of state and hundreds of miles away from Rocky Gorge. So, I had no delusions that the same thing wouldn't happen with Alexei. Sure, he would stand up for me in the beginning. They usually did. Being a hero was an ego boost for a while. Defending my honor would get old, though. A man could only fight so many battles before he began to wonder if it was even worth the bother.

No matter how much Alexei thought he wanted me, he didn't know the truth. He didn't know the real me.

If only I could deal with the damned loneliness. Knowing nothing was going to change regarding my relationship status, it almost made me angry that I'd ever met Alexei. I'd been fine before he started making my heart go all aflutter and shit.

I checked on the boys before plating their scrambled eggs and making a conscious effort to shake off my pity party. It wouldn't do me any good. I had two little boys to play with and that was enough. Especially if I took things one day at a time.

I turned the TV off and woke the boys up. "Rise and shine, little monsters! We have a big day ahead of us and it's time to get started."

12

HEIDI

Jonas whined while eating his eggs, but still somehow managed to finish and ask for more. Jaydan just ate in a state of grogginess and most of his eggs ended up on the floor. I let the boys each eat a squeezable yogurt while I gave them baths and got them dressed for the day.

Maria and I had discussed the boys' morning activity schedules and we'd both agreed that it would be beneficial to include educational pursuits. So, our morning was full of learning activities. We colored and played on the beach, but they also listened while I read to them and we worked on the alphabet.

I was proud of how smart and how well rounded they were. They could both sing the entire alphabet song and could write out some of the letters. They were going to be well prepared for entering preschool. In fact, I wasn't trained in early childhood education and they were quickly surpassing what I knew in regards to teaching kids. I'd soon need to do research to keep up with them if they kept sucking up everything I taught them so fast.

I handed them each a half of a sandwich before we left the house, or I knew there was a possibility of hangry tantrums. Then, we were off. I didn't trust them at all in public. I knew them better than that.

While I'd always felt so sorry for children when I saw them in those leash contraptions, after dealing with Jaydan and Jonas in public, I understood the necessity.

Maria didn't use the leash system when she took them out, but they were her kids. If she lost one, they were hers to lose. If I lost one...well, I wasn't taking any chances. Plus, I kind of liked the little brats. I didn't want them getting into any danger.

The leashes weren't as awful as they sounded. They were little monkey shaped backpacks that clicked closed around their little tummies and I looped the ends of the animals' tails onto my wrist. So, technically, the animals were on leashes, not the kids. I still felt slightly awkward about the leashes and I hoped the boys didn't hold it against me when they were older. But, if they did, at least they'd be alive and well while they blamed me in therapy.

We walked down Bluefin Boulevard to Coral Road and then connected to Main Street. Another reason for the leashes, Main Street was sometimes busy enough that I wouldn't trust one of them not to dart out into traffic the moment the opportunity presented.

It was lunchtime and our little island was busy with locals and the tail end of the tourists for the season. We passed plenty of people we knew and made small talk before going on. Outside of Pete's Pets, the boys stopped to pet Pete's big dog, Blossom. We waved at Mann Family Dentistry because, even though Maria couldn't see us, the boys knew where Mommy worked. On the other side of the dentist office was Clotilde's Creamery.

Clotilde had passed years earlier, but her daughter, Cameron, ran the place just as well as her mother had. Clotilde's had a big statue of a cow on top of the building. It was rumored that Clotilde had grown up in Idaho before moving to the Keys and the cow had been modeled after her favorite cow from childhood. I thought all cows looked alike, but apparently the big cow on the roof was the spitting image of Moona Lisa.

Cameron was at the counter when we walked in, the bell over the door announcing our entrance. Despite the customers lined up, Cameron's eyes were drawn to us. "Hey, guys!"

Jayden and Jonas waved to her and pulled me to the counter so they could press their noses up against the glass of the ice cream display and look at all the flavors. They were lost in a world of potential when I felt the air shift around me with another ring of the bell. I looked over my shoulder and couldn't help but smile when Alexei walked in.

He grinned as he sidled up to me, not even bothering to hide his stalking. "I saw you walk in and couldn't stop myself from following."

"Some would consider that creepy."

He stepped closer to me as someone edged by us. "And you?"

I narrowed my eyes at him and fought another stupid smile. "I consider it concerning behavior. You should definitely be checked out."

He held his arms out to the side as though offering himself to me. "Go right ahead."

I laughed and rolled my eyes. I was saved from having to respond by a tug at my hand. I looked down at Jayden and found him watching Alexei. His big blue eyes were curious, the new man presenting an interesting puzzle. I knelt in front of him and held his little waist in my hands while pulling Jonas closer.

"This is Auntie Heidi's friend, Alexei. Have you decided what ice cream you want?"

Jonas nodded and pointed back at the display, not concerned about Alexei. "The pink one."

I grinned. "Good choice! The pink one looks delicious. It's strawberry. You want strawberry?"

Jayden tugged at my hand again and leaned in to whisper in my ear that he wanted the pink one, too. His eyes were still focused on Alexei.

Alexei squatted next to us, his powerful looking thighs stretching his jeans as he did. "Hi. I'm Alexei. I want the pink ice cream, too."

Jonas immediately went to Alexei and held out his arms to be picked up. "You big."

I laughed, surprised at him. There was something deeper than surprise, something warm and fuzzy at seeing Jonas in Alexei's arms, but I ignored it. "We don't tell people they're big, Jonas."

Jayden had watched silently, but suddenly, he wanted Alexei to hold him, too. I pursed my lips, not enjoying being an outcast in my own group. Alexei, wearing an ear to ear grin, easily picked up Jayden, too, holding each boy in a thickly muscled arm. His expression was one of victory.

I watched them for a second while he leaned them over the case, showing them the ice cream closer up. Part of me worried that Maria would be pissed about a stranger holding her boys, but for some stupid reason, I trusted Alexei. They weren't my kids, though.

As if she'd been reading my mind, Maria popped into the shop. She waved at Cameron and then came over to us. Her eyes raked over Alexei and then focused on me. I could tell she had something brewing behind those brown eyes and when she got closer, I could see it was mischief. "Hi, babies!"

Jayden and Jonas waved at their mother, still content to remain up high in Alexei's arms. I nervously tucked my hair behind my ears, feeling flustered at being caught out with her kids and a man that she didn't know. "Hey! We came to get ice cream and ran into a friend."

She wagged her eyebrows at me. "Uh huh."

Alexei extended a hand, despite having the kids wiggling in his arms. "I'm Alexei. You're their mother?"

Maria grinned. "I am. Maria. You must be the reason my best friend has been so mysterious lately? She's all daydreams and secret little smiles, but she won't breathe a word about why."

He met my eyes and a heated expression passed over his face. "I hope so. I've been trying my hardest."

I groaned while Maria floated away on some romantic cloud. *Lord have mercy.*

13

ALEXEI

Heidi was in a short sun dress that showed her long, smooth legs. The dress was yellow with little white flowers all over it. The swells of her breasts were showing just slightly over the scooping neckline of the dress. Her toes were painted a seashell pink and her fingernails matched. Her thick, wavy caramel colored hair was tied in a ponytail and everything about her made me think thoughts and feel feelings I had no business thinking and feeling while holding two innocent little boys in my arms.

Spotting her had been a happy accident. I'd been grabbing lunch for the team, but after seeing Heidi slip into the ice cream shop, I'd quickly decided it wouldn't hurt them to go without a meal. Watching her interact with the two little boys had been an extra perk. She was sexy as hell, and so beautiful that she stole my breath. Observing her motherly interactions with the children stole my heart.

Fuck, I sounded like a teen romance, but there it was. Heart stolen. It was the moment that I *knew*—without a doubt I knew. She was my mate. My bear had been in love with her since day one, minute one. I supposed it took me longer because I couldn't believe that it'd been so easy to find her. There was no arguing it, though.

Standing in that ice cream shop, I knew it just as well as I knew my name. She was the one.

Maria cleared her throat and I realized I was standing there staring at Heidi amidst an awkward silence. Maria broke the silence. "I've got to get back to work. I just ran over because I saw you walk past the dental office with my little guys."

Heidi pulled her friend a few steps away, her eyes still on me. She whispered something privately, but I was a shifter. I had amazing hearing. "I'm sorry, Maria. I didn't plan this. If you're uncomfortable with the boys being around someone you don't know, I'll tell him to go."

Maria scoffed. "You act like I don't trust you. Those are practically your kids, too, Heidi. Judging by the way you look at him, you like him. So, I do too."

Heidi's cheeks tinged pink, but she just rolled her eyes and waved her friend off. "Want me to get something for you while I'm out?"

"Would you? I had a couple of people schedule for this afternoon, so I won't be home for a little while."

The little boys wiggled in my arms and one of them tugged at my hair. "Ice cream?"

I grinned at him. "I get it. It's hard to wait while the grownups stand around talking, isn't it?"

Heidi came back to my side and glanced back at Maria. She mouthed something and then looked up at me, face red still. "Sorry about that. I just had to ask her something."

I looked down at her, impressed with the way she put the kids first. Cocky, or not, I thought she wanted to see me. Yet, she was willing to send me away if Maria was uncomfortable with a random man hanging out with her kids.

"Ice cream!"

She cocked her head to the side and gave the screaming boy a look that said she disapproved. "We don't scream for things we want."

He pouted at her and big tears welled up in his eyes. "Ice cream."

"Remember the magic word? Can you say please?" When the

little ones both said please, she smiled, her face lighting up. "That's better. Now, we're still all getting pink?"

"So *that's* the magic word! I've been wracking my brain for the right word to get you to go out with me." I winked at her and laughed when she gave me an exasperated look.

It felt strange to be standing there, two kids in my arms, waiting on my mate to order our ice cream. And by strange, I meant wonderful. It wasn't hard to look at her and imagine a future with more of this in it. I liked Sunkissed Key. It was hot, yeah, but I could deal. Heidi and I could buy our own house here and start a family of our own. I liked the idea of it. Matter of fact, I loved the idea.

"I'll pay. Just grab my wallet." I turned so she could see my wallet in my back pocket.

"Nice try. I'll pay." She did just that, chatting with the woman at the register one minute, holding four cones stacked high with ice cream, the next. "Come on, guys. We can eat outside."

The boys were suddenly wild animals in my arms. Shrieking and wiggling to get free and run. The slippery little guys were like greased piglets. I held on, ending up with my arms around their waists, holding them parallel to the ground. They let loose laugh-like squeals that I wasn't sure was good until Heidi turned and laughed with them.

I held onto them for dear life until we got outside and I managed to put the boys on their feet. Heidi still had them by their…leashes? I made a face. "Are they on leashes?"

She handed them their cones and nodded. "I'm not losing them. They're like little magicians who can vanish with the snap of their little fingers. I'm not chancing anything in public."

I held our cones as she settled them into a chair together, right up next to her. She even tied the ends of their leashes to her arm before reaching for her ice cream.

"So, this is your day job?"

She nodded. "Yeah. I babysit and help Maria around her house during the day. Then, I bartend at night."

"You're busy." I licked the tip of my ice cream and nearly groaned when her heated eyes followed the motion.

Instead of replying, she just nodded and looked away. Then, she licked her cone, completely unaware of the torture she was putting me through. Her tongue stroked the cone in ways that my mind would not ever forget. I adjusted myself in my chair and forced my eyes away.

"Oh, crap."

I looked over and saw that she'd gotten ice cream all down her hand somehow. She passed me the leashes and stood up. "I'm getting napkins. Are you okay with them for a second?"

I nodded and looked at the boys. "We're good, right guys?"

They ignored me, the ice cream was far more captivating. I held their leashes and watched Heidi walk inside, a big smile on her face. She'd just grabbed a stack of napkins and turned to head back out when a woman stepped up to her and said something that made the joyful expression on Heidi's face drop like a lead balloon. The woman's expression was a snarl of disgust and anger and she poked her index finger into Heidi's chest as she spoke.

It was over in seconds, and Heidi returned with the napkins, her eyes misty. Her smile was gone and she looked flustered with her face red and her mouth pinched tightly.

"You okay?" I didn't realize I was standing until the boys cried out. I was pulling their kid-leashes too tightly.

She nodded and took the leashes from me. "We're going to go home. Come on, Jayden, Jonas. You can eat your ice cream on the walk home."

"Hold on, Heidi. Talk to me. What happened?" My stomach was in my throat and I wasn't sure what to do to help.

"It's nothing. See you later." And then she was leaving, rushing the kids off with trembling hands.

14

ALEXEI

Unable to let her leave like that, I went after her. I caught her arm and pulled her to a stop. When I saw that she was crying, I felt my bear rage inside me. "Come on. My office is right down here."

She let me scoop the boys up and pull her with me. Her hand gripped mine tightly and I could hear her heart racing. We were passing the ice cream shop again when the same woman who'd upset her initially stepped out and scowled. Heidi froze.

"Is that someone else's husband you've got your hooks into? Shame on you!" The woman's voice was harsh and cruel, her eyes just as condescending.

I put myself between the two woman and looked down at Heidi. "Come on, Heidi."

She shook her head. "We've really got to get home. I have something to do that I just remembered."

I felt my blood boil as she took the boys from me, a distressed look on her face. Before I had a chance to argue, she was rushing away, a child in each arm, sticky little hands in her hair, and ice cream dripping down one of the boy's cones and onto her shoulder.

Spinning around to face the woman who'd hurt my mate, I found her staring after Heidi with a vicious scowl on her face. I didn't like to yell at woman. I didn't like to hurt women. Of course, in my line of work, there were exceptions. I'd dealt with women who could make Osama Bin Laden look like Mickey Mouse. With the sour woman before me, I was sorely tempted to snatch her up by her ankles and shake her.

"Who are you?" My voice was barely more than a growl and when the offending woman heard it, she stepped back.

"It doesn't matter who I am." She shook her head but took another step back concerned for her safety. "Are you married?"

I frowned, confused by the woman's obsession with marriage. "Of course not! What's your deal, lady? What do you just go around spewing vitriol and hurting people?"

"Me? ME? Don't you know who she is? She's the one who hurts people. A shameless hussy who breaks up marriages with her selfishness."

It was my turn to step back. The venom coming out of the woman was overwhelming. "What are you talking about?"

"That's Heidi Garcia from *Love In An Instant*. The TV show?" She rolled her eyes. "She was on the first season that came out. She's a monster. She slept with people's boyfriends, just to cause trouble. Her motto was something about being a slut and proud of it and she certainly showed the world her true colors. A complete trollop."

I saw red and stepped closer to her. I lowered my voice and growled at her. "Watch your mouth. You're behaving this way because of something you saw in a TV show? You're the one who should be ashamed of yourself. I would say that you're lucky you're a lady, but I think we both know that you're no lady. So, I'll say you're lucky I'm a gentleman."

She blanched, her anger instantly replaced by fear. When I growled again for good measure, she whimpered and scurried away.

I shook my head and ran my hands through my hair. I wasn't proud to have threatened her, but what the fuck? She'd just verbally attacked my mate for something on a TV show?

I made my way back to the near-empty office and was glad to see Hannah inside. I dropped into the chair in front of her and sighed.

"Whoa. What's up, Alexei? I don't think I've ever seen you frown before."

Megan's head popped out from the back office. She looked at me and her eyes widened. Kerrigan's head popped out right below Megan's. She slapped her hand over her chest and hurried out. "Oh, my gosh! What's wrong, Alexei?"

Their mates, Serge, Roman, and Dmitry, stepped into the main office, their faces masks of confusion, too. Serge shook his head, like he was trying to clear it. "What happened to you?"

"You guys ever heard of a show called *Love In An Instant*?"

Hannah nodded. "Yeah, why?"

"I met someone from it, I guess." I hesitated. "What is it?"

Dmitry mock saluted. "I'm out of here. I'm going back to work."

Roman settled next to his mate. "I've got nothing better to do."

"This isn't important, then?" Serge held up his hands when I growled at him. "I meant *work* important. It's not *work*-related, then?"

Hannah shushed her mate and turned back to me. "It's a reality dating show. The biggest one on TV. They put together groups of people to see what happens and film it, basically. I mean, they pair you up with someone based on some kind of test you take, but then it's kind of this free for all. They try to pretend like it's this love at first sight thing, but it's just a ploy to watch people fool around and make asses of themselves. I mean, no one ever sticks with the person they're matched with.

"Who'd you meet from it?"

I frowned, not understanding most of what she said. My brain was trying to relate it to Heidi and what I knew about her but it wasn't computing. "Heidi Garcia."

Hannah's mouth fell open. "Holy shit."

"What?"

"Even I know this part." Megan shook her head and moved nearer to Roman who pulled her into his lap. She let out a startled, "Oof," but didn't lose focus on the conversation. "That poor girl."

I sat up straight and felt my bear fighting to get loose. He wanted to fight for his mate. "Tell me."

"The show has this cult-like following. There are so many people who think it's real and they are obsessed with it. Well, Heidi was the villain on her season. I don't know how much was real and how much was staged for dramatic effect, but to say she was not nice to the other women on the show would be a huge understatement."

Hannah nodded. "I mean, like Megan said, who knows if it was real, but if it wasn't, that's even more messed up. She was painted as a complete evil bitch."

"Well, yeah." Megan made a face. "When that one couple that everyone loved, Aaron and Ashley, were about to get engaged and they were the sweethearts of prime time TV, she was caught in bed with Aaron."

"I read something on Yahoo News a while back. A 'where are they now' type of thing. No info on Heidi. Apparently, or so the article stated, she was so hated after the show that she couldn't get any other work. She actually received death threats and just kind of vanished."

I stood up and slammed my hand down on the desk in front of me. "It's all bullshit. She's sweet and kind. When we were getting ice cream, she was confronted by some woman whose face looked like she'd just been sucking lemons. Heidi turned away, nearly in tears."

Roman growled at me, but it was just a warning to not yell at his mate. Megan patted Roman on the chest to placate him and gave me a warm smile. "Sorry, Alexei. Is she..."

"She's my mate." I stood straighter when I said it, filled with pride. No matter what they said, I knew what kind of person Heidi was. "And she's not an evil bitch. Not by a long shot."

Hannah smiled. "Well, she is gorgeous, I'll say that. She reminds me of, whose that actress from the show *Empire*?"

Megan nodded. "Nicole Ari Parker! She has the same coloring and they're both rare beauties."

"Yes! Nicole Ari Parker. I feel bad for Heidi. Even if she had been that person in the past, it doesn't give anyone the right to attack her. Everyone has a past."

I raked my hands through my hair and crossed my arms over my chest. "I don't like seeing her upset."

Roman grunted. "Welcome to the club, brother. Get ready to suffer for a while. Until it sorts itself out, anyway."

15

HEIDI

Work was hard that night. I wanted to call off and hide out at home, but there was no one who could cover my shift and I wasn't going to leave Mimi with the whole bar by herself. I was in a terrible mood though. I knew that I wasn't making anyone's night with my saltiness. I just couldn't shake my mood. Hearing that woman insult me so thoroughly at Clotilde's had thrown me. It hit me harder than normal because I was there with Alexei and the boys. They could've overheard the vile things she'd said about me.

It wasn't fair. I wanted to scream back at everyone who taunted me and reminded me of that stupid show. I'd done that in the beginning—flipped out and told them how I felt, but I'd since learned. It never changed anything. No one cared about the truth. They had their opinion and that was that. I could scream until I was blue in the face about how it was a fake TV show, how we were all following prompts and director's cues and everything was staged to make for good television, but they'd never believe me. My name was tainted. I was labeled a whore and a homewrecker. The Cuban slut, people called me. And, hell, they knew all about it, or so they thought, since they'd seen it with their own eyes.

If I knew when I'd signed on what that show would end up doing to my life, I would've run as fast as humanly possible to get away. I'd just seen it as a way to jump start my fledgling acting career. I thought that if I did the show, I could get an agent and, subsequently, some better gigs. Little did I know, I'd never get a call back again. I was branded by the character I played—a nasty, bitchy troublemaker. I would have accepted being typecast as a villain, but it was worse. Producers and casting directors assumed that I really was a difficult person, like the character, and that I'd be hell to work with. No one would come within a hundred yards of me.

At the end of the day, the missed career opportunity was fine. I was happy being a small-town girl in the Florida Keys—a bartender and babysitter. It was the harassment and judgement from fans of the show that I couldn't handle. And it would usually pop up from out of left field, like the woman in the ice cream shop.

I'd never actually slept with anyone from that show. I hadn't done any of the things I was continually accused of. I was just a foolish kid who'd mistakenly thought people wouldn't actually believe that reality TV was, well, reality.

My stomach ached from knowing that Alexei was going to hear those things sooner or later, and that he'd already heard some of them. I knew that I had no business worrying about what he thought of me. I had no intention of developing any type of relationship with him beyond a very casual friendship. I couldn't. That was how it had to be and that was *fine*. Everything was fine.

"Are you with me, Heidi?"

I snapped out of my trance, and turned to Sarah. "Sorry, what'd you need?"

She called out her order again and frowned. "You okay, girl?"

I nodded and started working on the drinks. I wasn't up to my usual self, but I was still faster than most bartenders. When I handed the drinks over to her, she was still frowning. "I'm good."

She looked away and then grinned. "Hottie's back for you."

I knew it was Alexei before I even looked. Sure enough, he was leaning against the end of the bar, looking every bit as handsome as I was trying to forget he was. He made it impossible.

The bar wasn't packed, but it was busy enough that I had to stop and pour drinks twice before I reached him. I was nervous. I'd left abruptly earlier and I was embarrassed. Who knew what he thought of me?

I had to remind myself that I wasn't supposed to care.

"Hey." He leaned towards me, his face drawn into a tight smile. It looked like he'd combed his hair. It was neatly brushed back from his face, a contrast to the shadow of stubble on his face that hadn't been touched. He was in a button-down shirt, jeans, and work boots. He looked like he'd just come off a modeling shoot and I loved it.

I swallowed an excessive amount of drool and reminded myself once again that nothing was allowed to happen between the two of us. "Hi."

He leaned even farther across the bar and his hand came up to gently brush a strand of hair out of my face. "Did I mention earlier that that dress is killer on you?"

I wanted to turn my face into his hand, but I resisted and he pulled it back into his own space. "You don't give up."

"Never." He rested his elbows on the bar and his smile was just as tight as ever. "You okay?"

I shrugged. "I'm fine."

"You don't look fine. You look like you could use a drink yourself."

I saw a hand go out with an empty glass down at the other end of the bar and nodded at it. "Sorry, I have to work."

It went like that for about an hour. He nursed the one beer he'd ordered and tried to talk to me between customers. He seemed genuinely worried about me and it was hard to face.

"What's a guy gotta do to get some attention around here?" Alexei grinned at me over his beer, the look on his face more determined than happy. "I mean, I dressed up for you."

I took his warm beer from him and gave him a cold one. "Is that all for me?"

He unbuttoned another button on his shirt then gave me a sexy, exaggerated pout like he was on the cover of GQ or something and winked. "This better?"

I rolled my eyes. "You can't possibly like this."

"Being ignored by the prettiest woman in the bar while I make a fool of myself to make her smile? What's not to like about that?"

"I'm fine, Alexei. Go home."

"Not without getting a genuine smile from you."

"Look, I've had a shit day. It's not a big deal. People have them."

"I know people have them, but I don't like that *you're* having one. I don't care about anyone else."

I stopped mid-pour of a tequila shot. Looking up at him, I couldn't help tilting my head to the side and trying to see him clearer. Had he just implied that he cared about me? Naw. He didn't know me.

"I'm not giving up. I'll dance on this damn bar if I have to."

"You can't dance on the bar."

"I can."

"It's against the rules."

"Do I look like I follow rules?"

I sighed. "Alexei, you don't have to worry about me."

He stood up and grabbed the edge of the bar. "You're really gonna make me do this?"

"You're not getting up there."

"Watch me."

16

ALEXEI

Heidi slapped her hands over her eyes when I swung up onto the bar and stood to my full height. I knocked my head on the ceiling, and a few colorful toothpicks fell off, but that didn't stop me. I wasn't going to stop until she smiled and I saw the pain in her eyes fade. If I knew one thing, it was that she didn't deserve her suffering and I'd do everything in my power to take it from her. That was two things, but I knew them both.

"Turn up the music!" I'd never danced on a bar before. But, hey, I'd try almost anything once.

Someone obliged and as the music got louder there was chanting and clapping as well as a few hoots and hollers. I ignored the hands waving dollar bills in the air. With plenty of eyes on me and nothing to do but entertain, I did just that. I moved to the music as best as I could, but I was a fucking bear shifter. Dancing wasn't in my DNA.

"Don't avert your eyes, Heidi. This is all for you!" I swung my hips and accidentally kicked someone's beer off the bar. "Sorry, man."

Heidi looked up at me, her hands cupped on either side of her face, like she wasn't sure what to do. "Get down! You're going to get kicked out!"

I unbuttoned a few more buttons. "What did you say? You want to see more skin?! Why, Heidi! I'm shocked!"

She shook her head and turned her back to me. "I'm not watching this!"

I unbuttoned the rest of the shirt and laughed when she looked over her shoulder and through her fingers at me before turning away again. "I'm not stopping until you smile."

She swung around and flashed her teeth at me. "There. Now, get down."

"Oh, but that wasn't a genuine smile. Nice try, though. I guess I'll just have to lose the pants."

She turned to face me, a real smile twisting her lips. "You're such an idiot."

I grinned back at her. "And you're the most amazing woman I've ever met."

"Come down from there."

I hopped off, onto her side of the bar, and smiled down at her. I was probably standing too close, pushing too hard. "You're beautiful."

"You're crazy." She hesitated, looked around, and then met my eyes. "Sometimes, you have to let people feel how they feel. Even if it isn't what you want."

I bit my lip and took a step back. "You're right. I apologize."

She shocked me by stepping into my space. "This wasn't one of those times."

"Heidi…"

She took my hand and stepped around me, pulling me after her. Through a swinging door, away from the bar, down a hallway, and into a small room with a desk and a chair that was missing a wheel. She pushed me until my back hit the wall behind me and then she moved closer, until she was a breath away.

I grabbed her waist and pulled her the rest of the way into my body. She fit just right against me, her curves soft and tempting. I stared down into her eyes, looking for any sign that she was opposed to what we were doing. There was nothing but fevered heat staring back at me, though.

I don't know who kissed who first. We both moved and then our mouths were sliding together and her taste was exploding on my mouth like a professional firework show. Her mouth was soft and hungry against mine. Her hands were on my face, holding me while our tongues entwined.

I wrapped my arms around her, pulling her tighter against me, and kissed her deeper. She even tasted sugary sweet. I moaned when she took my bottom lip between her teeth and nipped.

The kiss was intense and powerful. The only thing I was sure of in that moment was wanting more of her. Her fingers ran through my hair, grasping it, pulling me closer. I slipped my hands down over her ass and easily lifted her up against my body. Her thighs locked around my waist so our bodies pressed up flush against one another from shoulders to hips.

Her ass was firm in my hands, the rounded cheeks filling my palms perfectly. When I flexed my fingers, squeezing, her kiss grew wilder, and she moaned into my mouth.

I ran a hand up her back and gripped the back of her neck, holding her steady and moving us over until she was laid out on the desk and I was standing between her thighs. She opened her legs wider and I gripped them harder than I had to, but I had never been so turned on. Her skin was soft and silky, and it drove me insane. All of her drove me insane. I wanted to touch and taste every inch of her a million times over.

Heidi dragged my mouth back to hers, and I closed the gap that her thighs had made for me, feeling her heat through my jeans as I rocked my erection against her.

Her nails dug into my shoulders and she locked her ankles behind my lower back. Her mouth open, breathing heavily, she met my eyes with a half-lidded, needy gaze.

Holding eye contact, watching every nuance of her expression, I rocked my hips into her again and again until I knew the rhythm she wanted. Then, I gripped the back of her neck once more and held onto her hip with my free hand and rolled my hips against her while pressing my forehead to hers and breathing through gritted teeth.

Heidi in the throes of passion was the most erotic thing I'd ever seen. She wanted me. Her body was desperate for me. And the sentiment was mutual—I wanted her just as badly.

Heidi held onto me tighter as her small moans became higher pitched and breathier. Suddenly, she clenched her thighs tighter around me and her nails dug into my back. Her neck tensed under my hand and her body arched into me like a longbow. Her head dropped to my shoulder and her teeth clamped down on my shoulder as a muffled cry sounded.

As I felt her orgasm rock through her, I gripped her tighter, feeling my own release too close. I wasn't about to come in my pants and embarrass myself like a teenager. I squeezed my eyes shut and inhaled deeply. The scent of my mate's arousal was one I never wanted to forget.

"Hey, Hei—" A woman's voice abruptly cut off and a giggle followed. "Sorry! Never mind! Didn't see a thing!"

Heidi pulled back and covered her face with her hands. "Shit."

I pulled her hands away and kissed her, feeling her shiver against me. "I'm not done with you."

17

HEIDI

I slept better that night than I had since meeting Alexei. I felt like all the tension in my body had drained away and I was finally feeling at ease. At least, my body was. My brain was in a bit of a tailspin, but it wasn't enough to keep me up.

I got to the beach bright and early that next morning, fishing pole in one hand, tackle box in the other. I hadn't had my usual fresh fish dinner in a few days and I wanted some kind of normalcy back in my life. I'd already caught my dinner by the time Houdini showed up.

I should have been pissed at Mr. Zoo for being so goddamned lax that an almost 900 pound bear was able to repeatedly slip out of his supposedly secure sanctuary. But I was too excited to see my bear to be angry. I hurried down to the beach and he knocked me back on my ass in the sand and then covered my face in sloppy kisses. I laughed and gently pushed his huge face away. It went on like that for a few minutes. He was so excited to see me that he rubbed against me until he settled down beside me. Then, I wrapped my arm around him, as much as I could, and I leaned into him.

I talked to him more than I talked to anyone else. It was super weird, but there wasn't much about the entire situation that wasn't crazy, so why not just go for it? He listened. That was the kicker. The damn polar bear listened better than a best friend. He watched me as I spoke and seemed to reply with his little sounds when appropriate. I should've been more worried that I'd lost mind, probably.

That morning, I told him all about Alexei. I told him about the mean woman and then Alexei doing everything he could to cheer me up, including dancing on the bar and pretending he was going to strip. I couldn't remember anyone ever trying so hard for me—or caring like that. Finally, I told him about kissing Alexei. The kissing that had turned quickly to dry humping and then an earth-shaker of an orgasm. I left the orgasm part out, slightly red faced as I thought about it.

"And then Sarah walked in on us. Of course, she was like a dog with a bone during closing. She wanted to know everything." I sighed. "There's nothing to know, though. I don't know anything about Alexei. I mean, I know that he's funny and hot, and I know that he seems like a nice guy. I don't know anything else, though."

I grinned when Houdini put his big paw on my back and patted me. The things he'd learned in whatever circus he'd been rescued from were amazing. It was almost like sitting next to a person the way he responded and interacted.

"Thanks." I reached up to scratch his ear. "I'm just freaked out, I guess. I've been alone for so long that I've gotten used to it being that way. It's not easy to learn to trust someone. I don't know his motives. I don't know anything. And who's to say he won't be like every other man. It's not easy to have random people pop up and proclaim that the woman you're dating is a slut. It doesn't matter that I'm not. It can get to a person over time. Especially a man.

"I don't know if I have it in me to open myself up to more pain. And Alexei would be a hard man to not miss if he ran."

I hugged my knees and watched as a seagull landed close by, spotted Houdini, and then freaked out before flying off. Houdini huffed next to me and got to his feet. He paced back and forth in front of me, his head raising to let out little growls every so often. If I didn't know better, I'd have said it looked like he was trying to lecture me.

"It looks like we're both stuck in our feelings this morning."

He looked at me and actually rolled his eyes. Then, like he was tired of me, he strolled away, towards the sanctuary.

"Hey!" I got up and hurried after him. "What are you doing?"

He just trotted along until he got to the wildlife sanctuary's back gate and then he used his head to crudely knock on it himself. I just stood there, mouth open, and watched as he disappeared inside the gate and it shut in my face.

I stood there for a few seconds, unsure of what had just happened. Well, it did make sense in a way that he'd know his way back. And maybe he was hungry or something. Or maybe he was sick of hearing me complain about my complicated love life.

I strolled slowly back to the beach to get my fishing gear. I was still lost in my thoughts when the sound of footsteps approaching dragged me back to the present. I looked up and spotted Alexei jogging towards me. My mouth dropped open.

He was in nothing but a pair of low slung swim trunks, and holy mother of god, his hair was wet and wild; his body dripped water as he advanced. Muscles flexed and worked as he ran, all of them jaw-dropping.

"Close your mouth or you'll catch flies." He grinned and stopped in my space. He cupped my face and leaned down. His eyes flicked to my mouth and then back up. "Hi."

I swallowed, my brain needed the second of time to try to catch up. "You're wet."

He laughed. "Yeah, I am."

"You don't have many clothes on."

"Want to even the playing field?"

I rolled my eyes and stepped back, his joke giving me the chance to snap back to myself. "You're a smartass."

"And you're a goddess. Let me take you to breakfast?"

"I have work. Besides you're nearly naked. I know the dress code is pretty lax around the island, but what you're wearing—or not wearing—might be pushing it."

"Lunch then. I'll wear more clothes, promise." He wagged his brows. "Though, are you sure you want me to?"

Laughing, I looked up at him, trying to see through the exterior to what he really wanted underneath. I was nervous. It was easy to forget reality when he was in front of me, but it was still there. I felt as though I liked him, despite not knowing him. It scared me to think about how I would feel if I got to know him and it turned out disastrously. What if I liked him too much and he wanted nothing else to do with me?

Like he could read my mind, he caught my hands in his and smiled gently. "Just lunch. We can talk, get to know each other. We'll take a step back from last night. I'm good with that."

I licked my lips, still nervous, but nodded. I couldn't help it. I did want to know more. "Okay. I can meet you at one o'clock."

"Bayfront Diner okay with you?"

I nodded. Looking up at him, I felt something so familiar in his eyes, the way he watched so patiently. Nodding my head, I backed away. "See you at one."

He smiled and watched me go. "I could walk you home."

"Don't press your luck."

He laughed. "See you at one."

18

ALEXEI

Part of me felt guilty for using the things Heidi told me to get her to open up to me, but I had the best intentions. She was my mate and I wanted to be with her. I wanted her to learn that she could trust me. The end would justify the means.

She sat across from me at the diner, eyes cautious but curious as they flitted between me and the menu. She'd changed into another dress, a white one. The neckline was higher, but her shoulders were mostly bare and I found I was attracted by any skin she showed.

It must have been Kerrigan's day off since Susie popped up next to us, her expression revealing her own curiosity. "Well, well. It's been a minute since you've come by, Alexei."

The older woman patted my hand and smiled. "I've been busy with work, or you know I'd stop in more often."

She turned her eyes on Heidi. "And you, missy. You don't come by nearly enough. I can see your house from the front window. Yet, you never stop in and say hello."

"Oh, Susie, I'm sorry. I don't eat out much anymore." She grinned at the older woman. "Besides, you know I had an issue with your cooking. I couldn't stop eating it. Pretty sure I gained ten pounds from your cinnamon rolls alone."

Susie wagged her finger. "Well, it looks like you could use some. Put a little more meat on those bones."

Heidi laughed, a full laugh that drew the attention of people around us. It was infectious. "That's funny. You're a real hoot."

"Uh huh. Anyway. Sweet tea for both of you?" When we nodded, she walked off, just to come right back with a basket of cinnamon rolls. "Eat up."

I grinned at Heidi and then laughed when she stared hungrily at the rolls. "I didn't mean for you to have some kind of pastry crisis over lunch."

She sighed heavily and met my eyes. "I love these things more than almost anything in the world. It's a downward spiral, though."

"I'm sure you were still stunning with ten pounds of pastry weight."

"You have to say that. You're trying to get into my pants." She hesitated. "At least I think that's what you're trying to do."

"Amongst other things."

"What are the other things? Cue me in on the plan."

I leaned into her and plucked out a roll. "You'd think I was crazy."

"Try me."

"I'm not looking for a hook up. Not anymore." I took a bite of the roll and licked my lips. "I want more. In fact I'd like to see you with ten extra pounds of weight provided I was the one with you on all the dates where you ate enough to gain that much."

Her eyes went wide and she sank back in the booth. "You're not being serious."

I nodded. "I am."

"You don't even know me."

"I know enough." I shrugged. "Well, I don't know enough. I want to know more. There's a reason I keep showing up. I want to know you. I want you to know me."

"I don't date."

"Because of the cinnamon roll thing?"

She laughed suddenly, her face lighting up and the worry lines around her eyes fading. "No, not because of that. Because of...other stuff."

"A husband? Kids? You're actually a serial killer and afraid a relationship might blow your cover?"

"You're a smartass." She was still smiling, though. "Mostly because of stuff like that what happened with that woman at Clotilde's Creamery."

"You don't date because random psychos might come up and harass you? To be fair, I think having me next to you with a big snarl on my face would go a long way towards preventing those types of encounters. I do a mean growl, too."

"Alexei—"

I snarled and let out a loud growl. When half the diners turned to stare, I crossed my eyes and made a crazy face at them. "See? No one would fuck with you with me next to you, looking like this."

She laughed again and hid behind her menu. "You're nuts, you know? You're the strangest person."

"I'm not the one with a pastry problem." I leaned over the table and caught her hand. "I'm serious, though. I'm not into hooking up and running away. I'm not going anywhere, Heidi, not unless you really want me to."

She looked away for a second, a serious look settling over her face. When she met my gaze again, her expression was determined. "I don't date."

"Fine. You win. We won't date. We'll hang out until you decide you want more." I felt my body heat as she licked her lips. "We'll have to discuss whether we're doing a just friends or a friends with benefits thing though."

Her cheeks burned. "You're stubborn."

"I like you. There's something here and I'm not going to just turn away as though you aren't worth fighting for."

Susie came back over and took our orders, silently pushing the rolls closer to Heidi the whole time. By the time she left, the rolls were practically in Heidi's lap.

"Why?"

I raised my eyebrows at Heidi. "Why what?"

"Why are you so interested in me?"

"Some things are bigger than us. Fate, for one."

"And you think this is..." she gestured back and forth between us, "*fate?*"

I shrugged. "Something like that."

19

HEIDI

I was floating on a weird high that night at the bar. I couldn't stop thinking about everything Alexei had said. He thought we were supposed to be together—like through the guiding hand of fate or something. That sentiment was strangely romantic for a man. I liked it. It still scared me a little to fall for him only to have my past turn out to be too much for him in the end. But, I kind of knew what he was saying. I had this strange feeling like we were connected, too. I felt something so familiar when I looked at him.

It made it hard not to want to throw out every conviction I had about remaining single. Alexei made me feel hopeful, like maybe things could be different. Hell, one afternoon spent with him and I was having trouble not imagining waking up next to him every day.

I was excited, but scared. I couldn't help feeling giddy and eager for what was going to happen next, but I had made myself into a pessimist over the past decade. That didn't vanish with a little attention from a hot guy. Something had to be wrong with the picture. Right?

I didn't know. I was confused.

The bar was busy and I'd been working for a few hours already.

Alexei had already told me he had to work and wouldn't be able to stop in that night. Yet, I found myself still looking for him.

Stupid? Yep. Could I help it? Nope.

Lord, I had it bad.

When the three women settled at the bar, I felt a shiver of unease as their eyes raked over me. It wasn't so much judgement as it was curiosity on their part. I knew that they recognized me, though. More than from just around town. And, if I wasn't mistaken, I recognized one. She had owned a photography shop at the end of the island. The place had been leveled by the hurricane.

I put a smile on my face, despite feeling like I was walking into a trap. "Hey, what can I get you ladies?"

The one I recognized smiled brightly at me and stuck out her hand. "Hi. I'm Megan."

Another chimed in. "I'm Hannah. And this is Kerrigan. We're friends of Alexei."

After I'd shaken their hands, I just kind of stepped back and looked at them. I didn't know what to expect. Did they just want to meet me or were they there to warn me away from their so-called friend? Also, why did Alexei have so many female friends?

"We're all mates to other guys in P.O.L.A.R.—his task force." Hannah shrugged. "I doubt you've met any of the guys yet, though."

I shook my head. "Um, nope."

"You have no clue what we're talking about, do you?" Megan laughed lightly. "Alexei hasn't mentioned us? Or, maybe you two haven't had much time to talk." She waggled her eyebrows.

I bristled. *Here come the slut slurs.*

"I just mean that it's a mate thing. It's not uncommon to meet, screw like rabbits, and save the conversations for later." Megan nodded to the other women. "We've all been there."

I stared at her. What the hell was she talking about?

Kerrigan nodded. "She's not wrong."

"The joys of being mated to polar bear shifters." Hannah smiled a secret little smile.

My head snapped back like she'd slapped me. What the fuck were they talking about? Polar... I thought of Houdini. Was that a coincidence?

"What's wrong?" Megan's face wrinkled in concern. "Are you okay?"

"What are you all talking about?" I gripped the bar top and shook my head. "Why did you say 'polar bear'?"

Their faces all blanched at once. Kerrigan's eyes seemed to grow even larger behind her thick glasses. Megan's jaw dropped and Hannah gasped. It was Megan who spoke, though. "We... You don't know any of this, do you?"

"Any of what? What about polar bears?"

"Shit." Megan looked at the women on either side of her and muttered another curse. "I'm so sorry. We just assumed... Alexei has been spending so much time with you and he's even happier than normal. We just thought the two of you had already mated..."

I had a second to try to digest what she'd said before Hannah piped up. "We shouldn't have come. We shouldn't have said anything."

"He's going to kill us." Kerrigan groaned. "And he'll have every right to. I'm sorry, too. It wasn't our place to tell you."

"Tell me what?" I was getting pissed, feeling like I was the outsider in an insider's club.

"Alexei will tell you everything."

I stepped closer to them. "The three of you need to spill. You've already started, no way I'm letting you walk out of here without an explanation. I especially want to know why you mentioned polar bears."

Megan groaned. "Promise you won't be mad at him? He would've told you himself if we hadn't opened our big mouths."

I couldn't promise that. I was already upset and I hadn't even heard them out yet. I had a feeling I was going to be royally pissed at Alexei once I had.

I waved Mimi over and told her I needed to take my break immediately. She covered the bar while I went to a table in the back with the three women. All of them looked stressed and were casing the exits as though they might just decide to make a run for it instead. They didn't, though. I motioned for them to be seated, and when they were, I took a chair facing the three of them.

I eyed them sternly. "Spill."

"We didn't come to ruin anything between you two. We're not like that, honest. We just wanted to meet you. Alexei has been over the moon and he mentioned it was you he'd been spending time with, so we wanted to..."

"You wanted to see if I was really the bitchy, homewrecking whore from TV? I know you know who I am. I saw it all over your faces when you walked in."

Megan raised her hands in protest. "No! Alexei is a great guy and he wouldn't have a mate like that. Really." She looked at the other two as if wanting one of them to interject, but neither said anything. "We just wanted to welcome you to the fold, so to speak."

"The fold?" I frowned. "Fine. Explain all of this to me, though. The polar bear talk. There's been a polar bear running loose on South Beach. I've returned him the Sunkissed Wildlife Sanctuary several times now and he keeps getting loose again. I'm suddenly pretty damned sure that it's no coincidence that you three happened to bring up a polar bear. Is this about him?"

Hannah winced. "Um...okay, unless there is something really crazy happening on this island, that polar bear is Alexei."

I leaned back in my chair and sighed. "Is this some kind of prank? You all think it's funny to come in and mess with me?"

"No! No. It's nothing like that. Our mates, our men, are shapeshifters. I know it sounds crazy, but they have the ability to transform into polar bears. All of them. So, the polar bear you've encountered on South Beach? Probably Alexei."

"That's ridiculous."

"I thought so, too. Until I saw my mate, Roman, shift before my very eyes." Megan leaned forward and placed her hand over mine. "I'm sorry we jumped the gun and came in here before giving Alexei a chance to tell you himself. We weren't trying to judge you or ruin things between you and Alexei, I promise. We were just excited to meet you."

"And maybe we did want to make sure you were a nice person. We're sorry for that, too." Kerrigan smiled sheepishly.

Hannah took my other hand. "Alexei told us that you weren't like the character you played on *Love In An Instant*. And we totally believe him. We're not stupid enough to think reality TV isn't staged for dramatic effect."

I felt nauseous. "People don't shift into animals. You three are pulling my leg. I mean, you all seemed so normal and then you opened your mouths and…" But their faces told me they were dead serious and even a little regretful. "I think I'm going to throw up."

"We could prove it. We could have one of our mates shift for you and show you." Kerrigan scooted closed, not at all concerned that I might vomit on her. "I feel like your mate is the first person you should see shift, though."

I stood up, having had enough. "Don't say anything to him about you coming here."

"Not a problem." Megan groaned. "He's going to kill all three of us."

"I'm not saying I believe you, but I can't do this right now. I can't listen to this." I held up my hands when they tried to talk. "I'm sorry. Please just leave. Please."

I didn't wait to see if they'd leave. I just went to the back and hid in the employee bathroom. I bent over and braced my hands on my knees, completely thrown off by what had just happened. I'd have laughed at them and blown off what they said completely if it weren't for my prior interactions with Houdini. That was just too coincidental.

It would explain the feeling of familiarity I got when I'd looked into Alexei's eyes for the first time. What was I thinking?! There was no such thing as shapeshifters. People didn't shift into animals! There was no magic, and no fate. Just bullshit humans and their bullshit games.

Surely Alexei would have told me all this himself if it were true.

Wouldn't he? *Wait*—what if he was trying to get rid of me? Maybe this was all a ploy. He sent the three woman to Mimi's Cabana tonight to spread some weird story in the hopes that I'd drop him like a hot potato.

No, that didn't make sense either because he was the one pursuing me, not the other way around. If he wanted to get rid of me, all he had to do was say so.

For the first time in longer than I could remember, I went home early and crawled into my bed. I tried to make sense of everything as I lay there staring at the ceiling. Over and over, my mind sorted through every interaction I'd had with Alexei and with Houdini. Was it even remotely possible? A man who turns into a polar bear? I was crazy for even considering it.

When I finally did drift into a fitful sleep that night, it was only after coming to the conclusion that I would have to find out for myself. I wouldn't come right out and ask him, but there was another way. A way to test Alexei. I'd get to the bottom of what was really going on.

20

ALEXEI

I shifted into my bear in the water and hurriedly swam to Heidi that morning. I was eager to see her. I'd told her the day before that I thought we were fated to be together and I was ready to hear her thoughts about that. Maybe, if she was ready, I could explain the whole shifter thing.

She was sitting on the beach, her face blank, when I reached her. Instead of smiling and getting up to greet me with a hug the way she normally did, she just sat there. When I rubbed against her, she absently patted me on the head. She seemed a million miles away and I worried if something had happened. Maybe she'd had another nasty encounter with a diehard fan of *Love In An Instant*.

As I raged inside at the thought of someone being so rude and mean to her, she started quietly talking.

"You know what I really want, Houdini? I want a dominant man, one who tells me how it is. I've been thinking about it and as much as I like Alexei, I think he's a little too polite and respectful, you know?"

I bit back a growl. What was she talking about?

"I would be so turned on if he just pushed me around a little. If he walked up to me and said something like, 'Bitch, gimme a beer,' or grabbed me by the hair, dragged me down to my knees, and ordered me to service him. I need to be dominated—treated roughly. I don't think Alexei has that in him." She sighed. "I just feel...bored with him. We're completely mismatched."

My pride ached and my heart sank. What was my mate saying? What had changed overnight that I was suddenly boring? Had she met someone else?

She stood up and brushed the sand off her. "I'm sorry, Houdini. I wish I could hang out more this morning, but I've got to get to the boys early. Come on. I'll walk you back."

I was so thrown off that I just followed her, dumbfounded. I felt like I'd had the wind knocked out of me. She didn't even say goodbye when she knocked on the gate of that asshole Leon Zoo's place. She just turned and left.

There was something seriously wrong. She didn't seem like herself at all. Whatever was going on, I had to fix it.

I raced back to the pier, shifted and threw on my shorts before running down the beach to find her before she disappeared. I caught up to her just as she was going towards a small house right off the beach.

"Heidi!" I forced a smile and jogged up to her. "Hey. I was hoping I'd catch you again this morning."

Her expression was still flat and indifferent when she looked at me, although I thought I detected something else beneath the surface. "You caught me."

"Are you okay?"

She sighed, making it obvious that she was not okay. "Fine. Everything is fine."

I caught her hand. "Something's off. You seem different."

"I'm fine. I'm just...bored." She shrugged. "It's nothing."

Desperation can do crazy things to a man. I had no interest in pushing Heidi around or treating her "roughly", as she put it, but if that was what she wanted, hell, I'd do anything to make her happy. "If you're so bored, get on your damned knees and service me....uh...bitch."

If she'd seemed quiet, indifferent, and even bored before, she suddenly did a one eighty and her temper flared like a raging wildfire. Her features contorted and she turned a deep shade of red before her hand shot out like a cannon and connected painfully with my face. When I jerked back, shocked, she followed me, punching me in the chest.

"Are you fucking kidding me?!"

I was so confused. "I-I'm sorry. I thought that's what you wanted! I'm sorry. Jesus, just stop punching me before you hurt yourself."

"You thought that's what I wanted? Why would you think that? Huh, Alexei? How would you know that? I didn't tell you, did I? I told a fucking polar bear!"

She was in full freak out mode, practically foaming at the mouth. When she slipped in the sand and I caught her to keep from falling, she just exploded even more. She ran down the beach still hollering.

"I've told a fucking polar bear lots of things! Lots of personal things! About how I wanted to get to know you more and then you showed up, demanding we get to know each other. I told him how hot I thought you were and how I wanted you, but I was afraid. I told him everything!"

I'd caught up to her by that point. Somehow, she'd found out I was a shifter and set me up. "Heidi..."

"Fuck you. You want to be with me, you think it's fate?" She taunted. "Bullshit. You were just feeding me what I wanted to hear. What do you really want? Just to make a complete fool of me? To fuck me and then laugh about it later? What was the point?"

I tried to grab her arms to stop her and make her listen to me, but she just smacked my hands away. "Heidi! Stop and listen to me. I'm sorry! I wasn't trying to—"

"I thought you were different. I thought you liked me." She angrily wiped away a tear. "I thought a polar bear was my friend. So, I guess this is really my fault. I was the idiot spilling my heart out to a damned bear."

"Fucking stop and listen to me. I didn't mean—"

"Go to hell." She turned and ran up the steps to her house, slamming the door so hard that the walls rattled.

I stood there, looking up at that door, feeling the pieces of my shattered heart fall to my feet. I'd fucked up. Royally.

I stayed there for a while, trying to come up with something to say, something that she'd actually want to hear, but nothing came to my mind. I'd been an idiot. I'd let her tell me everything under false pretenses. Then, I'd used that information to get closer to her.

I'd be lucky if she ever spoke to me again.

21

HEIDI

I was on day two of calling in sick to work. Hadn't showered. Hadn't brushed my teeth. Had no motivation to do either again. All my anger had faded and I was left with a terrible, depressive sadness. It just hung over my head like a cloud of doom that rained mopiness on me. I wanted anger back, because at least with anger came motivation. Motivation to lash out at Alexei, or spend time visualizing kicking him in the balls, but still. With sadness, I just wanted to lay on my bed and stare at the ceiling. Or worse, cry.

Alexei was exactly why I'd stayed away from men since moving to Sunkissed Key. The whole situation was. Dreaming of something I couldn't have sucked. I hadn't felt so lonely before Alexei. I hadn't stayed in bed all day long and cried over the realization that no one was ever going to touch me again. Alexei. Alexei was never going to touch me again.

It was awful how I still wanted him. The anger had faded but thoughts of him were still driving me crazy. I didn't understand how he'd managed to get past all my defenses so thoroughly, but he had.

He was well and truly under my skin.

I missed Houdini... who was really Alexei. The whole concept was still insane to me. Alexei turned into a bear and...what? Sat and listened to women talk so he could find out their inner thoughts, and then use them to lure the women into bed? No, that made no sense. Alexei didn't need any tricks to get a woman into bed. He probably got propositioned daily. Well, whatever his reason for doing it, I did miss stroking his fur while I chatted away. I missed curling up against him and watching the ocean roll in over the sand and then back out.

I wasn't stupid. I knew I sounded like an idiot, crying over a lost friendship with a bear. Was I so lonely and pitiful that I thought a bear was my friend? The answer was sad.

I hadn't even begun to process what it meant that he could shift from man to bear. I just wasn't there.

I was still feeling hurt over the betrayal.

Had Alexei been laughing the entire time he'd been using what I told him to lure me in? Had I been such an easy target? I felt like I was going to be shamed and ridiculed all over again, even more. I'd dragged him into the back of the bar and had an orgasm against an old rickety desk. People were going to know I'd done that. They were going to feel like they were right in their judgements of me.

I was really working myself into a big crying spell when someone knocked on my front door. I cringed.

I knew it wasn't Maria. She'd asked her mother to step in and look after the kids for a couple days after I'd given her a brief rundown of why I'd gone into hiding. She knew better than to come over until I asked her to. Maria was the only person who ever stopped over, so... was it Alexei? I wasn't ready to face him. Especially not all smelly and gross and in the same clothes I'd worn for the past two days. I didn't want him to know how he'd affected me.

"It's us! Megan, Hannah, and Kerrigan. The relationship-ruiners."

I fell back into bed, planning on ignoring them. They'd go away eventually.

"We aren't leaving, Heidi. You're stuck with us on your porch until you let us in."

I groaned. "Go away!"

"No, ma'am." Evidently, Megan was their stubborn ringleader. "We'll camp out here if we have to."

The only reason I got up was so I could throw something at her. I scrunched my face into my best scowl and jerked open the door. "Go away. I don't want to see you. Any of you."

Megan shrugged and pushed her way past me. "Well, I suppose you'll have to get over it. We're not going anywhere."

Kerrigan moved past me next. "I like your house. It's cute."

When Hannah just stood there, a stupid smile on her face, I stepped aside. "Well. You might as well join your pals."

She patted my arm as she moved past. "I'm sorry we're barging in like this. We have to, though. We messed up and we owe it to you and Alexei to stage an intervention."

"Don't say his name."

Megan turned away from a picture of me with the boys and faced me. "Alexei, Alexei, Alexei. You'd best get used to it because you're going to be hearing a lot of his name today and for the rest of your life. We have a lot to explain. Where should we set up? And would you like to shower first?"

I gave her an incredulous look.

She laughed. "Okay, no shower."

Hannah groaned. "I'm so sorry. We're all so sorry. Megan doesn't mean to be so rude, but we've been watching Alexei mope around like his world came to an end. He's so sad and it's all our fault."

"Oh, your fault, huh? Were you the ones who told him to convince me that he was a polar bear escaped from the local animal sanctuary? You told him to sit and listen to me pour my heart out about this really hot guy I met? You told him to use the information to get me to agree to go out with him?"

Kerrigan whistled. "No one ever claimed he was the sharpest tool in the shed."

"He *is* the sweetest, though. He's not a bad guy, Heidi. He's just... clueless. He should've known better, yes. He should've done some things differently. He didn't, though. And it doesn't change that he's your mate and that the two of you are fated to be together." Megan put her hands on her hips. "Now, how about that shower?"

I scowled. "Rude, much?"

She shook her head. "You'll forgive us later."

"Doubt it."

"I'm really going to enjoy being friends with you when all of this is over. I'm always saying how these two are just too nice."

"You really just bullied your way into my house and are insulting me. Nice."

She just grinned. "You're going to enjoy us being friends, too. I mean, after you forgive me for all of this."

22

ALEXEI

I'd never felt worse in my life. I missed Heidi more than I thought possible. My chest ached. I was usually the most laid back of the team. Things didn't often ruffle my feathers, but this —my bear was slowly losing his shit and so was I. My world was falling apart. I'd even gotten my nose broken on the job by a nutcase rabbit shifter with a few too many beers in him who didn't want to be calmed. I didn't even know rabbit shifters existed. He'd gotten the drop on me and it would have been more than a little embarrassing except I didn't care about anything but my mate.

I'd gone to the beach every morning waiting for Heidi, but she never showed. She was making it more than clear that she didn't want anything to do with me. I got it. I'd pulled some stupid shit.

I should've come clean sooner, before she found out herself. I shouldn't have used what she told me to try to win her over. I shouldn't have let her spill her private info without letting her know it was me she was spilling it to not some dumb animal. Although right now, I supposed that description could accurately be applied to me—dumb animal.

I'd been pissed at Megan, Kerrigan, and Hannah at first for flapping their gums and assuming Heidi knew everything. They'd just dropped the whole thing on her like a bomb. They had to have freaked her out beyond belief. It wasn't really their fault, though. Not really. I'd been the idiot.

"How's the nose?"

I looked up at Serge and shrugged. "Fine. Healed already."

He chose the chair opposite me in the office, and sank into it with a grunt. "You okay?"

Frowning, I looked away. "Not really."

"She'll come around. It's just the way it works."

I wasn't so sure. I'd tricked her. I'd taken away the chance for her to want to tell me, the man, everything. "Sure."

"Hannah and the other two went over there yesterday." He grunted again. "Figured they'd try to repair what they'd broken."

I sat up straighter. "What happened?"

"They all argued a lot, apparently. Your mate isn't very trusting, it seems." He laughed. "Hannah said she's stubborn and is the perfect mate for you because you need someone strong enough to deal with your shit."

The ache in my chest grew stronger. "She has plenty of reason to not trust people."

"So, I hear."

I stood up and went to the window. There were people walking past on the street, but no one that I wanted to see. "Did they say how it all ended?"

"I got the impression that they weren't done talking to her."

"I should've been the one telling her everything."

"Well, it's too late for that now. So, you can either feel shitty about yourself, or you can go and fix it."

Frowning at him, I held my hands up in the air. "How? How do I fix it?"

"Not by sitting here and feeling sorry for yourself."

"I don't feel sorry for myself. I feel sorry for what I did to her. There's a difference." I shoved my hands in my hair and tugged. "I fucking miss her. It feels like part of me is dying."

Serge walked over to me and put his hand on my shoulder. "Make it right. You can do it. We've all been where you are, wondering how the fuck we're going to get our mates back. With Hannah, I thought I was going to fucking choke on the pain."

"I don't know what to do. I lost her trust. She fucking hates me, man. No big gesture is going to fix that."

He squeezed my shoulder and then let go. "Don't try for big gesture then. You're smart. You'll figure it out. She's your mate. You're literally made for her. Stop bellyaching in here and go get your mate back. You're on leave until you do. I need you on the team, but last night was bad. You could've been hurt. You could've gotten the team hurt."

I growled. "Serge, I have to work. I can't just...do nothing."

"Don't do nothing then, asshole. Go get your mate."

I watched him leave and sank back into my chair. I didn't know what to do. I didn't know how to make it right after breaking her trust. I couldn't think through the haze of pain.

Sitting there for the rest of the day, I was finally so stiff from not moving that I forced myself to get up and go out. I walked down the beach, no real aim in mind. At least, that's what I thought until I saw that I was outside of Heidi's house.

I had no plan. I needed to think of something before I tried to talk to her, but still, I walked up to her door and knocked. She didn't answer and I couldn't smell her sweet scent close by. I sank onto the top step and deflated. I felt like I was barely holding on. I needed her.

"Alexei?"

I looked up and saw Megan coming towards me. I couldn't pretend like I wasn't broken to save face, so I just shrugged and stared out at the ocean view that Heidi had. It was beautiful, but I couldn't truly appreciate it.

"Oh, Alexei." Megan sat next to me and sighed. "I'm so sorry that we did this."

"Not your fault."

"Some of it's our fault." She nudged me with her elbow. "She's going to come around."

I wasn't so sure.

"Just talk to her. Come clean about everything and put yourself out there. Show her your vulnerable side." She stood up. "She's stubborn, but she'll hear you eventually."

I just nodded and kept my eyes trained on the ocean.

"Ugh. You bears are all the same. You think you're so strong, but you're just lost little cubs without your mate." She patted me on the head. "Get your mate, little cub, before you melt away in a puddle of sadness."

"Too late."

She just laughed. "If you don't make some sort of effort soon, she's going to think you don't care."

I finally looked at her. "I care more than I care about anything else in the world."

"Well, act like it. This feeling sorry for yourself isn't solving anything."

I grunted. "You and Serge are pains."

"Yeah, well. So are you."

23

HEIDI

I didn't want to be at work, but I could only shirk my responsibilities for so long. My tips were going to be pitiful tonight since the only expression I could manage was a frown, but it wasn't fair to Mimi and Sarah to have to cover my shift for yet another might.

My mind was elsewhere and I kept screwing up drinks. I couldn't help it. All the things the trio of women had told me were running through my head on a continual loop. The women turned out to not be so bad. They were rather nice, really. But, the info they gave me...wow!

Polar bears and shifters of every kind existed. Men who shifted into animals, did whatever they wanted to do as animals, and then shifted back to men. It was mind blowing. And all true. I'd watched Megan's mate shift. They hadn't wanted to show me, but I insisted. If they expected me to believe something so off the wall, I needed to see it with my own eyes.

Not that I didn't halfway believe it already. That stupid test I'd put Alexei through had proven that he knew exactly what I told Houdini. I mean, what I'd told Alexei. As Houdini. Since they were one in the same.

I dropped a glass of ice and swore. It was going to be a long night. I would get over it and move on at some point. No matter what the women said. They seemed to be convinced that nothing would get better for me until I talked to Alexei. I wasn't ready for that, though. I still felt like such a fool. I'd opened myself—raw and exposed—never knowing I was spilling my innermost feelings to a man I'd just met and hardly knew. I mean, how the hell could I possible have known?

"You okay?" Sarah leaned over the bar, her worry evident. "You look like you're a million miles away."

I swept the broken glass and melting ice into the dustpan and tossed the whole mess into the trash. "I'm okay. Everything's okay."

"Mimi and I can do without you, if you need to go home. You look like you're barely holding it together." She ducked under the bar and came up to me. "It's obvious you're going through something, Heidi. Go home if you need to. You work hard for this place and no one is going to be mad if you need a little more personal time for whatever you're going through."

I blinked back tears and swallowed down the lump in my throat. "I actually do need a minute to myself."

She sighed and straightened my hair. "Okay, just...take a break. I don't know what's going on with you, but you look like seconds from an all-out sob fest."

She had no clue how right she was. As though I hadn't indulged in enough sob fests already.

I took a five-minute break in the back and when I came out, I was a little more together and could at least pretend on the outside like I wasn't such a wreck inside. Things were going better until I dropped another glass. This time, it shattered into the ice. Swearing, I braced myself on the bar and took a deep breath.

"Heidi?"

I glanced up at Sarah and shook my head. "I have to change this ice out."

I'd just gotten started pouring pitchers of warm water over the ice when a couple of guys settled themselves at the bar in front of me. I glanced up and tossed them an absent smile before going back to my chore of melting the ice.

"Ahem. Are you going to take our order?"

I strained to keep my faux smile in place. "Yes. It'll be just a minute. I'm in the middle of something. Sorry about this."

I went back to cleaning out the ice, making sure everything melted, drained and was cleaned, ensuring no glass shards were inadvertently sent out in someone's drink. I was just about finished when I realized the men were snickering.

My back instantly stiffened. I'd had snickers like that directed at me plenty of times over the years. They were never good. I looked up to find them recording me while I was bent over, working. Scowling, I turned to face them. "What the fuck is wrong with you?"

"Whoa, sweetheart. We were just enjoying the view. It's not a big deal." The guy with the phone put it down and rolled his eyes. "It's not like you're not used to it."

I had a job to keep, a level of professionalism I needed to uphold. That night, though, I couldn't calm down. I was pissed, all the anger and sadness I'd been feeling finally had a solid outlet.

"Keep your eyes and your camera to yourself or I'll break them both, you skinny little shit." I glared at both of them. "You can leave now. I'm not serving either of you."

Phone boy scowled back at me. "You don't have to be a bitch. Jesus."

"And you don't have to act like a creep."

"Fuck you." He looked down at me like I was something gross he'd stepped in. "It's not like either of us really wanted to look at a piece of trash like you. Everyone knows you've been around the block so many times that you'll spread your legs for any Tom or Harry... oops, I mean Dick!" His buddy laughed like that was actually funny.

"Get out." My hand reacted before my mind did, but I wasn't sorry that I threw a pitcher of warm water at him.

He was drenched, water pooling in his lap until he jumped up and tried to shake it off. His face was beet red and his expression said he wanted to strangle me. "You bitch!"

Sarah came rushing over, her eyes wide. "You okay, Heidi?"

"Is *she* okay? That bitch just poured water on me. I want to talk to your manager!"

"Call her a bitch one more time and you'll be scraping your jaw off the floor."

The deep timbre of Alexei's voice startled me, but it was nothing compared to how I felt when I looked at him and saw the dark expression on his face as he stared down the two men. His hair was disheveled, he was unshaven, and there were dark circles under his eyes. He looked rough. I got a sick satisfaction out of realizing that he'd been as miserable as I'd been.

"Fuck off, asshole. This doesn't involve you."

"That's where you're wrong. She's mine and you're a dead man if you keep talking to her like that."

Sarah held up her hands and moved between the two men. "Okay, that's enough. No one's fighting in here."

"So, your sorry ass got stuck with her? How does it feel to know your woman has been passed around like a bad cold?"

Alexei growled low in his throat. "Excuse me."

I watched with widening eyes as he picked Sarah up and placed her back on her feet behind him as though he were relocating a figurine. She gasped at what she saw behind her, but before Alexei could turn back around, the asshole with the cell phone swung his fist out and hit Alexei in the side of the head.

He really shouldn't have done that.

24

HEIDI

Alexei picked up the offending asshole like he weighed nothing and easily tossed him overhead towards the exit. The guy hit the door sideways, and tumbled onto the floor. "I'm letting you go. Make the right choice."

Asshole's friend swallowed so loudly that I heard it from where I was standing. "I don't want any trouble."

"Take your friend and get the fuck out, then."

Cell phone guy who was climbing to his feet wasn't nearly as smart as his buddy, though. "Fuck you and your ho bitch, man." This scene was going to get even bigger, apparently, because he then focused his gaze on me. "Everyone in here knows who you are! Everyone saw you on national television, fucking every guy with a pulse."

The bar had gone quiet, except for the music which was oddly loud without the buzz of conversation. It was painfully obvious that everyone was listening to what was going on and all eyes were on us.

I wanted to sink behind the bar and never come out again. Not only did I want to, I actually did it. I couldn't face everyone. It was one thing when I had to deal with people one on one, or two on one. A whole bar full of people was too much. I slid down behind the bar, my back to the bucket of ice that I'd been cleaning out, and wrapped my arms around my legs. It wasn't my proudest moment, but I needed to get away.

"What kind of moron are you?" Alexei's voice was raised, his anger palpable. "That shit isn't real. It was all staged—completely fake. Everyone on the show followed a script. She was cast as the villain and did her job the way she was supposed to. But, even if it wasn't all phony, that gives you no right to treat her like an object. Your vile behavior shows *your* character not hers."

Sarah's voice rose, too. "Yeah, you're the only trash here. You and anyone else who would harass someone based on what you saw on TV show almost a decade ago."

"She's a better person than you could ever hope to be. She's kind, smart, and caring. You'd be lucky to kiss her feet." Alexei growled. "Which isn't going to happen. She's mine. Even if I'll never deserve her either."

Mimi's voice rose from the back. "Okay, boys, this has gone on long enough. If you have an issue with one of my bartenders because you think you have the upper hand on some gossip about them, stay the hell away. Take your money somewhere else. Like back to the hole you crawled out of." I really loved my boss, Mimi.

"Yeah!" Sarah cheered along.

I heard Alexei's low, strong voice next. "I suggest you leave now of your own volition. If not, I will make you leave—now. One of those options ends with you in traction, eating your meals through a straw for the next six months. Your choice."

I listened with strained ears, but I couldn't hear anything. I couldn't figure out what was happening until the door slammed and people cheered. Then Sarah's head appeared over the top of the bar and her grin stretched as wide as her face.

"They're gone." She reached over and stroked my hair.

Mimi rounded the bar and stood in front of me. "You okay, honey?"

I shook my head and then nodded. "Yeah. No. I don't know."

"I think the hottie has a real thing for you! Did you hear him?" Sarah sighed, still hanging over the bar. "He said you're *his*."

Mimi's hand flew to her chest. "He's not the type a girl should let slip through her fingers. Trust me on that. I know. I've been married five times."

I forced a smile and pulled myself up. She was right. No more hiding. I had to talk to Alexei and at least thank him for standing up for me. When I turned, though, he was gone.

Sarah sighed. "Where'd he go?"

I looked around the bar. People were staring at me, but the looks were curious rather than cruel. The vibe in Mimi's Cabana quickly returned to normal, the drama forgotten, but Alexei was nowhere to be seen.

"I should thank him."

Mimi snorted. "You should marry him."

I groaned. "Things are more complicated than that."

"Oh, really? A man that beautiful wants you and is willing to fight for you and it's complicated? Okay. Complicated. Sure."

I stood up taller and scanned the place once more hoping to find him. "It's more than just that. He...he did some stuff."

Sarah's eyes widened. "He cheated?"

"No."

Mimi crossed her arms over her large chest and coconut bra. "He's abusive?"

"No."

Mimi nodded knowingly. "He's only into anal."

I jerked around to face her. "No! What's wrong with you?"

She laughed. "Then, it sounds like whatever he did is forgivable. Go, get him."

"I..." I blew out a shaky breath and looked for him again. "It's—"

"Take a chance," Sarah said. "You've lived like a nun the entire time you've been here. It's time for you go a little wild."

I looked at the door and wondered where he'd gone. "I don't like the consequences of living wildly."

"Maybe the outcome will be in your favor this time. How will you know if you don't take that chance? Now, go. I can't stand here and convince you to do what's best for you all night long. I've got tables to wait."

As I stood there after Sarah went back to work and tried to think through what I was going to do, Mimi took over pouring drinks. I could stay and let him get on with his life. We could both go back to the way things were. I'd forget him eventually, no matter what Megan and the other women said, and live the rest of my life the way I had been.

So, things weren't exciting? So, I was lonely? At least I was safe.

Or I could step out of my comfort zone and go after him—let him explain. We might even be able to work things out. Maybe the women were right and he was my mate and things would never be fine again because they'd be amazing.

"Two beers, please!"

I climbed over the bar, and ran out the door amidst cheers of the patrons who had been side eying me, second guessing what I was gonna do. Well, what I was gonna do was hear Alexei out. But, that was all. I deserved an explanation. Yeah, that was the only reason I was chasing him down.

25

ALEXEI

I crossed Main Street and walked to the beach. I was barely holding myself together, anger getting the best of me. I wanted to lash out and rip someone's head off. I wanted to hurt everyone who'd ever hurt Heidi, including myself.

The image of her crouching behind the bar, hiding, was scorched into my brain. I couldn't unsee it. She was hurt. She deserved better. I wanted to be the one who made it all better, yet I'd only made it worse for her.

I shifted, not concerned about my shredded clothing, and padded into the water. My bear was mourning the loss of his mate, his sorrow audible as he cried. We were both mourning. It was my fault. I hadn't taken things seriously enough and I'd ruined everything.

"Alexei!"

I turned towards the sound of my name being called and froze. Running toward the water was Heidi. She stopped at the water's edge and stepped out of her shoes before wading into the water.

"We have to talk. Right now." Out of breath, she was waist deep in the water, the bottom of her dress floating up around her hips.

I swam closer, still keeping my distance, and just waited. Had she really chased after me?

"I want to hear what you have to say. I need to hear it. Can you shift back?"

My bear retreated, leaving me there to face what I'd done. I swam closer to our mate and felt my stomach twist painfully. "I'm sorry."

Her eyes were wide and she blinked a few times. "Wow."

"I know. That doesn't really cut it, does it? I am, though. I'm sorry I wasn't honest with you. I should've told you right away. I should've shown you and let you decide what you wanted to tell me. It was yours to decide and I took that away from you. I know how wrong I was."

"You make it look so easy."

"What?"

She stepped closer. "Shifting. I saw Roman do it, but it's not the same. It's amazing. You're a bear one second and then you're...you. Wow...it's so...beautiful."

I stilled. "You think it's beautiful?"

She nodded. "Can you do it again? Right now?"

I wasn't going to tell her no. I shifted into my bear and chuffed at her. I was amazed when she smiled and held her hand out for me to come closer. I eased closer, but I let her decide if she wanted to touch me. I was done presuming things.

She scratched behind my ears the way I liked. "Again, please."

I shifted back and stared down at her. Her hand cupped the side of my face and I pressed my cheek into her palm greedily. "I'm sorry, Heidi."

"Did you mean to trick me? Was it supposed to be a joke?"

I shook my head. "I never meant to trick you in a bad way. At first, before I realized you were my mate, I thought it would be funny for a polar bear to be on a beach in Florida. But after that, it was just... me...hanging out with you any way I could. It was wrong of me, though, not to provide you with full disclosure."

"You think I'm your mate?"

I held her gaze. "I know you are. Everything about you calls to me. I meant what I said about fate. I understand you being angry. I knew I wasn't making the best choices, but I was so desperate to be with you that I didn't care. I should've thought things through."

"Megan told me that shifters need their mates. She said that you would be in physical pain without me."

I just nodded.

"And you were just going to leave and let me shut you out?"

I nodded again. "I'm not going to force you to be with me. I've done enough."

"So, what? You just suffer?"

"It's fine, Heidi. You don't owe me anything. Don't worry about me, okay?"

She stepped closer, the water up to her chest then. "You said you're sorry."

"I am. Very much."

"I forgive you." She came even closer. "I think…"

"What? What do you think?"

She let out a shaky laugh. "I'm terrified. I'm terrified that you might hurt me again. I want to believe all of the mate stuff, but it's not easy. It's been a long time since I've been able to believe the best of something."

Too eagerly, I moved closer to her. "I can show you. I can show you that you're bound to me and that we're meant to be together."

"How?"

I trailed my finger down her neck. "The mark. You'll feel what I feel. You'll know that this is real. It's serious, though. It's forever after that. There's no going back."

"You want to mark me?"

"So badly that my bones ache from it. If you're not ready, though, it's okay. We can go slowly. We can—"

"Alexei?"

"Yeah?"

"Stop talking and do it." She closed the gap between us and put her finger to my lips. "But then we both let it go. I forgive you. You have to forgive yourself, too. I'm not fragile. I don't need you apologizing and treating me like I'm going to break. I want you the way you are."

My hands went to her waist and I sucked in a sharp breath. "Can I talk?"

"I guess."

"I want to mark you as mine. I want to claim you so there's never a doubt that you belong to me and that I belong to you. No games, no jokes, just you and me, together."

She sighed and swayed into me. "Forever?"

"If there's anything longer than forever, then that."

"You won't change your mind?"

"Heidi?"

"Yeah?"

"Stop talking and let me do it."

26

HEIDI

I gasped as Alexei pulled me into his body and kissed me. God, the man could kiss. He made love to my mouth in a way that I'd never experienced. His lips moved over mine slowly and deliberately, tasting and teasing. He moved from my bottom lip to my top lip before running his tongue over them, seeking entrance.

I was a puddle as he stroked my lips and then my tongue. Short and teasing strokes built up to strong, deep strokes that drove me crazy. I couldn't get enough of his kisses.

I wrapped myself around him, longing for more. Locking my arms around his neck and my legs around his waist, I felt the thick ridge of his erection press against my core.

Alexei growled against my mouth and pulled back to look at me. "Fuck, you're beautiful like this, with lips red and swollen from my kisses and your pulse beating like crazy at the base of your throat."

I kissed his neck and ran my tongue over his skin, tasting him. "When are you going to mark me?"

He groaned and I felt his erection pulse against me. "Are you sure, mate?"

I liked hearing him call me that. I liked it a lot. "Yes. I want you to mark me. Will you be able to see it? When you look at me, will you see that I'm yours?"

Another pulse. "You're killing me. It'll be visible. All shifters will know. I'll feel you, too. We'll feel each other—through the bond."

"Do you know what you'd feel right now? If you could feel me?" I ran my fingers through his hair and peppered kisses on his lips. "You'd feel that I don't want to wait anymore. I want you—now."

He swore and his mouth descended over mine again as he pivoted us. The pier where we'd first met was behind him, and he pressed my back against it. We weren't immersed so deeply that the water covered us completely, but we were far enough out that were cloaked by darkness.

Alexei pinned me to the thick wooden pillar with his lower body and slid the top of my dress down over my shoulders and even farther, taking my strapless bra with it. As the waves rolled in, the cool water kissed my bared breasts seconds before his mouth did.

With lingering strokes of his tongue and deep, hungry, open mouthed kisses to them, he only stopped when I pulled his head up and silently begged him for more. The blue of his eyes were glowing a bright sliver in the moonlight. "What's the magic word?"

I dropped my head back as his hand trailed down my side and worked its way between us. When my panties were shoved aside and his thick finger was easing into me, we both moaned.

I reached up and behind me to grab the pier, trying desperately to brace myself against something firm and solid. I was light-headed and had the feeling that I was floating away. "Alexei, more."

He slid another finger into me and ran his tongue over my breasts again, sucking and nibbling. He was purposefully driving me crazy. "Say the magic word and I'll take you right now. I'll make you scream my name and mark you as mine. All you have to do is say it."

"Please!"

He grinned, resting his forehead against mine as he pumped his fingers back and forth and his thumb swiped over my clit sending shivers of pleasure through my body. "That's a good one and we may use it later, but it's not the magic word I want to hear from you."

And suddenly, I knew exactly the word he was waiting for. He was waiting for a concrete confirmation. "Mate...you're my mate. You're mine, Alexei, and I want you in me."

He groaned and then his fingers were gone and in their place a crushing emptiness. But, before I could voice a protest, his cock was there instead, slowly filling me until I thought I couldn't handle another inch.

He gripped the pier, his hand partly over mine, and his other hand cupped my ass. His forehead pressed to mine, eyes focused on me, as he slowly moved. His hips gyrated with the gentle rocking of the waves, pumping in and out of me in a rhythm that sent me reeling.

I watched the strain on his handsome face, the way he held back, and wanted desperately to see him let go and lose control. I arched my back and met his thrusts harder. I used my hands, locked around the pier, to give me leverage to increase the friction between our bodies.

My move seemed to have its intended effect. He swore and thrust into me harder and faster, matching my pace. His grip on my ass was bruising. "I'm not going to last long like this, Heidi."

"Good. I want you to come with me." I shuddered, my body close to coming apart for him. "Mark me. Mark me, mate."

That was all that he needed. He used his chin to nudge my head to the side and then his tongue stroked over my exposed neck. I held my breath, but he just licked me again.

"*Mate.*" I moaned. "Please!"

He let out a wild snarl and then sank his teeth into my neck. It hurt for only a split second before the pleasure hit full force. It seemed to come from all directions and all at once. My body tightened... and then snapped with an orgasm unlike any I'd ever felt flowing over me, I trembled like an earthquake, the contractions rocking me to the core. The pleasure radiated, going out, coming back in, rolling through me. Everywhere.

And I screamed, lost somewhere in a blissful euphoria, not caring who heard, I screamed Alexei's name.

Alexei thrust a few more strokes and then went still, buried in me to the hilt. I felt his seed filling me, as another orgasm started up for me, even stronger, as though his climax had triggered mine. The sounds I made were helpless cries of surrender to a passion more powerful than I thought possible.

I wasn't sure how long we hung onto the pier like that, but the moon was higher in the sky when I was able to think clearly again. I opened my eyes to find Alexei watching me, a crooked grin on his face. "What?"

He bit his lip and that smile grew wider. "You're mine."

I couldn't help but smile back. I felt...him, his emotions toward me. An overwhelming sense of pride and warmth and joy...and love. I could feel through our bond the depth of his feelings for me. I held his face in my hands and tasted his lips, hoping he also knew through the bond what I thought of him.

Fate had given me a gift, for whatever reason, and I wasn't one to be ungrateful.

"Alexei, let's go back to my house. I want to hear *you* say please. Magic words work both ways, you know?"

He laughed and pulled me away from the pier. He insisted on carrying me up the beach and then up the stairs to my house. Anyone looking out their window would've gotten quite the view.

"You're not into just anal, right?"

He stumbled. "What?"

"Sorry, sorry. It was something that Mimi said." I hesitated. "I'm willing to experiment, just as long as it's not all anal, all the time."

"Stop saying anal."

"I'm just checking."

"Okay, well, no, I'm not into all anal, all the time."

I laughed as he tried to carry me into the bathroom while looking for the bedroom. "Next room on the right."

He found it and dropped me on the bed.

I pulled him down on top of me and kissed him. "Wait."

He stiffened. "What?"

"Why was Mr. Zoo just accepting a random polar bear into his animal sanctuary?"

"It's a long story."

"No wonder he was so rude to me." I laughed. "I kept bringing him an animal that he didn't want."

Alexei buried his face in my shoulder and growled. "Enough talking about another man. In fact, let's stop talking altogether."

I tangled my hands in his hair and shifted my hips so he brushed against my entrance. "I could talk about anal some more."

He laughed and sank into me in one deep thrust. "Heidi?"

"Yeah?"

"Please."

THE END.

TACTICAL BEAR

P.O.L.A.R. 4

Parker is fighting extinction—
Of her own shifter species!
She'd already be mated.
If not for those bullying polar bears.
They've scared away all decent prospects.

Maxim has met the one
But, she's an activist with silly notions.
And she wants nothing to do with him.

As a Tactical Bear, he'll need all his strategic skills.
Not for military advancements,
But to win over his mate!

1

PARKER

The bell over the door at Rise and Shine Bed and Breakfast had a shrill, piercing peal. I'd fussed with Penny about the damned thing almost nonstop since I'd started working for her, right out of high school. It practically shattered my sensitive eardrums every time it went off. And a cranky employee wasn't great for Yelp reviews. Neither was a front desk clerk who was scowling in pain every time a new guest walked through the door. That sort of thing made it hard to get off on a good foot, customer-service wise.

Penny thought the bell made the house feel vintage, and Penny pretty much did as Penny pleased. Which, of course, was her right. So, the bell stayed.

I trained my pain-induced grimace on Penny since she was the one I was standing with in the small entryway at that moment. She just flashed a wide grin back at me and then turned to the young couple who'd stepped inside and were looking around expectantly. "Hello, folks! Welcome to Rise and Shine B&B. I'm Penny, the owner and proprietor."

Facing the couple, I took in their tightly clasped hands, eager smiles, and slight nervousness.

Newlyweds.

"You must be Mr. and Mrs. Gaines from Birmingham?"

Mrs. Gaines grinned so wide her back molars showed. "Yes! How'd you know?"

"Oh, there's a 'just married glow' about you two." I smiled back at her and held in the bitter sigh trying to escape. It wasn't the glowingly happy Gaineses that bothered me. It was having my own not-so-glowing reality thrown in my face. And my reality was that I was twenty-seven, single, and without a prospective mate anywhere in sight. Happily ever after came easier for some than it did for others.

Others, like me.

The only glow I had these days was from the sparkly lotion my teenage niece had gifted me with for my birthday.

Penny put on her figurative innkeeper hat and took both of the new guests by the hand. "We're so glad that you chose us for your honeymoon. Parker will get you checked in and I'll have your bags carried up to your room for you."

"This place is just so quaint!" Mrs. Gaines squeezed Penny's hand right back and then turned to her husband. "Isn't it, Joe?"

"The quaintest." Mr. Gaines looked like he wouldn't have minded honeymooning in the bowels of hell as long as he was there with his new bride. He nodded and kept right on staring at her.

"There's coffee or tea and cinnamon rolls in the dining room right now, if you're interested. Sweet tea, or a nice rose blend, and the rolls are made by a woman here on the island who could bake Martha Stewart right out of business."

I cleared my throat. "And before you slip away, we have a petition here for you to look over while you're spending the week with us. We're petitioning to get a name change for an endangered rabbit subspecies indigenous to this island."

"Why? What's wrong with the name?"

I could feel Penny shooting daggers at me, but I ignored her.

"We're—uh, *they're* named after Hugh Heffner. Those cinnamon rolls, by the way, even better than Penny described."

"Why would anyone name a rabbit after Hugh Hefner?" Mrs. Gaines looked at her husband and then it must have dawned on her.

She slapped a hand, laden with a diamond the size of a marble, over her mouth. "Oh! Of course, we'll sign."

I grinned and slid the clipboard their way. "Thank you. I really appreciate it."

Penny mouthed something at me from behind the guests that looked suspiciously like a vulgar curse. When Mr. and Mrs. Gaines turned to face her, she was all smiles, though.

"We've put you up in the Swan Suite. It's a perfect honeymoon suite, with a patio that opens right out onto the beach. You two will have your own jacuzzi just outside the room, completely private, of course. Marvin will bring you anything you require, including breakfast in bed each morning, if that's what you'd like."

"Marvin?"

"Oh, yes, Marvin. He's been with the house since it opened in 1960. He likes to work, even though he could have retired years ago..." Her voice trailed off. "Anyhow, whatever you need, he'll be more than happy to accomodate you. Just let him know."

After another few minutes of checking them in, Penny escorted them to the dining room to enjoy the tea and cinnamon rolls, then called in her son, Jacob, to take their bags up to their room.

As soon as Jacob was out of sight, she leaned over my little counter and poked me in the chest. "What have I told you about that damn petition? Knock it off."

"What kind of unsupportive friend are you? Do you not even care about my cause?"

"*Nobody* cares that some local rabbits are named after Hugh Hefner."

I narrowed my eyes at her. "I care. You just don't get it."

"I get that you'd better hide that clipboard and keep it hidden, or I'm going to smack you over the head with it."

"Is that any way for a boss to treat her subordinate?"

"I think you mean *in*subordinate."

"Pot-*ay*-to, pot-*ah*-to." I put the petition under my desk, but I fully planned on asking everyone I could to sign it. Penny was not only my employer, but a close friend. Even so, she didn't know everything about me, and she didn't know anything about shifters. It wasn't just any rabbit species that was named after Hef. It was the local rabbit *shifter* population. Of which I was a part.

Jacob came back down the side stairs and winked at me. "All done, Mom. Can I go?"

Penny, who rarely missed a beat, caught the wink. She lightly smacked him on the arm and frowned. "Leave her alone."

His face burned bright red, but he kept his chin up. "If she wants me to leave her alone, she'll tell me herself."

I smiled sweetly. "Leave me alone."

Jacob pouted instantly. He was barely sixteen and for some odd reason, considered me his dream woman. It was cute and made me a little envious of the woman he'd genuinely fall for some day.

I wasn't a slender supermodel type. Nor was I conventional. At five foot five, I had curves and a little extra weight around the middle that wouldn't go away no matter what I did. Not that I did much. I also had a multitude of tattoos, a few odd piercings, and my current hair color was a lovely shade of pastel lavender. I liked that Jacob wasn't solely focused on stick thin, conservative women. If only I'd had someone like Jacob around when I was his age. All the boys at the high school I went to had wanted supermodels.

"I'm just teasing, Jake. But listen to your mother." I winked back at him, unwilling to crush his spirit. "Hey, do you have any friends over eighteen that would want to sign—"

"Oh. My. God. Parker, quit with the petition. Jacob, go help your father with yardwork." Penny pointed at us like she was mom to the both of us. "I need a vacation."

Just to mess with her, I pulled my clipboard out and smiled. "Granted. I'll take over while you're gone, but sign this petition first."

Jacob grinned. Penny scowled. Mr. and Mrs. Gaines emerged from the dining room, still glowing.

My smile became a wince when the bell over the door rang again and another happy couple stepped inside.

2

MAXIM

Mallory, Melanie, Minnie, or whatever her name was looked up at me with her mascara running down her face and smiled. Her lipstick was smeared all over her mouth from doing things that I was pretty sure were illegal in some states. "Are you sure I can't talk you into staying the night?"

I buttoned my pants and looked for my shirt. "I'm sure."

She pouted and let the sheet she held around her chest drop down to her waist. Her tits were great, I'd give her that. She leaned towards me, pushing them together. "We could have more fun, Maxim."

I found my shirt half under her bed and pulled it over my head. The neck was stretched out and ripped a little, a casualty of foreplay with what's-her-name. "Sorry, babe. I've got work in the morning."

She pouted. "No fun." Then, she stood up, baring all, and stalked over to me. Running her hands down my chest, she batted her lashes at me. "At least take a shower with me?"

I considered it for second. She was hot, crazy wild, and kinky as hell. She'd done things and let me do things to her that were off the charts. She also had all the makings of a stage five clinger. Better to shut that down early. "No, thanks. I've got to go. Thanks for a good time, though, uh...babe."

She ran her hand down to my crotch and grabbed a handful of my junk. "We can do it again."

I lightly removed her hand and looked for my shoes. Had I kicked them off in the front of her house? Had I worn a belt over? I needed to start keeping up with that shit.

"Hey, was I wearing a belt when I got here?"

Her voice raised a few octaves. "Seriously?"

I followed her gaze to see what she was getting so worked up about and noticed my belt hanging from her bedpost. Oh, yeah. I walked over and snagged it before spotting one of my shoes. "Thanks."

"You can't be serious right now. You didn't remember that?"

Red flags began waving all over the place. I swore as I stepped into my shoe and still couldn't find the other one. "Of course, uh, I did. Sorry. I was just distracted."

Judging by the hiss from her side of the room, she didn't buy my flat tone. "They said you're an asshole, but I didn't believe them. I guess I should have."

I spotted my other shoe and grabbed it. Knowing my time was running out, I didn't even bother to put it on. I unbuckled my belt from the bedpost, and headed towards the door. "Who said I'm an asshole?"

She didn't bother covering herself as she followed me. "People. And they were right. You don't have any feelings about what happened here between us at all, do you?"

It took me a second to get all three of the locks on her door undone. "What? Yeah...sure I do. I *feel* that, uh, it was fun...but I have to go." What the hell did she want from me?

"What's my name?"

I had the door open and I should've beat feet the hell out of there. I definitely shouldn't have turned to face her trying my hardest to remember her name. I knew it was something like Minnie. Mipsy? Moopsy? Fuck, I had no clue.

"Oh, my god! You don't even remember my name!" She came at me, tits swinging, and shoved me the rest of the way out the door. It was barely midnight and there were people walking along the beach, typical for a Friday night. She gave them all a show as she stood in her doorway naked, yelling. "It's Karen, you jackass. My name is Karen!"

I shoved my foot into my other shoe and kept moving. I was on the other side of the island and had to walk all the way home to the P.O.L.A.R. house. I nodded to the teenagers who were giggling at what they'd just witnessed.

Early November, the weather was cooler on Sunkissed Key, but it still fucking sucked compared to home. I hated Florida. I hated Florida so much that I'd been keeping a tally of each nightmarish day we were there. And I blamed Serge for every tally mark. I knew headquarters couldn't keep us stranded forever. We were far too capable at what we did for them to refrain from fully utilizing our skills forever. It was ridiculous of them to keep us away from where we could actually do the most good.

I couldn't wait to be back in the snow, and no longer sweating my ass off. Worse than ass sweat, was the ball sweat. I could barely remember a time when my nut sack wasn't stuck to my thigh. I wasn't even comfortable engaging in oral intercourse without a solid shower and scrub. No one deserved that.

I wanted to be able to fuck without worrying about ball sweat. I wanted to be able to walk outside without feeling like I was either going to melt into the pavement or go up in flames at any moment. Fucking Florida.

By the time I got to the house, I was drenched in perspiration. I knew that some of the guys didn't abhor Sunkissed Key anymore. Alexei even seemed to thrive in the heat. Not me. I felt every fucking degree of the thermostat.

Serge was sitting in the kitchen with Hannah on his lap and they were whispering to one another when I walked in. He looked me over and shook his head. "Another walk of shame?"

"I didn't know there were any women left on the island that you hadn't slept with." Hannah's words were harsh, but her tone was light and teasing. She seemed to like me for some reason.

"There are still tourists." I grabbed a glass and poured myself some water. "What are you two doing up?"

Serge grinned and Hannah blushed. "None of your business."

I nodded at them and headed for the stairs. "Just keep it down, you crazy kids."

Upstairs, I could hear someone else going at it. A couple of the other guys had been staying at their mates' homes, but they randomly stayed at the P.O.L.A.R. house, too. Now that four of the six of us were mated, it was rare to walk into the house without hearing the groans and pants and whatevers of lovemaking in progress.

Shaking my head, I climbed to the third floor and locked myself in the bathroom intending to shower off my night. As the cold water shot from the showerhead, I undressed and stepped under the frigid spray letting it wash over me as I did my best to block out the sounds of mates being mates all throughout the house.

3
PARKER

Latte Love was my absolute favorite place on the island. It was the local coffee shop, owned and operated by Penny's twin sister, Paige, and it was right next door to Rise and Shine B&B. Plush, comfy, and decorated with huge potted palms, flamingos, and every other kitschy thing you could think of, I loved it. I could sink back into one of the overstuffed, furry chairs and be hidden away by a couple of massive palm fronds. I did that frequently—hide away from the world with my laptop, earbuds, and java. Paige made coffee that could rival Starbucks.

I tucked my feet under me and leaned forward. I was surfing the web for a date. Not just any date. A rabbit shifter date. There were a couple of secret shifter dating sites online, but they were sad, sparse things, only utilized by those shifters that were hard to match like porcupines and skunks. Online dating in the human world had finally gotten less taboo, but in the shifter world, it was almost unheard of. Shifters just met—where and when they were supposed to. It was considered by many to be fated.

A shifter who needed the internet to find his or her mate was a pathetic loser. Or so they said. I disagreed. I was a rare rabbit, trying to find another rare rabbit on an island where rabbits were few and far between. More than that, I was an endangered subspecies of rabbit. It wasn't going to be so easy for me to casually bump into a mate of the same species at a social event, for instance.

I scrolled through the few men listed. Just a couple snake shifters and a lone wolf who looked like he'd been in one too many brawls. No rabbits.

Sighing, I pushed my laptop away and took a long gulp from my mug. I was ready for a mate. Not only a mate, but the whole nine yards—a mate, kids, a happy family. I could close my eyes and imagine little bunnies running around my house and yard, playing their little hearts out.

Laila pushed aside a palm leaf and poked her head around. "Thank God it's you. I've invaded the privacy of three other people already."

I raised my eyebrows at her. "You could try your nose."

She scrunched it up. "It's still weird for me."

She'd only just found out she was a shifter over the course of the past year. She was a wolf shifter, though. There was absolutely no reason she shouldn't be using her heightened sense of smell to her advantage.

"I'll get there."

She glanced at my computer screen and made a face. "Online dating? Come on, Parker. I don't think that works. Online people are illusions. They're half-truths, and then your own mind fills in the blanks with imaginary preferences."

I grunted. "I have to try. I haven't seen another rabbit on the island since those damn polar bears showed up."

She sighed dreamily. "Oh, yeah. The polar bears. They're sooo hot."

"Hot? They're scaring away my chance of finding a mate." I finished my coffee, stared into the mug, and blinked, wondering how I'd finished the entire cup so fast. "I'm going to die old and alone because of them. Hell, I'm practically an old maid now. Do you know I'm a decade older than my mom was when she had me? A decade!"

Laila shut my laptop and shook her head. "You're going to meet your mate and live happily ever after. Stop stressing. It'll happen when it's supposed to. Just relax and let it."

"I don't think I know how to relax."

"No kidding. You remind me of the energizer bunny. You have no chill mode."

I gave her a blank stare, unamused. "First of all, *no chill mode?* What are you? Eighteen? Second of all, don't play up stereotypes. They're insulting."

She just waved me off and pulled my mug towards her. "Want some more? I'm going to get a hot chocolate."

"Sure. Decaf, though." I waited until she was gone and then opened my laptop again. I logged onto a different dating site. No rabbits and even scarier looking options.

Someone needed to build a site for shifters that was legit. Not a sketchy, backwards, hook up site, but something modern and tasteful. Shifters needed help meeting one another, too. I had to wonder how many shifters were walking around living a lonely existence because they had yet to find "the one". I bet there were tons who would jump at the opportunity to search for a mate right from the comfort of their own living room. Surely fate couldn't orchestrate every pairing itself. Maybe fate needed a personal assistant from time to time.

I lifted the palm leaf to call to Laila. "On second thought, make the coffee regular. I'm addicted to the caffeine." I frowned. "Actually, make it an espresso. Double."

Paige laughed. "I'd already ignored the decaf order. I know you better than you know yourself, Parker."

I lowered my leaf again, ensconcing myself in my hidey hole. My fingers flew over the keys, composing an email to a distant cousin in Jacksonville. She'd found her mate at a young age, a wolf shifter, but she still had friends who hung out in the single shifter crowd. Desperation was getting the better of me and I shamelessly requested she ask around her friend group about any single rabbits in the state.

"Okay. A double espresso and a muffin, your favorite—chocolate/chocolate chip."

"Oh, I love you. And my fat rolls love you even more."

Laila shrugged and flopped herself into her own fur-lined chair. "How was work today?"

"Boring. The rooms filled up yesterday and no one has checked out. All I had to do was clean rooms and give walking directions to various attractions." I frowned. "No newly arriving guests to sign my petition."

"I still don't understand why you need to have the name of your species changed. It's been the same since the eighties."

I narrowed my eyes at her. "Because my species isn't some sort of crude joke. That's why."

She held up her palms in surrender. "Hey, at least you get the energized and sex hungry reputation. I'm supposedly some terrifying monster who howls at the full moon wants to eat your children."

"What children?"

She slapped my arm. "Stop. It'll happen when it happens. Now, come on, relax and stop trying to force something."

We both knew her advice was in vain.

I had no intention of sitting back and waiting for a mate to fall into my lap. No, this girl was nothing if not proactive.

4

MAXIM

The AC units in the office were still going full blast despite the slightly cooler weather and the fact that Hannah, wearing a thick sweater and wrapped in a blanket, sat at the desk answering the phone with chattering teeth. I tuned in, waiting to see if we were needed for anything important.

"Police scanner 411. 719 with 212 at 901 Dockside Drive." Hannah repeated the call, louder, and then hung up.

We were all hanging around the office, so everyone heard it. Serge translated aloud, "Rogue shifter. Domestic situation."

"Rabbit with a reported firearm," Roman added.

Dockside Drive was on the north end of town. We swung into action immediately and, after piling into the van outside with Serge behind the wheel, pulled out onto Main Street. We didn't need gear for this one. Not for facing down a rabbit shifter. Not much of a threat there, even with a firearm.

"What kind of pussy shifter uses a gun?" Alexei shook his head. "And what's with all these batshit crazy shifters down here?"

"Probably the weather. The heat would drive anyone loco," I growled audibly, angry all over again about being sent to Florida. "We're never going to work a real assignment again. The main office is going to hear about the work we've been doing here and they're going to laugh us right out of every fucking special ops mission ever."

Serge sped from the south end of the island, dodging what little traffic there was this late in the tourist season. "This *is* a real assignment. It may not be what we're used to but, in the event you hadn't noticed, these are real people and real situations and they need real assistance."

"A rabbit shifter waving a gun around is a real assignment?" I stared ahead, seething. If it hadn't been for Serge chasing Hannah instead of focusing on the job, we'd all still be in Siberia executing recon missions or hostage recoveries instead of responding to a domestic involving a fucking bunny rabbit. My grandma could handle that.

"Get over yourself and take this seriously, Maxim."

Serge slowed and took a right. We pulled up in front of a little white cottage with a small but growing crowd gathering out front. One sniff told me the crowd was a mix of humans with a couple shifters thrown in.

We were out of the truck and parting the crowd in seconds. Just as we got to the front porch, the door of the house flew open and a woman came running out with a small man chasing after her. His eyes were crazed and had a drugged-out glaze. He was waving a small caliber pistol in the air and shouting something unintelligible.

As the woman flew down the steps, he was right behind her. "Get back here, Marisol!" His speech was slurred and it was clear he wasn't in complete control of his senses.

I stepped between them just after Marisol ran by. The rabbit came up short and pointed his gun at me. My fist shot out and landed a solid uppercut to his jaw, but instead of the blow knocking him out cold as it should have, his eyes spun wilder and he squeezed the trigger—firing the weapon. The shot missed my head by millimeters and only because I'd jerked to the side as a precaution.

Furious that the puny fucker would dare fire at me, and at point-blank range, no less, I yanked the gun away from him and lifted him by his throat. "Look at me, you stupid little cotton-tailed rodent. You just attempted to shoot me in the face! You're lucky I don't snap your worthless neck. Me and the guys would love a hearty pot of rabbit stew for dinner tonight."

Serge relieved the perp of his weapon and grunted. "Alright. You can release him."

I dropped the asshole to the ground and swore when he instantly sprinted away down the beach. I rolled my eyes. "Give me that gun back. I'm going to shoot his ass."

Alexei and Dmitry took off after him and Serge stepped over to the woman, Marisol, to talk to her and determine whether she needed medical care. Roman stood next to me grinning. "So. Not a real assignment, huh? Thumper almost blew your head off."

I scowled, about to respond, but something distracted me. A delicious but light scent of...carrot cake. It floated atop everything else, including the stench of the rabbit junkie. The aroma had my mouth watering and my cock jumping in my pants. I ignored Roman as I scanned the crowd trying to determine where it was coming from. There, near the back. A short, curvy woman with light purple hair, facial piercings and a mean scowl. She was evidently pissed about something, but she smelled like absolute heaven on earth.

I caught only a brief glimpse of her before she was swallowed by the crowd. Just a glimpse of pale purple hair and an angry glower. But, that was all it took to pique my interest and spark a strong urge to go after her.

Serge was yelling my name, though, calling for more restraints. Konstantin cuffed my shoulder, urging me forward, and then I was running through the sand, away from the scrumptious scent of carrot cake.

When I reached the guys, they'd made it pretty far down the beach. They were wrestling the rabbit, trying to hold him down. The drugs he was on had apparently given him some crazy superstrength. He shouldn't have been able to hold his own with one polar bear, much less the group of us.

By the time we got him restrained and back on his feet, he had a bloody nose and a black eye and his bottom lip was starting to swell.

He was also spitting mad, screaming and calling us every name in the book. We were all pretty much covered in sand and sweat and Alexei had apparently suffered a broken nose in the scuffle.

Back at the van, I caught another hint of that delicious aroma drifting through the air and I jerked around to search for its source. I found her standing behind a group of shifters, her eyes burning with fury as they raked over the drugged out rabbit shifter. I willed her to look at me, but she avoided my eyes as though she knew that's what I wanted and instead intentionally chose to be defiant. Before I could do something to make her look, she was gone. I growled, frustrated that again, she slipped away.

I had felt her anger as though it was a living, breathing entity. It was almost as though, if I tried, I might've even been able to hear her thoughts. I didn't try. I was tempted, but something held me back. There was some little niggling at the back of my brain, some little recognition of what that kind of connection might mean.

"Maxim?" Serge was staring at me, *his* anger visible, too. "Get in the fucking van."

I scanned once more for "Carrot Cake" before getting in and slamming the door shut. She was hiding from me. That was fine. It was a small island. I'd find her.

5
PARKER

I sat behind my desk at the bed and breakfast, still fuming over what I'd witnessed the day before. I hadn't been able to sleep much last night, I was so angry. A local rabbit shifter had been beaten by those big, muscled, testosterone-fueled bully bears. Sure, the rabbit, Jamie, had been crazy and strung out on drugs. He hadn't been acting right, but they didn't have to beat him. And what the hell was Jamie doing getting hooked on drugs? Our population of rabbits was less than two hundred—worldwide! We couldn't afford for a single one of us to be lost to street drugs.

God, once it got out that Jamie had been beaten up by a group of apex predators, I was most certainly going to die a withered old spinster. No rabbit was going to set foot on Sunkissed Key. The males of my species were careful. A little too careful at times, but who could blame them for not wanting to face off with a bunch of polar bears.

I groaned out loud and leaned back in my chair. "I'm destined to go through life alone."

Penny popped her head out of the dining room and frowned. "Who are you talking to?"

"Myself? Mother nature? The universe? I don't know."

She furrowed her brows and shook her head. "Just...keep it down."

I groaned louder and was rewarded with Penny throwing a leftover cinnamon roll at me. Of course, I caught it. I was a shifter with quick reflexes. Plus, I'd skipped breakfast and was ravenous.

I kept picturing that one especially cocky looking polar bear from the day before. He'd almost gotten his head blown off by Jamie because he was so confident that he could handle a little rabbit shifter. Ha! Then, he'd made that comment about rabbit stew. Disgusting. It was unfortunate he was such a Neanderthal because he smelled so good, like pine forests and spiced oranges.

The bell chimed and I looked up to greet whoever was arriving. "Welcome to—"

"Save your spiel. It's just me." Laila waved me off as she entered holding a wrapped sandwich that I could smell as soon as the door opened. "I brought you food, since you always seem to be starving to death."

I tore into the vegan sandwich and moaned as it hit the bottomless pit that was my stomach. "Thank you! I can't stop thinking about food today. I don't know what it is."

"Your period?"

I shook my head and shoved more food into my mouth.

"Pregnant?"

I snorted. "That would require sex with someone other than myself."

Penny poked her head back out of the dining room. "Do you mind?"

I glared at her. "I'm sorry that I'm interrupting your polishing the silverware routine."

"I'm sorry that I don't want to hear about your masturbation sessions."

"I don't have to take this abuse, you know?"

"Quit. I dare you." She laughed. "No one else on this island would be loco enough to hire you."

I pouted at her and took another bite of my sandwich. Talking with my mouth full, I complained. "Lay off, boss lady. I'm having a bad day."

"Because of the gorgeous guys who roughed up the asshole who was beating his old lady yesterday?"

I scowled at Laila. "Do you have to put it that way?"

"What way? Like they're heroes?"

"They're literally predators. Not heroes. And they're scaring off all my potential baby-making partners. No decent prospect is going to come to this island if those ruffians are on the loose."

Penny wagged her brows. "They're more than on the loose. They're wild and hot and if I wasn't happily married, I'd let any one of them get loose on me. Come rough me up a bit."

"Are you serious? Go back to your silverware, ya' freak." I pursed my lips. "How are all the women on this island blinded by the looks of those cretins. They have muscles, so what? They're handsome, so what? They smell really good, so what? That stuff doesn't matter in the long run."

Laila giggled. "They smell really good?"

"Not the point."

"What *is* the point, Parker?"

"Well, Penny, the point is that I want a man who has the right qualities to become decent marriage materials. Qualities like loyalty, and commitment and, oh yeah, *humility*! Someone who will be as dedicated to my causes as I am and who will marry me and have little…Parker babies with me." I couldn't say rabbit babies, but that's what I meant. "No man like that is going to come here while those beasts are on the loose."

"Those beasts, as you called them, are helping this town and its unique brand of crime. Plus, they're beautiful. And you'll find your significant other whether those beautiful creatures are here or not."

She didn't get it. I wasn't going to meet a rabbit with those polar bears on the island and without a rabbit, I had no chance of doing my part to help save my species. There was a very real possibility that in another couple generations, we would become completely extinct.

And that damned Hugh Hefner moniker would follow us to our graves.

I groaned and flopped back in my chair, letting my arms hang limply out to my sides. "You don't get it!"

"I have to get back to work. I just wanted to drop off the sandwich, and you're being weird."

"And I have silverware to polish. You *are* being weird, Parker."

I rolled my eyes to the ceiling. "You're both fair-weather friends."

Laila just laughed. "I'll see you later. Your place after work?"

"Let's do Mimi's. I need a drink. Or a couple."

Penny popped back out of the dining room. "Maybe you'll run into one of those good smelling hunks there."

God, I really hoped not.

6

PARKER

I usually just drank at home or had a little "Irish coffee" at Latte Love. Even though Paige didn't technically serve alcohol, she kept a bottle of whiskey behind the counter—hush-hush and only for her close circle of friends.

I'd been to most of the bars on the island a few times each, but not for a while. As I settled onto a stool at Mimi's Cabana, I wondered why I wasn't doing this kind of thing more. If I wanted to meet someone, I needed to get out and mingle. The dark cloud that was my reality crept over me reminding me that there were very few rabbits hanging out on the island, so it wasn't likely I'd run into one at Mimi's anyway. Damn polar bears.

I'd gone home and changed after work, though, because one never knew. I might just get lucky and the perfect marriageable rabbit shifter might just happen to be passing through our small island and might just happen to come waltzing into the bar, lost, thirsty, and looking for love. I'd put my hair up in space buns and thrown on a curve-hugging short, black dress. I'd even added a little glitter around my eyes to spice things up. I maintained a strict goal of finding a rabbit and mating to help further our species, but a girl could still have some fun without it affecting her social activism.

Laila had on a slinky little light blue dress and it looked amazing with her pale skin and thick, white-blonde hair that curled out around her head in every direction. Her human self was every bit as stunning as her wolf form probably was.

If I was a lesser woman, I would've been jealous of her. She was a badass wolf shifter and looked the part. I was an endangered rabbit and, unfortunately, I looked the part, too—round and fluffy.

Sighing, I nudged her and smiled. "You look stunning."

She grinned back at me. "You look amazing, yourself. I love the space buns. Fun."

I narrowed my eyes. "What kind of fun?"

Her eyes lit with mischief. "The kind you need handlebars for."

I slapped her arm but couldn't help laughing. "Should I take them down? No. No, forget I asked. I like them. Even if they look like BJ accessories."

"Yeah, fuck it." She paused in lifting her hand to signal the bartender. "Um... Fuck feeling self-conscious about them. Not fuck it like...you. Or your mouth."

"God, Laila!" I rolled my eyes and turned to the bartender coming our way. "Hi! Can I get a whiskey?"

"For me, too."

The woman quickly and efficiently poured our drinks, her pretty green eyes on my hair all the while. "I like it."

I groaned. "You heard?"

She nodded. "But I do like it. You look spunky."

I twisted my mouth. "Do I want to come off as spunky, though? I'm trying to find a mate. I mean boyfriend! I'm trying to find a boyfriend."

She suddenly leaned forward, "Did you say *mate*?"

I narrowed my eyes and inhaled her scent, searching for any hint of shifter to explain why she'd know about mates. She was human, but she had the scent of bear all over her. "Yeah."

"Are you...?" She suddenly pushed back from the bar and held up her hands. "I'm sorry. That's rude. It's none of my business. I hate when people invade my privacy, so I should know better."

I studied her a second longer and extended my hand. "Parker. I'm a...what you're thinking. Rabbit."

Laila pointed to herself. "Wolf. New at it, though."

"Heidi. I'm just...uh, normal, but my mate is a bear."

"One of those hunky polar bears walking around the island?" Laila threw back her shot and gave me a big, shit eating grin. "Isn't that a funny coincidence, Parker?"

I tossed my own shot back and kicked Laila. "I saw a couple of them yesterday, working. Small world."

"Small island." She smiled. "Well, you ladies enjoy yourselves tonight. I have to work the bar." She gestured with her head to the opposite end of the bar where a young couple was trying to get her attention. "Another shot before I go?"

We both nodded gratefully as she poured us new shots. When she walked away, I wrinkled my nose at Laila. "She seems so nice. What's she doing with one of those cocky jerks?"

"Maybe they're not the jerks you think they are."

"Maybe they are."

"Maybe you need to stop being size-ist."

I scoffed. "That is not why I don't like them!"

She scoffed right back at me. "Well, whatever the reason, could it be that you're, oh, I dunno...*wrong*?"

I glanced down at Heidi and watched as she smiled sweetly at an older man in a Florida Marlins baseball cap. She said something that made him laugh. She honestly did seem nice, yet I couldn't help feeling the way I felt. It was in my nature to be cautious. My kind had a sense of self-preservation built in, particularly against large, predatory, carnivorous animals. Plus, look what they'd done to Jamie's face.

I shrugged off Laila's words and threw back my shot. "It's not like it matters. It just is what it is. I don't have anything to worry about unless you plan on bringing one of them home."

"I think four of them are already mated. That only leaves two. Hey, maybe you and I should each take one."

When I looked over at her, about to give her a piece of my mind, she barked a laugh and slapped my leg, clearly thrilling in her little game of 'mess with Parker'. I just scowled. "You're not as funny as you think you are."

"Yes, I am."

Heidi came back a while later and poured us another drink, her smile warm and genuine. "I haven't met any other people like you two. Besides my mate and, you know, the other guys in his unit."

I shrugged. "We're around."

"Even here? Like in this place, now?"

I looked around the bar and inhaled deeply. "Yeah. Two other wolves, a snake, a flamingo, and a couple of—"

Laila touched my arm. "You okay?"

I motioned to Heidi for another shot as the scent of pine forests and spiced oranges washed over me. Warm and sultry, it stirred my rabbit into a heated frenzy. "More whiskey," I croaked out.

"Oh, hey. And three polar bears." Heidi grinned. "Really, though? A snake?"

I pointed to my empty shot glass and repeated myself. "Whiskey, please."

Laila looked over and suddenly laughed, drawing more attention to us. I was tempted to knock her ass off the barstool to get her to shut up. The last thing I wanted was for the source of that seductive scent to come any closer to me. My rabbit was up wiggling her stupid nose and thumping her stupid little feet in excitement. Bitch was all but sticking her cotton-tailed ass in the air.

"Really small island, indeed." Laila wrapped her arm around the back of my stool and leaned closer. "Should I call them over?"

"I'm leaving. I've had some whiskey, a little chit-chat. I think it's time we take off." I lifted the flap of my purse and rifled through its contents in search of my wallet. Petition, fliers, pens, pencils, ketchup packets from a take-out joint, the other half of the sandwich that Laila had brought me for lunch. Where was my damned wallet?

"Oh, look! Here they come."

7
MAXIM

A s if I'd conjured her with my very thoughts, the angry little rabbit was sitting at the bar talking to Heidi. I could only see the back of her, but the light purple hair and the delicious aroma of carrot cake was a dead giveaway.

Her ass was a beautiful sight on that worn leather barstool. I suddenly wished I was familiar enough with her that I could walk up and greet her with a kiss and nuzzle her neck while I slid my hands over her luscious curves. The dress she wore looked soft to the touch. Soft and clingy. My eyes traced the path of her spine all the way down to her lower back, where the dress ended. She had a tattoo, an intricate design of flowers. I inadvertently leaned closer, desperate to get a peek at the end of that tattoo that was hidden beneath the dress.

"Dude, why are you growling?" Alexei punched me in the shoulder and shook his head. "You're being weird today."

I ran a hand through my hair and followed Konstantin to the booth where we usually sat while Alexei went to the bar to talk to his mate. Damn, he stood next to the sexy little rabbit—he stood right next to her! I didn't like how close he was to her. That was where I wanted to be, slipping my arm around her waist and letting my other hand curl over her thigh possessively. Her skin looked as though it would feel incredibly soft under my touch.

"Still growling, fucker." Konstantin slid across the booth and sank into the dark corner with his back against the wall.

I sat across from him and angled myself so I could keep an eye on my angry little rabbit.

She leaned into the woman next to her and said something that made Alexei, on her other side, laugh. Her head snapped around to him and I felt the sting of the glare she shot him all the way to where I sat. I couldn't make out what Heidi said through the dull roar of the crowded bar, but she was smiling as she said it.

I suddenly needed to be there. I wanted to shove my way between Alexei and the little bunny and hear what she was saying. I could only imagine it came with a hefty dose of firecracker.

"Who's the bunny?" Konstantin leaned out of the shadows to smirk at me. "She got a target on her ass or are you just that horny?"

I growled and stood. "Enjoy your solitude, asshole."

He just chuckled as I walked away leaving him alone in the booth. He wouldn't have to be alone for long—not if he didn't want to be. Although, he probably preferred seclusion.

I skirted around the crowd and came up to the little group on Alexei's other side. He nodded in acknowledgement and then looked back at his mate.

"Hey, Max, tell Heidi that we didn't purposely rough up a helpless little bunny rabbit yesterday." He nodded over his shoulder and grinned. "Seems that we have an 'excessive use of force' complaint, brother."

Heidi leaned over the bar and patted Alexei on the cheek. "It's all fun and games until someone gets a bottle of whiskey cracked over his head. C'mon babe, leave her alone. It's time for my break. Come help me in the back with…a thing. Wink, wink, nudge, nudge."

Alexei's lascivious grin spread from one ear to the other and, quick as a flash, he vanished and I was face to face with the petite rabbit shifter who'd been on my mind since we dealt with that lunatic druggie the day before. When I met her gaze, I sucked in a sharp breath, taken aback by the intensity of the flames in her eyes as she stared at me.

Fuck, she was sexy. Rounded cheeks and pouty lips, oddly colored hair styled into two little knobby things on either side of her head. She should've looked like a sweet little cherub or something, not a sex kitten. Sex *bunny*? Whatever, damn, she was all appealingly sexy to me. She had a piercing under her bottom lip, one at the side of her nose and another through her left brow. Her lovely golden eyes were enhanced by glitter and I suddenly had a fantasy of waking up in the morning with glitter sticking to my chest...and stomach...and everything.

I stared, mesmerized, as her pouty lips turned down at the corners and her eyes narrowed. "Go away."

I coughed out a shocked laugh and, just like that, she turned to her friend and gave me her back. If sexy bunny knew how intent I was on running my tongue all over her floral tattoos, she wouldn't have been so comfortable showing me her back.

"Excuse me?" I felt my adrenaline kick up and my half-hard dick grew to full mast.

She downed a shot of whiskey, her throat working as the liquid slid down, and ignored me. "Time to go. I've got work in the morning."

Her friend was nearly suffocating in an attempt to disguise a fit of giggles. "No, you don't. Oh, my god, Parker. What are you doing?"

A man stepped into the space between us and leaned up against the bar. His ignorance of his own actions was the only reason I didn't knock his ass to the ground with a single punch. He motioned for Mimi, and kept his eyes to himself.

"Parker, is it? Cute name."

I wasn't too far that I couldn't see goosebumps spread over her back and shoulders. So, I was having an effect on her after all.

The guy between us looked over at me. "Um, it's Dave, actually."

I heard her snicker and growled out, "Not you, Dave."

He looked behind him and nodded. "Oh, uh, sorry. Switch places with me?"

Parker's head snapped around and she pinned Dave with a look of sheer savagery. "Stay."

Dave stayed.

I grinned at her. "Parker, this is no way to get to know each other."

"I'm not interested in getting to know you. You're a ruffian and a bully. I saw what you did to poor Jamie yesterday." She narrowed her pretty, glittery eyes and shook her head at me. "I'm not even speaking to you. You're about three times his size and five times his strength. I'm so not speaking to you. You could've easily restrained him without hurting him. But did you? No. I'm definitely not speaking to you."

"Yet you're still talking, Bunny."

The little knobs on top of her head rocked when she snapped her head back around to me. "Bunny? Really?"

"So, you're pissed because I defended myself against an out of control, raging drug addict who was using his mate as a punching bag and tried to shoot me in the face?" I raised my eyebrows. "Does crazy run in your kind?"

I was half sure I saw smoke shoot out of her ears. She leaned across a wide-eyed Dave and jabbed her finger at me. Her fingernail was painted neon green. "By *your kind*, do you mean what I think you mean?"

Dave had had enough. He sidestepped her neon green pointer finger and hurried off to the other side of the bar. I slid closer to the little demon bunny and had to ball my fists up tightly to keep from brushing a stray piece of hair behind her ear. "If you *think* I mean rabbit shifters who have clearly lost all sense of reason and rationality, then, yeah, I mean what you think I mean."

"You don't know me. You can't say I have no sense of reason. You just think you're so high and mighty, top of the food chain, no natural predators and all that. Well, whoopty-fucking-do! Aren't you Mr. Bigbad?!" She made contact with that finger, one solid poke to the middle of my chest and I felt it all the way down to my toes.

"You realize you're literally poking a bear right now. I'd say that amounts to a clear lack of sense. *And* you're arguing in defense of a wife beater."

"Girlfriend beater, technically, and I'm not defending *him*, I'm criticizing *you*." She poked me again. "And I'm not afraid of you. I will poke you until I'm blue in the face if I feel like it."

I grabbed her hand and yanked her into my chest. "Is that so? Go out with me, then. You can poke me all you want."

The statement just about shocked us both equally, but I recovered faster. I'd meant it. I wanted to fight with her more. I wanted to fuck her and fight with her. I wanted to fuck, fight, and then fuck some more. I wanted everything I could get with her.

Parker's eyes flew open. Her apparent shock seemed to cool off some of her anger. Her mouth opened and closed a few times before she reined her emotions in and went right back to glaring. "You have got to be kidding me."

I was still holding her against my chest and I was pretty sure she could feel how much I wasn't kidding. "Go out with me, Bunny."

She suddenly jerked away from me, slid off the barstool, and straightened. Standing in front of me, she barely reached my chin. She was a tiny, curvy little thing, but when she glared up at me, size was no issue. "No. Fucking. Way."

She turned on her heel and marched off, her hips swaying as she went. I watched her go, every part of me longing to chase her down. She was prey and she was running away. Like she knew what I was thinking, she looked back at me over her shoulder and flipped me the bird before stomping out of the bar.

I stared after her, not even sure what had just happened. I knew only that, whatever it was, I wanted a whole lot more of it.

8
PARKER

"Hello. We have a reservation for Alan and Mary Jo Hill."

I forced a smile and nodded. I went through the motions of checking in the happy couple and then watched as Penny picked up where I left off. She did her whole welcome spiel and offered cinnamon rolls and tea or coffee, then came back to me with a frown on her face.

"That was subpar, at best."

I frowned right on back at her. "Well, I'm in a crap mood."

"You didn't even pester them to sign your petition."

Shit! "You think I can still catch them before they lock themselves in their room?"

"No!" She snorted out a laugh. "Finish telling me about last night before someone else comes in."

"I'm so pissed off, Pen." I shoved my hair out of my face but it immediately flopped back. "That bully guy, the one who made all the nasty comments about rabbits? He was there at Mimi's last night, hitting on me."

"Which one is he?"

The one who smells like heaven. "The one with the big ego that's probably a mask for a small dick."

She raised her eyebrows. "Really?"

It wasn't true. I'd felt too much at the bar to be able to say that he had a small dick with a straight face. I'd felt *way* too much. "Whatever. He's the one with the perfectly styled hair—not a strand out of place."

Her eyes went wide. "Oh, that one! Maxim, I think. He's the bad boy of the group, I hear. Lots of broken hearts left in his wake."

I made a face. "Really? If by bad boy, you mean loud-mouthed conceited jerk, then that's him."

"Okay, just get on with the rest of the story."

"He was there, hitting on me. Still talking crap about rabbits and being a general, all around dick, but yeah. He asked me to go out with him. No, actually, he *told* me to go out with him."

"And that's a problem, because…"

I grunted. "*He's* the problem. He and his Rambo buddies are running around the island scaring off all my potential future baby daddies."

"You know I love you, right?"

Sighing, I shook my head. "I don't want to hear it right now, Penny. I'm not being unreasonable. He's dangerous *and* problematic! Not to mention a complete arrogant ass!"

"Do you remember Eric Granger?" She gave me a teasing look. "You spent six months telling me what a jerk he was and then you nearly wet yourself when he asked you to prom."

"Eric Granger moved to Detroit and got arrested for feeling up a woman on a bus."

"Still. You practically shouted from the rooftops about how much you hated him. When, really, all you wanted was for him to notice you."

I faked a gag. "I'm not a teenager anymore, Penny. I no longer think that a boy teasing me and dipping my pigtails in the ink well means he likes me. I'm not saying this about Maxim, or whatever his name is, because I want him to ask me to the high school prom. He's rude. He fucking calls me Bunny. What the hell is that?"

Jacob rounded the corner, a scowl on his face. "Who fucking calls you Bunny?"

Penny pointed at me. "This is why you have to watch your mouth."

"Mom, come on. I'm not a kid. Plus, you say fuck all the time."

Penny's head looked like it might explode as she angrily pointed back the way Jacob had come from. "Go to your room."

"I'm supposed to be helping with the luggage."

"Well, go to someone else's room, then. I don't care. I just don't want to see your dirty little mouth in my face right now." She shook her head. "I don't swear that much, I really don't."

Jacob, grinning because he knew his mom was a pushover and wasn't as mad at him as she pretended to be, winked at me. "See you later, *Bunny*."

"Don't call me that."

"Don't call her that."

"Whatever."

Penny glared at me. "I blame you. He gets that attitude by emulating you."

"I kind of think he has a great attitude. Besides hitting on me, kid's got an awesome sense of humor."

"Tell me again why I continue to employ you?"

"Anyways. Laila thought the whole thing was great. She's completely fooled by him. She said I need someone like him, someone who stands up to me. I think she's lost it." I winced as the bell rang, but cheered up when I saw it was Paige coming over with coffee. "My favorite twin!"

"Don't let it go to your head, sis. She's hating on me right now because I pointed out that she's crushing on one of the guys from that rescue group."

"I am *not* crushing on him." My stupid little rabbit was up and hopping around, though. *She* seemed to like polar bears just fine. Matter of fact, she seemed to looove polar bears, and one in particular. Why she wasn't afraid was beyond me.

"Ooh, which one? I've heard the one with the perfectly styled hair is a total playboy."

There was a word I abhorred. Playboy. It reminded me of the man for whom my species was named. Not that I had anything against Hugh Hefner personally, but who wanted to be the namesake of a man considered to be the world's largest-scale and longest-running pimp? It was utterly disrespectful and bordered on defamation.

Of course, Maxim was a playboy. No wonder I found him so off-putting.

"Look at that, she's at a loss for words. Her brain just short circuited, or something."

I tilted my head and leveled Penny with a glare. "You are going to end up doing this job with just 89-year-old Marvin to help if you don't behave yourself."

The threat fell on deaf ears, though. Both sisters giggled and poked at me, having fun at my expense and acting like unruly children. Penny even ended up singing that childhood song about kissing in a tree before I surrendered and went upstairs to see if I couldn't find something to clean.

Still, as I stripped a bed and laid out clean sheets, I could hear her singsong voice in my head, taunting me about love and marriage and a baby carriage with the goddamned polar bear.

9

MAXIM

That night, P.O.L.A.R. house was full. The entire team was seated around the dining room table as were the new mates. Serge and Hannah had cooked a great big Italian meal. The smell of garlic and oregano filled the house and made my mouth water and my stomach rumble. I had plans to go out later, but I wasn't about to miss a good, homecooked meal.

The dining room table wasn't big enough for the whole crew, but the guys preferred their mates on their laps anyway. I was seated at the end of the table, watching as the food was passed around. When it got to me, I piled my plate high with spaghetti and meatballs and dug in.

The table was quiet for a while as we all got busy stuffing our faces. I was always hungry; I was a bear, after all. Even as I ate, though, I couldn't help stealing glances at Heidi. I wanted to ask her if she knew anything more about Parker, but not in front of the others.

I couldn't help but wonder about the hot-headed little rabbit shifter. Where did she live? What did she do? How did she like her eggs?

Nope, not going there. It didn't matter what breakfast food she preferred or how she liked it prepared. I was never going there with her. I drew the line at overnights. Too messy.

Still, I found myself starting to open my mouth and ask about her. It wasn't my business, though. Plus, I wasn't some dweeby high school nerd who couldn't get a girl's number without going through her friend.

"What is it, Maxim?" Heidi put her fork down and narrowed her eyes at me. "You keep looking at me like you have something to say and it's driving me crazy."

Alexei growled at me, clearly not appreciating that I was looking at his mate. "Keep your eyes to yourself, fucker."

"Hush for a second, Alexei. Is there something you want to ask me, Maxim?"

I looked at Heidi and shook my head. Nope. I wasn't about to ask about Parker. Especially not with a live audience sitting around. "No, nothing. Nothing at all."

"Come on. Out with it."

I let out a slow breath. "I was just wondering who's working the bar tonight."

She rolled her eyes. "Something tells me that's not what you really want to say."

Alexei continued to glare at me as we finished our dinner. Everyone else went back to normal, but I was ready to get away. I didn't like that I seemed to be preoccupied by Parker. I needed to go out and do something to get her out of my head.

After everyone had finished eating and we had all helped with the cleanup, Heidi sat down next to me. "Spit it out."

I feigned complete ignorance. "What?"

"Is this about the new bartender? Or Sarah?" She grinned suddenly. "Or that feisty little woman you were eyeing last night?"

"What feisty little woman?"

"Nice try, Maxim, but I'm on to you. So, it was the rabbit shifter who caught your attention?"

"I have no idea what you're talking about. I've got to go, though." I stood and patted her head as I walked past her. "Tell Alexei I said he's a dick-faced loser."

"Uh huh. Well, before you go, I don't know anything else about her. I liked her, though."

I forced myself to keep walking—one foot in front of the other—out of the house and down the street to the bar. In minutes, I was back at Mimi's, hoping I could forget about Parker. I had no idea why she had gotten under my skin. My bear was all freaked out by her, too.

The pervasive thoughts were threatening to ruin my night, but I wasn't going to let that happen. I was going to have a good time and get her out of my head. Maybe for good.

Mimi's Cabana was busy when I got there, but I found a seat at the bar and ordered a beer. I scanned for single women but didn't see anyone who held my interest.

Mimi came over right away with a cheeky grin for me. Her coconut-covered breasts swayed. It was always a gamble whether or not one of those suckers was gonna pop right out of its coconut. "Hey, honey. What can I get you?"

"Whiskey. Neat." I answered before I even thought about it. I realized I'd only ordered that because that was what Parker had been drinking. "Scratch that. Make it a beer, actually."

"Having an identity crisis, Mr. Maxim?"

I gave her a grin and shook my head. "Not me."

After she handed off my beer and waddled off to her other patrons, I turned to face the crowd. There was an eager looking blonde on the dance floor making eye contact and adding a little extra sway to her hips. I wasn't interested. In truth, as attractive as she was, she did nothing for me. But I had something to prove, so I forced myself.

I joined Blondie on the dance floor and we danced a few songs before she dragged me to her table and sat on my lap while telling me about herself. I tried to listen, I really did, but only a few words here and there registered. I didn't give two shits about her and would have preferred to stand up and let her just slide right off my lap and onto the floor, but I had to do this. When Blondie snaked her arms around my neck and leaned in to kiss me, I couldn't do it. I flinched reflexively and drew back. She giggled, thinking I was teasing, and arched her body against mine. I felt nothing.

I was determined, though. Maybe I just needed to get her away from the crowd and let things heat up a bit, I thought. Blondie was quick to invite me back to her place and I pretended I was as excited as she was when she pulled me by the hand toward the door.

I was forcing myself to appear interested as Blondie stripped for me. It was a good show, one I normally would've been really into. She put work into it and when she straddled me and leaned in to kiss me again, I should've enjoyed it. Instead, I dodged her lips and tried to think of an excuse to get the hell out of there.

Panic started to creep up my spine when she went to her knees and tried to unbutton my pants. Oh, hell no. No, no, no, that wasn't gonna happen. I wasn't attracted to her. Not even a little bit. I mean, I *wanted* to want her, but no go. My dick was limp as a wet noodle and I was getting close to losing the contents of my stomach all over her.

Instead of sticking around to find out if I was having a bad night, or a *really* bad night, I did the low down cowardly thing and got the hell out of Dodge. I faked a phone call and pretended that urgent work-related business had come up and then I ran off with my tail between my legs.

I wanted to go home, but the thought of listening to a house full of my buddies screwing their mates…naw, it wasn't a good one. Instead, cussing up a storm, I headed back to Mimi's Cabana, and settled in our usual booth. In the dark shadows of the back of the establishment, I drank enough beer to sedate a whale all while keeping watch over the crowd, searching for a set of light purple hair knobs.

10
PARKER

My cousin came through for me. I had a short list of names of single, male rabbit shifters all of whom resided in the south Florida area. The list was golden. It might very well hold the name of the guy who would be my future mate and my partner in helping to perpetuate our species.

Turned out Ralph Riley wasn't that guy.

Ralph had answered my text right away.

Ralph had been willing to meet up for a date that very night.

Maybe I should've smelled something fishy when he'd called me twice to confirm that the date was still on.

I definitely should've smelled something fishy when he'd shown up in what I'd assumed was an Uber. Or, when the older woman driver parked and watched raptly as Ralph entered Tuna's Seafood House.

But, when he turned and gave her a big thumbs up before greeting me, I just told myself that the fact Ralph hadn't driven himself to the restaurant could simply mean that he didn't own a vehicle. Maybe Ralph was environmentally conscious.

When Ralph revealed that the older woman, who ended up

remaining outside of Tuna's and watching us through the front windows, was his mother, *that* smelled pretty darn fishy.

But I was a woman on a mission—to nab herself a rabbit mate. I still held out hope that there was a remote chance that Ralph and I could make it work.

By the time we'd finished our salads, all hope was long dead and buried. Unfortunately, Ralph, who still lived with and was supported by his parents, was about as exciting as a six hour layover. No job. No house. No car. No money. And no real interests—at least none he cared to share, which made me think he probably spent his days in his underwear holed up in his parent's basement playing video games and watching porn. What was worse, Ralph didn't seem to see anything wrong with his status in life. When I tried to tactfully question him about goals and aspirations, he gave me a blank stare. According to Ralph, his parents owed him since, after all, they'd brought him into the world.

By the time our vegetable lasagnas arrived, I was ready to pluck my eyelashes out from sheer boredom. I was getting an antsy feeling in the pit of my stomach, wondering if I was going to be able to find a rabbit mate that would pass muster. I also kept comparing Ralph's beady eyes to the heated gaze of the polar bear.

Midway through my lasagna, I was actually considering setting the place on fire—just a small bathroom fire. Anything to get away from Ralph. And if I couldn't get my mind off the damn polar bear, I might just throw myself into said fire.

Little did I know that things were about to go from bad to worse.

The door opened and the air in the place shifted suddenly. I looked up to see the polar bear striding cockily towards our table. With him came the irresistible aroma of pine forests and spiced oranges and I nearly drooled down my chin.

He looked pissed, his face pinched tightly, but when he got to our table, he forced an easy smile and nodded down at Ralph. "Hey, there."

Ralph looked like he was about to shit his pants. He looked every bit the defenseless, helpless rabbit facing down an apex predator. He stammered out a greeting and paled even further when the bear pulled up a chair from a nearby table.

"I hope I'm not interrupting anything. I was just passing by when I caught the loveliest scent of carrot cake." He extended his hand to Ralph and grinned. "Maxim. I'm a *very* close friend of Parker's."

Ralph hopped to his feet suddenly and nearly turned the whole table over on me. I was saved from being doused by Maxim's quick reflexes. His hand shot out to catch the water glass that was nearly upended. "S-sorry. I have to go. Mother is waiting."

I crossed my arms over my chest and glared at Maxim. "What are you doing here?"

He watched Ralph leave and quirked an eyebrow at me. "Was that your date?"

I was so angry that I was practically frothing at the mouth. Just by showing up, the stupid, asshole, cocky, dickhead bear had run off a potential mate. Well, in truth, Ralph had already been mentally crossed off my list, but what if he hadn't been? Then what?

"You are a dick."

"Moi?"

"You did that on purpose, scared him away like that."

"How?"

"By showing up!"

"You didn't go scurrying off like a timid little churchmouse. Why is it that *you're* not afraid of the big, bad bear, Bunny?" He leaned a little closer, that sweet yet spicy scent warming my whole body. "It occurred to me that instead of fleeing, you bare your teeth and prepare for battle. Is there something perhaps a little more vicious than helpless rabbit in you?"

I threw my head back and barked out a sarcastic laugh. "Why the hell would I be afraid of you? You're nothing but an arrogant bully!"

The waiter appeared at the table and made quick work of whisking away the plates. He made no acknowledgement as to the change of my dinner companions; he just smiled politely and asked if we wanted dessert.

"Do you have any carrot cake?"

I glared at Maxim as the waiter flashed him a warm smile, nodded and left. Feeling betrayed by the waitstaff, I sank back into my chair and grunted. "You were not invited."

"You didn't answer my question. Why aren't you afraid?"

"Because you're not scary. If I was afraid of every knuckle-dragging mouth-breather who roamed this island, I'd never leave my house." Then, just to insult him, I nodded to his hair. "Plus, who'd be afraid of a man who styles his hair with more precision than a beauty queen?"

I had to give him credit. He didn't even react to my insult about his hair. He just sat back and studied me.

"What were you doing with that guy?"

"I was on a date, for your information. A date that you just ruined."

Bear boy sat up at that and pointed to the exit Ralph had recently run through. "With *him*?"

I leaned forward. I shouldn't have entertained Maxim's questions, but anger got the better of me. "What is wrong with *him*?"

"You mean besides the fact that his mommy still wipes his ass for him? What's with you and the rabbit obsession, anyway?" He shook his head. "A woman like you would eat a spineless doormat like him for breakfast."

My mouth fell open. "A woman like me? Eat him for breakfast? Is that a fat joke? That's a fat joke, isn't it?"

I could have sworn Maxim's eyes went all heavy-lidded and seductive as they trailed over my body. "Not even a little bit, Bunny. It was a statement on how an overgrown adolescent like him could never handle a woman like you. A woman with the fire you possess...that sorry excuse for a male would be reduced to cinders by your flames."

I rolled my eyes. "You don't know me."

The waiter appeared again with a sizable slice of carrot cake, which he placed in front of Maxim, along with a glass of water, and then vanished again.

Maxim used a spoon to scoop a hefty bite into his mouth. His eyes closed, his jaw worked, and the growl that rumbled from his chest affected me way more than I cared to admit. "Fuck, I never knew how much I liked carrot cake until you."

I watched as he licked his lips and dove in for more. Only, instead of lifting the spoon to his own mouth, he moved it towards mine. My mouth opened instinctively and he slid the spoon in. His eyes glowed as he watched me, the gray in his irises glowing like molten steel. I enjoyed cake as much as any woman, but being fed by Maxim turned the experience into something shamelessly provocative. Suddenly everything felt electric in my mouth.

Maxim growled again, louder, and the spoon bent in his grip. He leaned into me, his blood pumping so loudly that I could hear it. "Go out with *me*, Bunny."

I snapped back to reality just in time—before I did something stupid like accept his offer. I swallowed the cake and leaned back in my chair, putting a few more inches of much needed distance between us. "No, thanks."

"Well, at least you were polite that time. We're getting closer."

I scowled. "You should leave."

"Why? Your skittish little date is long gone by now. His mommy took him home." He snorted and shook his head, like he couldn't believe any of it.

"Yeah, thanks to you. Look, I don't need you showing up, running my prospects off. You and the rest of your polar buddies. It's hard enough to find rabbits around here as it is."

"Prospects? *He* was a prospect? Why the low standards?"

"I don't have low standards. It just so happens there aren't many of us to choose from."

"*Us*? Who's *us*?"

"Rabbit shifters."

"Yeah, see, why are you limiting yourself like that?"

"None of your business."

"Come on, Bunny. Talk to your big, bad polar bear. Tell me what's wrong." He smirked. "Why are you so worried about me chasing all the scared little rabbits away?"

Fuming, I leaned into his space and poked him in the chest. "Stop being such a dick about rabbits."

He reached up and used his thumb to scratch his eyebrow, then twisted his mouth as though he was contemplating my request. "No. Probably not going to happen. It's just too tempting." He leaned forward and poked me back. "Now, tell me why it's so important for you to find rabbits. Did one of them steal all the Trix?"

I glared at him. "Oh, my god, you really are a complete dick!"

"So, they didn't steal the Trix?"

"I'm looking for a mate, you asshole." I hissed it out with another jab of my finger to his chest. "It's not easy to find a decent rabbit shifter who hasn't been scared away from the island by you Commando wannabes. Good enough answer for you?"

He caught my hand and held it, his smirk gone. In its place was a dark scowl. "Why does your mate have to be a rabbit?"

I jerked at my hand, but he was too strong. "So, I can have pure rabbit babies! Now, let go of me."

He let my hand go and watched as I stood up and pulled money out of my wallet.

Still, he was silent, that jaw working.

I threw down cash for the meal and shoved my wallet back in my purse. Glaring at him, I pushed in my chair in and skirted around the table, farthest away from him. "Keep your damned paws to yourself from now on, bear."

11

MAXIM

A few days had passed since I'd crashed Parker's date, but she hadn't left my mind the entire time. Worse, she hadn't left my bear's mind. He was infatuated. Every second of every day he urged me to find her—go to her. The whole thing was making me incredibly cranky.

Work had been busier than usual, so I'd at least been able to pretend to have some self-control. I hadn't been able to look for her and I hadn't embarrassed myself by admitting to any of the guys how much space in my head was dedicated to her.

Every hour that passed, I wondered if she'd found another fuck head rabbit to date like the one she'd been with at Tuna's Seafood House. I couldn't help wondering why a woman like her would resort to dating a loser like that. Rabbit babies? There had to be more to it than that. The thought made me want to hunt down the little underachiever who'd been with her at dinner that night. Hunt down, sink my teeth in, and rip his loser throat out.

It was late in the afternoon and I was slowly going insane. Work had slowed down and everyone else was checking out for the day. They were either rendezvousing with their mates or...doing whatever Konstantin did. I was proud of myself for staying away from Parker for a couple days. It had been a struggle, but I'd managed it by keeping busy with work. In the quiet of the office that afternoon, though, I felt my resolve caving in. I had an irresistible urge to find her, even if it was just to see her lips twist in annoyance when she saw me coming her way.

I went home and showered before dressing and getting ready. As I was styling my hair, I remembered Parker's barb about it and smiled to myself.

Not sure where to go, I ended up heading to Mimi's Cabana and settling in my booth. I hoped she'd show up there again and I'd get a chance to talk to her. I didn't know where else to look for her.

About ten beers and three hours in, I started to feel like a complete pathetic moron. Not just for waiting around the bar on the off chance that she'd stop in, but for thinking that if she did stop in, I'd have the remotest chance with her. She'd made it crystal clear that she wanted nothing to do with me.

She was a rabbit shifter who only wanted to meet another rabbit shifter to have rabbit babies with. Her intentions were clear, and they excluded me.

I was man enough to admit that I wasn't used to being rejected and it wounded my ego a bit. When she was with me and I could see the heat in her eyes, I didn't mind her words of rejection, or insults, or whatever she dished out. But not seeing her at all, that was hard, and it was leaving me with an empty feeling that was fast growing as I sat there pounding beers.

God, I was pathetic. Why was I sitting there crying in my beer over a woman who had told me over and over she didn't want me?

Plus, there was the whole issue of her wanting children. The last thing on my agenda was being someone's baby daddy. Hell, I had yet to graduate from wham-bam-thank-you-ma'am. One-and-done's were way more my style. Hell, I'd never woken up next to a woman—or wanted to. I didn't do relationships.

And I sure as hell didn't do children.

Parker...well, she was clearly not a one-night kind of girl. That much was obvious. I was barking up the wrong tree with her.

The longer I sat there, the more I was able to convince myself that I should overcome my obsession with Parker by spending a few hours of quality time with someone who *did* want to be with me and who *was* on the same wavelength as me. What was that old saying? The best way to get over someone is to get under someone else? There was a brunette at the bar who'd been giving me the 'come hither' eye all night.

My bear was not only outraged at the very thought, he was disgusted, repelled and nauseated. But, he wasn't my judge and jury. It wasn't often that I went against what he wanted, but he was just a polar bear, after all. What the fuck did he know?

Heidi was behind the bar watching as I approached the brunette. Her eyes rolled so hard I was afraid they'd fall out the back of her head, but she turned away and went about her business.

I bought a drink for the brunette and a few cheesy pickup lines later, we left. She was all over me by the time we got to the beach and even though I wasn't into her, I was ready to try anything in hopes of forgetting Parker—even for a night. Down in the sand we went, the brunette kissing me and both of us rolling around as she attempted to make out with me. I felt nothing but revulsion, though.

It only took me about two and a half minutes of forcing myself to endure her kisses and trying to summon feelings of arousal to realize that nothing was going to happen. My bear was roaring so loud in my head that I couldn't have focused even if I wanted to. I didn't even bother to fake a phone call that time. I just rolled off of her and told her it wasn't happening. She pouted, but she left pretty soon after, realizing that I was serious.

I stayed there in the sand, accepting that my dick was broken. It refused to react to anyone other than Parker. Who could blame it? No one looked as pretty or smelled as sweet. No one spit words of fire at me quite the same way, either. My bear was pissed at me for even thinking another woman might have been an option. Parker was the one. He wanted me to find her and apologize.

Oh, Jesus, my bear had turned into some sort of romantic sap while I wasn't looking. My bear? Hell, *I* was becoming the same sap.

I knew what was happening. I knew exactly what all this meant. Parker was my mate. And just like with the other guys, the mate bug was about to sink its teeth into my ass, bite down hard, and turn me into a mushy, cuddly teddy bear.

I groaned and flung my arm over my eyes, needing to just hide away on the beach for a little while longer. I wasn't ready for all that mate shit. I'd seen the guys become ultra-possessive and pissy. Grown ass men, all needy and helpless without their women.

I wasn't ready for that.

I knew it didn't matter what I was or wasn't ready for. Ready, or not, I was about to become Parker's bitch.

12

PARKER

As part of my foray into the social scene on the island, I'd been heading to Mimi's when I saw Maxim step out of the place with a sleazy brunette on his arm. She clung to him like Saran wrap as they headed towards the beach. I shouldn't have cared. I should have been grateful he was with someone so he would leave me alone. I should have just going on into Mimi's and minded my own business. I damned sure shouldn't have stood outside the bar long enough to hear the sleazy chick's heated moan coming from that direction a minute or so later.

My plans to hang out at the bar were completely ruined. I was overcome with anger, so much so that all I could do was march myself home and crawl into bed.

My rabbit was crushed. She'd had some stupid fantasy about Maxim, but clearly she was played for a fool. Maxim was a player. He was an arrogant, cocky, philanderer and I wanted nothing to do with him, no matter what my sad little rabbit said.

I hadn't seen him for two days, anyway. Maybe he'd done what I'd told him to do and forgotten about me. It was for the best. After the stunt he pulled with my last date, I didn't need him around.

I slept like absolute crap that night and the next morning I was basically a zombie as I got dressed and headed to Latte Love to fuel up on caffeine. I ordered a giant mug of black coffee and sat behind a palm leaf while I drank it in peace.

Hidden away there, I dragged a book out of my purse and tried to get in a little reading it before going to work. It was a romance novel, though, and as I read, I kept thinking of Maxim. Grunting, I slammed the book closed and drained the rest of my coffee. I couldn't even enjoy my morning without it being ruined by him.

"There's a lot of grunting and swearing coming from over here in this corner, Parker. You okay?" Paige stuck her head over my leaf and raised her eyebrows. "I've got customers concerned that you're losing it."

"They're not too far off."

"What's going on, babe?"

I frowned at my book and shook my head. "Romance novels are such utter crap. These men are so chivalrous and honorable."

She settled into the chair across from me. "And that's not been your experience?"

"Hell no!" I laughed. "Not even close."

"Yeah, I don't know many women who've found the perfect man." She grinned. "When they do, he's usually gay."

"Honestly, even a man who was halfway decent would be a rare find." I shoved the offending book back in my purse and stood up. "I've got to get to work. It's time to spread this sunny disposition to the lucky guests at Rise and Shine."

Paige hurried over to the counter and grabbed a basket of goodies. "Take this with you, will ya'? Penny beat me at gin rummy last night, and this is what I owe her."

∼

Work went by slowly and by the end of the day, I was ready to snap and rip the bell from over the door. I was cranky, hungry, and feeling just about as dragging-on-the-ground as I could get. When Laila canceled our dinner plans because she had to handle work late, I ended up going straight to Mimi's when I got off.

It was too early for the place to be busy and probably too early to be drinking, but I ordered a basket of wings and some mozzarella sticks and topped it off with a spiked sweet tea from the bartender anyway. I'd just been served the food and was digging in when Heidi appeared from the back.

A grin spread across her face as soon as she spotted me. Coming over, she leaned against the bar in front of me and looked me up and down. "You don't look like you're having a fun day."

I shoved the rest of a mozzarella stick into my mouth and finished chewing. "You know what my problem is?"

She poured herself a glass of coke and shrugged. "Hopefully not me. That'd be awkward."

I paused, dipping a buffalo wing in bleu cheese. "Why would I have a problem with you?"

"A lot of people do."

"I don't." I chomped on the wing and licked the sauce off my fingers. "It's men. I hate 'em. All of them. The big ones, the little ones, the scared ones, and especially the cocky ones."

"Uh oh."

I nodded. "Yeah. Uh oh is right."

"What happened?"

"I don't think you want to hear it." I bit into another mozzarella stick. "Especially since it's about your mate's buddy."

"Maxim?" She clapped her hands together and leaned in closer. "I do want to hear it. Talk to me."

"He crashed my dinner date a few days ago. Scared off the guy I was with and was just an all-around arrogant dickhead. Then, I see him hooking up with some brunette last night. He's a total player."

Her face twisted in confusion. "He hooked up with... I was sure he was going to..." She paused. "I thought there was something happening between the two of you."

"Nope."

"He was being all weird, hinting around about you without

coming right out and asking. I thought maybe you two were, you know, like mates or something."

I dropped wing I was holding and reached for my tea with trembling hands. I drained half the glass in one swallow.

"Mates? Not a fucking chance."

"Are you sure about that?"

"Yes! I'm sure. You don't fuck around with other women if you've met your mate." I realized I'd sounded really sharp and sighed. "Sorry. I don't mean to be nasty to you. I'm just…"

"Hurt?"

"Hurt?" I looked away. "No. There's nothing to be hurt about."

"Again… Are you sure about that?"

"Positive."

She motioned to my glass and smiled. "Need a refill?"

"In a big way."

13

MAXIM

It took me another two days, but I finally sniffed Parker out. Turned out she worked at Rise and Shine Bed and Breakfast. I'd tried to find out more from Heidi without it being so obvious, but she'd instantly called me on it. Apparently, she and Parker were hanging out a little more which made me think Heidi had lots of things she *could* tell me, but none that she would. It'd been slowly driving me crazy.

We'd been in the middle of a job assisting the coast guard, rescuing passengers of a capsized catamaran, when I'd spotted Parker entering the B&B. Deducing that she worked there wasn't rocket science, so I went back later in the day to find her. I didn't care about how it made me look, chasing after her like I couldn't stay away. I couldn't. It had been entirely too long since I'd seen her and I was feeling a little bit like I was going through drug withdrawal. Parker, being my drug of choice.

Rise and Shine B&B was a huge, pink house with a beautiful front porch that had been decorated for fall. The front entrance was warm and welcoming, which I knew couldn't be said for the little rabbit shifter inside. At least not once she saw me.

When I opened the door, a bell rang so shrilly that I cringed. It was loud for anyone, but earsplitting to a shifter. I glared up and then grabbed it to keep it from ringing again when the door closed. The first thing I saw when I looked around the place was a wide-eyed, open-mouthed Parker sitting behind a desk.

Her pastel hair was piled into a loose bun atop her head and she was wearing black rimmed glasses that immediately filled my wicked mind with visions of her playing naughty librarian. Shit. I had to clear those lusty thoughts away if I was going to have a rational conversation with her without tripping over my own tongue.

Her mouth puckered like she'd been sucking on a sour lemon and she shoved a pen into her hair before standing up and shaking her head. Her Rise and Shine T-shirt had the sleeves rolled up, revealing an entire tattoo sleeve down her arm. Once again, my mind wandered to the goodies that were hidden beneath her clothes—more tattoos? Other piercings? What, where and how many?

"Oh, hell no! You have to leave."

I grinned and moved closer to her. "Why, hello, Parker. It's lovely to see you, too."

She absently searched her desk and I worried that she was looking for something to stab me with. "I don't want you here."

A middle aged woman came out of nowhere and slapped Parker's arm. "Parker Pettit, what has gotten into you?"

The answer to that question was not me, not yet. I smiled at the other woman and extended my hand. "Hello, I'm Maxim. Parker's very good friend."

"Will you stop saying that? We are *not* friends. We are *so* not friends. In fact, you better get the hell out of here before I find my taser."

I edged closer, gambling on the hunch that she didn't actually have a taser. Not that it would do much to me other than sting for a minute or two. "Bunny! You'll hurt my feelings."

The other woman laughed suddenly, her face going mischievous. "You're *that* Maxim. I'm Penny. I've heard a lot about you. Parker can't stop talking about you."

Parker hissed. "What? That's not true! Don't tell him that! Why would you say that?"

"You've been talking about me, Bunny? I'm flattered." I leaned against her desk and over just enough to catch a glimpse of bare thigh below her shorts. "Is this like a high school crush type thing?"

Penny giggled. "That's what I said!"

Parker was red faced with fury and the amber of her eyes was glowing, definitely in a rage way. "Not funny. Neither of you two are the least bit funny. And Maxim, you were just leaving. Hint, hint—GO!"

I scanned her desk and spotted a clipboard with her name across the top. I grabbed it and read over it before glancing back at her and laughing. "Hugh Hefner? You're kidding."

Penny did a cut throat motion and winced, trying to tell me that I was heading in the wrong direction.

"You think that's funny, do you? I bet you do. It's probably freakin' hilarious to name a respectable, noble species after a creepy guy who walked around in a smoking jacket and who was most noted for his objectification of women and promotion of extremely narrow standards of beauty. How would you like if your species was named after him?"

I studied the drapes for a second while I pondered her question. I didn't see a problem.

"Wait. Don't answer that. Do NOT answer that."

"C'mon. How do you not see the humor? Bunnies... Hugh Hefner..."

Penny held up her hands and backed away. "I tried to warn you." She shook her head from side to side as she headed toward the staircase leading to the upper floors. "I did warn you. I did."

Parker stood up and somehow managed to stretch across her desk to poke me in the chest with her neon painted fingernail. That seemed to be a thing with her. "It's not the least bit fucking funny. That is a slanderous and defamatory stereotype. Go ahead and laugh, though. Laugh it on up. Just do it on your way out the door."

"Calm down, Bunny. It's just a name."

"Out!"

I sighed. "Fine. What time do you get off? Let me take you out to dinner as an apology for...uh...offending your species."

She huffed a laugh. "Not a chance in hell."

"Why? Because of the bunny baby daddy thing?"

She scowled and her fist flew out and flipped me the bird before pointing to the door.

I rolled my eyes. "Look. You're my—"

The bell rang and in walked a teenage kid. He frowned at me before turning his eyes on Parker. "Everything okay, P?"

She smiled at him and nodded. "Everything's okay, Jake. Your mom just went upstairs."

He edged around the counter and crossed his arms over his chest. "Is this guy bothering you?"

If he hadn't been a kid, I would've knocked him out cold. As it was, I kind of admired him for attempting to defend Parker. That kid was half my size. So, I just growled and glared at him.

Parker leaned across and poked me again. "Don't do that."

"Jacob! Come up here, please!" Penny called from upstairs, saving the kid from any further embarrassment.

He ran off and Parker scowled at me. "What's wrong with you?"

"I think you know what's wrong with me."

"I don't."

"You do."

She hissed her anger becoming even more apparent. She rounded the desk, her sharply pointed finger ready to jab me again, aiming for me like a heat seeking missile.

14

PARKER

The nerve of that damn bear. I rounded the desk and jabbed my finger into his chest. It was solid as a rock. Why did an arrogant ass like him have to be so hot?

For him to come to my place of employment and bother me was one thing. For him to laugh at my cause was a whole other thing. Worst of all, though, he'd growled at Jacob and had hinted that I was his...*something*. He had a lot of balls to even show his face around me.

"You've clearly fallen, bumped your head, and rattled your brain. Why else would you come in here and act like you had a chance in hell of me agreeing to go out with you?" I poked him again and then decided I wasn't finished. "I saw you. I saw you the other night, going down to the beach with the sleazy brunette like you couldn't get in her pants fast enough."

I should've felt satisfied at the way his face blanched, but I didn't feel anything but pure rage.

"It's fine that you're a complete man-whore and want to stick your dick into anything with a pulse. Do whatever you want, honestly. But you don't get to ruin my dates or come in here acting like I owe you a goddamned thing."

"Dates? Plural?" He was growling again and I was tempted to knee him in the balls.

Penny popped her head down from the top step and nodded at the door. "Take the afternoon off, Parker. You two are scaring the guests."

I went back around to grab my purse. "Gladly."

"You've had more than one date, then?"

I stomped out of the front door and headed down Main Street, toward home. I knew Maxim was following me, but I was so angry that I didn't care at that moment. "Are you for real? You're out fucking every woman with a pulse but you've got a problem with me dating?"

"Yes!...No!...Yes!"

"First of all, you don't know me. I don't know you. You're a stranger. Which means this possessiveness over who I date isn't cute or endearing. It's psychotic. Second of all, if you're going to be possessive, the least you can do is act like you have some dignity and keep your dick in your pants." I turned and poked him in the chest again—just because it felt so damned good to do it. "And third of all, where do you get off growling at a sixteen year old boy?!"

He grabbed for me, but I was fast. I backed out of his reach and kept moving toward home. Down Main and then Toucan Boulevard, all the way down to Shipwreck Way. He just kept following me, arguing with me, and driving me utterly insane.

"I didn't put my dick in the brunette—or anyone else. You're wrong." He growled. "Would you stop walking and talk to me?"

I shook my head. "No! I'm not stopping for you. You're a total man-whore."

"Okay, that's just not true." He hesitated. "Well, maybe, it's a little true, but that's not... Just stop walking!"

I snorted out a laugh. "No."

"Bunny, I'm trying to talk to you."

"And I'm trying to ignore you!"

"Fine, the whole beach can hear, then. I didn't fuck anyone else. I didn't even have the slightest desire to. Not since the moment I met you. The only reason I was with her was to see if I could conjure up any feelings for anyone else. But I couldn't. I didn't. I haven't been able to get you off my mind since I met you. No other woman compares." He nearly ran me over when I stopped short and glared at him. "I wanted to be absolutely sure about you and me. And I am."

His words got through to me. They sliced right through my anger and terrified the hell out of me. I knew what he was getting at. I could read between the lines. I just didn't want to accept it. I wouldn't accept it. No way! I was meant to have a rabbit mate, and pure rabbit babies, to keep the bloodline pure and going strong.

"Are we talking now?"

I jerked back into gear and swore as I nearly stumbled up my front steps. "No, we are not. I'm not interested. I'm looking for a nice rabbit shifter who hasn't slept around with every woman on the island. Someone loyal and decent."

He stomped up behind me. "You and this rabbit bullshit!"

I yanked my front door open and stormed inside. "Bullshit? It's not bullshit! It's who I am."

"Why is this door not locked? Are you trying to get yourself killed? Have you ever heard of basic safety?" He followed me into the kitchen and cornered me against the fridge. "Why are you obsessed with a rabbit mate?"

"Because, you overgrown bully, that's what I want." I ducked under his arm and turned, scowling up at him. "And it's none of your business."

"It *is* my business." He turned and braced himself on the counter, an arm on either side of me, cornering me again. With his face right up against mine, he growled low in his throat. "And you know very well it's my business. I know you do."

"I don't know what you're talking about."

"Yes, you do."

"Look, my mate is out there somewhere and he's a nice rabbit shifter with manners and a healthy respect for personal space." I bared my teeth at him and was rewarded with him pressing his lower body into mine.

"Your mate is never going to be a rabbit shifter." He lowered his face and stared me in the eyes. "We both know that, Bunny."

I pushed feebly at his chest. "Wrong."

He grabbed the back of my head with one strong hand and gripped my hair. Using it to hold me still, his lips crashed over mine. Momentarily shocked by the vehemence of his kiss, I pushed at him and twisted my hips to get away, but my struggle ended in just a few seconds.

My body reacted to Maxim like a flame to a candle. Instantly, I was ignited, my body on fire for him, and my hands, instead of pushing, began stroking and exploring. My brain went to mush and all I knew was that I needed more.

15
MAXIM

I hadn't meant to start anything physical. My intent really was to simply talk. The kiss was meant solely to try to get her to shut the fuck up about rabbit shifters for a minute before I lost my temper. As soon as my mouth landed on hers, though, electric sparks shot through my body like fireworks. For a second, I'd wondered if she'd brought out the taser after all.

I gripped her hair tighter and devoured her mouth. Her nails raked down my chest, her hips wiggled against mine. She was liquid heat, her lower body rubbing and caressing until I thought my head would blow. Kissing down her throat, tasting and nibbling the tender flesh of her neck, I grabbed her ass with my free hand and pulled her into me harder.

Parker's hand reached around and grasped my ass, too. I growled into her throat, nipping her hard. She gasped and arched her back, locking her leg around my hip. The position put my cock against her pubic bone and the heat coming off of her made me crazy.

Her tantalizing laugh was half moan as she gripped my head and guided my mouth to her chest. I yanked her shirt up enough to grip her bra and shove it up, too. Then, my mouth was on her breasts, tasting and teasing her hard, pink nipples. I bit and sucked while she worked her hips against me, working us both into a frenzy that teetered right on the edge.

"*More.*"

That one breathy word from her kicked things up another notch. I spun her around and with a hand on her upper back, pressed her down so her body was leaning over the counter. She shoved down her shorts as her ass wiggled out of them. They tangled around her knees, her perfect ass on display, and I felt every last bit of control vanishing. I leaned down and bit the curve of her ass hard enough to leave a mark. Parker moaned and arched her back, pressing her ass into me.

I swore and jerked my pants down low enough to unsheathe myself. Lining our bodies up, I thrust into her. The way her body squeezed around me was almost too much and I gripped the counter on either side of her hips and growled into her shoulder.

"Fuck, Bunny."

Bent over with her chest on the counter, I was curved overtop of her and, as she panted under me, her hands reached back clawing at me, urging me into her deeper. Her walls pulsated around me, her sweet pussy trying to suck the life out of me. "*Maxim...*"

"Parker, are you here?"

My little bunny gasped under me and, like she was waking up from a trance, jerked upright shoving me backwards. She spun around and wiggled back into her shorts, staring at me in wide-eyed shock. "Holy Fuck!"

I heard someone coming closer and yanked my own pants up, tucking my still rock hard cock away. "You can say that again."

The soft, needy look that had been in her eyes was gone, replaced by anger—at me. She jabbed her finger at me and then pointed to the way we'd come in. "Out!"

"Parker?" Her wolf friend appeared in the doorway to the kitchen and her eyes grew even wider than Parker's. She burst into a fit of giggles and slapped her hand over her mouth. "Oh, my god. I'll go!"

Parker shook her head, her messy bun even messier as it flopped over to the side and several clumps of hair escaped. "No, stay! He was just leaving."

My hands ached to touch her again, but I could see the threat in her eyes. She was not about to allow an encore. I licked my lips, longing for another taste of her. "Okay, fine. But, you and I aren't finished, Bunny. Not by a longshot."

Her cheeks turned bright red and she clenched her thighs together hard. "We are more than finished."

I winked at her and, forcing my feet to move, left as she requested. Leaving was the hardest thing I could ever remember doing, but I knew for sure that the little bunny was my mate. Her taste, her smell, every inch of her body was addicting. I couldn't imagine ever touching another woman. I couldn't imagine not being with Parker for the rest of my life.

All of that should've freaked me out, but it didn't. Not anymore.

I didn't want to leave, but I forced myself to walk down to the beach and to wade straight into the water. It was cool compared to the hot sun that was beating down on my back. I needed a cold shower and to work off the rest of the energy I had coursing through my veins. The ocean was a piss-poor replacement for making love to my mate, but it would have to do. Besides, it beat walking home with a massive hard on and blue balls. I swam out and then shifted, shredding the clothes I'd been wearing.

My bear wanted to swim back and go to Parker. He wanted her just as much as I did. He didn't understand leaving her that way, and he pouted, angry at me like it was my fault.

I swam deep under the water and, oddly, found myself for the first time not hating Florida. The water felt good against my fur, the fish tasted great fresh from the source. I swam deeper and farther until I couldn't see the shoreline.

Only then did I roll over and float, letting myself hang there, in the ocean, while I thought about how drastically my life was going to change. No more random hookups. No more walking home at midnight after sleeping with some nameless, faceless female. From now on, it was only going to be Parker. Parker for the rest of my life.

I waited for panic to hit, but I found, instead, that I liked the idea. She was fire and, as it turned out, I had a penchant for getting burned.

16

PARKER

Laila sat next to me on my couch, both of us staring at the TV. Animal Planet was on, *Pit Bulls and Parolees*, but neither of us was really watching it. I hadn't said a word about what had happened yet. My heart was still racing and I could still smell Maxim all over me, even after a quick shower. My lips still tingled from his kiss, as did other places, and my libido was still worked up, craving more.

How had I lost control like that? Ugh, how had I let it happen? I mean…he was a total player. I was just another notch in his bedpost, no matter what he said. My rabbit was angry that I was thinking so negatively about him. She kept screaming "mate" at me, as though the word was going to make Maxim any less of who he was.

"So…" Laila kept her eyes on the TV. "*That* happened."

I glanced over at her and she glanced back at me. She broke first, falling over into a fit of hysterics. Something about her giggling lessened the gravity of the situation and I laughed, too. I'd been caught with my shorts down.

"God, that was embarrassing."

She fanned her face, trying to stop the tears from leaking out of her eyes. "You should've seen your face!"

I shook my head. "Ugh. I can't believe that happened. Thank God you walked in when you did."

She froze. "Wait, what?"

"I mean, not that it wasn't too late, but at least we didn't...finish." I groaned and sank back into the couch. "I can't believe that happened."

"You said that already." She curled up and turned to face me. "What do you mean by at least you didn't finish?"

"I mean you came in before we finished."

"Did the hot dog go in the bun?"

I stared at her. "Are you serious right now?"

"Yes! I need to know!"

"Yes. Yes, the hot dog was in the bun. Not for long, though." I shifted and tried not to think about it. "It doesn't matter. It was a mistake. I temporarily lost my mind."

"So... just out of curiosity, are we talking cocktail weenie, bun-length hot dog, or meaty, jumbo bratwurst?"

"Are you not listening?"

"I'm listening and choosing to ignore your cold feet and misgivings. Cocktail weenie or bratwurst?"

I hesitated then sighed loudly. "Gastro pub brat."

She screamed. "We're talking a sixteen dollar sausage! Hand-crafted, no less!" Her hand flew to her chest.

I doubled over laughing. It was the lighthearted fun that I needed to help me get over feeling like I'd just buried my dignity in the sand.

"I'm so jealous. He's beautiful and he has a high quality wiener. Not fair."

"You're forgetting the part where he's a man-whore, though."

She wagged her eyebrows at me. "I don't know. Maybe Mr. Gastro Pub is looking at you like you're the one for a reason."

"He is not my mate!" I yelled it so loudly and sharply that Laila jumped. I took a deep breath and repeated myself more calmly. "He's not my mate."

"O-kay. He's not your mate." She leaned back and sighed. "Can I have him, then?"

I hissed at her, which gave away entirely too much of my inner turmoil. When she smirked knowingly, I knew she could read through my bullshit. I just continued the act, though. "I have a date tomorrow."

"With Maxim?"

"Of course, not." I grabbed my phone and pulled up the picture of Mitch. He was handsome and smart, according to a friend of a friend of my cousin. And he lived in Miami, so not too far for a date. "This is Mitch. He's a rabbit shifter."

"Oh, Parker." Laila stood up and looked down at me, a frown etched deep onto her face. "You're so stubborn."

I gritted my teeth. I wasn't being stubborn. I was protecting my species. And myself. Maxim was a threat to everything I held dear. I wasn't willing to give up my convictions or be just a number to him.

"Alright. Go out with your rabbit shifter and be bored to death again. You're courting trouble, though. I hope you know that."

I watched her leave and sighed. There was a chance she was right. On the other hand, there was also a chance that I could meet a nice, rabbit shifter guy who would affect me more than Maxim affected me. I had to try.

I didn't sleep well that night. Normally, I would have shifted and let my animal take over and roam the island for a few hours to tire myself out. But, it was my rabbit that had me tossing and turning as she kept bugging me to let her get to Maxim. No matter how much I tried to quiet her, she was too busy yearning for the man she kept trying to convince me was our mate. I was too afraid to shift for fear of what she'd do.

That next day at work was rough. I'd never been so sleep deprived before in my life. By the time the end of the work day rolled around, I was ready to go home, climb into bed, and pass out, but I couldn't. I had the date with Mitch. Safe, well-mannered Mitch who worked as a branch manager for First Federal Bank.

I went overboard primping in order to make myself feel better about the evening. Hair spiral curled, the latest trend in autumn makeup, according to the YouTube tutorial, low cut dress with a back cutout. Heels up to my ass. I was dressed to impress. Or fall on my face.

I'd suggested we meet at Tuna's Seafood House, despite the last 'disastrophy' that I'd weathered there. When I arrived, I found Mitch already waiting for me. He was early, dressed to the nines, and had adorable dark, curly hair that lent his looks a boyish charm.

Still, when he looked at me, there was zero spark. Zero. None of the heat I felt when Maxim was anywhere within fifty yards of me, and none of the passion. My sour mood turned even worse as I sat across from a perfectly respectable option for a mate and had to stifle a yawn.

Mitch was sweet and kind. He complimented me and made sure to point out how nice I looked. He kept his eyes above my cleavage and held so much eye contact, I started to get itchy.

It wasn't fair that my reaction was so insipid. He'd driven his own car, respected his parents, paid his own bills, and was charming. He would've made a perfect mate and our kids would've been adorably cute. Yet, I couldn't stop thinking about Maxim's cocky smirk and confident swagger. I wanted to rip Maxim's head off. Or stick my tongue down his throat. I couldn't decide which.

It wasn't until I noticed Mitch's eyes trail over the waiter's ass that I realized why he wasn't having any trouble not looking at my cleavage. Our waiter *did* have a nice ass, and Mitch was gay. Of course, he was.

Why did I feel so relieved?

17

PARKER

"Can I get you to sign my petition?" I pulled my clipboard out of my purse and waved it in front of Mitch. "I just... We face enough stereotypes as it is. I hate that we have to be labeled with this name, too."

Mitch looked like he wanted to decline, but the clipboard was in front of him and I was handing him a pen, so he hastily scribbled his name on the paper before smiling. "I don't actually mind it, but I can see how it might feel more derogatory for a female."

Before I could launch into my spiel about our species being the namesake of one of the biggest playboys in American history, the door to Tuna's flew open and Maxim came storming in like a raging bull. Or raging polar bear. Whatever. He practically had steam shooting out of his ears as he scanned the place until he spotted me. Then, his eyes narrowed into dangerous slits and he stomped our way. Next to me, Mitch looked as though he was trying to crawl inside of himself. The scent of his fear permeated the area. I couldn't say I blamed him. Maxim was a pretty imposing sight all pissed off like that.

"Are you fucking kidding me, woman? You can't seriously still be on this kick!" Maxim didn't stop until he was standing over our table, his fists balled at his sides. He glared at Mitch. "If you touched her, I'll rip your intestines out and use them to decorate my Christmas tree."

Mitch raised his hands in surrender as he scrambled away from the table and made a hasty exit, wisely refraining the entire time from showing Maxim his back. A couple seconds later, the loud squeal of tires as Mitch peeled out of the parking lot could be heard above the quiet din of dinner conversations.

I chewed on my bottom lip in an attempt to fight the urge to lay into Maxim in front of all the other diners. Over and over I tried to convince myself not to make a scene, but *myself* just wasn't listening.

I was going to make a scene.

I stood up from my chair and glowered at Maxim. In my heels, I was almost eye to chin with him and those few inches gave me a little extra confidence. "What the actual fuck is wrong with you? How could you think it's okay to burst in here like a maniac and scare away my date?! We're not cave people. We don't beat our chests and throw people over our shoulders to claim them, asshole."

He leaned into me. "No, we sink our teeth in to claim them. I'm pretty sure you're still wearing a temporary mark on that gorgeous ass of yours right now. You're mine, Parker. What more do you need to understand that?"

I jabbed my finger into his chest. "Don't talk about my ass in public!"

"Don't try to make babies with strange men in public!"

I let out a frustrated squeal and stomped my foot. "You're a complete barbarian!"

"And you're a stubborn brat."

I felt steam building in my head and felt like I was going to explode. "I am not yours. I am never going to be yours. Get that through your thick, Neanderthal skull."

"Um, excuse me? Ma'am, sir? I'm going to have to ask you to please sit down and lower your voices." The waiter looked like he was going to pee himself as both Maxim and I swung our angry glares around to him.

I grabbed my purse and rooted around for my wallet, a déjà vu of my last disastrous date. "You can't just ruin every date I have. And stop saying I'm yours. You and I are not together."

"The fuck we're not. I don't know what you think you're doing, but you and I both know that we're mates. We're—"

"Nothing! We're not anything! Yesterday was a mistake. I shouldn't have let that happen."

"You really think that meek little shit that ran out of here like the place was on fire is your mate? You think he can handle a woman like you, Parker? You think he's going to satisfy you the way I will? Did you forget that I can hear how hard your heart races for me? Did you forget that I can smell your arousal, Bunny? I know what you're feeling right now and those feelings have nothing to do with the rabbit turd that just ran out of here."

"What I'm feeling right now is complete and total fury." I threw money on the table and glared at him. "And you're right. That has nothing to do with Mitch. It's all for you."

"Don't say his name."

"Mitch! Mitch, Mitch, Mitch! What are you going to do about it?" I marched towards the exit but stopped and turned back on him. "Mitch was sweet and kind. Mitch complimented me and was interested in me. Mitch would make a great mate."

The waiter poked his nose in. "Again, I need to ask you two to keep it down. And, not that I want to get in the middle of this or anything, but your date, uh, Mitch, slipped me his number."

I threw my hands in the air and let out a frustrated scream before storming out of the restaurant. Maxim was right behind me, his angry growl making me weak in the knees.

"Bunny, you're making me fucking nuts. Stop trying to mate other men."

I ignored him and kept walking. I was so angry and embarrassed that I couldn't even process what all I was feeling.

"Fuck, Bunny, I know you feel the chemistry between us." He caught my arm and pulled me to a stop. "What happened yesterday, that intensity, that connection, it's a once in a lifetime thing. We've got something special, you and me."

I shook my head. "No. I refuse to believe you're my mate. You're about as likely to stay committed to me as a cab in rush hour."

"That isn't true. I couldn't touch another woman, if I wanted to. And even if I could, I wouldn't. I don't want to." He shook his head. "What's wrong with you? Why are you acting like this?"

I jerked away from him. "You *did* touch another woman. I saw you. I heard you. Did you forget that? God, you're so full of it. *You're* why I'm like this. Men like you."

"Come on, Bunny."

"Don't call me that!" This time when I walked away, he let me.

I drove back to my house and made a beeline straight to my liquor cabinet. My hands were shaking and I felt nauseous. I needed a drink of something. Anything. I didn't know what I was doing anymore, but the feeling of dread was growing. I didn't know what it was from. Should I be running harder from Maxim, or should I give in and run *to* him?

My rabbit thought she knew the answer, but I had plans for my life—a mate, children, a happily ever after—and none of that involved a polar bear shifter.

18

MAXIM

I went to my room and slammed the door shut. When that didn't make me feel better, I opened it and slammed it shut again, this time so hard it fell off its hinges. Still didn't feel better. Turning to face my room, I let out the anger that I'd been holding in, and trashed the place. I punched holes in walls and ripped shelves down before shoving my dresser over and kicking the shit out of it. I wasn't sure how long it went on, but at some point I noticed Serge was standing in the room with me. At that point, the whole place was destroyed and I still didn't feel better.

"You want to explain why the hell you just ripped a hole through your bedroom wall into the bathroom?" He stood with his hands on his hips, looking pissy.

I surveyed the damage and growled. Fuck. Nothing left to break and I still had excess aggression to release. I needed to get away. No, I needed my mate to stop rejecting me. My bear was pouting like a little cub and I felt awful. I was angry at Parker and I was angry at myself for being angry at Parker. She was so stubborn, though. Why she thought she could deny fate was beyond me.

"Maxim?"

I shook my head. "It's nothing."

Serge rested his hand on my shoulder and sighed. "Talk, bro. What's this about?"

I glanced back to see Roman, Dmitry, and Alexei standing outside of my door, concern on their faces. I envied every single one of them. Serge, too. They were all basking in the disgustingly syrupy sentimentality of newly mated men. You could just look at any one of them and practically see little red hearts flooding their eyes like in the cartoons. I couldn't tell them about Parker. Not with them being so happy and all. I wasn't ready to say anything yet, anyway.

"What the fuck are we doing here? Why are we sitting on this island squandering our talents, not to mention wasting the extensive and rigorous training we've received? Fuck, we're doing bullshit that anyone who has gone through a two week security guard course is qualified to perform. What's next, directing traffic and issuing parking tickets? This place is turning us all into pussies."

Alexei rolled his eyes and walked away. Serge groaned and moved towards the door. "You need to get over yourself. We're here now. And the work that we're doing, although it may not exactly be adrenaline pumping enough for a thrill-seeker such as yourself, is still valid and important."

"Don't you guys even care that we're stuck in the armpit of one of the hottest climates on the planet?"

Roman shrugged. "Well, some of us have come to the conclusion that fate guided us here. Me, Dmitry, Alexei, we've all found our mates here. Trust me, man, a little heat is a small price to pay for that."

"Oh, so since fate gave you three your mates, you're advice for me is to shut the fuck up, keep doing jobs that a twelve year old girl can do, and drown in my own ball sweat? That's it, huh? I'm just supposed to the sacrificial lamb so the rest of you can live a life of happily mated bliss?"

Serge pressed a hand to Roman's chest to keep him at bay. "What's going on with you, Max? You're usually not this much of an asshole."

"Maybe this is who I really am. An arrogant asshole and a man-whore." I shoved past them and took the stairs down three at a time. "I'm getting the fuck out of here."

Heidi was standing in the kitchen with Alexei, her eyebrows drawn together. "What happened, Maxim?"

I just kept moving without replying. I felt like I was about to explode and the best thing was to get far away from all of them. I stormed out and stomped down the beach, sand flying as I trudged angrily away from all the mated fucking mates and their mated fucking mates. When I realized I had marched my seething self in the direction of Parker's house, and was in fact only several yards away from her front door, I knew it was a bad idea to confront her in the state I was in.

But I couldn't stop myself.

Climbing the stairs to her porch, I stood outside and pounded on the door. "Bunny!"

A couple of seconds later, I heard a rustle coming from within. "Go away, Maxim."

"I'm not leaving. I'm tired of this shit. Just admit that I'm right and open the door."

"Go home. I'm not doing this." She sounded sad.

I smacked the door with my palms. "Let me in. I'm not playing games with you anymore."

"You know nothing about me, Maxim."

"I know that you're my mate. What else do I need to know?"

"You seem to think that you can tell me what's what and then I'll just cower submissively and expose my neck. If you actually knew me, you'd know that I don't respond well to orders—or threats. I'm going to bed. You can stay here and knock all you want, but I'm not opening the door to you. Not now. Not ever."

"Fuck! How can you say that?"

"I can say it because it's the truth. You're not interested in me. Not really. You don't know my likes, dislikes, the things I care about—do you even have the slightest bit of interest in knowing any of that?"

I leaned my forehead against the door. "Just open up and talk to me face to face, Parker! I don't want to have this conversation by shouting back and forth through a closed door."

"Goodnight, Maxim."

I heard her muffled footsteps as she walked away. I smacked the door a few more times. "This isn't right! This isn't how mates are supposed to treat each other."

But, she'd already closed herself in her bedroom, and was probably tucking herself under the covers. Meanwhile, I felt like I'd been gone over with a baseball bat.

I sank onto her front steps and sat there with my head in my hands for what felt like hours. I couldn't believe where I was, the situation I was in.

I'd never given much thought to finding a true mate, but I certainly never would have guessed that having one would leave me feeling so awful.

19

PARKER

"What's going on, Parker?" Penny waved a cinnamon roll in front of my face and snapped her fingers. "Earth to Parker?"

I looked up at her and frowned. "Why are you waving that around in front of my face? What am I, a dog at the race track?"

"Well, you're just sitting here staring into space. I was starting to worry that you'd been body snatched, but I can see you're still your normal, snarky self. Nothing to worry about."

"I'm fine."

She took a big bite out of the cinnamon roll, just staring at me while she chewed. "Uh huh."

"I'm *fine*, Penny." I brought my coffee mug to my lips and took a big gulp, only to find it was ice cold. When I realized it had to be at least twenty-four hours old, I spit it back into the mug and gagged. Had I forgotten to get coffee before work today?

"Yeah. You don't act fine. What's going on? Talk to me."

I shook my head and leaned back in my seat. "Nothing's going on. Nothing at all."

Penny stared intently through narrowed eyes with her mouth

drawn tight. Knowing Penny as well as I knew Penny, it was pretty obvious she wasn't going to walk away without an answer.

I waited for a few seconds and then groaned. "Fine! I'm not feeling my best. I didn't sleep well last night."

She nodded. "Why not?"

Truth be told, I hadn't slept well since meeting Maxim. Last night had just been the icing on the insomnia cake. "I don't know. I just didn't. So, I'm tired."

"Would this sleeplessness have anything to do with that hunk, Maxim?" She leaned against my desk and finished off her roll. "Laila told Paige she walked in on you two doing the dirty."

"Oh, my god. I'm going to kill her." I scowled. "Who else knows?"

"Um, it's Paige we're talking about."

I threw up my hands. "The whole friggin' island knows."

She shrugged. "Probably."

"Great. Just great. Now, I'll be even less desirable to Florida's eligible bachelors." I was so frustrated. I was even farther from my goal, all because I dropped my pants for Maxim. The worst part was, that I missed him, and I hated that I missed him.

"Parker, come on. You're talking crazy. Are you sure you feel up to being here today? If you need some time, Marvin and I can hold down the fort for the day."

I shook my head. "I don't want to go home."

It was true; I didn't want to go home, but I didn't want to be at work either. I was ready to crawl right out of my skin from the restlessness and frustration. I still wanted Maxim even though I didn't want to want him. My body was in pain from the cravings.

We weren't compatible though. The man didn't give a single fuck about me, about the fact that my species was endangered, or about my mission to have our name changed to something more respectable.

So, my resolve had wavered slightly in my kitchen. I'd let my body and my rabbit win out over my rational mind. It wouldn't happen again. I wasn't about to give up something that mattered to me for a guy who didn't care about me as a person. Or, rabbit.

Even if he was my mate.

Not that I was admitting that he was my mate or anything. My rabbit thought so, but not me. I refused to be bullied by fate into having to accept a man who was clearly not right for me, nor would I turn my back on everything I believed in. I would choose my own mate, not have one chosen for me.

At the end of the day, even if Maxim changed his playboy ways, even if he wasn't actually a callous, pompous jerk, he wasn't a rabbit.

I had a goal. I was going to demand respect for my species and bring them back from the edge of extinction. That had been my dream for so long. I planned to do my part by having a huge family of my own full of rabbit shifters who would each go out and start their own big families. In a couple generations, my family line could number in the hundreds, thousands maybe. They—*I*—could single handedly save the species.

It mattered to me, and if Maxim was truly my mate, it would matter to him, too. It sure as hell would matter to another rabbit shifter. One of our own wouldn't write off my petition as frivolous.

"Parker? You still down here with us Earthlings?"

Snapping back into reality, I nodded. "I think I will take the day off."

Penny gave me a quick hug. "Go. Get some rest and call me if you need anything."

I grabbed my purse before she could change her mind. The B&B was always full and there was plenty of chores to go around. And, while Marvin tried his best, he wasn't as quick or as efficient anymore as he once was.

Once I got home, I pulled out my list of eligible rabbit males. The most productive thing I could do with my day off was to find myself a rabbit mate who would make me forget all about smug, pretentious polar bears.

Yeah, I didn't want to think about polar bears anymore, ever.

Sitting at my kitchen table, I ran down the list to determine who would be the best candidate to meet up with next. There had to be someone that was perfect or, if not perfect, at least passable.

At least better than a polar bear.

20

MAXIM

"We found out why you've been such a fucking asshat lately. Heidi spilled about your crush." Alexei laughed. "We heard you two got caught going at it like," he cleared his throat, "rabbits."

The guys laughed like that was fucking funny or something and I felt myself tense. "Fuck off. All of you."

Serge slapped me on the back. "Is she your mate?"

I growled. "We're not talking about this."

Roman grinned. "So, the rumor's true. Hey, as long as you're *hoppy*."

I stood up and glared at him. "Fuck you."

"You sound fed up with the *hole* thing." Alexei chuckled.

"Must be a bad *hare* day." Dmitry was even getting in on the teasing.

Serge was the person standing closest to me and he suffered for it. I swung a punch and hit him in the gut before grabbing Alexei around the neck and throwing him across the office. A desk collapsed in a flurry of papers. A file cabinet toppled. Someone tackled me, and I went down fighting. Someone slugged me across the nose and blood splattered. I managed to drag Roman under me and got him good across the chin before Serge grabbed me in a chokehold and dragged me out of the fray.

Panting and still seeing red, I wanted to hurt them all. I wanted to lash out and hurt each one of them as badly as I was aching inside.

Serge shook his head. "Why you assholes always go after me, I'll never know! Get out. Go find your mate and make it right. You're going to be hell to deal with until you do."

"She doesn't fucking want me!" I ripped away from him and shoved him hard enough to make him stumble into the wall behind him. "She doesn't want me."

The guys blinked up in silence from the floor.

Then, Konstantin crawled up and plopped himself in a chair. Dmitry sat up, but remained on the floor. Alexei rolled over, rested his elbow on the ground and propped his head on his fist. Roman remained on his back staring up at the ceiling and shook his head, smiling. "Brother, they always do that. It's just part of the process."

"I agree. I think it's just the way it works." Alexei shrugged. "You need to go out there and win her over."

I backed away, holding up my hands. "She won't even let me. She doesn't want…a polar bear. She's determined to have a rabbit shifter mate."

"What? You're at the top of the goddamned food chain!" Serge scoffed. "Alright, I guess it's up to you to show her that fate paired the two of you for a reason. Quit picking fights with these goddamn dickheads and go work on convincing your mate that you're the right man, shifter, and species for her. Go!"

I ground my teeth. Serge had a point. I couldn't give up on her; we belonged together. And, I *was* a better match for her than any rabbit shifter she could find. She had to see that.

I left the office and headed straight to the bed and breakfast, but when I entered, Parker wasn't at her desk. Penny emerged from a back room and as soon as she spotted me, her eyes went wide and she rushed over. "Oh, my god, Maxim! Are you okay?"

"Where's Parker?"

"She went home. What happened to you? Do you need a first aid kit?"

I didn't answer. I just turned and ducked back out, heading straight to Parker's. My heart was racing. My body was strung tightly. I was determined to do exactly what Serge said and convince Parker that she needed me. I got to her house and stomped up the steps. She must have heard me coming because by the time I reached the door, Parker was already opening it with an expression of shock. Okay, so she heard someone coming but clearly had not been expecting *me*. Before she could slam the thing in my face, I grabbed her and planted a kiss on her plump, pouty lips.

Her mouth responded instantly. Her hands grabbed fistfuls of my shirt and she let me walk her back into her house. Apparently, I'd caught her off guard, because it only took another second or two before she yanked out of my grip and turned her back to me.

"What are you doing?!" She flew to the other side of the room and ran her hands through her hair. "You shouldn't be here."

"Stop, would you? Just stop this nonsense. We're mates. I know it and you know it. We're meant for each other. There's no use fighting it. Stop the nonsense." I took a step closer to her and growled. "No more of this looking for another mate bullshit. You won't find anyone else. Your options are me...or me."

She suddenly turned and looked as though she was about to lay into me when she seemed to notice my appearance for the first time, and paled. "What happened to you?"

I waved it off. "Scuffle with the guys. It's nothing. Did you hear me?"

She shook her head and her eyes shifted to her dining room table. "You need to leave."

"Fuck no I'm not leaving. You're my mate, Parker. Do you understand that?"

"I'm not your mate." She glanced at the table again and then over my shoulder. "I'm not anything to you."

I walked over to the table to see what was so damned interesting to her. There was a sheet of paper with what looked like information on different men—names, addresses, phone numbers. All fucking rabbit shifters, I'd stake my life on it, and all men she was considering as potential mates. I glared at her. "Are you fucking serious?"

She snatched the sheet of paper off the table and held it behind her back. "I told you to leave."

I snapped.

I knew it was counterproductive and wouldn't help my standing with her, but I was hurt—maimed by the feeling of extreme rejection. I wasn't acting like myself, or maybe I was. Maybe, I was just so desperate that the only way I knew to deal with it was to fight it head on as hard as I could. Even if it was another of my bad decisions.

I took her shoulders in my hands and glared down at her. "You think you can just ignore fate, is that it? You think having a stupid, weak little rabbit for a mate is more important than being with your *fated* mate? Why? Because you're so obsessed with making more rabbits? Jesus, Parker, so what if you don't have a rabbit kid? So, what if your ludicrous petition doesn't go through because it has all of, what, ten signatures on it? Is all of that bullshit more important than true mates? You're willing to throw away your future for something so ridiculous?"

Parker's eyes filled with tears. *Oh, shit.* I suddenly felt like the biggest dick on the planet. I hated myself for losing my temper. I wanted to take back all the nasty things I'd just said in anger, but how?

When she spoke, her voice was steady and calm, quiet even. "I asked you to leave."

"Wait, Parker..."

She spun away from me and stalked across the room, nearly putting herself in a corner to get away from me.

"I'm sorry I said those things. I didn't mean them. Can we please just talk first?"

She turned to face me, a tear rolling down her cheek. "I don't want to talk, Maxim. I want you to leave. *Please.*"

I swore and moved towards the door. "Fine. I'm going."

As I pulled her door shut, I heard her whisper. "Don't come back."

21

PARKER

In the bathroom of Cap'n Jim's, Laila sighed heavily before stepping behind me to work on my hair. She stared at me through the reflection in the mirror and frowned. "Aww, babe. I hate that you're so gloomy."

I looked away and shrugged. "I'm fine. It is what it is, you know?"

"And you're sure you can't just sit down with him and open some lines of communication? Maybe together, the two of you can make sense of everything." She pulled a few bobby pins out of her purse and slid them into my hair at different angles. "I mean, this situation doesn't seem ideal, either. You're clearly unhappy."

I swatted her hands away and turned to face her. "Would you be with a man who cared nothing about your feelings?"

She blew out a deep breath and twisted her lips. "No, but maybe Maxim—"

"Don't say his name, Laila. I don't want to hear his name. I came here to drink and forget about you know who." I swiped mascara smudges from under my eyes and shrugged. "Besides, I'm not unhappy. I'm perfectly happy." It was a bald-faced lie, and we both knew it.

"Maybe we should go back to your house."

"No!" I was having difficulty stepping into my kitchen without reliving the wild sex that was started and interrupted, and I was having trouble stepping into my living room without reliving the angry reaction of a certain bear shifter when he'd discovered the list of single, available male rabbit shifters in the area. No, home made me feel hollow and empty and way too tempted to run out and find the polar bear-who-will-not-be-named for a makeup session.

Laila finally nodded and gave me a side hug. "I'm here for you, Parker. Whatever you need to do."

I brushed her off and opened the bathroom door. Music from the bar was instantly deafening and cut off any chance of having a normal conversation. Which was awesome and exactly what I needed. I didn't want to talk about mates, bears, rabbits, or anything of the sort. I wanted to pretend to be a human for a night and drink enough to forget that my chest felt like an elephant was sitting on it.

I'd never been to Cap'n Jim's. On the north side of the island, it was somewhat of a tourist trap. Club music played too loudly, the drinks were marked up and watered down, and Jim wasn't even a real guy, much less a captain. The owner's name was Kenny and he wasn't a captain. The one thing that Cap'n Jim's had going for it, though, was a distinct lack of polar bears.

Back at our booth, Laila and I ordered drinks and settled in to people watch. I felt her eyes on me more than once, like she was taking my vitals. She was worried about me. Everyone seemed to be. And they all wanted to fucking talk about it.

I didn't.

When two men slid into our booth, blocking us in, I pretended that I wasn't thoroughly repulsed. Laila didn't seem put off by the guy who was next to her, so I played along. I leaned in to try to hear what the guy next to me was saying, but the music was too loud for my shifter ears. Between songs, I caught that his name was Nathan and he liked Bud better than any other beer.

Nathan talked, whether he realized I wasn't listening or not, I didn't know. I pretended I was and nodded along. He smelled like cheap cologne and trying-too-hard and I wished I didn't have to breathe him in. When he touched me, an innocent brush against my shoulder, I felt my skin crawl. I leaned away from him.

Laila glanced over at me and smiled, but I could still see the worry etched in her features. Nathan's mouth kept moving, and I was getting to the end of my rope. I wanted to scream. I wanted to shove Nathan out of the booth so I could run the hell out of there for some fresh air. A night out had been a mistake. I was in no condition to be around normal people.

"Can you let me out?" I raised my voice and leaned closer to Nathan. "I need to go."

He squinted at me and yelled something back that I couldn't hear.

"Let me out!" I put my hand on his shoulder and pushed, hard, trying to emphasize my point. I needed to go. I was panicking, for some reason. The loud music and cloying scent of his cologne were wreaking havoc on my heightened senses and I felt a sense of panic beginning to surface.

Nathan was instantly gone. I stared at my hand for a second, shocked and wondering how I'd somehow managed to gain the super-strength of twenty rabbits. Until the scent of pine and spiced oranges hit my nostrils.

I told myself not to look, but there was no stopping me. Maxim was already halfway across the bar, dragging Nathan by the back of his shirt toward the door. I watched as he kicked open the exit and threw the guy out on his butt. Maxim looked back over his shoulder. Our eyes met, a shared gaze that made my pulse race and my heart leap in my chest. The searing intensity in his eyes touched me to the core. Then he turned and walked out.

He just left.

Laila pushed at the guy next to her, but he was already getting up to chase after his friend. She put her mouth right against my ear and shouted. "I think we've worn out our welcome."

I bit my lip and nodded. I felt as though I was crumbling. I was going to lose my composure and I didn't want to do it in front of people. I followed her through the crowd and towards the back door, grateful for her quick thinking. Laila had realized that the front door was a no-go and had, instead, dragged me out the back door. We were hurrying down the beach, toward my house, in no time.

I wasn't normally much of a crier and I didn't want to have to talk or explain the tears that had started trailing down my cheeks. Laila and I locked eyes. Everything that needed to be said was conveyed with just a single glance between us, and Laila nodded. She understood that right then what I needed was to leave my body. I needed to shift.

My rabbit was small, but she was fast and smart. I ran past Laila, who stopped to grab my clothes, and skirted the edge of the water towards the southern tip of the island. I wanted to go farther. I wanted to run south until I couldn't go any farther. It was an attempt to escape the extreme and confusing emotions.

I hesitated at the edge of the road.

"Come on, Parker. Let's get you home. Stay shifted, if it helps." Laila scooped me up and held me against her chest. "I'm going to take care of you tonight, okay?"

As embarrassing as maybe it should have been, being picked up and carted around like a child, it was actually cathartic. I let her carry me back to my house and then she sat down on the couch and stroked my fur while she spoke.

"You know I love you. You're my best friend and I'd do anything for you, babe. I think you're making a mistake, though. I only know about mates from what you've told me and from what I've learned in the last year or so, but it's never sounded like something you can run from.

"I guess I had this idea in my head, from what you've said, that fate doesn't get it wrong. I still think that. I know you know what you want, but maybe that's not what you need. Maybe, just maybe, this is hurting so much because you're fighting the best thing that's ever happened to you.

"Obviously, he's not perfect. He really seems to care about you, though, and that's a pretty good foundation to build on, isn't it? They say communication is key to a healthy relationship. Maybe that's what you need, the two of you. I mean, you could talk to him and explain what's important to you and why. Make him see. If he's truly your mate, I think he'll listen and care about what's important to you. You could at least give the guy a chance."

I buried my head in her stomach and tried to block out what she was saying. It made far too much sense.

22

MAXIM

I ended up getting permanently barred from Cap'n Jim's for throwing that twatwaffle out on his ass. It was worth it. He shouldn't have been talking to my mate, and he damned sure shouldn't have touched her.

The problem was, now I was having a hell of a time convincing my bear that running after Parker was a bad idea. No, we shouldn't follow her home. No, we shouldn't show up at her front door. No, we shouldn't break it down to get in and make sure she's okay.

In order to keep what was left of my already tenuous hold on my sanity, I needed to get far away from Sunkissed Key. I drove north and didn't stop until I ended up at some dive club in Miami.

The place was so much bigger than the bars on the island and I found myself irritated by how many people were there. So many sights, scents and sounds. I also realized that I probably looked like a vagrant. I hadn't changed clothes in...I didn't remember how long, but awhile, and I hadn't shaved or fixed my hair in longer.

Settling at the bar, I ordered two double shots of whiskey and threw them back one after the other. Motioning for more, I rested my elbows on the bar top and held my head in my hands. I was such a hot mess. I hadn't slept, couldn't remember when I'd eaten last, and I ached all over. I missed arguing with Parker. I missed any and everything with her, but I knew she was done with me. I'd screwed things up without even completely understanding how.

"You okay, big guy?" The bartender was a pretty redhead with a neck tattoo.

I slid my empty glasses back and motioned for more whiskey. "Fine."

She filled the glasses higher than normal and nodded at me. "Keep it together tonight, honey."

I laughed and threw those shots back, too. I had no intention of keeping anything together. I intended to drink until my chest stopped aching and I could convince my unruly bear to leave Parker the hell alone because she hated us.

The night went on like that for...I don't know how many hours. I drank hard, ignored the crowd around me, and proceeded to get so hammered that I forgot where I was. I must've blacked out at some point because the next thing I knew, I woke up on a hard ground.

I was shifted into my bear and everything around me stunk like wild animal and rank, stagnant water. I sat up and looked around, immediately ascertaining that I'd fucked up majorly.

I was in a zoo, a goddamned zoo. Not the small wildlife refuge on the island, either. This was a big goddamned zoo and I was in what looked like some sort of quarantine containment area. Still, zoo goers could observe me. There was a group of children staring at me and tapping at the glass.

I groaned. I felt like shit. Just what I needed, an audience of curious onlookers to witness the rapid descent of my dignity and its culmination in a fiery crash—at rock bottom. How the hell I was going to get out of this mess? It would have been better if I'd woken up in the slammer. At least in jail, I'd have been able to post bail. If my head wasn't pounding so hard and I didn't have to concentrate on choking down the bile creeping up the back of my throat, I'd have been more panicked.

Serge... I called out, hoping our telepathic link would reach all the way to Sunkissed Key. I had a feeling he was going to need time to get me out.

A pimple faced teenage boy started pounding on the glass and shouting. The sounds were like a sledgehammer to my cranium and I snarled viciously at him.

What?

I have a slight problem. I looked up as a man wearing a uniform stepped cautiously into the containment area. Miami-Dade Zoological Park was emblazoned on the right breast of his shirt and he held a big bucket of dead fish in one hand and what looked like a cattle prod in the other.

Oh, fuck, scratch that. I have a BIG problem.

Just tell me.

I gagged and turned away from the fish. They weren't fresh and, even though I was half animal, I couldn't do old, stinky fish—especially not while fighting a hangover from hell. *I just woke up in a cage. No idea how I got here. Get me the fuck out!*

After a long period of silence, Serge came back to me. It was clear by his tone he was having a field day with this. Fine. Great, laugh it up at my expense.

You fucking jackass. I'll do what I can. Any idea where you are?

Miami Zoo.

He growled in my head, all his humor gone. *Fucking hell, Maxim. I thought you meant you were here on the island. I'll get you out, but it may take a day or two.*

A day or two?! Get me the fuck out of here fast or I'm going to fucking lose my shit. I growled at the worker coming closer to me with the dead fish. *They're trying to feed me fermented fish.*

I sank back against the fake rock wall behind me and growled louder. Fuck. I was in for a miserable time until Serge figured out how to get me out.

Time crawled as plethora of employees each came at me with different foods and medicines. I did my best to chase them away by growling and viciously baring my teeth, but that only made them bring out a tranquilizer gun. At that point I ended up running around the enclosure to keep away from them.

I felt like I was in a Three Stooges film, running, weaving, leaping and doubling back as the team of zookeepers chased me. I'm sure I looked like a complete idiot, but I couldn't exactly shift back and walk out of the place. I was hungover as hell and all the running was making me feel like death warmed over.

After a while, I just gave up and let them sedate me. When they finally left me alone, I sat in a drugged out haze and contemplated life.

Had I really sunk this low? I was caged in a zoo like a goddamned halfwit while Parker was out there hunting herself up a rabbit mate. Serge was right. I was a jackass. Instead of setting about convincing her that I would make her a good mate, that she didn't need a rabbit, I'd acted like an entitled dick and made demands that pushed her further away.

Night was settling over the zoo and the keepers had left me alone for a while. I stared up at the little bit of sky I could see. I needed to fix things. Drinking myself into an oblivion had been a poor decision. Getting locked in a zoo was an even poorer decision. I was full of poor decisions lately.

Things weren't just going to fall into place for me. The guys seemed to think that mates always ended up together, but they were basing that on their own experiences. Maybe it didn't always work out. Maybe this whole waking up in a zoo experience was a sign that it was time to throw in the towel.

No.

Fuck, that. I wasn't a quitter and I wasn't going to give up on Parker. Maybe a change in tactics...yeah, that was it. I'd utilize my tactical skills and knowhow to work out some strategic, calculated moves. I could do it! I had to do it—life without Parker wasn't an option. Not anymore. The thought of going back to the emptiness of sleeping with nameless, faceless women every night just to try to ease the hollow ache inside and keeping every one of them at an arm's length made me want to retch. There was only one woman I wanted and I wanted to get as close to her as possible.

I had years of training to fall back on. I just had to tap into my skill set.

Step one: Analyze past and present tactics and pinpoint failed tasks and maneuvers. Shame settled over me as it dawned on me that I hadn't really done anything at all to win Parker over. What had I offered her? Just me. Like that should make her drop everything and run into my arms. No wonder she called me a Neanderthal. No wonder she was still looking, still going on dates. I hadn't made much of an effort to get to know her or to determine what made her tick—what she liked and cared about.

Step two: Formulate a new tactical mission that removes and eliminates all enemy forces. Fix things. I just had to convince her that I was worth her while. That I was worth her changing lanes on the direction she'd planned her life to go in. For that, I had to put in an effort to learn everything I could about her. Find out her likes and dislikes, what makes her tick. Prove to her that I would make a good mate. No, the *best* mate.

Step three: Implement newly formulated tactical mission. And I would... as soon as I could get my furry butt out of the zoo.

23

PARKER

"She's drunk." Laila laughed and pulled my glass away from me. "I am too, actually."

"Yeah, you're both pretty far gone. We didn't need an announcement to notice." Penny shook her head. "I suppose Paige and I have some catching up to do."

Laila and I exchanged a glance. "Not much."

Heidi immediately poured more tequila, Penny's drink of choice, into her glass. "And, there you go."

Paige stood up and cheered all of a sudden. "I love this song! Come on, Pen. Dance with me! Do you remember when this came out? That summer you were dating Pauley Ford?"

"I wasn't dating him! *You* were dating him."

"I never dated him! He was a weirdo."

"Then what makes you think *I* did?"

I watched them merge onto the dance floor and fade into the swaying crowd, still arguing. Every single time those two had a little alcohol in them, they argued about their childhood and teen years. I grinned and turned to Laila. "Think we'll see them again tonight?"

"Not a chance."

That was another thing about Penny and Paige. Once they got

going squabbling about the good old days, they tended to just…leave. No matter where they were, they just took off together. I was convinced it was because they were bickering so much that they didn't even realize that they'd walked themselves right on home.

"Like I did that time with Maxim."

"What?"

I blinked. "What?"

"You did what with Maxim?"

I frowned. I hadn't meant to say that out loud. I looked at Heidi and shook my head. "We're not talking about him. I have nothing nice to say and he's your friend so that would be weird. I'm not talking about him. I'm not even thinking about him—or wondering where he is. At all."

Laila rolled her eyes and grabbed what was left of Penny's tequila. "Okay."

Heidi just grinned. "Of course, you're not talking about him. Why would you?"

I pointed at her, suddenly excited that she understood. "Exactly! Why would I? Why would I talk about that…that…conceited, arrogant, buff, beautiful, sexy man?"

"So, you think he's buff, beautiful, and sexy, huh?" Heidi wagged her brows at me. "I thought you weren't thinking about him?"

I rested my elbows on the bar so I could get serious. "I'm not! Because I'm going to find a rabbit mate. That's my destiny—a rabbit. I don't need any big, sexy polar bears in my life and bossing me around. Did I tell you the way he spoke to me?"

"Yes."

"Yes."

I stared at both women and sighed. "Well, it was rude. He just laid down the law as though he could tell me to jump and I'd ask how high. Demanding, cocky, arrogant, rude, overbearing, did I say rude? Yeah, rude, I said rude. He didn't even care about my petition. Oh, Heidi, can I get you to sign my petition?"

Heidi took my empty shot glass away and, laughing, just shook her head. "I already did."

"Oh, right. Good. I just hate being named after Hugh Hefner. I mean, have you read some of the stuff those women said about him? It's so insulting. Why couldn't we be named after like…a saintly priest, or Nobel peace prize winner or something? Someone noted for something other than whipping his junk out of his pants." I sighed. "Why didn't Maxim keep it in his pants?"

Laila shrugged. "Why are we still talking about him?"

"We're not! I'm not talking about him." I hesitated for a minute. "I just want to know, is all. If he thought I was his mate, why did he take another woman to the beach and suck face with her? Who does that?"

"We're definitely not talking about him." Heidi grinned.

"And did I mention how rude he was?" I felt like crying. "Do you think I'll ever find love?"

Laila wrapped her arms around me. "I love you."

"Do you think a man will ever want me?"

"A polar bear already wants you." Heidi slid a glass of water towards me. "He's a mess without you."

I scowled at her and held a hand up. "We're not talking about him. I don't want to hear anything about him."

She just waited.

"Okay, tell me. What do you mean he's a mess? A mess how? Is he sad? Does he miss me?"

"No, you shouldn't have to listen to any of this stuff. You don't need to hear about how sad he's been, or about how he hasn't even used hair products lately. You especially don't need to hear about how he got so hammered that he blacked out and ended up locked in the Miami Zoo."

Laila jerked upright. That was her worst nightmare. "No!"

Heidi turned towards her. "Okay, I guess I can tell *you*, Laila. Cover your ears, Parker. So, yeah, he's still trapped there. The guys are all trying to work out how to get him out. It's a mess working with state and federal agencies for retroactive permits to house exotic animals and certificates of veterinary inspections. Before that, he completely trashed his room he was so frustrated—knocked out walls even, which isn't like him at all. He's usually way more laid back. He just hasn't been himself."

I leaned in closer, absorbing the information about him like I was a sponge.

"It's good that you rejected him, I guess, Parker. Otherwise, something like this might stress you out and get you down."

Deflating, I leaned back in my chair and gasped as I realized there was no back to the chair. The barstool I was on had no back to it, so I kept leaning, and kept leaning. Just before I crash landed on the floor, Laila used her lightning reflexes to catch me and prop me up. Since I hadn't actually hit the ground, it didn't faze me.

My mind was full of images of Maxim being stuck in his animal form and being callously poked and prodded. I felt my eyes well with tears. "Do you think he's okay?"

Heidi grinned suddenly and shrugged. "Who knows? It's nothing for you to worry about, though. I'm sure he'll find someone to clean up his messes. Probably some beauty queen, knowing him."

I was growling and all but foaming at the mouth before she even finished the sentence. My heart squeezed like my rib cage was trying to juice it.

"Oh, babe. We're just trying to get you to see that you care about him." Laila wrapped her arm around me and hugged me.

"I'm sorry, Parker. I didn't mean to upset you, well, yeah, I did, but with the best of intentions." She hesitated and then squared her shoulders. "Laila and I both think you're being incredibly stubborn. If you feel this strongly about him, you should do something about it."

24

MAXIM

Getting out of the zoo had cost us an arm and a leg. What was worse, we now owed Leon Zoo, the owner of Sunkissed Wildlife Sanctuary, another huge favor that I was sure he would call in at some inopportune moment. Serge had to grease quite a few palms along the way, but I was finally free and on my way back to Sunkissed Key. I stunk like the fucking zoo, so I let the window down on the drive back to get some fresh air in my lungs.

Serge wasn't pleased with me. To say the least. He was griping that he'd had to put so much time and effort into getting me out of a situation that I shouldn't have been in in the first place. "I don't even know where to start with you."

I just grunted. "Then don't."

"Nice. Great. Good way to express gratitude." He swerved around a slow moving car and glared at me. "Look, I get that you haven't been yourself lately, what with dealing with all the mate stuff, but the truth is you've been acting like an overgrown cub lately. In fact, you've been a dick since we got to this island. You're not the only one of us that was uprooted and sent here. Newsflash, we're all in the same boat."

"Yeah, well, we wouldn't be on this fucking island if not for you and your fuck ups." It was a low blow, blaming Serge, but I was feeling dirty, smelly, and antsy as hell from being in a nightmare for over two days, not to mention agonizing over what Parker had been doing while I was locked up. I was ready for a fight, apparently.

"Because I broke protocol to find my mate. It was worth it. I'd do it again—every single day, if I had to. At the end of the day, Maxim, fuck this job. Fuck P.O.L.A.R. and fuck the main office. The most important thing to me is Hannah. I'd throw everything else away in a heartbeat if I had to for Hannah. That's what being a mate is. If you pulled your head out of your own ass for a moment, you'd know that." He slammed on the brakes and pulled off the road. "You're dissatisfied? You're welcome to leave the team. Go back to Siberia and grovel at the main office. They'd let you join another league—maybe the grizzlies. You've always been a good operative and you'll always be one. They'd be lucky to have you."

I swallowed. I hadn't expected him to hand me an out like that. I hadn't expected it at all. "Fuck, Serge. I'm not leaving our unit."

He grinned suddenly. "I know. I was calling your bluff. None of us would actually let you leave, anyway. We're a family. You're stuck with us, so fucking deal with it. This is where we are now. You might find you don't mind the heat so much if you stopped setting your whole life on fire all the time."

I raised an eyebrow. "Spare me the lecture. I've had nothing but time to think for days and I've done plenty of it."

"Then you know how to fix it?"

I laughed but didn't answer.

"You're telling me you've had all this time to figure shit out and you didn't come up with a plan on how to fix everything?"

"I came up with something—a tactical plan of operations. I think it might work." I blew out a rough breath and stared ahead. "Not treating her like a notch on my bedpost would probably be a good start. I didn't mean to—didn't even realize I was doing it."

"Hard to fix a habit that's never been a problem before." He pulled back onto the highway and hit the gas hard. "I've heard through the gossip grapevine that she's been talking about you a lot. Not all good things, but still. That means something."

That made me laugh. It seemed that I was still driving her crazy and pissing her off. It wasn't hard to picture her angry face while she ranted about me.

"I deserve it." I rolled the window up and turned the AC on higher. "She's a little firecracker, and I like that. I think I could've handled the whole thing better. I've been replaying everything over in my head on a loop and I keep kicking the shit out of myself for how often I treated her like what she cared about was insignificant—stupid, even. In my defense, she kept talking about wanting a rabbit mate and having rabbit babies and...I just saw red. I should have listened, though. I should have tried to understand what was important to her and why."

"It's not too late."

I hoped not. I had to make it right. "Can you drop me off near her house?"

"You sure you don't want to get cleaned up first? You look like hell." He sniffed and then winced. "You smell worse."

I grunted. "Drop me off by the water. I'll go for a swim first."

"Whoa. The perfect hair bear isn't going to go home and get his gel on?"

"Fuck you."

"Yeah. Fuck you, too."

I looked over at him and shook my head. I'd blamed Serge for us ending up in the Florida Keys, and I'd been so bitter about it that I'd started to resent the guy. He'd been like a brother for nearly as long as I'd been alive, though. We'd been through thick and thin together. It shouldn't have taken me finding my own mate to understand why he did what he did, but it had. That was my bad.

"What? Do you want to kiss me now? Stop looking at me like that. You're creeping me out."

I grinned and punched him in the arm. The car swerved, but he chuckled. A tension had been released and I felt one brick in the tower of my life slip back into place. "Am I really supposed to feel the heat less because I found my mate?"

He snorted. "Fuck, no. That's just something we say. It's still fucking hot as a bonfire in a desert at high noon. Swamp-ass city every day and every night. None of us are cutting down on AC units anytime soon and none of us are going to suddenly need a jacket this winter."

"Are you fucking kidding me?"

"Nope." He glanced over at me. "It doesn't suck as bad, though when you get to come home to the woman who holds your heart. That makes anything bearable."

I sighed. "*Bear*able. Got it."

"Plus, it's hard to notice how much your balls are sticking to your thigh when your dick is rock hard ninety percent of the time."

Groaning, I shook my head. "Alright. That's a little too much sharing for me."

25

PARKER

I never wanted to get out of bed ever again, but someone was knocking on my door. I felt like my head had been used as a rock tumbler and my back had doubled as a trampoline. I rolled over to answer the door and fell out of bed. Groaning, I opened my eyes and realized that I wasn't at home. What the hell was I doing at Laila's?

"Parker, let me in! Parker? I got locked out!"

I pulled myself up on the side of her bed and stumbled towards the front door. "Why the hell did you do that?"

She pushed in as soon as I unlocked the door and flopped herself onto the couch. "It was an accident. I went to get coffee and then I realized I forgot my wallet so I came back but when got here I realized I also forgot my keys. I've been locked out, without coffee, for almost five minutes."

"Really?"

"And you hogged the whole bed last night. I had to sleep on the couch and you know my couch has that one lumpy spot with the spring that pokes you in the back if you try to sleep on it."

"Well, take your bed back. I need to go home. I should water my plants...or something. What time is it?"

She pointed at the large wooden clock on the wall. "Learn to tell time, bed hog."

It was already close to one in the afternoon and I was going to regret sleeping in so late. "I've got to go. I have a date tonight."

She sat up and grabbed her head. "With Maxim? Did you call him?"

My stomach lurched. "No. And hell no. I've gotta go. Bye."

"You're hopeless."

I slammed her door a little harder than necessary on the way out, instantly regretted it, and winced from the sharp head pain.

My place was just a few streets from hers. The island wasn't that big. But trudging through the sand made it feel like running a marathon that morning. By the time I got up my front steps and inside, I was sweaty and tired. Still, I forced myself to make a pot of coffee and get in the shower. One glimpse in a mirror was all the motivation I needed.

I'd just pulled on a t-shirt and pajama bottoms when I heard a knock at my front door. I gathered my wet hair out of my face and on top of my head in an elastic and went to see who it was. Before I got too close, the smell of pine forests and spiced oranges gave him away. Maxim.

"I'm not here to fight, Bunny." His voice was subdued, calm, almost like he wasn't even the same person. What had they done to him in the slammer? My heart raced.

I opened the door almost expecting to see a broken, beaten man. Clearly, I had watched *Shawshank Redemption* one too many times. Maxim looked weary and a little rougher around the edges than normal, but he was still Max. Handsome, devilish, and with a smile that was like the issuance of a permanent dare. His hair was mussed and he hadn't shaved, but he looked good. And he wasn't wearing a shirt. His low-slung shorts were damp with ocean water; I could smell the salt on his skin.

"Hey."

I swallowed a lump of desire and emotion. "Hey."

He forced a smile and ran his hands through his hair. "Sorry to just show up. I... I wanted to talk. No pressure. I was just thinking about that petition of yours and wondered if maybe I could sign it."

That was unexpected and caught me completely off-guard. I took a step backwards.

"May I come in?"

I had already stepped back enough to give him space to enter, so I just nodded. I watched him walk in and look around. Suddenly, I was wary of how my house might look to him. He'd been in before, of course, but we hadn't exactly been comparing home décor.

"I like this." He touched my couch. "Looks comfy."

I had no clue what we were doing or what was happening. I just slipped into hostess mode and gestured towards the couch. "Sit. Do you want some coffee or tea?"

He nodded. "Coffee would be great."

In the kitchen, I leaned against the counter while staring at the coffee pot. What the fuck was I doing? Had we both lost our minds?

"Seems like so long since we were in here." He sighed when he saw me jump. "Sorry."

I couldn't handle the weirdness. I turned to face him and crossed my arms over my chest. "What are you doing here, Maxim?"

"Uh, your petition. I want to hear about it and sign it—the way I should have the first time I saw it."

I shook my head. "What are you really doing here?"

"Apologizing?"

"Maxim..."

"Even if you don't want to hear it, I need to say it. I'm sorry. I shouldn't have been such an arrogant dickhead to you. What you care about is important to me. It truly is. I should've signed the petition and listened to you about why it's important. Maybe then, I could've understood more why you have your heart set on another rabbit so much."

I looked down at the floor, not sure what to do with him.

"I'm sorry for being a jerk to you. I like arguing with you. You're a spitfire and don't take any shit from me. For some reason, I love that. But I was an asshole."

My stomach twisted. "I was an asshole, too."

"I wish we could've talked like this before. It could've saved some headaches."

"Are you okay? I heard...about the zoo."

He grinned sheepishly and shrugged. "Yeah. Not exactly my finest hour, but it gave me time to think."

I wanted to do things I had no business doing—like hug him. I felt like he could use one and, if so, I wanted to be the woman who gave it. Seemed I couldn't handle Maxim being a decent guy who wanted to talk to me. He was like kryptonite to me.

"Maybe we can talk more? I'm wide open tonight if you want to go out to dinner, or something?"

Reality hit me and I turned back to the coffee pot. I figured a fight was coming. "Um... I'm busy tonight...I, uh, have plans." I didn't say it, but I was pretty sure he assumed that "plans" meant I had a date. If so, he was correct.

There was silence for a beat and then he cleared his throat. "I hope it goes well." His voice was strained and it was obvious that it took a lot for him to say that.

I jerked around ready to fight, or make excuses or justifications, but he was already gone. He was just letting me go out with some other guy? He wasn't even going to protest? Or, show up and ruin it?

My heart sank. He was giving up on me.

And I couldn't blame him.

26

PARKER

I was miserable.

My date, Tom, was a nice rabbit with nice manners and nice sense of style. He had nice, normal sized, stereotype-breaking teeth, and a decent amount of smarts. He was a doctor. He also was attentive enough to know that I wasn't the least bit interested in him. He stayed through dessert, though, no matter how awkward it was that my eyes were magnetically drawn to the door throughout the entire meal, and that I was desperately waiting for a certain someone to stomp through it and chase Tom off.

Even the waiter at Tuna's Seafood House was eyeing me like I was pathetic. When Tom finally gave up and left, after paying the bill and wishing me all the best, the waiter took his break and sat down with me to finish the cheesecake that Tom hadn't touched.

"The big, angry, muscular guy didn't come bursting in tonight."

I frowned. "No, he didn't."

"So, what's with you two, anyway?"

"Nothing. There's absolutely nothing between the two of us."

"So, what are you resisting? These guys you keep meeting in here? Dear god, send a life alert. You look like your head is going to nod off right into your vegan bouillabaisse. But when the big guy comes in, you shine, girl. You're all fire and sass."

"The guy tonight, Tom, was perfectly fine!"

"For your mother, maybe."

I narrowed my eyes. "You're awfully involved in this."

"Honey, you've been the live entertainment so often lately that I'm invested. It's like watching *Days of Our Lives*. What will she do next? Stay tuned for tomorrow's episode... So, why aren't you with the big guy?"

"We're just different people." I shook my head. "I think. I don't know."

He sighed and rolled his eyes. "Oh, my god. What is it with you women? That is one fine hunk of man meat there. Not only that, he comes bursting in here, wasting his time, letting you know he's more than interested. He looks at you like you're literally the last morsel of chocolate on earth and it's so damn hot, the chef could sear a steak on it. I don't get it. The rest of the servers here are wondering the same thing. Why the hell are you rejecting him?"

I just stared at him. I had an answer. I did. I just couldn't tell him. He wouldn't understand that I needed to find a rabbit mate. That I felt it my duty to do my part to perpetuate the species.

My stomach sank to my feet as I realized how lackluster I felt any more about the idea of a rabbit mate. I didn't want to touch any other man but Maxim. How I thought I could mate someone else, I didn't know. I still wanted rabbit babies and I still felt strongly about saving my species and getting rid of the ridiculous moniker, but I found I didn't hate the idea of little polar bear cubs. I didn't hate the idea at all.

"I..um...I'm pretty sure he's reached his limit. I think he's washed his hands of me." Maxim had finally done what I'd been telling him to do from day one. The fact that he hadn't crashed in here and interrupted my date made that painfully obvious.

"Are you going to accept that? Because, if not, there are about fifty other women who would be more than willing to take him off your hands. Hell, men, too."

"Back off." I growled at him and stood up. "He's mine."

"Yes! There's that show of passionate possessiveness I was hoping for!" He smirked. "Feel free to name your firstborn after me."

I looked at his name tag and nearly choked. "Um. No. Sorry, Hugh, but you're out of luck."

∽

I HAD an idea of where the polar bears lived. Heidi had talked about it some and, once I was in the general vicinity, it was easy for a rabbit shifter to scent out where a bunch of apex predators lived. I felt hesitant and I was second guessing myself as I got closer to the large two story bungalow. The scent of dominance was strong in the area and my rabbit sat up and twitched her ears. The idiot little thing was eager to go inside. The fuck? Did she have a death wish?

I could smell Maxim inside. My stomach flip-flopped and I began to second guess myself hard. What was I doing? I had a plan. I had a goal in life. I had...

The front door of the house opened and a huge guy nearly ran me over as he was leaving—one of the polar bears. He barely stopped before turning me into roadkill. "Fuck, sorry."

I backed away. I was making a fool of myself—I should just go home. "Excuse me."

"Wait, are you Parker? Maxim is inside. Go on in." He stepped out of the way and all but pushed me inside. "To the left."

He pulled the door closed after leaving and then I was left standing in the entryway of a house full of polar bears, wondering what the hell to do now.

"I smell rabbit!" A voice yelled from upstairs.

Annoyance tore through me. "Well, if it helps to mask the stink of bears, you're welcome."

Maxim immediately appeared from the left, like the other bear had said, a confused and shocked look on his face. "Parker. Is everything okay? What are you doing here?"

At that moment I wished I could fade into the wallpaper. It had clearly been a terrible idea to just show up unannounced. He probably didn't want me there, invading his space. "Um...you know, I'm not really sure... I'll go."

I didn't even get a chance to turn around before he quickly stepped around me and blocked the exit. "No, don't leave. Did you come to talk? What's on your mind?"

"You." I blew out a quick breath and shivered. "It's freezing in here. Why is it so cold in here? What, do you guys have the air conditioner up full blast?"

"Want to take a walk?"

I nodded. It was better to get out of that house. Being in an enclosed space and surrounded by Maxim's scent while trying to think clearly wasn't likely to yield the intended results. It was hard enough to make sense of what I was doing, with my rabbit jumping loops like a lunatic inside me. She was so happy to see her mate.

Maxim ushered me outside but kept out of my space. He didn't even speak as he started us walking in the direction of my house. We had to cross Main Street, but still, neither of us spoke. It wasn't until we were at my porch that Maxim shrugged. "I figured it'd be easier for you if we were on your own territory."

He was right. We sat on my front steps and it was easier to spill my guts. "I wasn't always like this. When I was younger, I didn't care who I slept with."

He dropped his head into his hands. "Not the thing to say to me, Bunny."

"I meant it wasn't so important to me to find another rabbit shifter. I wasn't so—neurotic. Things happened... I don't know, I got older. It became important to me where I came from. My parents died and I kind of felt alone in the world. About the same time, I also realized how few rabbit shifters there are like me left in this world, and the combination freaked me out.

"What I'm trying to say is that I think I might've gone a little overboard."

27

MAXIM

I didn't want to breathe for fear of pissing Parker off and drawing her away from where I hoped she was going with all this. She also looked vulnerable for the first time since I'd met her, and I didn't want to say anything that might take advantage of that vulnerability.

"I'm sorry." She turned to face me and rested her hand on top of my thigh. "I got carried away. I should have known better than to think I could ignore this thing between us and just find a rabbit that I feel *meh* about to mate with."

I was holding my breath and leaning closer to her. "What are you saying?"

"I can't help but argue with you."

I nodded. "Ditto."

"And you make me a little crazy."

I nodded again. "Ditto."

"I've never felt this way about anyone else, Maxim"

I flashed her a huge grin. "Ditto."

"When we're together, I'm not sure if I want to kiss you or punch you. I dream about kicking you in the shin and then kissing you to make it all better. None of this makes sense to me. But, I feel it."

I scooted closer to her. "I have something for you."

She raised her eyebrows. "As in a gift, or a restraining order?"

"A gift. I got some signatures for your petition."

"What? How?"

I grinned, feeling hopeful. "Half coercion, half seduction."

When her lips turned down, I leaned forward and pecked a kiss on her sweet lips. She pulled away and shook her head. "What do you mean?"

"I made all the guys help. We got topless on the beach and begged women to sign. The men, we threatened." I pulled her closer. "I have a stack of pages at the house, three thousand two hundred twenty nine signatures. You're not going to have that name attached to you anymore, not if you don't want it."

Her eyes filled with tears. "Three—that's over two thirds of the population of Sunkissed Key! You did that for me?"

"And for our future children. So they can be named after someone else. Someone inspiring, maybe. Someone who's done great and noble things."

"Future children?"

"That's another thing I wanted to talk to you about. I want a family with you. I want everything with you. I never wanted any such thing—never even thought about it—until I met you, but I do now. And, if it's important to you to have little rabbits, we can do that. I looked it up. There are ways. There's artificial insemination—with a donor.

"You looked it up? You'd do that? Are you serious?"

"I don't need our kids to have my DNA, Bunny. I just need you."

"I-I..." I hadn't expected her to fall into a puddle of sobs against me. I wasn't sure if I'd said the right thing or the wrong thing, but I scooped her into my arms and held her while she cried. As she tried unsuccessfully to compose herself, I carried her into the house, and —surprise, surprise—she let me. She didn't even struggle to get away when I settled us on the couch with her on my lap.

"I didn't think you were going to turn out to be the good guy." Her voice was small, ashamed.

"I'm the *best* guy."

"And still arrogant."

I stroked her hair away from her face and sighed. "Have you been getting any sleep?"

"None."

I stood up with her still in my arms, and carried her to her bedroom, the only other room in the house. I pulled back her blanket and placed her in bed before crawling in behind her and drawing her against my chest. Tucking the blanket over us, I buried my face in her hair and blew out a content sigh.

"What now?" She wiggled against me, her little body butting up perfectly.

I grunted and gripped her hip to keep her still. "Just rest, Bunny. You need some sleep."

"But..."

I held her tighter. "Sleep, little bunny."

She sighed, but her body relaxed against me almost instantly and within seconds she was fast asleep. I smiled into her hair and let myself relax. It'd been so long since I'd been able to fall asleep without feeling like there was a deep empty hole in my chest. Having my mate in my arms filled up that emptiness. I fell asleep nearly as fast as Parker, and for the first time since meeting her, slept hard.

At some point during the night, I came awake with a start to the feeling of Parker sliding down my chest. She stopped only when she got to the top of my pants.

"Bunny..."

She looked up at me and gave me a slow smile before sitting up and pulling her top over her head. She unhooked her bra and tossed it aside. "I had a dream."

Wide awake now, I reached for her, but she pushed my hands away. I growled as I watched her unbuckle my belt and pull the zipper down.

"In my dream, you told me that you'd gotten my petition signed and that you'd be willing to have rabbit children with me. Even more, you told me you wanted to have a family with me. Long term, big commitment, *children and family*." Her voice broke as she got emotional, but she blinked it away. "Only me? For the rest of your life?"

I sat up, ignoring her attempts at being in charge, and flipped her over so she was under me. Staring down at her, I grinned wickedly and shook my head. "I don't know how fate decided that I deserved a woman as fine as you, but I'm not asking questions. It's you and me, forever. I'm all yours, Bunny."

"I'm all yours, too."

I dipped my head and kissed her. "Mine."

She arched her body into mine and batted those beautiful amber eyes at me. "Are you going to do something about it? I've never heard of a shifter male bringing his woman home to nap."

My bear growled from within me, rising to the challenge. "Is there ever going to be a time with you don't push my buttons?"

"Doubt it. Can't handle it?"

I extended my claws just enough to rip through her jeans and panties, taking them off in one swipe. Having her bare in front of me, I sat back and marveled. "Spread your legs."

She kept her thighs closed and narrowed her eyes at me. "Those were expensive jeans."

I gripped her thighs and pulled them apart, exposing her sweet sex to my hungry eyes. She hissed at me and tried to squeeze her legs shut. I just smirked, watching as she struggled in vain against me. "I'm in charge tonight, Bunny."

"That's not fair."

I moved my right hand up enough that I could run my thumb over her wet folds. Her sharp intake of breath told me she was ready. "I'm in charge."

A beat passed. Then another. Then, her legs went limp and she dug her hands into the bedding under her. It was the only sign of submission I was getting.

28

MAXIM

I growled as I lowered myself in front of Parker and pressed an open mouthed kiss to her inner thigh. She trembled under me, her body tense. I wanted to take my time and devour all of her. I wanted to taste and touch and learn every inch of her body. I rubbed my nose over her the sensitive folds between her thighs listening as she growled back at me.

"Dammit, Maxim. Do something."

Feeling like I was entering the hottest, most satisfying battle I'd ever took part in, I lightly flicked my tongue over her core tasting her deliciousness. She tasted sweet and spicy like carrot cake and the way her body reacted, the way her voice broke as she called my name, I'd never experienced anything so thrilling.

Parker wasn't giving up control that easily, though. She couldn't help herself. She dug her fingers into my hair and yanked, trying to get me where she wanted me, but I didn't give in. I moved where I wanted to, drawing out and prolonging her pleasure. I sucked and nibbled and flicked my tongue everywhere but where she wanted me.

When she screamed my name, I finally focused on her clit and nibbled gently until she cried out—spasming and shaking, orgasming on my face as her body twisted and writhed.

I wasn't done with her, though. I'd waited so long for this, there was no way I'd let her rest already. I dragged my shirt over my head and tossed it away before sitting back on my knees to work on my pants.

Parker sat up with a growl and, in a flash, my pants were in shreds around us. I looked down at them, at my naked body and hard cock jutting forward, and dragged a rough breath into my lungs. My little mate wasn't anyone's sweet little innocent. She was just as rough and wild as I was. I had a feeling my little bunny just might kill me before the night was over. If so, I would die a happy man.

"*More.*"

I swore and grabbed her to me, kissing her passionately. I wanted everything with her and wanted to give just as much of me back. She was a lovely contradiction of sugary sweetness and stinging bite. Curvy and soft, but with plenty of nails and teeth. She sank those teeth into my chest and raked her nails over my back, heightening my pleasure.

Desperate and starving for each other, we were both just as fevered and just as needy as the first time we'd tried this, in her kitchen. I spread her thighs and slid into her in one solid thrust. She screamed and pulled at my hair before arching her back and rolling her hips.

"Fuck me, Maxim." She stretched out under me like a fucking siren, luring me to my death. There was no going back from her. There never was. And I was all-in.

I pulled out of her temporarily and flipped her over so she was on all fours in front of me before slamming right back home. Holding the back of her hair, I pumped and growled loud enough to shake the walls. We'd slipped into animalistic rutting, but it was what we both needed. I felt every part of myself connecting with her, imprinting myself onto her, just as she was tattooing her very essence on my soul.

Loud, sweaty, rough, we slammed our bodies together again and again. I pulled her hair, dug into her hips, smacked her ass. She grabbed the headboard, her head thrown back, my name a constant on her breath.

When I felt her body start to constrict around me, I tried to hold back, but feeling her come undone under and around was too much. I brushed her hair off her shoulder and sank my teeth into her neck, marking her as mine for all the world to know. She came with a wild scream, her hands turning into little claws as she ripped the bedding and bent the metal headboard.

I followed her over the edge with a roar, my fingerprints bruised into her hips. I released my seed in her in warm jets and when she collapsed under me from weakness, I went down with her.

I panted, trying to catch my breath while listening to her do the same. It'd been rough and fast and probably nothing like what a claiming should be, but I was so filled with happiness that I couldn't even remember my own name.

When I was starting to put too much of my weight on her, I rolled to the side and pulled her with me. On my chest, curled around me, her arms and legs hugging me, my heart was full.

I stroked her hair and back and did everything I could think of to let her know how much she meant to me without having to speak and ruin the moment. She let me hold her there for so long I'd been convinced she'd fallen asleep when she finally spoke.

"So. That happened."

I grinned. "Yeah, it did. You okay?"

"Is that a real question?"

"Woman."

"Yes, I'm okay. I feel like butter someone left out in the sun. I could melt right off of you and puddle on the floor." She sighed. "I can feel you."

"I hope you can."

She snorted. "Not like that, idiot. I can feel you in here."

When she tapped my chest, I grunted. "That's just gas."

Laughing, she sat up and pulled me up with her. Straddling my lap, she pressed her forehead to mine and kissed me. "You *are* a good guy."

I made a face. "You know I can feel you, too, right?"

She made a face back at me. "I'm just as mushy as you, right? We're pathetic."

"Absolutely disgusting."

"We should probably do this all again, just to make sure it sticks." She shrugged. "Maybe slower this time? I feel like the first time is supposed to be romantic."

"Am I not romantic enough for you?" I grinned, poking her and enjoying it fully. "I already went to dinner with you twice. That's just about as romantic as I get."

"What?! You did not go to dinner with me! You showed up and ruined my dates."

"Damn right! And I'd do it again! You should be glad, woman."

She bit her lip and rocked her hips against me. "Let me show you just how glad I am."

29

PARKER

Two weeks of rolling around with Maxim and bearing permanent rug burn later, two weeks in which I'd taken and given pleasure every which way, and I was head over heels in love with the big, cocky bear. He'd proven that he was so incredibly sweet and patient with me when I needed him to be. He was also infuriating and purposely did things to drive me crazy just because he liked to see me get angry. Of course, make up sex was extra wild during those times. No denying that.

He was amazing. And frustrating. And amazingly frustrating. I wanted to push him down stairs at times, and jump his bones at others. The whole thing worked for us. We were each better with a little bite to us. Too much mushiness and we both tended to get a little over emotional.

My rabbit had really come into her own with him, too. She was bossier than ever and had taken to nipping at his heels on our midnight runs down the beach. If anyone ever saw us, they'd think they'd gotten a bad batch of something, because a giant polar bear being chased and messed with by a small rabbit must have been a sight to see.

The only problem I had was that a part of me that felt like I'd let down my rabbit shifter community. I felt as though I'd turned my back on my social activism and abandoned what I believed in. I hadn't, not in my heart, but it was hard to find a balance. I had no doubts I was meant to be with Maxim, my angst was all about failing to do anything concrete to save my species.

There was no way I was going to agree to artificial insemination to ensure I had a rabbit baby. No way. I wanted Maxim's child. But, Maxim's offer had touched my heart in a huge way. Knowing that he was willing to honor me enough to do whatever it took for me to have a rabbit child, even if it meant that he wasn't the biological father, was selfless. I didn't want that, though. Fate did a pretty good job of pairing us up and I would let fate handle our future as well. Whatever was supposed to happen would happen. If our kid was a rabbit, I'd be over the moon, but if it was a polar bear, I'd be equally as happy.

I still wanted to save rabbits and, after wracking my brain, I thought I had come up with a pretty good way that combined my activism with a new business idea. It was something I'd been giving a lot of thought to—a way to make a difference without me having to buy rabbit sperm.

"You're deep in thought." Laila pulled back the palm leaf from my hiding spot in Latte Love and grinned at me. "You picked a pathetic leaf today. I spotted you right away."

I smiled at her and shrugged. "I was wondering how you found me so fast. I'm working on a new business venture."

"Oh, it wouldn't have been hard to find you, even if you'd been behind the biggest leaf in the place. You *smell*." She wagged her brows at me.

I scoffed. "What the hell does that mean?"

She grabbed my hands and leaned in. "My nose is working better than ever today. I can smell you so clearly."

"Oh, gross."

"You smell like rabbit, polar bear and... a little something extra." She winked when she said that last part and her smile stretched wide across her face. "That little something extra is going to make me cry."

"What?" My heart leapt to my throat, not sure if she was hinting at what I thought she was hinting at.

"You didn't know that you're pregnant?"

I screamed. Full out, blood curdling, send people scrambling for cover. I screamed and then I jumped up, knocking over the puny potted palm and scaring everyone in the place. "No!"

Laila was right there with me. "Yes! You're pregnant!"

I screamed again and grabbed my hair. "Holy shit! Holy shit!"

Laila clutched at her chest. "I'm going to be an aunt!"

I laughed. "I'm just so excited! I'm having a baby! You're sure? You're absolutely sure?"

She nodded, tears in her eyes. "I'm sure. You're having a baby, Parker."

"I'm having a baby." I gasped. "*We're* having a baby! I have to go find Maxim!"

"Wait, what about this super important new business venture?"

"I'm going to start a better online dating site for shifters!" I hugged her hard. "I'm going to match other rabbits together. That'll be how I make my difference with my own species. Of course, it's for all shifters, not just rabbits. I'll match any kind of shifter, but it's going to be updated and nice. Not some sleazy hook up site or something that shifters balk at."

"Online shifter dating, huh?" Laila smiled brightly. "Okay, I'm game. Sign me up."

"I have to go! I'll tell you more later!"

I ran out of there like a maniac and ran straight to the P.O.L.A.R. office. I'd been to the office plenty of times since mating Maxim and I'd met all the other women mates and found myself excited to tell them, too. Maxim, first, though. Hannah was the only person in the office when I bounded in. She jumped up, startled, and stared at me wide-eyed.

"Where's Maxim?"

"At West Beach. Something's going down with a rogue female snake shifter."

I thanked her and ran back out. I hurried to the beach, panting and sweating by the time I got there.

Maxim was easy to spot. He was the one with the snake coiled around his leg. He was trying to shake her off and very obviously trying awkwardly not to hurt her. I didn't think twice about running straight to him, grabbing the head of the snake bitch and squeezing until she let out an awful hiss and let go of my mate. She was fine, just a little shaken, but whoever it was would get an earful from me later.

"What the fuck are you doing here?!"

I put my hands on my hips, still holding the snake a little too tightly, and scrunched up my face at him. "Is that any way to talk to your pregnant mate?"

He stumbled. "What?"

Serge came up beside us and cleared his throat. "Maybe you should drop the damned snake, Parker?"

"Yeah, and you guys out here cursing in front of me. That's got to stop."

Serge looked confused. "The cursing?"

"Yeah, you boys are going to have to watch your language now." I cocked my head. "Cause of the baby." I rested my hand on my lower abdomen.

Serge's eyes widened. He looked at me and then at Maxim who was grinning from ear to ear like a fool. "You're pregnant?"

"I'm pregnant!"

Maxim grabbed me and yanked me into his chest and as he did, I tossed the snake at Serge. It immediately locked itself around him.

"Are you sure you're pregnant?"

"How many times are you going to ask that?" I grinned. "Yes, I'm pregnant."

He lifted me in the air and buried his face between my breasts. "I'm going to be a daddy!"

"Someone should really help Serge." Alexei shrugged. "But congrats, kids! I can't wait to be an uncle!"

I wrapped my arms around Maxim's neck as he peppered me with kisses. I'd never been happier in my life. My future wasn't unfolding exactly as I'd envisioned it. It was so much better!

Maxim was the best mate I could've ever dreamed of and we were beginning to grow our little family. While Serge was slowly getting eaten by a snake.

Serge was getting eaten by a snake! I gasped and pushed against Maxim's chest. "Max, you better help him!"

He grinned down at me, refusing to release me from his grasp. "Naw, those guys can handle it. I'm taking my pregnant mate home for a little alone time, just the two of us."

Then, smiling at one another, we both corrected his statement at the same time.

"Just the *three* of us."

THE END

ROYAL BEAR

P.O.L.A.R. 5

*In the search for her missing brother,
Free-spirited Grace
finds some **firsts**—
friends, family, a home,
and a hot shifter who captures her heart.*

*To claim Grace as his mate,
Konstantin must not only renounce his title
and shun his duties,
he must betray his friends.*

Being a Royal Bear is a royal b*tch.

1

GRACE

Mid November mornings were colder than a witch's tit in South Dakota. The seasons had snuck up on me this year. Normally, Freebird, Damocles and I would have already headed farther south by this time of year.

Freebird was my home on wheels, a converted sprinter van. Even though her single pane windows were covered with thickly-padded blackout blinds at night, she wasn't insulated well for these colder temperatures.

Usually the only tools I had in my arsenal to combat the chill were a hot water bottle for my toes, a thick down comforter, and my not-so-friendly tabby cat, Damocles. This morning, I had an extra tool. He was still asleep.

Ted was sawing logs on the pillow next to mine. Or was his name Ed? Maybe Fred. Pretty sure it was something that rhymed with *dead*. Which was appropriate considering the quality of our party in the sheets last night.

I rolled off the 4-inch foam mattress and padded naked over to the little cubby where I stored my clothes. Shivering, I threw on a pair of yoga pants and a sweatshirt with *#vanlife* written across the front, then started the propane burner under my mini coffee percolator.

I lived a roving existence, traveling from state to state wherever whim—and weather—took me, and Freebird enabled me to remain off-grid.

My peripatetic lifestyle gave me the opportunity to appreciate all the beauty this country had to offer, from the quaint fishing villages of coastal Maine to the flat prairies of waving Kansas wheat, to the old western ghost towns that dotted the Nevada desert.

It also meant I never put down roots, never developed friendships, and was never anything but an outsider, a nomad—a perpetual stranger. This was the life I'd always known. The life I'd lived ever since I could remember.

My current place of residence, if it could be called such, was the Black Hills of the South Dakota Badlands. For four months, I'd been parked out in wilderness shaped by buttes and harsh, white-clay terrain washed nearly barren from centuries of flash flooding. Most mornings, the grassy mesas were speckled with prairie dogs, grazing wild bison, and the occasional big horned sheep.

As I tore the blackout pads off the windows, hoping it would serve to rouse Fred, Damocles sat coolly giving me the evil eye. Not sure if it was because I slept late and his breakfast was delayed, or because he was pissed at having to share our tiny living space with Fred. Ed? To say he wasn't keen on strangers was an understatement.

As a peace offering, I opened a can of his favorite 9 Lives, seafood flavored, and set it on the floor in front of him. Then, I glanced over at the sleeping Ned. He needed to go. I was eager to head into town to check my emails. I'd been waiting impatiently for an email from my brother Gray for the past two weeks. Five years older than me, Gray was just about as nomadic and hard to pin down as I was. With each of us always on the move, and frequently in different time zones, we'd tired of trying to reach each other by phone years ago. A simple email on the first and the fifteenth of every month was how we kept in touch and assured one another we were still alive and kicking.

And, for seven years now, like clockwork, we emailed on our scheduled days. Seven years without fail. Never missed...until two weeks ago. When I didn't hear back from Gray on the first of

November, I told myself not to panic. I waited a full two weeks without panicking. Yesterday was the fifteenth and I emailed again. Nothing. If I didn't hear from him today...well, I wasn't sure what I'd do. My stomach twisted into a knot at the thought.

"Debbie..."

"Debbie...?"

I suddenly realized Jed was awake. Damn, I had to start remembering what name I gave my overnight guests. Not that Damocles, Freebird and I entertained many overnight guests. It wasn't a frequent habit, but hey, a girl had needs. I smiled at Ned, which apparently served to encourage him.

"So I was thinking, Debbie, there's supposed to be a storm front moving in later tonight. Maybe you and me could head to town this afternoon and take in a movie or something? What do you say?"

"Er...not today. I have a full workday planned."

Ted looked dejected. "Okay, maybe an early dinner?"

Gee, Ed, take a hint.

I smiled tightly then cleared my throat. "Look, last night was great and all..."

As I paused to select my words carefully, an old Janice Joplin tune ran through my head: *"Don't you know that you're nothing more than a one-night stand. Tomorrow I'll be on my way..."*

Fortunately, Ed was intuitive enough to pick up what I was putting down. "But you're kicking me to the curb, is that it?"

I shrugged. "Well, I wouldn't exactly put it that way..."

"Naw, it's okay, I get it." To give Ned credit, he didn't try to persuade me that he was the next great love of my life if only I'd give him a chance. He merely nodded, said his goodbye, and even tried to pat Damocles on the head before he left. Damocles hissed and the hair stood up along his spine. Typical. The cat would have gotten a chunk of flesh if Ned hadn't pulled his hand back so quickly. Grumpy cat.

Relieved that my overnight guest wasn't a cling-on, I folded my comforter, tucked away my bedding and transformed my bed platform back into a bench sofa. Then, sipping on my first cup of liquid energy, I grabbed a granola bar and slipped into the driver's seat for the daily half hour commute to Wall. As if on cue, Damocles leaped into the copilot's seat, curled up, and began his morning tongue bath.

The sky was gray and overcast as I pulled onto the road that led into town. Sure looked as though the weather forecast was on point. A storm was predicted to come in later that night and was supposed to bring in even colder weather and maybe some snow.

I figured that was a good enough sign as any that it was time to get out of South Dakota and head for warmer weather.

2

KONSTANTIN

"Watch out!"

I'd already seen the volleyball sailing through the air, headed my way, and twisted easily to lob it back. I nodded to the grinning bikini-clad players before turning back to continue staring out at the ocean. As I breathed in a lungful of warm, salt air, I committed as much of the scene as I could to memory.

The sea was a gorgeous dark blue, and the setting sun was fast becoming a palette of fiery oranges and reds. The evenings here in the Keys were exquisite. The days weren't half bad either with white sand, green palms, and bright pink and purple bougainvillea that seemed to bloom everywhere on the little island.

Sunkissed Key was a far cry from the vast frozen tundra and snow-capped mountains of Siberia. Sure, the heat here was torturous some days, but the extreme heat was quelled by the fact that I was thousands of miles from my stuffy family and my familial obligations. I knew it was impossible, but I'd have been very happy staying on the little island—far away from Siberia—indefinitely.

"Dinner's ready!" Serge called out the back door of the house and waved at me. "And I ain't waitin'."

I took another long, mental photograph of the ocean view before standing, brushing the sand off, and heading inside. I knew my days as a member of the P.O.L.A.R. team were numbered and I wanted to etch everything about this amazing adventure I was living into my memory banks. I would undoubtedly need to tap into the pleasant, carefree memories to sustain me through challenging days and long, cold nights ahead. *Cold* in both the literal and metaphorical sense. Once I returned to Siberia and assumed my title, the legacy of my birthright, and the duties that accompanied it, this life I loved, and the comradery of being just one of the guys, would come to an abrupt end.

Hannah, Serge's mate, gave me a wide smile as I stepped into the kitchen. She'd been with us since before Sunkissed Key and in a not-so-indirect way was the reason we'd ended up on this on the island. "I made tacos."

My stomach growled and I patted the top of her head, the way I knew made her laugh. She'd quickly grown to be a friend over the months and I was going to miss her warm smiles. Hell, I'd miss all of them. "Sounds delicious."

"Hands off my woman." Serge pointed the tongs he was holding at me and growled.

Hannah leaned into him, wrapping her arms around his waist. "Look at my big, strong polar bear, getting all jealous."

"Don't say it like that, woman. You make polar bears sound like cute, cuddly teddy bears."

Kerrigan, Dmitry's mate, grinned at Hannah before goading her own mate. "To be fair, you guys are rather cute and cuddly. In a big, strong, muscular kind of way."

Roman and his mate, Megan entered the dining room and sat next to Alexei and Heidi at the large table. Across from them, Maxim, and his shifter mate, Parker were already seated. Although most of the guys and their mates stayed elsewhere now, the team frequently gathered at the P.O.L.A.R. house for dinner, and there was a happy, lively energy in the room. I'd never seen any of the guys so carefree and content before. Not even Alexei.

Serge looked at how crammed everyone was, even with most of

the women sitting on their men's laps. "We need a bigger table. This is getting ridiculous. When Kon brings home a mate, we won't all fit."

I paused with a taco halfway to my mouth. My back to the group, I afforded myself a wince. There would be no mate for me, not in the traditional sense. None of them knew that yet, though.

"That would mean Kon would have to be even remotely interested in finding a woman. Never going to happen." Alexei joked. "He really does just go to the bars to drink and unwind."

Heidi scowled at her mate. "And what do the rest of you go to the bars for?"

I glanced back to find Alexei holding up his hands and looking like a deer in headlights. "I meant *before*. I was talking about, like, *before* you. Before when we were still searching for mates."

"Speak for yourself, Alexei." Maxim leaned into Parker and nuzzled her neck. "I was a choir boy before I found my Bunny."

Parker rolled her eyes at him. "If you're going to keep lying, I should move before you get struck by lightning or your nose grows six inches." She rubbed her expanding baby bump. "I hope your fibbery doesn't rub off on our baby."

"Speaking of..." Roman held Megan closer. They stared into one another's eyes and Megan's began to water. "Speaking of baby, it looks like our kids are going to grow up together, Maxim."

It took three seconds for the impact of the words to be absorbed and digested by everyone. The women all jumped up squealing and giving Megan hugs while the rest of us clapped Roman on the back and congratulated him. A second P.O.L.A.R. baby on the way. The team was becoming a real family. I stood back and watched, committing yet another warm scene to memory, studying every detail as the group of people I cared for deeply stuffed themselves with tacos, laughed jovially, and looked forward to their future. Together.

My future weighed heavily on my shoulders as I watched the women toss out baby shower ideas while the guys made bets on whose kid was going to join the P.O.L.A.R. team first. I knew I wouldn't be around to see whose child joined P.O.L.A.R. My time here was running out. Chances were, I wouldn't even be around long enough to attend a baby shower.

With my obligations looming ever nearer, I felt as though I was trying to tread water with a boulder in my stomach and my ankles weighted with bricks. Sometimes, even in a room full of friends, it was as though there were a million degrees of separation between me and the others. As though I was a complete stranger.

I slipped away to my bedroom without finishing dinner.

3
GRACE

Once I reached the small town of Wall, population, 872, I parked outside Wall Drug—the combination drug store, restaurant, gift shop, and tourist attraction—where you could get everything from necessities like clothes and food, to hunting licenses, to cowboy hats, to touristy junk like postcards and jackalope trophies. Me, I came for the free Wi-Fi.

I earned the majority of my living as a graphic artist and had my virtual shingle hung out on several sites like Fiverr and Upwork. I supplemented the income from my digital art by making bead jewelry, which I sold on Etsy.

As soon as I fired up my laptop, I immediately logged onto my email. The last email I'd gotten from Gray had been short and vague with no clues about what he'd been up to. When nothing popped up from him, I refreshed the page and waited. Again, nothing. Other than a couple of junk emails, and one from my latest client, a sci-fi author for whom I was designing a series of e-book covers, my inbox was as empty as ever.

After another three times refreshing, I finally admitted defeat. My heart sank as I refreshed the page once more, just to be absolutely positively sure. An icy chill ran through my veins. Gray would never miss on purpose. Never.

I slammed my laptop closed and hurried over to the post office. I had a couple jewelry orders to mail out. As I walked, I tried to rationalize the situation and quell the terrible, ominous feeling brewing deep in my belly. Gray was a badass. Tough as nails. He may have gotten caught up in something. He was always pushing limits and ignoring the boundaries of what a normal person should and shouldn't do. He wasn't normal though, not by any means. Neither of us were normal, but growing up had been a heck of a lot tougher on Gray than it had been on me. By far.

When I entered the tiny Wall Post Office, I recognized the postal clerk, an older woman with an inquisitive nature. Her eyes lit up when she saw me. The fact that we both recognized one another was another sign that it was time for me to be moving on.

"Hi, dear! I was wondering if I'd see you again."

I smiled and dropped my outgoing packages on the counter. "Temperature's dropping out there."

She nodded as she placed one of the packages on the postal scale. "It certainly is. There's a storm front coming in. Tell me, honey, what's your name?"

"Jennifer." The lie slid off my tongue as easily as butter and I didn't feel one iota of guilt about it.

"Jennifer. Well, isn't that just a co-inky-dink. My son, Thomas, is a huge Jennifer Lawrence fan."

"Small world."

She batted her eyelashes at me. "There's not many single young ladies around here and I've been telling my Thomas all about you. He's eager to meet you."

Ugh, I definitely needed to be moving on.

I forced a smile. "I'm so sorry, but I'm married."

Her face fell. "Happily?"

I laughed at that. "Yes, ma'am, blissfully. I'm sure your Thomas is wonderful, but my Henry has already captured my heart."

"Well, shucks. Thomas is going to be so disappointed." She shrugged it off and sighed. "Oh, well. There's still young Mandy in town. She'll be eighteen soon. Do you know her? Mandy Brown?"

I held back a wince for poor young Mandy and hoped she managed to steer clear of Thomas's matchmaking mama. "I don't."

The woman's face turned more curious and her eyes narrowed slightly. "Where *are* you from?"

My smile turned brittle. I couldn't help it. I didn't like being interrogated, even by a nosy old lady who was probably completely harmless and only wanted to ensure she had grandbabies to spoil in her later years. "Oh, here and there and all over the place." I shrugged, running my fingers along one of the packages, eager to get them both posted and get the hell out of there.

She laughed and backed away. "Well, you're all set, Jennifer." She handed me the receipt and I slipped it in the pocket of my denim jacket to add to the shoebox of business receipts I kept under the passenger's seat of Freebird.

"I'll see you next time." She wiggled her fingers in a wave.

I grinned on my way out the door. *Not if I can help it.*

As soon as I was back in the van, I checked my inbox again. No matter how many times I refreshed the page, still nothing from Gray. My stomach sunk to my toes. My pulse pounded out a staccato rhythm. Was Gray in trouble? Or worse? I tried not to imagine what "or worse" might mean. My brother was all I had in the world.

Growing up, our dad had moved us from town to town never staying anywhere long enough for the local authorities to get wind of the fact that he never paid taxes or sent us to school or did any of the other things that he considered means of suppression by a tyrannical government.

I always hoped that maybe someday we would finally settle down and live like a normal family. Then, instead of running to avoid the truant officer or IRS, I could make friends with other girls my age. I used to dream about having sleepovers where my friends and I would do each other's hair and gossip about boys.

It never happened.

Neither Gray nor I had ever had any other roots—no friends, family, or anything at all—except each other. And Dad. Our bi-monthly emails were as important to Gray as they were to me. It was weird to say, but they tethered us to one another and that kept us both grounded. When you lived a roving existence like we did, it was huge to know that in this great big world, there was one other person somewhere who cared.

Tears formed in my eyes as I thought about my brother being hurt...*or worse*. As much as I wanted to believe otherwise, he wouldn't just forget to contact me. He wouldn't. I had to find him.

I knew Gray lived life on the edge. That was just who he was. But, there had to be some way to begin searching for him. Some clue as to his whereabouts. I didn't even know what he did for a living. I began pouring through the old emails for clues—any mention of towns or plans or jobs or what he might be involved in...anything.

I found a few references to the ocean, but east coast? West coast? There were too many possibilities to narrow it down. I kept reading over the emails, lingering on every word until I noticed the numbers in very small font at the bottom of one of the emails, under his name: 243333n814703w. A smile stretched across my face. To anyone else, it would have looked like a random jumble of numbers and letters, as though maybe his pet had stepped on the keyboard. I knew otherwise.

Gray, you sly dog you.

I pulled up an app on my computer and entered the numbers, grinning like a fool, despite the situation. I'd found exactly what I'd been looking for. I hadn't even noticed at the time. I hadn't bothered to scroll down and take a closer look at his sign off. Gray had slipped map coordinates into the old email: 24°33′33″N 81°47′03″W.

A geo atlas app quickly gave me the location on a map—somewhere in the lower Florida Keys. I figured if I drove straight through, stopping only to boondock in Walmart parking lots for a few hours of shuteye, I should arrive in about two days.

Jittery with nerves, I ran into Wall Drug for groceries, packed my mini fridge, gassed up Freebird, and hit the open road.

Sunkissed Key, Florida, here I come.

I hoped to god that if Gray had moved on from the Keys, he'd at least left a breadcrumb trail so I could figure out where in this world my brother was.

4
GRACE

As I exited the Overseas Highway, the sun was just beginning to peek above the horizon welcoming me to the sleepy little island. I arrived early enough in the morning that as I drove down Main Street, Sunkissed Key looked deserted.

I'd been driving all night, was exhausted, and desperately needed a shower and some deodorant. My eyes felt gritty; my throat felt scratchy. My body was screaming at me to pull over, curl up with Damocles and take a power snooze. But as tired as I was, I didn't think I'd be able to sleep until I knew more about Gray

As soon as I pulled Freebird up to the small cottage on the ocean, I knew it belonged to Gray. A beat-up old pickup was parked under the pillars of the raised cottage— the same two-toned, white and aqua colored 1969 Chevy short bed he'd been driving the last time I saw him, seven years ago. I had to smile. Only Gray would drive around Florida in a vehicle that lacked air conditioning.

My heart soared as I shifted Freebird into park, jumped out and raced across the sandy ground and up the stairs, two at a time. Even though I hadn't seen Gray in forever, I had no qualms about waking him up and kicking his ass for scaring the crap out of me.

When I reached the top of the stairs, I found the front door slightly ajar. The hope that had been bubbling inside me suddenly became lodged in my throat and I reached up brushing my neck with my fingertips as though I could physically push the lump back down.

With a shaky hand, I silently nudged the door open a little more and stepped inside. Planting my back against the wall, I took in the open floorplan while keeping alert for villains. Or boogeymen. Empty, but trashed. Drawers in the small kitchen had been yanked from the cabinets and upended. Couch cushions were ripped to shreds. The place had been thoroughly ransacked.

Any doubt I had that Gray had gotten himself into some sort of trouble vanished. I inched through the small cottage inspecting every room, bathroom, and closet, making sure there was no one still hiding out. From the look of the place, my brother had gotten involved in some serious doo-doo. But what? And where was he?

To say Gray and I'd had a bizarre upbringing would be putting it mildly. We'd been raised by a single father who was not only an anarchist and a doomsday prepper, but also a conspiracy theorist to the point of paranoia—and fury. It had taken years to quell the constant fear and anxiety I carried thanks to their cultivation by my Dad and the loony bunch of fringe dwellers we met up with from time to time at gun shows or militia field training gatherings.

As I flipped a chair upright and sat to contemplate my next move, I quickly came to the conclusion that my big brother wasn't the only one in over his head. I had a host of survival skills thanks to dear old Dad. Yeah, I could start a fire with two twigs, identify over 250 species of wild, edible plants, and survive for months in the wilderness equipped with only a pocketknife.

I could also pick a lock with a hairpin, hotwire a car in less than fifteen seconds, and build a homemade incendiary device with regular household items found under the kitchen sink. I was even trained to live through a zombie apocalypse with nothing but a slingshot and a bucket of rocks.

What I wasn't skilled at was the art of investigation. I knew a whole lot more about running, hiding, staying off-grid, and erasing my tracks than I did about finding someone. In that regard, I was useless.

That lump in my throat burned and tears threatened to spill. I didn't let them fall, but they put up a damned good fight. This was no time to break down. If I couldn't handle the situation, I had to enlist the help of someone who could—and pronto.

I debated going to the police, but it didn't feel right. When you had a childhood in which you and your brother had been taught to be wary, not only of the government, but also of law enforcement on any level, it was hard to shake that particular brand of paranoia. While I wasn't proud of it, I wasn't going to get over my ingrained distrust overnight. Besides, I didn't know what Gray was involved in. For all I knew, I'd ask the police to find him only to end up having my brother locked up and charged with a criminal offence. No, I needed someone who wasn't the police. Maybe a local private investigator.

I went back outside and sat on Freebird's running board with Damocles and my laptop nervously searching for PI firms in the area. There were pages of results, most based in the Miami area, but a Reddit thread popped up in the search results. It had been started by someone locally. Some of the respondents were complaining and others were praising the new "security force" on the island. There seemed to be a dispute about whether the group was working in opposition to or in tandem with local law enforcement, but both sides of the dispute agreed on one thing—they were not an officially government-licensed agency. Bingo.

Another search landed me a name and address—P.O.L.A.R., 44 South Main Street.

There was next to nothing online in the way of information on this group called P.O.L.A.R. Just a couple articles in the local paper— one about the group helping clear out the island in the aftermath of Hurricane Matilda and another about the rescue of a family after their pontoon capsized. I still wasn't convinced of anything except that the group was my best option, at least for the moment.

I tended to be a good judge of character—another throwback

from being raised by a neurotic parent—and I figured I'd decide whether or not to trust them once I saw them in person, face to face.

My van contained a small wet-closet, a toilet room that doubled as a shower, but it was miniscule and in warmer climates, I much preferred to shower outside. I set up my outdoor shower and rushed through my cleaning routine. Deodorant, some clothes, and a good toothbrushing later and I was off. I swung Freebird back out onto Main Street and headed toward the south end of the island.

It was still early and Sunkissed Key was just waking up, so I parked in front of 44 South Main and waited for them to open. I hoped they were still in operation. The place was unmarked and the front window was tinted. Antsy and nervous, I locked the van and made my way through the alley to the back of the building and down to the beach.

The ocean was serene and calm. Gentle, rolling waves eased up onto the shore before retreating back across the sand. I stretched my neck back, lifting my face to the rising sun to let it warm me as I waited for the little offices and stores along Main Street to start opening to admit their first customers of the day.

Gray had always liked the ocean. When we were kids, he'd light up with excitement when we landed somewhere next to water. Of course, as soon as Dad figured that out, it was all deserts and mountains from then on out.

Where are you, Gray?

My arms ached to grab my big brother and hug him close. It'd been too long and the fear that I'd never get the chance again was gnawing at me. I had to find him.

5
KONSTANTIN

There was something unsettling in the air that morning. It seemed to prickle my skin in a way that I wasn't sure I liked. At the very least, it had me feeling uneasy and restless. It felt almost as though there was something coming—as though the ether held a premonition of something big. Earthshattering.

I got up and dressed for the day as usual. As I went about my morning routine, I tried to ignore my uneasiness, but as soon as I arrived at the storefront that housed our office, something in air had me in a state of bewilderment.

The scent of honey cakes was wafting from somewhere near the beach. Someone was baking my favorite treat and, no matter that I'd just eaten a full breakfast, I wanted to gorge myself on the sweet. I had turned that way and was walking towards the delectable aroma before I even realized I was doing it.

"Kon, know anything about this?"

I glanced back. Serge was gesturing to a white sprinter van parked along the curb. It appeared to have accrued its fair share of mileage.

"Looks like a stealth camper. It's the latest thing, don't you watch YouTube?"

Serge gave me an *aren't you just the cleverest dickstool on the block* look, but when I tipped my head back and inhaled, more of that delicious aroma wafted from inside the vehicle.

"What is it?"

I frowned and strode over to the van. I tried the door, but it was locked. "Don't you smell that?"

Serge raised a brow. "Smell what?"

I inhaled deeply again and my fist clenched unconsciously on the door handle of the van snapping it clean off. I swore and shoved the chrome handle into my pocket. I smelled...medovic, the multi-layered, Russian honey cake from back home, fresh baked and warm from the oven.

"This is gonna sound strange but is it possible that someone parked here and is selling medovic down at the beach? C'mon, you have to smell that?"

His eyebrows bunched together and he tilted his head back, his nostrils flaring. "I smell soap and cheap coffee."

I just kept taking deep breaths of the intoxicating smell, my mouth watering. My dick stirred in my pants and I stared down at it in shock. The guys could make all the wise cracks they wanted about me being asexual but that wasn't the case at all. Not by a long shot. I noticed women. And I avoided them. For a reason. I'd gotten so good at it that I couldn't remember the last time I'd sprouted wood in reaction to a woman, yet the smell of honey cake was giving me a boner? I was losing it.

"Come on. Let's get the office open."

I backed away from the sprinter van and nodded. "Yeah, right."

Dragging myself inside, I plopped down at my desk in the back and turned on the window AC unit so that it blew directly over me. I was burning up. My skin felt like it was two sizes too small suddenly and I was on fire. Nerves fluttered in my stomach until I couldn't stand it and stood back up, unsure of what the fuck was happening to me.

As the rest of the team filed in, whatever they were conversing about that morning was lost on me. Settling in their chairs, the guys began the day filling out reports and catching up on the drudgery of our job—paperwork. Serge was the only one who hadn't gone right to work. He was watching me out of the corner of his eye with a look of suspicion on his face.

When I couldn't take anymore, I stood up, intending to leave the office and go on a hunt for—I didn't exactly know what. Something was up, though, and I had no intention of waiting for it to come to me. I was going to find *it*.

Before I got to the door, it opened and a warm breeze brought in the enticing aroma of delicious honey cake, freshly glazed. My mouth watered, my stomach clenched, and my dick turned to solid stone.

Everyone in the office turned to witness the petite woman step through the door. Her dark hair fluttered around her as the wind caught it and tousled it into her face. Wearing short, frayed, denim cutoffs, a t-shirt that said *home is where you park it,* and a pair of sandals, she tucked a lock of hair behind her ear and looked up, meeting my intense gaze. I could almost hear her little intake of breath.

A jolt shot through me, prickling my skin into goosebumps that tingled from my head to my toes. She stood facing me, her lush pink lips parted, her cheeks slightly flushed from the sun and I could almost feel the pulsing of her blood as it flowed through her veins, that's how connected I felt to the woman in front of me.

Her full breasts rose and fell rapidly with her breath, a sign that she was as affected as I was. I knew instantly who she was.

She was *the one*. The woman who was meant for me—made for me, and I for her. My mate. Was it possible to fall in love with someone at first sight? I didn't know how it worked for the rest of the world's population, but I damned sure knew that in that single moment, I had fallen head over heels. Head. Over. Heels.

My dick tried to pop a hole through my cargo pants and my mouth watered so much that I had to swallow before I drooled on myself. That swallow sounded like a bomb going off in the silent room. My bear fought and clawed to push forward to get to her, sweep her up, to make her mine. I fought to keep him down.

She cleared her throat as she forced her eyes away from me. "I need help."

I took a step forward without even realizing it. "I'm here."

Serge shot me a miffed look. "What can we do for you?"

She glanced from me to Serge and I watched her hands ball into fists at her side. "My brother...he's missing."

Serge moved closer to her, ignoring my low warning growl. "What do you mean, missing?"

She licked her lips nervously. "I mean he's *missing*. He hasn't contacted me in over a month so I tracked him to this island, but his house has been ransacked....and he's not there."

"What's your name?" I'd moved even closer to her, shoving Serge aside. It was as though she had me in a tractor beam from one of those old sci-fi movies and I couldn't stop myself.

Serge grunted, elbowing me back, but I stood my ground. "What's your brother's name?"

She cast a quick glance at Serge, but when I growled again, her eyes shifted back to me. "I'm Ann...uh...I mean Grace. Sorry. I'm *Grace*. Grace Lowe. My brother is Gray Lowe. I need help finding him and I can't go to the police because I'm afraid of what he might have gotten himself into. Can you help me?"

Serge and I spoke at the same time.

"Yes."

"Perhaps."

Serge scowled at me and repeated himself. "*Perhaps*. Let's get some more information and see."

I turned a hard look at him—a look that left no doubt that we, or *I*, was going to help her. No matter what. My bear was so close to the surface, restless, pacing, needing to know more about her, wanting to spend time with her and willing to do anything, up to and including brawling with Serge to please her. If that meant finding her missing brother, then that's what we'd do.

"We email each other every two weeks, on the first and the fifteenth of every month, without fail. He's never missed, not in seven years, until two weeks ago. I didn't get anything from him. I waited until yesterday and checked for another email, but, again, nothing. It's not like him." She wrung her hands together in front of her and blinked back tears. "His place, here on the island...the front door was unlocked and slightly ajar when I arrived. His truck is still there, parked at the cottage, but inside, the place was ransacked. Trashed. Something is very wrong."

It took everything in me to maintain my professionalism when what I really wanted to do was offer comfort, holding her in my arms, mold the whole world to whatever she desired. "We'll go to his house and see if anything stands out to us. You can tell us more once we get there."

Serge's jaw dropped at my statement, but Grace nodded quickly and stepped back out of the office and on to the sidewalk. I followed closely behind her and only stopped when Serge grabbed the back of my shirt to pull me to a stop.

"What the hell's gotten into you, making promises and barking orders?" He glared at me. "Did you forget that you're not the Alpha of this team?"

I pulled myself up to my full height, a few inches taller than him, and glowered. For the first time since I'd been accepted into P.O.L.A.R.—the first time in my life—I was tempted to pull rank. A few words from me were all it would take to flip the seat of authority in my favor, and those words were right there on the tip of my tongue. But I held back.

I wasn't *that* guy.

I wasn't going to start being *that* guy just because my mate had walked into my life.

"Yeah, fine, whatever."

6

GRACE

I was insanely aware of the hulk of a man following me. He was, hands down, the sexiest man I'd ever seen. His black t-shirt strained over his broad, heavily muscled chest and shoulders. He was so hot, my nipples squeezed themselves into hard little points and were attempting to slice their way out of my shirt. My pulse hadn't settled to a normal pace since I'd laid eyes on him. The reaction I was having to this man was almost...otherworldly.

Trying to appear casual, I glanced back at him and tugged my lower lip between my teeth. For as big as he was, he carried himself with an air of mystery that felt both dangerous and seductive at the same time. Giving him my back hadn't been easy. I had all kinds of warning bells going off in my head. I knew how a gazelle felt in the vicinity of a lion.

I took another glance over my shoulder. *Oh, sweet Jesus.*

What the hell was wrong with me? Gray was missing. This was no time to go all googly-eyed over a hot local. Not until my brother was safe, anyway. I took a deep, calming breath—which didn't calm a damn thing.

"I just need to get something from my van." In truth, I needed a minute to compose myself before I did something stupid like rub myself up against him and behave like a sex-starved hussy in front of the men of P.O.L.A.R., but when I reached for the door handle of the van, it was missing. "What the…"

A throat cleared behind me. I turned and he held out his large hand displaying my broken handle and wearing a sheepish grin. "Sorry."

Confused, I took the handle from him, careful not to make skin to skin contact. "No problem. No problem at all." I swallowed, suddenly overproducing saliva for some reason, and stepped around him. "I-I'll lead the way to Gray's."

"I'll ride with you."

I turned back to him and took a shocked step backwards when I found him too close. I blinked and looked up—way up. He looked like some sort of Nordic Viking god with his strong, chiseled jawline, blonde hair and striking violet eyes. Were they actually violet, or was it an illusion? He was intimidating in both size and stature, but it was the smoldering heat—the intensity of his gaze that really had me forgetting to breathe. I was quite sure the flames in those eyes had the potential to leave a path of scorched devastation.

In the interest of self-preservation, and dry panties, I shook my head no. I didn't think for one second that I would walk away from this man without being burned to a crisp. Plus, *Gray—missing* I reminded myself. "Um, or you can just follow…"

He opened my passenger door and put one long leg in. "I'd rather ride with you."

Okie-dokie then. There would be no arguing with the set of that jaw. Instead, I saved my breath and walked around to the driver's side. I climbed in, tossing the broken door handle over my shoulder into the back.

I'd never felt like Freebird was too small before, but with the Viking beside me it felt tiny and almost cramped, or was that just because of how flustered I was? He was too big. Too strong. And too masculine. Holy hotness, Batman.

"I'm Konstantin." He looked over at me as I maneuvered the van out of the parking spot. "Or Kon. Whatever you want to call me."

Whatever I wanted to call him? I cast him a side glance. His biceps bulged and his forearms were corded with a dusting of light blonde hair and tight muscle that tapered to strong, male hands. Capable hands. Oh the fantasies those hands could fulfill. What I wanted to call him was my trampoline for the evening. *Girl, get a grip!* "Um, yeah, nice to meet you."

"Likewise." His intense gaze didn't stray from my face and I thought I could feel a light sheen of sweat breaking out over my brow. "I wish it were under different circumstances."

At that moment, my grumpy cat emerged from the back and leapt up on Kon's lap. The Viking grinned and stroked the cat's head.

"Huh. That's odd. Damocles doesn't usually like strangers." The cat made me look like a complete liar as he broke into a purr and rubbed himself against Kon before curling up on his lap. Right there on his lap. I'd never been so jealous of another creature in all my life.

"You travel a lot?"

"Well, my home does have wheels." I made a conscious effort to keep my eyes off of him and on the road, though the temptation to ogle him was extreme. "Do you know my brother?"

"Not that I'm aware of. His name isn't familiar."

"Yeah, about that. There's a distinct possibility that he may be using a different name. An alias."

Out of the corner of my eye, I noticed Konstantin raise his brows questioningly.

"It's a long story," I mumbled. When the few seconds of silence stretched to a few minutes, I realized Kon was waiting for the long story.

"My dad was distrustful of our government. Gray and I learned to be evasive and somewhat paranoid. We grew up preparing for an apocalypse, Armageddon, or at the very least some sort of cataclysmic devastation. We were taught to expect everything from martial law to nuclear attacks to bioterrorism. And yes, I do know how ridiculous all that sounds." *And why was I babbling on like a fool?*

"Family can be rough to deal with sometimes."

I parked in front of Gray's cottage and turned the van off. I wasn't normally such a blabbermouth, especially with a stranger. I wasn't sure what had come over me. There was something straightforward and sincere about Kon that inspired trust. And apparently I wasn't the only who felt it. He seemed to have bewitched grumpy cat, too.

"What do you think happened to Gray?"

I blinked as tears welled in my eyes. Turning away as I got my emotions under control, I shrugged. "I don't even know what to think. This has never happened before. I'm afraid to let my mind wander too far into the realm of possibilities. Worrying about what could've happened won't do me much good."

Kon's large hand rested on my shoulder and he squeezed lightly. "I promise you, I will find him."

I stared into his gorgeous eyes that I now noticed were, strangely, actually violet, and inhaled sharply. I could feel his touch down to my toes and it shocked me silent. There was such a thick air of awareness between us—an unearthly connection—and I didn't know what to make of it. He was a stranger and I was in the middle of a crisis. Yet... my girly parts were practically screaming for this man.

There were so many things wrong with that. Mainly, the fact that I was looking for Gray, not a hookup. But who knew, maybe after Gray was safe and before I moved on to the next location, Kon and I...oh, lordy, I needed to kick my raging libido in the ass.

A loud knock on the passenger window startled me, jerking my head out of its lust-filled haze. I looked up to see the other guy frowning angrily at Konstantin, but Kon didn't seem to care.

I got out of the van mumbling. "I'll show you guys in."

"By the way, I'm Serge." The other man introduced himself as we walked up the steps to the cottage entrance. Serge shook my hand, despite Kon making a growly noise behind us. "The sooner we figure this out, the sooner we'll be out of your hair."

I chanced a quick glance back at Kon, but he was looking around at the little slice of land around the cottage. His eyes seemed to take in everything, which I found comforting, a sign that he took the job seriously and that I'd chosen well.

I led the two men up to the door and pushed it open. "The lock's been smashed, so the door won't catch properly now. When I arrived earlier, I was careful not to touch anything, uh, except that chair."

Serge moved around me, while Konstantin came up behind me and rested his hand on my shoulder. "You're not going to be staying here, right?"

Licking my suddenly dry lips, I shook my head. "I have the van."

"I wouldn't suggest staying anywhere near the cottage, even parked outside. Whoever did this could come back." Serge's eyes landed on Kon's hand where it had moved from my shoulder and now rested possessively on my lower back. "There's a RV park on the beach."

When I shivered, Kon stroked his hand up my back and cupped the back of my neck. "Nothing will happen to you, I'll make sure of it."

Feeling overwhelmed by whatever was happening between the Viking, me and his uber-possessiveness, I got a little freaked out and, making an excuse, ducked under his arm to go back outside for fresh air. "I need to grab something from my van."

KONSTANTIN

As soon as Grace stepped out of the small house, Serge turned to me with a scowl. "Care to explain what the fuck that was?"

I peeked out the door to make sure she'd gone downstairs before answering him. "She's frightened. I was attempting to comfort and reassure her."

"Bullshit. You were..." His scowl suddenly turned into a grin so wide I thought his face might crack. "Wait a minute, she's *yours,* isn't she? Ha! You've found your mate! Sonofabitch, it's about goddamned time!"

Despite the fact that I knew to the very depths of my being that Grace was my mate, it was at that moment, faced with Serge's direct question, that for the first time since I'd set eyes on her, I remembered my obligations. Due to the responsibilities I bore, the name I was born with, the title I carried, mate or not, she could never be mine. That realization couldn't have left a deeper cut if it had hara-kiried me with a samurai blade. "No, she's not my mine."

He didn't say anything, but with the incredibly skeptical look he gave me, he didn't have to.

I balled up my fists and forced myself to look around. The house was trashed. Couch cushions ripped to shreds, furniture smashed and broken. Someone had searched the place thoroughly. I tipped my head back and inhaled deeply, searching for something, anything. All I was getting was freshly baked honey cake.

I looked at Serge. "What do you smell?"

He snorted sarcastically. "What do *you* smell?"

I growled. "Stop."

He grunted. "I smell humans...and, interesting...wolf. The humans are male. A group. Here more recently than the wolf. I think your little non-mate might have some explaining to do about why this cottage that she claims belongs to her brother smells like a wolf shifter."

"Anything more specific?"

"One of the male humans had a serious case of body odor." He inhaled deeper and groaned. "One of them was wearing cologne that smells like charred ass."

I moved around the house trying to pick up anything I could, but my mind was distracted by the sweet, honeyed scent of Grace, her quiet voice, her dark, flowing hair, her gentle curves.

The footsteps coming back upstairs were soft and stayed quiet for a few seconds at the door before entering the house. A shaky breath escaped her lips before she stepped inside. "I can forward all of the emails I've received from Gray. They don't say much, but maybe I've missed something. I don't know what he was doing or what he might have gotten mixed up in. We...we didn't talk about stuff like that, not in an email that might be intercepted.

Serge swung around to face her. "Intercepted by who?"

"No one...er...it's a long story. Not relevant. At any rate, I always suspected that he might be earning a living by slightly illegal means —off the books, under the table, whatever. I don't know that for sure, though."

She looked heartbroken, like she felt guilty for not knowing what her brother had been up to. I desperately wanted to comfort her. I had to fight hard to stop myself. To do so would only add fuel to Serge's suspicion.

"We'll do some searches and see what we can come up with." Serge sighed. "This certainly looks like he got himself involved in something, but there's still the possibility that it's nothing. Maybe it's merely a routine break-in and your brother is holed up at a girlfriend's place completely unaware his cottage has been ransacked. He could still show up."

"Of course, yes." Grace lifted her quivering chin and planted her hands on her hips. "Just... Just find him. Please. Whatever the cost, I'll pay. It doesn't matter—"

I stepped forward. "I will cover all costs. And we will find him. That I promise, Grace."

Serge rolled his eyes, but to his credit, he kept his mouth shut. He merely cast one last searching glance around the room. "I'll get Roman to come in and fingerprint the place, just in case. We'll get back to the station and start the search for your brother."

Grace nodded. "What should I do?"

I felt my chest tighten at the despondent tone in her voice. She was brave but terrified. No way I'd allow her to feel as though she was going through this alone. "I'll accompany you to the RV park and help you find a spot. Then, we can talk more about your brother and try to sort out what he might have been involved in."

Serge barely refrained from another eye roll. "Alright. Help get Grace set up at the park and then come hightail it back to the office. Both of you. I texted Maxim and he's conducting an online search of the deep web as we speak, so we should have something by then." Serge kicked aside a few pieces of a broken coffee table with the toe of his boot, and grunted. "Whatever they were looking for here, I doubt they found it. If they had your brother, they wouldn't still be searching like this."

"How do you know they haven't found him since...since looking here?"

"You said he hasn't contacted you in a month. This place was searched less than a week ago. It's possible that in the last week they might have caught up to him, but based on experience, I tend to think that they haven't."

"Because it's unwise to give up hope?"

The way she said it was so unconvinced and forlorn that I couldn't stop myself this time. I moved across to her and wrapped my arm around her shoulders pulling her tight against me. Fuck what Serge thought. I gazed down into her eyes. "Because your brother is a wolf shifter. The people after him are human."

She gasped. "How did you know that about Gray?" Her eyes narrowed and I could almost see the wheels turning in her head. "You aren't...wait, are you guys wolf shifters, too?"

Serge threw his head back and barked a laugh. I glared at him for laughing at Grace. "We are shifters, but not wolves."

Grace squeezed her eyes shut and then blew a breath out with a small laugh. "Of course not—P.O.L.A.R.! Duh. Don't I feel like a big dummy? You're polar bear shifters!"

Serge nodded. "And we have excellent tracking skills. Just let us do our jobs. We got this." He lightly rested his hand on her shoulder and gave her a reassuring smile.

I was able to bite back a possessive growl, but I glowered at the fucker as I brushed his damned hand off her. "I'm taking Grace to the RV park. We'll meet you back at the office in a bit."

Serge just shook his head and smirked. I knew what he was thinking, and while he wasn't incorrect, what Serge didn't know was that it didn't matter whether or not Grace was my mate. My life wasn't my own. I wasn't free to claim a mate as the others had done. I already had a mate waiting for me back home, one I'd been promised to since before I could walk.

As early as I could remember, I'd known my destiny was plotted out for me. I needed to remember that and keep it at the forefront of my consciousness at all times—especially with Grace around.

As I settled next to her in her sprinter van amidst her deliciously enticing aroma that made my head swim, I reflected on how bitterly cruel fate could be.

8

GRACE

Konstantin directed me to a small RV campsite right on the beach. The fee for parking there was steeper than I usually liked to pay, but before I could grab my wallet, he'd already settled up with the guy and was gesturing for me to pick the spot I wanted. I didn't know what to make of that. I wasn't sure whether to be to be flattered, grateful, or offended.

On one hand, if his intent was to be friendly and welcoming, it was kind of a nice gesture. On the other hand, if he thought that little old me needed to be taken care of and couldn't stand on my own two feet in the world, he could fuck off. I wasn't into ultra-possessive men. And if he was trying to buy his way into my pants, well, he might as well think again. He didn't need to spend a dime for that. Truth.

"Charge that to my bill from your office." I climbed back into Freebird before he could argue with me.

Choosing the spot closest to the water was a no-brainer. On a slight incline, I'd be safe from the incoming tide, but I could wake up and walk right out onto the beach. In that way, I felt a comradery with Gray. It was easy to see what had attracted him to the tiny island. Warm sand, salt air, beautiful ocean. A wave of melancholy washed over me. I should've caught up with Gray sooner. Why had we let seven years go by without seeing each other? We should've made time for one another.

Kon seemed to sense what I was thinking as he moved to stand beside me. He gazed down with a look of utmost sincerity on his handsome features. "I'll find him. It's what I do."

"I'm lucky to have discovered you. Er, your team, I mean." I looked away and wondered if I was blushing.

"Most humans wouldn't have. Most would have gone to the police."

I rubbed at my cheek with the back of my hand in case I had a noticeable blush. "I grew up with a brother who's a shifter and a father who taught us to distrust cops."

"What's the story there? With your brother, I mean. You don't carry the scent of a shifter."

"I'm not. Unfortunately. I've had to lean on whatever human skills I learned, instead of the ability to shift into a badass animal. Gray inherited his ability from his mother. He and I have the same father, but while his mother was a wolf shifter, mine was a plain jane from the middle of nowhere, Indiana, who died giving birth to me."

Gray's mother hadn't revealed the fact that she was a shifter to our father until after Gray was born. I didn't know the full story, but once Gray was born, she took off, choosing to follow her pack, and left both Dad and Gray.

"I'm sorry. I lost my mother when I was very young, too. Were you and Gray close growing up?" Before I could answer, he chuckled darkly. "I'm trying to imagine what it would have been like if my sister had been human while we were growing up. She would've hated not being able to shift and snarl at me or nip at my tail."

I wrapped my arms around myself and smiled. "We were as close as we could be. It wasn't easy. My father was...*surprised* by Gray's shifting, to say the least. Surprised, and then angered."

"Poor kid. As if shifting into a big dog wasn't enough."

I laughed before I could help it. "Gray would kick your ass if he heard you call him a dog."

Kon's grin said he might enjoy a brawl. "He could try. Come on. Let's get back to the office and find your brother."

It didn't go unnoticed by me that Kon had managed to turn my *on the verge of tears* mood into light laugher and optimism. I reached out and grasped his arm, shocking both of us. "Thank you. I can't tell you how much more comforted I feel knowing you're helping me to find him."

He hesitated and wrapped his strong arms around me, pulling me against his chest. His hand stroked the back of my head and a low, growly sound rumbled in his throat. I could have sworn I heard him whisper, "I would do anything for you." But that was probably my overactive imagination.

He smelled so good. My hands gripped his shirt, and I buried my face, comforted by his warmth and strength. With his thick arms wrapped around me, I felt safe. I breathed him in, trying to place his unique aroma. Arctic breeze and sunshine. He carried the contrasting scent of crisp, clean arctic air and, warm, radiant sunshine. Something in the back of my mind was alerted. *Beware, the two natures of this man*, it said. But at that moment, his scent made me feel calm and at ease. Like a hammock swaying in a cool, gentle breeze. In the cocoon of his arms, I felt safe.

Guilt suddenly stuck a pin in my serenity balloon. I *was* safe. Gray was the one who needed safety, not me. I pushed away from Konstantin.

He seemed to sense my guilt and anguish without me having to explain. "Let's go, Grace. I want to get started looking for him right away. The less time you spend worried sick, the better." He took my arm and guided me around to the passenger side of the van. "When's the last time you slept? You look exhausted."

I frowned. "Gee, thanks."

"Beautiful, but exhausted." He pulled open the door and gestured for me to get in.

"No way. I drive." When he didn't move, I crossed my arms over my chest stubbornly. "The driver's seat is broken. It'll never go back far enough for those long legs of yours to fit behind the wheel."

He grunted and released my arm. "Why do I feel like you're lying?"

I flashed him a quick grin before rounding the van, opening my door and climbing behind the wheel. No one drove Freebird but me. "Because I am."

I drove us back to his office and found myself yawning by the time I pulled into a parking spot out front. I was going on 36 hours of no sleep, but I wanted to see them start on the search before I gave in to the exhaustion.

Like he was reading my mind, Kon looked over at me with a knowing frown. "You need rest. After this, maybe you'll go back to the RV park and sleep? I'll come to you as soon as I have something. I promise."

I nodded, agreeing. Leaving them to find Gray was something I was feeling more and more comfortable doing. They would be better at it than I could ever be. But after I got some sleep, I was going to go over to Gray's house, after it had been fingerprinted of course, and clean up. I didn't want Gray to have to see that mess when he came home.

"Come on. Let's see if Maxim discovered anything."

I followed him inside the P.O.L.A.R. office and he led me to a table in the back. Serge sat across from me, while several other guys stood around and introduced themselves before the one who introduced himself as Maxim started speaking.

"Your brother is a ghost, Grace."

I rubbed at my eyes and tucked my hair out of my face. "A ghost?"

"There's no trace of him online."

I scowled. "There wouldn't be much. We were raised...uh...differently. Taught to stay off grid, but in this day and age, there must be something, no? It's impossible to not leave some sort of online fingerprint."

Maxim was nodding. "That's the thing. There's not a trace. The house is linked to a man who died thirty years ago. His truck is registered to the same man. No birth certificate, no social security number, no tax records, medical records, employment records, DMV records, school transcripts—nothing. According to the United States, no one named Gray Lowe born August 8, 1986, or using any alias that I can find with his description, has ever existed."

I sat up straighter and braced my arms on the table. "What are you saying?"

"From the looks of it? I'd say your brother is a spook." He frowned. "No other way someone is completely untraceable. Unless you don't have a brother."

I gave him a flat look. "I have pictures. I assure you, my brother is very much real. And very much going to have a lot of explaining to do. When you say spook, you mean…a spook as in someone with one of those 3-letter name agencies?"

"Yep."

"Huh." My stomach twisted. My first reaction was to adamantly deny it. Not with our upbringing, being taught to distrust the government. But, had those childhood lessons carried over to adulthood for me? No, not really. Sure I was a cautious nomad, but I had no beef with the government. I paid my taxes—played by the rules. Was it far-fetched to assume that Gray used the skills he was taught in childhood to work for the government rather than to evade them? "What do I do now?"

Konstantin cupped the back of my neck. "You need some sleep. Let us handle the rest. We'll find him."

"How?"

Kon's grin was dangerous. "We have our ways."

I took a long gaze at the men around the room, each of them large and lethal looking. Kon was bigger and more foreboding than the rest of them. Yes, if anyone could find Gray, it was these guys.

9
GRACE

Despite it only being late morning when I got back to the RV park, I fell into my bed and slept until early evening. I woke up for a few hours only because Damocles was sitting on my face. I fed him and laid back down staring at the ceiling and thinking of Kon's delicious muscles and tight ass until I fell back asleep. When I woke up the next morning, I felt refreshed and full of energy but damned if my mind wasn't still on the big, handsome polar bear shifter.

After making a call to check in with Serge—nothing new yet—I headed over to Gray's cottage to start cleaning and putting things back in order. There wasn't much else I could do and I wasn't about to sit on my hands all day while my brother was god only knew where knee deep in god only knew what.

I trusted that the guys at P.O.L.A.R. were doing everything they could to find Gray, so I could focus on getting his house back in shape. I still felt stressed, but I didn't doubt Kon's abilities. I was pretty sure he would find my brother. And then I was going to kick Gray's ass.

My brother working for the CIA? I was still having trouble

processing it. If I was being completely honest, not that I believed the same shit that Dad had, but my fearfulness of the government was still there somewhat. I'd incorrectly assumed it was the same for Gray. I'd incorrectly assumed lots of things about him, apparently.

I'd only been there a couple hours and had barely made a dent—most of the time had been spent trying my damnedest to keep my thoughts off the big, sexy blonde Viking—when the front door flew open with a loud crash. I let loose a startled scream and my hand flew to my chest as I glared at Kon. "What the hell? You scared the devil right out of me!"

"WHAT are you doing here?" He glared right back at me.

I waved my arms around gesturing at the room which, granted, wasn't quite up to showroom standards yet, but did look a little better. "Uh...cleaning. I would think that would be obvious."

He looked at me as though I'd lost my mind. "It's too dangerous! If the people who trashed this place happened to come back and find you, do you have any idea what they might do?"

"I..." I looked around. I hadn't thought about that. Not really. I'd just figured they'd already searched the house once. Why would they come back to do it again? It looked to me as though they'd done a thorough enough job the first time. "You assume I can't take care of myself. Oh, ye of little faith."

He strode across the room and grabbed me. "Against a group of men possibly—probably—armed? It has nothing to do with my faith in you. You can't be here by yourself, Grace."

The force of his words put me on the defensive and, despite the fact that he was right, I opened my mouth to argue. "I have to do something, Kon. I can't just sit around in the van and twiddle my thumbs."

I crossed my arms over my chest and leveled him with my *I mean business, buster* look. "I'll go crazy waiting for news about my brother."

He caught my arm and turned toward the door pulling me after him. "I can get myself back to the campground, thank you very much. I don't need you dragging me."

"I'm not taking you to the campground. I'm taking you to the P.O.L.A.R. office. Serge's mate Hannah is there. She's nice and she'll keep you company."

I pulled my arm free. "Do you hear yourself? You're not my keeper, Kon. I don't need to be babysat like an unruly child."

He spun around and bent low. Because he caught me off guard, he was able to push his shoulder into my stomach and lift me off of my feet. I dangled over his shoulder, all the blood rushing to my head. "I can't focus on your brother if I'm worried about you," he grunted out.

Okay, tossing me around like that was unexpected and highly erotic in a *me Tarzan, you Jane* kind of cavemannish way. My eyes couldn't help staring at the way his ass moved in his jeans while he carted me downstairs. I crossed my arms and tried to be as stern and as dignified as I could while upside down and draped over the shoulder of undoubtedly the hottest man on the island.

"This is ridiculous. Is this the way you polar bears operate? Y'all throw your clients around like a sack of potatoes? Or is it just you? Would Serge, or one of the other guys, do the same if they'd been the one to come check on me?"

"They wouldn't dare." He rasped out all growly-like, and his hand which had been on my thighs moved up to my ass. "They touch you and they lose their hands."

A strange streak of pleasure coursed through me at his possessiveness. Okay, maybe I did like possessive men after all, or at least *this* possessive man. I played along. "Um. Excuse me? Your hand is on my ass, sir."

He just grunted and left it there. If I was expecting him to be any type of normal and put me down next to a vehicle, or some other form of transportation, I was mistaken. He continued to carry me all the way down Main Street that way, slung over his shoulder. Someone honked and I heard a cheer call out but I couldn't wipe the grin off my face. I kinda liked being manhandled by the hottest man on the island and I kinda didn't care who saw.

"Is this how you treat all your clients, Konstantin? If so, I feel like someone should give you a lesson in public relations." I squeaked when his hand landed firmly on my ass. Had he seriously just spanked me?! "How would you like it if I did that to you?"

"Do it and find out."

I tried to wiggle out of his grip, but it was useless. "Where are you taking me?"

"I told you, I'm taking you to the P.O.L.A.R. office to hang out with Hannah for the day. I'm following a lead and I won't be able to concentrate unless I know you're safe."

I was torn between frustration, humiliation, arousal and flattery—yeah, I was flattered that this hunky muscle man with incredibly smoldery violet eyes was carrying me down the street with his hand resting proprietorially on my ass. But I was just frustrated and humiliated enough to not want to let him know how turned on I was. "Kon, I appreciate you worrying about me, but I'm a grown woman. I've lived on my own since I was eighteen and I don't need you mothering me to death."

"Mothering you?" His grip on my ass tightened. "Is that what you think? Woman, if you only knew…"

I felt my face go red and crossed my arms again. It was a little ridiculous, hanging upside down and all, and I wasn't sure what to do with my hands. No way was I wrapping them around him. That spelled trouble. In all caps.

"I can only imagine your reviews on the Better Business Bureau. Bossy beasts who bully their clients. Hot, but real pains in the ass." I was mostly mumbling to myself, but Kon laughed. "The big one has a real issue with personal space, but at least he smells nice."

"So, I'm hot and I smell nice?"

"Actually, I was calling the others hot."

When Kon tossed me back over his shoulder, easily caught me, and put me on my feet in front of him, it was only to snarl at me. His glowing eyes told me the bear was more in control than the man, I watched as his nose began to lengthen to a snout and his voice emerged as a nearly inhuman gravelly growl. "Don't look at them."

I was stunned stupid.

My mouth was still hanging open when he tossed me back over his shoulder and continued walking.

10

KONSTANTIN

I was breathing heavily by the time I threw open the office door. It had nothing to do with the walk and everything to do with holding myself back from devouring the woman in my arms. I wanted desperately to claim her and mark her. Every inch of her called to me. My heart thundered in my chest and my bear was so close to the surface that I knew he was visible in my eyes, but there was not a damned thing I could do about it.

"Kon?!" Hannah jumped up from where she'd been sitting at the dispatcher desk, and gaped at us, wide-eyed.

I forced myself to put Grace down and back away from her. I was barely holding onto the sliver of self-control I had left. I needed to distance myself from her and regain composure. I kept walking backwards. She was having none of it, though.

The little minx goaded me. "What? You spend the past ten minutes gripping my ass like it's the last cheeseburger on earth and now you just turn tail and run away?" Grace put her hands on her hips and tilted her head, the challenge evident.

I told myself to leave. I told myself that leaving was best for both of us, but damned if I listened. I crossed the room in two strides and grabbed her before the squeal could make it out of her mouth. My lips crashed over hers. I pulled her flush against my body, and gripping her hair, licked at the seam of her lips. They parted with a groan, and angling her head back, I stroked my tongue into her mouth, tasting, plundering, owning that sweet mouth that tasted like honey cakes.

I gripped her delicious ass yanking her higher up and into me so she could feel the hard as steel erection I was sporting for her. When her thigh came up and wrapped around my hip, I growled and pulled her head back farther so I could kiss down her throat. Nipping and sucking her sweet skin into my mouth, I was desperate to put some kind of mark on her, no matter how temporary.

What the fuck was I doing? I was seconds from ripping her clothes off and fucking her right there in the office—in front of Hannah, no less! I dragged myself away and balled my hands into fists to keep them from grabbing her again. I rolled my head back and closed my eyes. I could barely get words out and when I did, they were stilted. "I'll be back in a few days."

I didn't wait to hear what she had to say. I practically ran from the place, but not before filing away the mental snapshot of Grace flushed and breathless from my kiss. That was an image I would hold onto forever, but if I didn't run out of there, god only knew what I'd end up doing. Never had I been so tempted to shirk my duties to the crown, my family and my species.

That, I couldn't do. There was too much at stake. No matter how much it pained me, I couldn't have Grace. Damn, I needed to do better at remembering that. The sooner I found her brother and got things settled for her, the sooner she'd be able to go on her way and I...well, I would have to go on mine, too.

I couldn't give Grace much, but I could leave her with something. And I'd move hell and highwater to do it. I'd get her brother back for her.

Unfortunately, gaining access to such confidential and protected information required tapping into all the intelligence at my disposal. If Gray Lowe was working for the CIA, then he would have covered his tracks pretty well. There was only one place I could go for access to the kind of information I needed—our King, my father.

I waited on the phone for nearly ten minutes before my father picked up the line. And if that right there didn't show exactly how little clout a Prince of the species carried these days.

When he answered, my Father's voice sounded older, tired. "Konstantin. To what do I owe the *extreme* pleasure?" I winced at my father's unbridled sarcasm. It had been months since the two of us had last spoken.

"Hello, Your Majesty—Father. I trust you are well."

He grunted. "Please tell me you have you finally decided to grace us with your return."

I cringed. I knew it was coming, but I cringed nevertheless. King Vladimir was a staunch traditionalist who hated change and held fast to old policies and traditions. He believed fully in the authority of the royals and the separation of classes and had done everything in his power to see that archaic traditions continued.

It had been near miracle that he'd allowed me a few years to live anonymously amongst what he referred to as *the masses*. I might add that it took all my persuasive powers to convince him and in the end he only agreed because I assured him it would make me a better ruling monarch.

"Soon, Father, I will be returning very soon." I prepared myself for his reaction to that statement.

"Unacceptable! Completely unacceptable, Konstantin. I've allowed you your foolish meandering. Now, it's time to leave this adolescent folly, cease your playacting and return home. The kingdom awaits you, as does your betrothed."

My heart was in my throat. No one denied a direct order from the King. No one but me, anyway. I knew my father was eager to hand the mantle of reign over to me. I also knew that I would first need to mate a woman I hardly knew, certainly didn't love, and who had been chosen for me only months after I was born. I accepted all that as my fate. But, I wouldn't leave before reuniting Grace with her brother.

As my mind searched for the words to say that would placate

him and give me more time, I wanted to kick my own ass. I was educated in diplomacy, for Christ's sake, tutored by nannies and governesses, fluent in six languages as well as a myriad of other subjects that it was determined would someday serve me as ruler of our kind. It was merely a matter of tapping into what I'd been taught.

"I understand Father and agree wholeheartedly that it is time to assume my royal duties and ascend to the throne and I am prepared to do just that." My face twisted into a wince as I said the words. "As I am nearing the tail end of a crucial mission, I must extend our deadline for a short time more, merely until the mission is completed at which time I will return immediately."

He huffed. Then grunted. Then paused. Then sighed. "And the time frame for completing this mission?" He sounded completely skeptical.

"I—I am afraid I have no definitive date, however I assure it will be in the very near future. Very near." I could hear my father's exasperated sigh. How the man could communicate so much with just one sigh, I'd never know. And here was where I needed to make my critical move. I cleared my throat. "Your assistance in the matter would greatly expedite the culmination of this mission."

Another sigh—this one large and loud and seeming to say *I'm tired and weary and my sons a royal pain in my royal ass.* Maybe that was my imagination. "What is it you ask from me this time, Konstantin?"

"I need information on the whereabouts of a certain wolf shifter believed to be working for or in cahoots with the CIA." I relayed all the information to my father who in turn, transferred it to his head of security.

"My patience is running thin. VERY thin."

"I understand, Father. I give you my word."

He grunted again. "Need I remind you of the consequences should you not honor your word, Konstantin."

No he did not need to remind me. I knew just what was at stake if I happened to withdraw from our agreement. He'd made it very clear

—an unveiled threat he held over my head to ensure I would comply with our traditions. "I am well aware of the stakes."

Should I fail to return to Siberia and mate my betrothed, I would be banished from the kingdom. And worse. Much worse. The guys on the P.O.L.A.R. team would suffer. The team would be disbanded, defunded and the guys, my friends, would be exiled from our homeland—indefinitely. All to punish me.

And that, I would not allow.

My sister and I had been fortunate enough to have grown up out of the public eye—something my mother had sworn my father to on her death bed. And, to his credit, King Vladimir had kept his word. There were no photographs of us, no sightings of us, and the media referred to me as the *Hidden Prince*—only not so hidden. Hidden in plain sight.

I received a call back from my father's head of security not more than thirty minutes later. Which was impressive by any standard. Turned out, Gray had been involved in something rather serious and he had, indeed, been working undercover for the CIA.

I still wasn't sure exactly where the guy had disappeared to, but thanks to my father's connections, I had a good solid lead on where to start digging.

My father had come through, and soon it would be my turn to keep my side of the bargain—just as soon as I found Gray Lowe. My next step involved going undercover myself for a few days to follow the leads and see what info I could dig up.

11

GRACE

"If you don't stop feeding him, I'll have to roll him home."

Heidi grinned as she held out another piece of raw fish for Damocles to gobble up greedily. "I caught this myself just this morning, little fella."

"I'm surprised he isn't frightened with all the big bear pheromones that must be floating around this place." Kerrigan patted the top of the cat's head and giggled as I tried to figure out what sorcery had turned my grumpy cat into a sweet, purring, overfed, spoiled rotten attention whore.

Hannah and I had hit it off so well, that she invited me to the P.O.L.A.R. house where she and the other women—mates of some of the guys—were gathering to fix a big, home-cooked meal. I tried to beg off by saying that I couldn't leave Damocles alone so long, but instead of accepting that excuse, she insisted I bring my cat along.

Right as Parker was putting the finishing touches on the table settings, since she was the only one of the women who had zero cooking skills, the doorbell chimed.

"Can you grab that, Grace?" I was closest, so I hopped up to greet whoever was on the other side of the door and opened it to a tall, statuesque woman who looked me up and down wrinkling her nose with a sneer of disgust. *Well, smell you, too.*

Her voice was harsh and grating. "Where is Konstantin?"

O-Kay. "Uh, and you are?"

She looked down her nose at me. "Here for Konstantin. Where is he?"

I suddenly felt defensive and had to reminded myself that this wasn't my house and despite him trying to lick my tonsils earlier, Kon wasn't my man. I had no reason to get all protective and defensive. Still, the hair on the back of my neck stood on end.

"Uh, he's not here."

Megan stepped up next to me. "Can I help you with something? What do you want with Kon?"

"*Kon*?" She spat the word out like it was vile and distasteful. "Have you no respect? His name is *Konstantin*... *Prince* Konstantin Nikolaev and he happens to be my fiancé. Now, I'll ask only once more. WHERE is he?"

A flush ran through me as the words hit home. Wide-eyed, I turned to Kerrigan. She turned to Parker who turned to Heidi. After several seconds of stunned silence, Megan was the first to regain her composure and speak. "*Prince*...there must be a mistake. You can't be talking about the same Konstantin who lives here. The one we know."

Suddenly, Serge descended the stairs from the second floor. As he took in the scene at the front door, he must have realized there was something strange going on. He stepped forward and took charge, eyeing the tall blonde suspiciously. "And who might you be?"

"It's not who I might be, it's who I *am*—Lady Valentina Vasiliev, betrothed to Prince Konstantin Nikolaev. Who happens to be your crown prince, Bear. You might show a bit more respect."

Serge's face went white as a ghost as he processed the information. "*Prince* Konstantin?!" Then, he turned a raging red as the implication sunk in. "I'll be goddamned. The Hidden Prince." Apparently, I wasn't the only one who was blindsided by this information.

"Are you going to stand there gaping at me like an open-mouthed carp, bear, or are you going to invite me in?"

"Er, of course, Lady Valentina. Won't you please come in?"

The only thing worse than crushing on some hot Viking god who disappears after practically dry humping you in front of a potential new friend was meeting his fiancée only hours later. And now, my circle of shame was complete.

As Lady Valentina entered P.O.LA.R. house with five of her "attendants" in tow, all eyes in the room swung to me.

Lady Valentina, it turned out, was sharp as a tack. She saw the heads turn my way and seemed to catch on immediately why they did so. She stared daggers at me while simultaneously barking orders to her attendants who were hauling in what looked like a truckload of luggage. Then, she turned her order barking to Serge, who ended up directing each of the attendants to one of the upstairs bedrooms.

I was more than aware that I probably reeked of Kon's scent, which would be especially noticeable to a shifter. So, when her sharp eyes raked over me while her delicate nostrils flared, I knew what she was getting—the scent of her man all over me.

I was furious and ashamed all at once. Although, was it really fair to be angry with Kon? What did he do anyway? There was an extreme mutual attraction between us to be sure, but that kind of thing couldn't be helped. It wasn't anyone's fault. Although, there was that kiss. That panty melting, jaw dropping, heart-pounding kiss... hell yeah, I could be angry at Kon! He deserved to have his eyes scratched out for making out with me when he already had a woman.

I took another look at Lady Valentina—gorgeous, tall, blonde, statuesque, with legs that didn't quit. And perfect hair and an awesome manicure and designer clothes that looked like they were tailored to her—they probably were! Her dress managed to show off her flawless figure while at the same time reflect impeccable taste. No wonder Kon was engaged to her. Or, should I say *Prince Konstantin*. I could picture them side by side. They actually made a beautiful couple in a Barbie and Ken sort of way. Him, a large, muscled Viking-looking warrior prince, and her a stately and regal blonde princess. What the hell had he been doing with me? Slumming?

The pièce de résistance was when Valentina, staring directly at me, insisted her things be placed in Kon's bedroom. *Ouch.* If I hadn't been humiliated before, at that moment, I would have paid good money to have the floor swallow me whole.

She was clearly marking him as *hers*. It couldn't have been more obvious if she'd lifted her leg and peed on the man. Actually, it was too bad Konstantin wasn't around to be peed on. I would have enjoyed that right about then.

I was ready to tuck tail and scram out of there, but my humiliation wasn't yet complete—oh, no. As I tried to sneak out of the room, Lady Valentina ceased barking orders at her staff long enough to level me with a sinister gaze. "Where are you off to, human?"

I straightened my shoulders and met her gaze. I felt terrible for making out with her almost husband, but I hadn't known anything about her and it wasn't fair that I should be made feel like scum because of Kon's betrayal.

I flashed my biggest fake smile and waved. "Home. Bye-bye!"

Hannah tucked her arm through mine and smiled. "I'll come with you." At that, all the others, Heidi, Megan, Kerrigan, and Parker, piped up expressing how they were all concerned about me walking home by myself and it was only right they accompany me.

Valentina snorted a laugh. "A girl's trip? Maybe I should come along and we can all gossip about whose fiancé we've been fucking."

Serge growled and stepped forward. "That's my mate you're talking to."

"And I'll be your queen soon, bear." Her eyes moved back to me and pinned me in place. "Have you no mate to step forward and defend *you*?"

I shrugged. "Just me."

"A bear to fuck you, but no one to love you. Pity."

Hannah's hand tightened on my arm in support, and suddenly I felt as though I was in a group of friends facing off against the mean girl. Her words were bitchy and petty, but they cut deeper than I cared to admit. I wasn't the type of person to engage in a catfight, though, so I let it go. I'd always kept my head down and chin up when things got rough—taken the high road, so I swallowed the lump in my throat.

"Oh, my god. What?" Valentina narrowed her eyes, provoking me. "Are you going to cry? Humans and their emotions. It's been five minutes and already you're in tears."

She's not worth it. She's not worth it. She's not worth it. I chanted to myself to keep from slugging her one in her perfect nose.

I lifted one shoulder in a casual shrug and attempted to narrow my eyes the same way she did. "No, I was just noticing that you have lipstick on your teeth. Pity."

Hannah giggled, pushing me out of the house and the others followed. The door slammed shut behind us and Parker snorted. "You just pissed off the soon to be queen of the polar bear shifters."

I made an unflattering fart sound. "Who cares? She's not my queen. She's no one to me."

"You've got that right, sister." Kerrigan looped her arm through mine on the other side while Megan and Parker tried to one up each other as they both attempted to perfect their Valentina impersonations. Heidi chuckled as she followed carrying Damocles.

As horrible as that whole scene had felt, there was one silver lining. For the first time in my life, I experienced what it was like to have girlfriends.

12

KONSTANTIN

Where the fuck are you? Serge was in my head and as angry as I'd ever heard him.

Undercover. We need a boat.

What the fuck do you think you're doing going undercover without saying something? You think you're some lone vigilante or something? Did you forget about the rest of us? That you're part of a fucking team? No, just go on, run off undercover. Don't let anyone know if you're alive or dead.

I'm alive. And, I've got a pretty good lead on Gray. In fact, I think I found him. But, we need a boat. Something small. We're going to have to slip under the radar of the coast guard and Uncle Sam.

Fucking hell. He hesitated for a moment. *When you get back on land, you have more than a little explaining to do. You've got a damn shitstorm waiting for you here.*

My stomach twisted. *Is Grace okay?*

Oh, she's great. Super. So's your fucking fiancée, Prince Charming.

A cold dread washed over me. *Fuck.*

Yeah, that pretty much sums it up. When did you think you were gonna tell us?

I...uh... Oh, fuck. Valentina in Sunkissed Key? I could only imagine how that must have gone over with Grace. Not to mention the team finding out about my title. I'd worry about the team later. It was Grace that had my stomach twisting itself in knots. My bear was raging—urging me to go to her immediately. Explain. Beg forgiveness. And I really wanted to, but I knew the best thing I could do for her right then was to find her brother and see to his safe return.

Is she okay?

Who?

Grace! Is Grace okay?

How the fuck do I know? Who do you think I am, her therapist?

It occurred to me that the phone call to my father must have triggered Valentina's surprise visit. He probably put her up to it.

Look, I can't blow my cover just yet. Can you get a boat and meet me the night after tomorrow at dusk, just off the port of Miami?

A few minutes passed and I was almost certain Serge was going to tell me to fuck off and get my own boat.

I'll arrange it and contact you once I know details.

I let out a breath I hadn't realize I'd been holding. *Thanks, brother.*

I hadn't missed the anger in his words. I also was under no illusion as to why it was there. The guys probably all felt betrayed by me. I'd hidden my true identity from them for years. I'd hidden it from everyone. Serge, more than anyone, deserved to have been made aware of my title, but I'd never wanted to stand out or be treated any differently. I wanted to be appreciated on my own merits.

Swearing, I turned back to the small hotel room I'd gotten for the night.

I hadn't seen Valentina since we were kids. I had no clue of the person she was or what kind of woman she'd grown into. I remembered her as a vapid, spoiled rotten brat. To be fair, we were both seven at the time. For all I knew she may have changed into a kind and generous person in the intervening years, but it wouldn't matter if her heart rivaled Mother Theresa's. I would go through with the mating, ascend to the throne, do what I was bred and groomed to do. Fulfill my duties. But as of three days ago, I knew there was only one woman who would ever claim my heart.

I would find Grace's brother and then mate Valentina. I didn't see another way.

13

GRACE

Everyone avoided P.O.L.A.R. house like the plague. Everyone except Serge who was in charge and had nowhere else to go. Even Hannah slept with me in the van as Valentina took up residence in the P.OL.A.R. bungalow with her entourage.

While Hannah was dispatching at the P.O.L.A.R. office, I worked on my jewelry making and finished the e-book covers I'd been working on. Then I went from new friend to new friend, doing anything I could to pass the time and avoid thinking about Gray and Kon and any danger they might be in. I helped Megan take pictures of a wedding. I helped Kerrigan rearrange the new furniture she and Dmitry had purchased. Heidi let me keep her company while she bartended, and Parker had me attending a birthing class with her while Maxim was on a job.

It was strange how easily I fit into their friend group. A good thing, too because I needed to keep busy. I was riddled with stress about Gray and hoping Kon was safe. I'd gotten no new information about the search for my brother except that Kon had gone undercover for some reason.

Just when I thought I was going to snap from the anxiety, Serge revealed that Kon had a line on Gray and they were attempting some sort of rescue. That's all the information I could pry out of Serge, but at least it was something. They were bringing Gray home.

Ignoring the warning Kon had given me about staying away from Gray's place, I went and worked the entire afternoon bagging up trash and hauling out broken furniture pieces, getting his house in livable order. He was missing a few essential items of furniture, things that had been destroyed beyond repair, but Megan came through with some secondhand pieces her neighbor was getting rid of. By the time we finished, his house looked pretty good if I did say so myself.

All the girls were with me at Gray's. Since the guys were on an overnight job, they'd decided to hang out with me for the night. Secretly, I suspected they were trying to distract me and take my mind off Gray. And Kon. And Lady Royal-stick-up-her-butthole.

Hannah had stopped into the P.O.L.A.R house to grab a bottle of wine and a few DVDs. "She's driving me fucking crazy."

Heidi snorted. "Tell us how you really feel."

"I feel like I want to strangle her. I've never been violent before. I didn't think I was the violent type, but I changed my mind. She never shuts up and it's all complaints and judgments. And she keeps calling me *human*, as though I don't have a name!"

Parker sniffed. "If you ask me, any man who'd want to marry her is completely off his rocker." She suddenly realized what she'd said and her eyes widened as she turned to me. "Sorry."

I shrugged. I was curled up in the corner of the couch Megan's neighbor had donated. "She's so beautiful, though. Her skin is flawless."

Kerrigan giggled. "Makeup. I saw her coming out of Kon's room the other morning and believe me, most of her face is painted on. She's got no eyebrows, no eyelashes. Nothing."

"She's still perfect, though."

"She's not perfect, Grace." Hannah reached over and held my hand. "She's ugly on the inside and that sort of thing shows through."

"No shit." Megan was stroking Damocles behind the ears to his great delight. "Not a one of us can stand to be anywhere near her."

"Evidently, Kon can stand it just fine." I pressed my lips together so hard it hurt, regretting saying the pitiful words as soon as they snuck out. "Ignore that."

Hannah came in from the kitchen carrying a bowl of popcorn. "If Kon is into her, he's an idiot. What am I saying? Of course he's not into her. I saw how he was with you, Grace. He's totally into you. None of us have ever seen Kon act the way he acted with you."

"And, just so we're clear, you're pretty perfect, too, you know?" Heidi grinned at me.

"Yeah, but I'm definitely not princess material. I suspect Lady Valentina wouldn't be caught dead living in a converted cargo van. She probably grew up in a mansion. Maybe even a palace with servants and butlers." At any rate, the woman was high-bred in every way and knew it. All I knew is the sooner Gray was found, the sooner I could leave Sunkissed Key and put this whole painful mess behind me.

"Maybe she's lying. You know, making the whole fiancé thing up."

Parker gasped and sat straight upright. "Wait a minute! If Kon's this Hidden Prince, like the guys said, maybe he has to marry her. Like an arranged marriage. That kind of stuff goes on all the time with royalty."

Megan grinned teasingly and did a mock curtsy in front of Parker. "Oh, does it, *Your Royal Highness*?"

Parker laughed and tossed one of the new throw pillows at her. "Girl, you better shut it before I stick my royal tiara up your commoner backside."

We talked late into the night, but I was exhausted and ended up passing out on my little corner of the couch. I woke up in the middle of the night to find them all stretched out around me. Heidi was on the couch with me, Kerrigan was curled up in Gray's new-but-used recliner with Hannah. Megan and Parker were on a pallet on the floor, Megan spooning Parker. I almost got my camera for that one.

I realized with a wave of emotion that I had friends and I was in the middle of my very first sleepover. I felt an incredible loss that I would never be able to explore the feelings between Kon and me.

Silly, since we hardly knew each other. But, as I looked around the living room, I knew it would be hard to say goodbye to these guys.

Heidi stretched in her sleep and shoved her feet into my lap. Someone in the room snored and Kerrigan mumbled something that sounded like the *toadstools are singing*. A weird little group of friends. I fit in like the last puzzle piece, I realized as I shoved Heidi's feet off of me and got comfortable again.

Still, Gray would soon be home, I would soon be on my way, and soon Kon would be committing himself to someone else.

14

KONSTANTIN

Gray Lowe was a pain in the ass. We found him alright. Turned out the rescue mission was a bust, though, since he hadn't needed rescuing. He'd been voluntarily holed up on a fishing vessel in Cuban waters and he had no intention of leaving.

Unfortunately, he was a big guy, almost my size, and it appeared as though we were evenly matched as far as combat skills. Just when I was getting ready to pound some sense into him, Maxim mentioned Grace. Learning that his little sister had come looking for him and that it was, in fact, Grace who sent us to find him let all the wind out of his sails and affected him in a way that made me grudgingly respect him.

After that, he came with us willingly and we crammed into the speedboat that Dmitry had acquired. I knew better than to ask *where* or *how* he acquired it.

On the ride back from Miami to Sunkissed Key, Gray relayed his story about how he'd gotten burned by the agency he worked for. With an especially nasty group of illegal arms dealers after him, and a near-fatal gunshot wound, he'd had no choice but to lay low for a while. He'd been hiding out, healing and trying to figure out a way to get back on dry land without costing several lives.

After hearing Gray's story, there was a lull in conversation inside the van as Serge drove us back to the office. I felt eyes on me, several side glances directed my way. And it was entirely too quiet. The guys were pissed at me, and rightfully so. I'd been lying to them.

When I couldn't stand Maxim's gaze burning a hole in me anymore, I turned to meet his eyes and raised my brows questioningly. He spoke quietly. "Why did you never say anything?"

Aw, fuck. Instant guilt. I rolled my head back, let out a slow breath, and spoke to the ceiling. "Would you?"

Serge's scowl was dark as he caught my gaze through the rearview mirror, straightened and shook his head. "Well someone sure as shit should have, *Prince* Konstantin."

"What do you want me to say, Serge? Sorry that I hid who I was because I wanted to be treated like everyone else? Sorry that I didn't tell you that my family thinks they're something fucking special and I have this title I carry around like a ball and chain?" I scrubbed my hands down my face. "It's not anything I asked for. I am sorry that I kept it from you—all of you, but do you think I would even be here if you knew? Would I have even made it onto the team if you knew that I carried a title?"

Serge grunted. "Fuck no. The last thing I need is some royal asshole under me."

"Exactly." The van grew quiet again. I wasn't sure if the guys were silently cursing me to eternal damnation or if they were considering how it might be to stand in my shoes.

Suddenly, Alexei started snickering.

I shot him a nasty glare. "Something funny?"

"*King Kon.* Kinda has a ring to it. Reminds me of…hmm.. let's see… a thousand pound gorilla on top of the Empire State Building, perhaps?" At that a few more chuckles before the others joined in.

"He's got a face like King Kong," Roman ribbed.

"More like King Dong," Dmitry chimed in.

I grinned at Dmitry. "King *Big* Dong, thank you."

Maxim snorted. "King *Ding* Dong."

And it didn't stop there. The guys continued to razz me the whole way back from the port of Miami as Gray watched snickering. I took it, honored to the core of my being to know them. Loyal, brave, friends to the end, these guys were the best group of guys I'd ever known.

~

WE NO SOONER PULLED THE van up in front of the P.O.L.A.R. office when any further talk was interrupted by squealing tires and a wild screech of joy. This elicited a laugh from Gray who was standing beside me on the sidewalk. Grace had pulled her sprinter van up behind us and was up and out of the vehicle rounding it at breakneck speed, the engine still running. She threw herself at Gray, crashing into him with a painful sounding *thud* that had him groaning.

She hugged him hard, her arms stretched to wrap around him fully, then kissed his cheeks, her eyes brimming with tears. Gray seemed taken aback by the display, but his shoulders straightened and his chest puffed out, pride evident in his haggard expression. It was clear that he adored his sister.

She pulled away from him and threw herself at me next. If Gray had been shocked, I was completely blown away. Her arms looped around my neck pulling me close and planting a kiss on my jaw. "Thank you for bringing him home, Kon."

Before I could react and keep her right there like I wanted to—with her breasts smashed against my chest and her soft curves pressed against me like they belonged there—she'd pulled away. That quickly. Standing in front of Gray again, she reached up and slapped him. "Do you have any idea how much you scared me? You have some nerve, Gray Lowe. I should kick your ass for this. I thought something had happened to you. I thought you'd gotten caught in someone's trap again, or shot. I thought you were…"

Gray winced and wrapped her in a hug as her voice started to crack. "I'm sorry, Gracey. I'm sorry I scared you, but I'm here and I'm okay."

"Are you going to tell her you *did* get shot?" Alexei chuckled.

Grace pulled back with horror written all over her face. "You were shot?!"

I rested my hand on her shoulder and squeezed gently. "Why don't we go inside and talk there?"

She shrugged my hand off, and the attitude of gratitude she'd shown me earlier evaporated in thin air. "Your fiancée is inside and she doesn't really like me, not that I blame her. I think I'll take my brother home. Thank you for finding him. I'll get the bill from Serge and settle it."

I'd told her several times that I'd take care of the bill. It was a clear dismissal and not at all something I was willing to accept. Not yet. First, I had some explaining to do to her—apologizing, actually. "I'll drive you both home."

"Prince Konstantin?" A high-pitched, whiny voice pierced my eardrums, and then I caught waft of perfume that smelled like a cross between cabbage and cat piss. My dick shriveled. "It's about time!" Valentina. The woman clicked her stilettos over to me, flashed a sickly sweet fake smile and ran her hand up my bicep.

Grace's eyes flashed pain—only for a split second, but I saw it—before her gaze moved back to Gray. She cupped her brother's face and sighed. "Let's get you home, big brother. You can get cleaned up and then tell me what exactly happened to you."

Serge cleared his throat. "Things aren't completely wrapped up, Grace. Your brother is still in danger."

"What?" With wild eyes, she suddenly shoved Gray towards the office. "Get inside, then. What are you doing, standing out here, in the open? Jesus. Do you want to get shot again?"

Gray laughed and hugged her to his chest again. "Relax, Gracey. Your new pals here are going to help me clean up my mess. For now, I'm fine. We can go back to the house and talk."

"That's right. I'll have someone outside guarding the house at all times at least until your brother's 100%. You'll be safe there. We'll be keeping watch." Serge smiled at her and then shot me a look of annoyance. "Kon, why don't you take care of your business?" He nodded at Valentina.

"Yes, Konstantin. We have lots of plans to make." Shiny pink fingernails landed on my shoulder and tugged. "We have lots of things to do. Including getting to know each other a little better."

Grace stiffened but kept her gaze on her brother. "Come on. Let's go."

Serge followed them. "I'll come for first watch. According to Hannah you ladies spent some time at Gray's house." Serge growled lightly. "I believe you were told to stay away from the place without one of us there."

Gray just watched his sister with a proud smile on his face. "I wouldn't get on her bad side, man. She has the face of an angel, but she's got mad combat skills. She could take any of us down if she had to."

Valentina scoffed. "A weak little human? That would be the day."

I turned to her and frowned. "Lady Valentina, please wait inside."

Grace was already leaving, though. When I glanced back, she was fussing over Gray, getting him into the van and buckling him up as though he wasn't capable of doing it himself. He was allowing her to fuss, watching with an amused grin.

Serge gave me a pointed look. "We'll talk later."

"I'll come by the cottage."

Serge's eyes shifted from Grace to Valentina and back. "I don't think that's the best idea."

Valentina grabbed my arm again. "He's right. You're a prince, Konstantin. You're going to be king soon. You're better than this running around, tracking people down, playing some god-awful military bad boy."

The guys gave me a disgusted look as though Valentina was my fault, and filed inside the office. I was stuck there, Valentina was still grasping my arm. She was wrong. I wasn't better than any of these men. I'd spent several years with them, knew who they were, and was honored to be among them and accepted by them.

I stood there a few more seconds watching as Graces' van, Freebird, backed up and pulled out onto the road.

15
GRACE

All the anger I was feeling toward Kon vanished the moment I witnessed his reaction to Valentina. While she clutched him and stroked his bicep, the man looked as though he was seriously thinking of chewing his own arm off. That was definitely not the reaction of a man whose betrothed showed up for a surprised visit. Not if he was in love—or even like. I had no doubt Kon was either.

The whole thing made me hurt for him. I wasn't sure what was worse. Granted, watching him sweep her into his big arms and welcome her with a passionate kiss would have sucked donkey balls, but watching him cringe and recoil at her touch? Damn. Poor guy. Parker was right. The engagement couldn't have been his choice. Not that I forgave him completely, I mean he could have said something, but I was beginning to better understand his actions.

"I figure we can get some rest tonight and I'll start packing up in the morning." Gray stared at me over the cold beer he'd been chugging, pulling me out of my thoughts. I glanced at the door. Serge was outside somewhere standing guard.

"It's still not safe here and I'm in no condition to be battling anyone. I like Sunkissed Key, but it's time to move on." He flashed his boyishly charming grin.

I crossed my arms over my chest and frowned. "Who's after you that you think you and the polar bears can't handle?"

He sighed as though he knew the question was only a matter of time and he was surprised it took this long for me to ask. "I was undercover with a small time weapons dealing operation when my cover was blown. They supply a big time drug cartel. I have enough on them that they're probably not just gonna throw their hands in the air and say, 'Oh well.' They're not done with me. And, it's not that I don't think P.O.LA.R. can handle 'em. It's that I don't think it's worth it, Gracey. Not when I can just disappear. It's one thing you and I know well, right? It's what we do." He gave me that crooked half-grin that Gray used to charm the heck out of women of all ages. I's seen it work on everyone from schoolgirls to 80-year-old great-grandmas.

"Yeah, but we don't hide out from each other."

Gray winced. "Sorry. I would've emailed you as soon as I healed a little more. I was only in hiding to give myself time to get over the wound."

"They'd still be after you, though."

"It wouldn't be the first time, baby sis."

I scowled at him, the shiny newness of having him home safe was beginning to wear off. "Who are you?"

"Come on, Gracey. That's not fair."

"Isn't it? I feel like I don't know my own brother. You work for the government? You're some spy?" I shook my head. "I thought you were doing illegal stuff this entire time. I thought you were…like Dad."

Gray tensed. "Do not compare me to that man."

"Then stop running. Stay here and face this, so you don't have to look over your shoulder for the rest of your life." I gestured out at his back deck, visible through French doors at the back of the house. "Look at this place. It's beautiful. A good place to settle and put down roots."

He just shrugged without looking at the view. "You know, as well as I do that a view can change in an instant and there are beautiful ones all over the country."

"Gray, I want to stay." I blew out a rough breath. "I want to stay here and I want you to stay, too. We haven't seen each other in years. Don't you miss me?"

He leaned forward and squeezed my knee. "Of course, I do, Gracey. Just 'cause I leave Sunkissed Key doesn't mean we couldn't visit in other places."

"It won't happen. You and I both know it. We both leave here, who knows when I'll see you again. The next time you don't email me, what if you're not just hiding? What if these people find you? I want this to be over. I want it to be over and I want us to be a normal family."

With a giant sigh, Gray leaned back on the couch. "Come on, Grace. You know that's not us."

My mocking sigh was just as loud. "Don't you think it could be? I mean, if we wanted? If we tried?"

He didn't say anything. His eyes shut and he let his head rest on the cushion behind him.

"Gray, I made friends here—five amazing women. I have friends for the first time in my life. And we even had a sleepover! I had my first sleepover at the age of 28." I pinched my thumb and forefinger together. "I'm this close to having friends, family and a regular life. What if we both stayed and you and I didn't run anymore and instead we got to be like a normal brother and sister." I sucked in a huge breath and blew it all out just as fast. "There's only one problem with that. Neither of us can stay if we don't settle this mess."

"Fuck, Gracey, you know I'd do anything for you.... I don't know if I can do that."

"Don't be like him. Don't run from this."

"I'm not fucking like him, dammit." He stood up and stomped to the kitchen. "This is bigger than our daddy issues. Staying here could put people in danger. You could be in danger."

"You said yourself that I can handle myself, Gray." I stood up and marched over to him. "Want me to show you that I can still handle myself?"

He stepped back. "Grace, don't. I'm still healing."

I sent him a dark grin and nodded. "That's what I thought. Scared of me. Ha! I'm not some helpless damsel. If it came down to it, I could hold my own."

He stared at me for what felt like forever and then grunted. "You really like this place, huh?"

My shoulders sagged. "I do. More than that, though, Gray, I love you. I need you in my life—more than what we've had. I didn't even realize how lonely and isolated I've been until I got here and was surrounded by people. I'm thinking that maybe there's more to life than moving from town to town never really knowing anyone or letting them know me."

"In all the years since you could talk, you've never asked me for anything." He wrapped me in a hug and sighed into my hair. "You know that? All these years and you never needed anything. Or, if you did, you didn't mention it. Which is probably more likely what it was, right?"

I just shrugged.

"Hell, you gave way more than I ever gave back. You fought for me when no one else would." He pushed me away and held my shoulders. "You remember that time in Kansas City? I was getting bullied and you ran in like some miniature badass and tried to fight boys five and six years older than you. You would've willingly gotten your ass handed to you for me."

"You shifted, though. Scared the meanness right out of them." I grinned. "It can still be like that. We can deal with this together."

"Ugh." He threw his hands up and looked up at the ceiling. "Fuck it. Fine. We'll stay. I won't have you getting in the middle of this fight, though. Understand me? It's not happening."

I started to argue but stopped myself. Best to quit while I was ahead. "Fine."

He rolled his eyes and pushed me away from him. "Get out of my face now. I need to shower and change into something that doesn't smell like week old dead fish."

"I didn't want to say anything…"

"Hardy-har-har. Funny." He got to the doorway to his bedroom before looking back at me over his shoulder. "What's up with you and that prince guy?"

I felt my cheeks redden. "Nothing."

"Didn't look like nothing to me."

16

KONSTANTIN

My brain was melting. There was no other explanation for the headache that was blooming behind my eyes. Valentina's voice and constant yammering were slowly killing me and I'd only been in her presence for twenty or so minutes. Twenty minutes that felt like twenty million years.

As I sat listening to Valentina, the boner-killer, and my nuts tried to dig their way up inside my groin to get away from her, my thoughts kept straying to Grace. The way her arms had swung around me, her soft body pressed tightly against mine in gratitude as though we were two halves of a whole coming together. God, I wanted that woman.

Valentina was pacing the room, her hands gesturing wildly as she continued to speak animatedly. "...and we must have a festival to celebrate the coronation. We owe it to our subjects. I've already hired a personal photographer of my own for the event to be sure my social media pics are from the best angle and with the best lighting..."

I had hated the composed, almost embarrassed way Grace had retreated from me once she realized she'd had her arms around me. I hated that almost as much as I hated the empty ache in my chest that followed.

"...wedding dress, of course, will be a Givenchy, but I've found a marvelous up-and-coming designer for the gown I'll wear to the formal engagement party. She's..." Valentina's voice had not changed in all these years. Astonishingly, it still hit the same abrasive pitch as when we were kids—nails meet chalkboard.

The pained look on Grace's face when Valentina had stepped out of the office was one I'd never forget. I'd watched her cheeks instantly flush before she'd turned toward her brother. That hurt so much my lungs constricted to the point it was hard to breathe. I couldn't stand it that I was responsible for her pain.

"...an off-shoulder cream satin with handtied lace. It will be the envy of every she-bear alive. Let them eat their hearts out is what... Prince Konstantin, are you even listening?"

I blinked, trying to make sense of what she was saying. The idea of spending the rest of my life with the woman was about as pleasant as shoving thumbtacks through my eyeballs.

Valentina's eyes narrowed suspiciously. "I asked how soon you can be ready to leave. Estelle can have my things packed in ten minutes. I'll be relieved to be rid of this place. It reeks of a zoo." She picked invisible lint off her tailored skirt. "Honestly, I have no clue how you've managed for so long. These bears are all so...simple. And what is with the fascination with humans? Between you and me I find it vile how the lower classes behave." She huffed indignantly. "Prince Konstantin?" This time she stomped her high heel on the carpet. "Are you listening to me?"

"Hmm? Er, no. No, I'm not listening. Lady Valentina, I'm afraid this isn't going to happen."

Valentina jaw dropped as she stared at me. Then her face turned a nasty shade of crimson and she looked as though her head might explode. "Excuse me? Wha—which part?"

I stood to my full height. "All of it. The formal engagement party, the wedding, the reception, the coronation...none of it is going to happen."

Valentina's look of complete and utter indignation said she'd have liked to have a flame thrower right about then to create a new dish—Konstantin flambé.

"I'm sorry. I'm sorry you've come all this way, at my father's insistence no doubt, but the whole idea of this betrothal is archaic, not to mention cruel. We hardly know each other. We damn sure don't love each other."

Her face contorted in a furious death stare. "You cannot do this! I will not allow it!"

"It's done. And done." I stood up and moved towards the door.

"It's that human, isn't it?! With the dog brother. She's weak, Konstantin. No backbone and the genetic clarity of a sponge!"

I growled willing to ignore her insult to Grace only because of the shock breaking our engagement must be to her. Not that she gave a rat's ass about me. I knew she only craved the title and power becoming my mate would grant her.

"I hope you find your true mate, Valentina." I also hoped the poor guy had a hearing problem. "And I apologize for any embarrassment this may cause you or your family."

"Oh, no you don't. This mating *is* going to happen Konstantin. It's going to happen because I have your father on speed dial." She waved her cellphone back and forth in front of her face. "His Majesty has assured me that either you come back and this mating takes place or both you and your little army buddies will never be allowed to set foot in Siberia again. And your precious P.O.L.A.R. unit will be disbanded and defunded as of yesterday. YESTERDAY!"

The smug, humorless grin—vicious and malicious—that spread across her face reminded me of a gaping wound. But, she had the upper hand and she knew it. She'd just played her trump card. Either I followed through with this ridiculous and archaic mating, go back to my homeland and ascend to the throne or I hang my team out to dry. I loved those guys like brothers.

I slammed the door so hard as I left that it cracked the frame. I didn't care. What I really wanted to do was go back in and throw Lady Valentina out of my bedroom window.

~

Despite Serge suggesting I stay away, I went straight to Gray's cottage. I didn't know what I was going to say to Grace, but I had to see her. I needed to at least explain that none of this was my choice. I'd never meant for her to be hurt by anything.

I looked up at the house and saw Grace peering out at me from behind a curtain. Her eyes widened and then she was gone. Swearing, I held out my hands to Serge, conveying I meant no harm. "I just need to talk to Grace."

"You're soon to be mated to a woman who's been spending all of her time making us absolutely miserable. Wonderful lady, that one."

"She's not my choice, man." I looked back up, hoping to catch another glimpse of Grace.

"She your true mate?" When I looked at him in horror, he laughed. "Grace. Not Valentina."

I blew out a deep sigh and nodded. "Yes."

"What are you going to do?"

"Not much I can do."

"Bullshit." Serge appeared concerned, but he didn't know the whole story.

"Look, about keeping everything from you and the guys..."

He held his hands up gesturing me to be silent. "I was pissed as hell at first. We all were. Except Alexei. We figured that all this time we didn't know you. But that lasted all of about five minutes. Then we realized we didn't know the *title* you carried, but we know *you*. Better than anyone else knows you. We've seen the real you. Hell, you're one of us. We're a team."

My throat suddenly clogged with a huge lump. Even after deceiving and keeping my identity from them, they stuck by me. I had mad respect for that kind of loyalty and they deserved my loyalty in return.

I headed towards the stairs. "We'll talk later, okay?"

He grinned and rolled his eyes. "Later, brother."

Brother.

I took the stairs two at a time and knocked much louder than I meant to. When Gray opened the door, he looked like he was ready for a fight until he saw it was me.

"Grace, Prince Boytoy is here." He walked back to the couch and dropped onto it.

Grace peeked out from the kitchen and frowned at her brother. Her arm snapped out and a wet rag flew across the room and slapped Gray in the back of the head. "Don't be an asshole."

Gray acted as if she'd poured a bucket of spiders on him, squirming to get away from the rag. "That's disgusting. You cleaned the floor with that!"

"He had you scrubbing floors?" I stepped farther into the room and scowled at the wolf.

"She wanted to. She's weird like that and who am I to get in her way?" He rolled his eyes at me. "Stick around some. You'll learn that, too."

"Why the fuck is everyone rolling their eyes at me?"

Grace let out a breathy snicker and then smiled. "I can think of a reason, or two."

I fought the smile that tugged at my lips. I didn't deserve her smiles. They were like Cupid's arrow through the heart. Her beauty was a beam of sunshine radiating, lighting the room. "Go for a walk with me?"

She nodded. "Okay."

17
GRACE

I was probably a fool for agreeing to go for a walk with Konstantin. The truth was twofold. One, I felt sorry for him because I didn't for a second believe that he was in love with the wicked witch from the North. And two, well, he was just tough to resist.

I knew he was either going to explain that he was engaged and I was a mistake, or tell me that I was nice and all, but he just wasn't that into me. I was waiting for the formal rejection, but he shocked me. He just silently took my hand in his and walked with me down the beach.

I took off my sandals and carried them in my other hand, settling in for a longer stroll. I knew he was not mine, but with our hands intertwined...was it so wrong that I pretended for a few minutes that he was? Ugh, yes! Yes, it was. It was certifiable. Pathetic. And I knew better, but my dumb, stupid, moronic, idiotic heart was stupid as fuck.

Minutes passed without him saying anything and I let out a little sigh. I wanted to know what he was thinking. Why was he there, holding my hand, and where was his mate-to-be? Did she know where he was?

I guessed I'd need to be the one to break the ice. "So, you're a prince."

"Grace, about Valentina—"

"I understand."

His brow creased and he turned to look down at me as we kept walking. He looked surprised. "You do?"

"Yeah, well, no...I don't know. Explain it to me?"

He nodded and stared down at his feet as we slowly strolled through the sand. "Shifter traditions are strange and archaic, but as heir to the throne, I have always known I had certain obligations. Adhering to old world traditions including mating a pre-selected female of suitable stature and breeding is just one of the sacrifices that will be asked of me in my lifetime."

He looked so sad that I gave his hand a little squeeze of support. "But you don't even seem to like her. Are you really expected to take her as a mate?"

The corner of his lips turned up in a wry smile that didn't reach his eyes. "It takes incredible effort to even be in the same room as her, but that doesn't matter. My life is not my own. Because of that, I've kept myself remote and unapproachable where women were concerned, knowing that romance could have potentially negative consequences...until you. You, I couldn't resist."

I felt a blush streak my cheeks. The whole situation was just awful for him. Awful for me—for both of us. We walked along in silence for a few minutes. Neither of us seemed to know what to say next.

"I'm glad your brother was okay." He glanced down at me and then looked away. "The team will stay around until it's clear that he's not in danger anymore. Neutralize any threat that comes his way. You don't have to worry about that."

I knew he was attempting to change the subject, but I didn't want to talk about Gray. I loved my brother and I was beyond grateful that he was okay, but he was safe and sound in his house with Serge guarding him. He was fine. What wasn't fine was that I was walking along with a soon to be married man, holding hands—and hearts—like he wasn't already taken.

"He's lucky to have someone like you."

I grunted. "He's lucky I don't shoot him myself."

"We all make mistakes."

That statement hung in the air between us and felt to me like a growing, pulsating living organism until I couldn't stand it anymore. "Was I a mistake? Is that how you'll think of me? I mean, if you think of me at all. You probably won't think of me…"

Kon let go of my hand to grab my waist and pull me into him. "You could never be a mistake. Never. You have been the best thing that has ever happened to me in my life. And saying goodbye to you will be the worst. I'll think of you often, every day, and every day I'll consider myself the luckiest bear in the world that I got to spend even a single second in your presence."

I wanted to be strong. I wanted to be the type of woman who would put another woman's needs over her own, but at that moment, I wasn't. I was selfish and greedy and I wanted Konstantin for myself.

"Kon…"

Like he was reading my mind, he swept me into his arms and carried me. His long legs ate up the sand and in seconds we appeared in front of my van. I hadn't realized we were that close to it, but I was sure glad we were. I didn't care if it had been his intention the whole time, or if it was just a beautiful coincidence. I just needed him touching me.

He didn't put me down as I reached to open the door for us before he could break it again, and hurried up the steps inside. Before I could turn around to face him, Kon was on me. Pressed against my back, his arms latched around my stomach. He buried his face into my hair and growled as he brushed it aside so he could kiss my neck.

I gripped his forearms as he raked his teeth over my tender flesh and left more marks on me. His large hands moved up to knead my breasts, his thumbs instantly finding my hard nipples. Stroking and squeezing me through my clothes, he nipped my ear and growled louder.

"I don't know if I can be gentle right now, Grace. Tell me to fuck off if you don't want this. Tell me to get the fuck out of here and I'll go."

I fought his grip to face him and gasped when I saw his teeth looked sharper. His eyes glowed a fluorescent violet. "Don't go. Stay with me. Even if we only have a couple stolen hours, I'll take it."

His hands gripped my ass and lifted me off of my feet. I locked my arms around his neck and held on while he spun us around and backed me against the side of the van. He was so tall, he couldn't stand to his full height and his cock was proportional to the rest of his size—huge—and it pressed against my core, his hips rocking at just the right angle to send delicious shivers through my body.

Pinned there, I tried to calm my fluttering heart. I was so turned on that I felt almost dizzy from the force of the desire pulsing through me. When Kon let go of my ass and grabbed both sides of my shirt, I wasn't expecting him to rip it off of me. I gaped at him, my shirt hanging in tatters around me.

He growled at the sight of my bra and reached for it, his finger extending into a claw to cleanly slice it in two. As my bare breasts tumbled out, he made a noise, a combination growl and purr and dove in, licking and nibbling my breasts. He sucked my sensitive flesh into his mouth and rolled my nipples in his tongue until my hips bucked against his.

I pulled at his hair, unable to stand much more of his attention, unless he was going to take me soon. "More, Kon. More."

He spun us around, lowering me onto my little tabletop. The old thing rocked dangerously, the few dishes I'd had on it toppled off and crashed to the floor, but Kon didn't notice. He pulled my shorts off and then buried his face between my thighs, kissing me through the cotton of my panties. I was ready to scream at him by the time he leaned up and pulled them down my legs, shooting me a dirty grin as he slipped them into his pocket.

He devoured me. I came hard almost instantly, calling out for him. My nails scored his shoulders, but he didn't stop. Two more orgasms slammed through me before he pulled back and stared down at me with a scorching gaze.

"More?"

I tried to squeeze my thighs together, but he wouldn't let me. "No more. Too much."

He dropped his pants revealing his beautiful, and enormous, erection which he stroked while watching me. "Do you want me, Grace?"

I shouldn't have been able to speak after three earth-shaking orgasms, and honestly it was an effort to get my mind and vocal chords to coordinate. Biting my lip, I nodded and breathed out, "Please."

His growl was louder and rougher than I'd heard before, his eyes glowing brightly. "I like hearing you beg for me."

I held his gaze as I spread my legs wider and cupped my breasts, taking my own pleasure. "I need you in me, Konstantin. *Please.*"

He planted his hands on the table on either side of my hips and lowered his mouth to mine. I raised up to meet him and kissed him with everything I had, needing to show him how much I wanted him. He slowly thrust into me, inch by inch, until he was fully in me and swearing viciously against my mouth.

"Fuck, Grace. You're squeezing me so perfectly." He watched my expressions as he pulled out and then thrust back in. "F-f-fuck."

I'd never felt more perfectly filled. I could feel him in me so deeply that I knew I would never enjoy sex again, unless it was with him. When he thrust harder and faster, I threw my head back and cried out for him, his name like a swear on my lips.

"Come for me, Grace." He bent and flicked my nipple with his tongue as his powerful thrusts continued. There was no way I could hold off another orgasm if I'd tried.

I screamed his name and shattered into a million pieces as pleasure washed over me like a tsunami. Almost painful in its power, all I could do was hold on to him as I was torn apart and put back together completely new and differently.

Kon followed me, growling my name and sinking his teeth into the flesh of my breast as he thrust into me once more and then stilled as his seed filled me. Another orgasm slammed through me, the bite transporting me to a place of white hot sensations that clouded my vision and threatened to drown me in a sea of pleasure. Growling through his orgasm, he slammed his hand down on the table. The old wood couldn't handle the added pressure.

The table collapsed under us, sending us both sprawling on the floor. Kon somehow managed to roll us so that he landed under me.

I was too raw, too shocked to laugh. Kon seemed to be in the same place. His body vibrated under me as his growl continued, a long and continuous sound that I wasn't even sure he knew he was emitting.

My heart hammered away in my chest, but the dizziness began to subside. I felt grounded so firmly to the man under me, that I knew there would never be anyone else. Terrified and unsure of what came next, I didn't protest when Kon slowly unfolded the bench sofa, converting it into a bed, and scooped me up, placing me on it and crawling in behind me, his huge body curled around mine.

I was floating on a cloud and I knew it would vanish in a poof and I'd come crashing down to earth, but damn if I didn't want to spend every last second I could with him.

18

KONSTANTIN

I didn't want to leave Grace's side, but Serge started shouting in my head about Valentina insulting Hannah and that he didn't care how high and mighty I thought I was, I needed to get my royal ass over there and straighten her out. And here I was worried he might treat me differently after finding out my royal status.

Grace was passed out and hadn't stirred. Curled up against me, her arm was stretched across my chest, her small hand over my heart. Her body was slightly bruised and marked from me. Maybe I'd been too rough with her. She didn't have shifter healing. I rolled away from her and pulled myself to my feet. I didn't want to wake her. She looked so beautiful.

I leaned down to pull the blanket back over her bare shoulders and paused. I'd left a nasty mark on her perfect breast and I felt immediately guilty. It was deeper than the rest. Just looking at made me want to crawl back into bed next to her and never leave. That mark... I shook my head. No, I would've had to bite her on her neck to truly place a claiming mark on her. Still, I felt...different.

I found my clothes where I'd finally kicked them off before crawling into bed and stepped into them before heading out. I wanted to get back to Grace as soon as I could. I didn't care that it wasn't the best idea or that my brain was taking a backseat to my heart. All I knew was that when you felt as deeply about a person as I felt about Grace, especially if you knew you'd soon have to leave and never see them again, you wanted to spend every second you could with them.

I walked briskly back to the P.O.L.A.R. house, hoping to clear up whatever storm Valentina was stirring up so I could hurry back.

Valentina was in the kitchen, chin out, nose in the air, haughtily facing off with most of the gang when I came in. Serge was snarling at her, holding Hannah to his side. Hannah looked like she contemplating throwing the tea kettle at Valentina. All heads turned to me and it struck me that there was no way they weren't going to smell Grace all over me. Not that I was ashamed of Grace, merely protective. I didn't know how she'd feel about the others knowing.

Alexei, Roman, and Maxim were all seated at the table, without their mates. They gave me pointedly blank looks and went back to eating. Serge scowled at me and held his mate closer.

"Are you fucking kidding me?!" Valentina screeched and flew at me, her nails coming dangerously close to my eyes before I caught her hands and held her away from me. "You stink of that human bitch!"

I roared so loud the house shook and I think I heard Valentina's teeth rattle. It certainly shut her up, but not for long enough.

Serge stepped forward. "She has to go. Royalty or not, I've reached my limit. She's worn out her welcome in this house."

"I was already on my way out, you ass, before your clumsy human spilled her drink on my luggage!" Pulling her wrists free of me, Valentina hissed at Hannah. "You'll pay for that."

My anger at being called away from my time with Grace to deal with Valentina's spoiled rotten behavior got the better of me. "Get out!"

Everyone went still. Serge froze, his mouth open like he'd been about to say something. Hannah hid a grin behind her hand and ducked behind Serge's back.

"Get the fuck out. You do not get to come into this house and treat these people as though they're beneath you. You may have a title that makes you think you fart unicorns out your butt, but I've got news for you: I. Outrank. You."

If looks could kill, Valentina would have incinerated me into a pile of ashes on the floor. She huffed and shoved past me on her way to the door. "I will be at a hotel. Fuck your little human while you can, *Your Highness*, but you had better be on that flight back home with me—or you'll be sorry."

The door slammed and everyone picked up what they'd been doing, avoiding eye contact with me and acting like nothing happened. Except Hannah. She looked at me with confusion in her eyes. I had the feeling she wanted to say something, but I was in no mood. I just shook my head and took the stairs, three at a time, up to my room. I needed to be alone for a few minutes.

It was impossible to have a productive thought when all I kept thinking about was how I couldn't give up Grace. Just being this far from her was making me cringe. My bear wasn't the only one who wanted to go back, curl up in her too-small bed with her, and never leave her side. I could easily and happily spend the rest of my life like that—with her arm draped possessively over my chest and me continuing to count the freckles on her shoulders.

I looked around for my phone. My spontaneous, gut reaction was to end this insanity and call my father—appeal to him, make demands or just flat out refuse to return. I'd tell him that my mind was made up. I was staying in Sunkissed Key with Grace, my true mate.

Fuck.

Breaking off the engagement, not following through with my duties to the crown would bring severe repercussions to Serge and the others in P.O.L.A.R. *We're a team,* Serge had told me in response to finding out who I really was. Double Fuck. I had no choice. I couldn't Benedict Arnold the guys.

That anger clawed at me dug into my throat until it was hard to breathe.

I slammed my fist into the wall and when that wasn't enough, I did it over and over again, until the wall was nothing but dust and pieces of sheetrock flung all around my room.

19

GRACE

Kon crawling into bed next to me woke me up. I shifted, reaching for him, while also peeking out the front window, trying to gage what time it was. The sun was still out. I'd been sleeping in the middle of the day. I grinned big. Kon had worn me out.

He kissed my temple gently and tucked my hair out of my face. "I didn't mean to wake you."

I stretched and groaned when my body protested. I ached everywhere. "I needed to wake up. I should be doing stuff."

"Like what?"

"Playing mother hen and clucking over my brother." I sat up and looked down at Kon. He was fully dressed and freshly showered. "Did you leave?"

He nodded. "You're worried P.O.L.A.R. isn't enough to keep Gray safe, aren't you? Not without you on guard duty." He was grinning, teasing.

I pursed my lips. "Shut up. I have other stuff to do, too. I should be working. I'm behind and I'm never going to meet my next deadline."

"What do you do?"

"Strange to hear that question *after* sleeping with a man." I gasped when I suddenly found myself under a growling Kon, his glowing eyes intense.

"I don't want to talk about any other men."

I scowled up at him. "One of us is engaged. It's not me."

With a loud groan, he flopped back on the bed and ran his hands over his face. "Tell me what you do."

"Tell me why you're engaged to Valentina and still here with me."

"Grace…"

"I'm a graphic designer." I shrugged. "I work remotely."

He studied me. "What types of things do you design?"

"Mostly book covers, e-book and print." I nodded to the stack of books on the small shelf on the other side of the camper. "Were you promised to her when you left?"

"Not because I wanted to be."

"Why can't you get out of it?" I blushed and tried to backtrack. "I mean… If you don't want to mate her, don't."

"It's not that simple. There will be severe consequences, not just to me, to people who deserve my loyalty."

"So, you're just going to go through with it?"

He looked away and I knew the answer wasn't one that he liked, either.

Groaning, I got out of bed and searched for my clothes. "This sucks. It's so unfair. You shouldn't have to take a mate that you don't love. You shouldn't be forced… She's… No, I'm not going to talk poorly about her. Not when I'm the one sleeping with her almost husband—mate, whatever."

"You're not doing anything wrong."

I finally found a t-shirt and pulled it on. "Pretty sure Valentina wouldn't feel the same way."

"Grace."

I stopped looking for shorts and met Kon's serious gaze. "This thing between you and me…it's more than a normal relationship. It's a melding of souls. You aren't doing anything wrong."

Butterflies took flight in my stomach. As corny as it sounded, I knew exactly what he was saying. I felt it too. "When does your official mating take place?"

"I'll have to leave in a week."

"You're sure you can't get out of it?"

He shook his head.

I blew out a rough breath and squared my shoulders. "Okay."

"Okay?"

I swallowed past the urge to cry. "I have a week with you. I don't want to throw that away. Maybe I'm wrong for doing this. I'm not proud of being the other woman, but given the circumstances, I just want to..."

Kon sat on the edge of the bed, his eyes intense as he stared at me. "Walking away will probably kill me."

I turned away to hide the tears in my eyes. "I don't want to talk about that. I can't. If I think about how much that will hurt, I'll want to run, protect myself. But, if I don't squeeze out every drop of happiness from whatever time I have left with you, I will regret it forever."

His arms wrapped around me and he held me. "No thinking about that, then. I need this week with you. I need you."

"Then, take me."

That time with Konstantin was softer, gentler. We finished together and he spent the rest of the day talking to me about my work while he stroked my hair. Even when I felt him tangling it, I didn't stop him.

When darkness settled over the camper and Kon fell asleep next to me, soft snores filling the space, I buried my face in my pillow and cried. I was overcome with emotion, most that I didn't even understand. How I could feel more for a man I'd barely known than I'd ever felt for anyone else in my life was hard to comprehend. It scared me. In the night, my bold declaration that I was willing to take the week with him instead of missing out seemed nuts. He was going to destroy me.

My heart already ached, knowing the expiration date on whatever we were doing was so soon. I somehow knew that there would never be anyone else. I would spend the rest of my life mourning him. He would spend the rest of his life mated to Valentina.

I wasn't sure which of us would have it worse.

Then, thoughts of him with Valentina invaded my mind. Would they grow to love each other over time? Have little cubs? Damn, that was probably one of his royal duties. They would share all kinds of firsts. I wanted to peel my face off to distract myself. Anything would be better than that tangent of thought.

I must've tossed and turned one time too many times for Kon. He reached over, grabbed me, and hauled me against him. With him arms locking me to him tightly, my panic started to ease. When his soft snores filtered through my hair, I finally fell asleep.

20

GRACE

Heidi was behind the bar at Mimi's the next night when I plopped my ass on a stool. I'd spent the day with Gray while Kon and the guys were working and then, just after he'd gotten to Freebird to see me, he and Alexei got called back out to work a small job near Miami and he'd had to leave. I'd barely gotten to say hello before he was gone again. The worst part was, I could smell Valentina's strong cabbage-and-cat-urine scented perfume all over him.

He could barely stand to be in the same room as her. So, whatever happened–whether she tried to hug him or leaned against him, or just sprayed the air near him—I knew nothing intimate had gone on between them. I also knew that that perfume was intentional. Valentina was marking her territory, as was her right. Which served to remind me of the awful predicament I was in.

When Heidi texted telling me to stop by Mimi's Cabana where she worked, a Polynesian themed bar with tiki masks, palm trees and coconuts, I jumped at the chance to hang out with one of my new girlfriends. Heidi and booze sounded like a great plan.

None of the other women knew exactly what was happening with Kon. If Heidi's questioning looks were any sign, they knew that Kon and Valentia's mating was still a go. On one hand, I wanted to be calm and rational and explain that sometimes we had to do things we didn't want to do in life, make sacrifices for the greater good of our country, and Kon was a man of honor and integrity. On the other hand, I wanted to cry in my beer until I was so shit-faced I no longer had emotions.

The bar was busy, but there was another bartender, a thick Samoan woman with a coconut bra, on duty and Heidi happily took a break when I got there. She leaned over the bar to talk to me, ignoring the patrons who tried to get her attention.

"You look upset."

I shook my head and dug my nails in my palms to keep from crying. "I'm okay. How's your night going? It's pretty quiet in here."

She narrowed her eyes at me. "Something strong?"

I nodded, gratefully. "Yes, please."

She poured me three shots of tequila and pushed them across to me. "Down those and then tell me the truth about why you're upset."

I downed all three shots, one after the other, wincing as I did. Then, I rolled my shoulders. I didn't even know where to start. I *didn't* want to talk about Kon. He was the beginning and end of my hurt feelings, though.

"Grace, honey, just talk to me."

"It's Kon!" I pulled a face and groaned. "Sorry. I didn't mean to yell. It's Kon. It's nothing, though."

She crossed her arms under her chest and waited. Her eyes went to my neck and her perfectly waxed eyebrows shot up. "Jesus."

I pulled my hair forward more, doing everything I could to hide the sucker bites that Kon had left. It was still warm out in southern Florida and I couldn't exactly wear a turtleneck to hide them all. "Maybe, it's a little more than nothing."

"Did he *mark you* mark you? Like a claiming mark?"

I shook my head. "I don't think so. I mean…"

"You would know if he did, Grace. It's…intense, to say the least. Massive orgasm intense."

I thought of the last bite he'd landed on my breast. "Can you be marked somewhere not on the neck?"

Heidi's eyes widened and she let out a scream that drew everyone's attention. Seeing everyone looking, she glared at them and made a motion with her hand for them to look away. "Nothing to see here!"

I leaned forward, the tequila loosening my body and mind, alike. "Does this look like a claiming mark?"

She looked down my shirt as I held it away from my chest. She hooked her finger in the neck of my t-shirt and pulled it out farther. Her eyes slowly came up to mine and she pursed her lips. "He marked your tit."

I yanked my shirt out of her fist and sat back down on the stool so hard that I almost fell off backwards. I motioned toward the bottle of tequila and gestured for her to keep 'em coming. When her eyes went back to my neck, I growled and pulled the hair forward again. "He did not mark my tit."

"He marked your tit." Pouring me more shots, she tipped her head back and laughed. "Holy shit."

My heart lodged somewhere just south of my mouth and I felt myself losing the battle of the tears. "He's leaving."

"What?"

"He's leaving with Valentina. He's not staying. He's not going to be my mate. You're telling me that he marked me, but he's leaving me." I slammed the shots back and wobbled to my feet. I suddenly felt as though the walls were closing in. "I need to get out of here."

Heidi was around the bar and slipping her arm around my waist in a second. She walked with me to the exit and once we were outside, she led me to the beach and helped me down. Sitting next to me, facing the ocean, she took my hand in hers and sighed. "Don't cry, Grace. You look like a sad angel when you do and it's confusing."

I laughed through the tears and shook my head. "I'm his mate and he's still leaving?"

"Tell me everything." She nudged me with her shoulder. "Then, I can decide if we all need to get together and use his balls for field hockey practice."

"Don't do that! He has beautiful testicles." I laughed and then hung my head in my hands. "I can't believe I just said that. That tequila packs quite a punch. I'm a hot mess."

"We all went through piles of shit to get our happily ever after with our men. Tell me about Kon's version."

So, I did. I told Heidi all of it.

"He's still going through with it? He's still spending time with her?" She was as confused as I was.

I nodded. "I don't know why. Or in what context, really. I know he doesn't like her. I know that. It's just I thought I could do this—spend the little remaining time with him, but I can't get off my mind the fact that she's getting him in the end. Happily or not, she's getting the *ever after*."

"Oh, Grace. I'm so sorry." Heidi wrapped her arms around me and sighed into my hair. "This is a little more intense than what the rest of us went through. There was no royalty or obligation to a kingdom and duties to a crown involved in our mess."

"I want to trash her hotel room." I shook my head. "No. Sorry. That was my father coming out."

A slow smile spread across Heidi's face. "Are you sure? It's not a terrible idea. It might make you feel better. Hell, it might make us all feel better." Heidi's grin was all mischief but she just watched me silently while I pondered the idea.

I pulled myself to my feet and grinned. "Fine. You talked me into it."

"Excellent! I'll call the girls."

"No, I don't want to interrupt their time with their mates."

Heidi cupped my cheek and then roughly patted it. "Trust me, they'll want to be interrupted. Valentina has ruffled more feathers than Colonel Sanders. They'll be ecstatic to get in some payback."

A dark thrill ran through me. I'd worked so hard to walk the straight and narrow my whole life, but maybe being a little bad was just what the doctor ordered.

21

KONSTANTIN

Dead tired, I sank onto the side of my mattress at the P.O.L.A.R. house. I would have headed straight to see Grace, but I needed a shower and I couldn't fit into the small closet in Freebird that Grace called her bathroom. I also needed to give myself a minute. I was in a foul mood and I didn't want to bring that to her.

I was having a hell of a time concentrating as I swam around the pickle jar I was in. I wanted desperately to stay with Grace and build a life, a future, with her. I would lose everything—the inheritance, the title, the kingdom—everything that I'd never wanted. I'd relinquish it all in a heartbeat.

The only real problem was backing out, staying here with Grace, meant the team would never be able to return to the covert operations and reconnaissance missions that they thrived on. They would never be able to see their families that remained in Siberia and their citizenship would be revoked.

I knew how much they all hated the heat, hated the never-ending sun beating down on them, and hated the inconsequential work that we were doing here. They were all antsy to get sent back to home. I could be selfish and take what I wanted, but they'd lose everything.

Desperate, I worked through scenarios in my head that would end with Grace and I getting to be together. None of them were the least bit acceptable.

I was showered and just about to dress when my phone rang. I grabbed it and answered without looking at the screen.

"Konstantin?"

"Hannah?" I stood up and searched for a shirt, knowing it wasn't good if she was calling me instead of Serge. "What's wrong?"

She giggled and covered it with a cough. "Um. So, we were all out and about. We just happened to stumble upon this hotel and now the police are here, accusing us of vandalizing it."

I swore. "Grace is with you?"

"Yep." She popped the p and giggled again. "She's in the police car. She wouldn't let us take the blame. She's one in a million, Kon."

I charged down the stairs and out the front door. "What hotel?"

"It's the Bogart & Bacall Inn just off Toucan Boulevard. And, Kon?"

"Yeah?"

"Um, Lady Valentina is here, too."

I groaned. The last thing I wanted to do was see her. "Why?"

"Well, because, maybe, just maybe, it was her hotel room window that we threw a stink bomb through." She fell into a fit of giggles. "Sorry. I'm sorry, Kon. Heidi brought us tequila and after a couple bottles…"

My brain fizzled into red. "I'm calling Serge."

"Oh, no! Kon! Don't call him. He's going to get all fussy and I'm going to have to listen to him lecture about safety and what his life would be reduced to if anything happens to me, blah, blah, all night."

"And I'm telling him you said that!" I hung up and growled as I jogged toward the hotel.

Your mates are with Grace, in trouble with local law enforcement for throwing a stink bomb through a hotel window. I shook my head and my jog turned into a full-out run. The idea of Grace in a police cruiser didn't sit well with me.

I got there in time to see an officer bent over, talking to Grace through the open squad car door. Resisting the urge to plow into him and knock his ass away from her, I cleared my throat and crossed my arms. "Officer Reynolds."

He jumped and turned to face me, hand on his firearm. "Oh, Konstantin. Startled me there, son. What can I do for you?"

I nodded toward Grace without looking at her. "The woman."

He nodded his understanding. "Sorry, Kon. She threw a stink bomb through a hotel window. The entire floor had to evacuate. There's some kind of VIP or something, or so she claims, in there demanding we press charges."

I growled. "No charges. I'll pay for whatever damages were incurred."

"I'm afraid it's too late. I'm taking her to lock up."

I tilted my head and tried to remember to breathe. "Don't move this car. I'll go clear things up with the owner and be right back."

I chanced a look inside at Grace, cuffed, wearing a t-shirt that read *life rocks when your home rolls*, and mouthing something out of the other window, at the rest of the women. They all fell into fits of laughter and I had to bite back a smile at whatever antics Grace was up to. It was damned hard to stay mad at that woman. Cuffed in a police car and she was making jokes.

I was able to smooth things over with the owner—after settling a large bill—before facing Valentina. Her perfumed scent was gone, replaced with the stench of rotten eggs, which might have been an improvement over the horrid perfume. She looked like a wet dog, drenched and half melted from the sprinkler system.

"I want her locked away for the rest of her life." She was seething and I was a little surprised she hadn't gone after Grace with her claws out.

"No."

"Excuse me?"

"No." I repeated. "She's going home. The hotel isn't pressing charges and neither are you. You want me to go with you and you'll drop this."

"We're leaving in two days, then." She jabbed her finger at me, wafting a new wave of rotten egg at me. "If I could get the plane back by tomorrow, I would. Two days and we're fucking out of this shithole, Konstantin."

I clenched my jaw. "Fine."

22

KONSTANTIN

Grace was not the least bit remorseful. If anything, she was even more belligerent than ever on our walk back to her van. "Why'd you have to go and call the other guys on them? You got them in trouble."

I hid a smile at the way her southern accent suddenly came out stronger than ever. Tequila seemed to have an interesting effect on my mate. "You women got together and decided that it was a good idea to throw a stink bomb through the window of a place of business. There's such a thing as consequences."

"Aw, bullpucky." She bent to scoop up a seashell and stumbled. "Oopsie. The sand snuck up on me there."

"How did you even know that was Valentina's window?"

"Ew. First of all, do not say her name. Second of all, Bunny, I mean, Parker has an amazing shifter nose. She just sniffed Valentina right out. Golly, I wish I had that." She suddenly threw the seashell she'd picked up at me. "But even I could smell that nasty perfume of hers from a mile away. I swear it smells like cabbage and cat pee. Gag! Like today, when you came over. I could smell her all over you."

I froze in my tracks. "Is that what made you do this?"

She scoffed. "Yeah, right. Like I even care."

I laughed, unable to stop myself. "Uh huh."

"Don't you laugh at me, Konstantin... Konstantin..." She licked her lips. "What's your middle name?"

I grinned. "I don't have one. Want to know my last name?"

Her eyes went wide. "I don't even know your last name? Oh, lordy. I need to go home."

"That's where we're headed."

"Oh, good." She yawned. "I'm exhausted."

"Criminal activities can take it out of you, huh?"

She took my hand, all her anger at me forgotten. "Don't tell Gray about this, okay?"

I had to push words out around the lump in my throat. Her hand was tiny in mine but it felt like the world. I never wanted to let her go. "Why not?"

"I'm usually a good girl." She faked a gag. "Scratch that. I'm not a girl. I'm a woman. A good woman. I don't do bad things. I stay in line. I always have. Until you. Now, I'm sleeping with someone's fiancé and vandalizing hotels. Oh, sweet lord above, I ruined that hotel. I'll have to pay to have it fixed."

I tugged her into my side as she teared up. "It's okay, mate. I took care of it. You didn't ruin anything."

"Mate. Ha." She scrunched up her face and mimicked me. "It's okay, mate."

"That had a bite to it. Something you'd like to say to me?"

"I'm not your mate. If I was your mate, you wouldn't be leaving. You wouldn't be stinking of another woman's expensive-but-stinky perfume. You...you would stay. With me. And love me."

I opened my mouth to tell her that I did love her and that I damned sure wasn't leaving her willingly, but she pulled away from me and shrugged.

"Whatever. One day soon, you'll be with your queen, living in some palace, making beautiful little babies who look perfect. They'll have her perfect nails and your perfect violet eyes."

I stopped moving. "Grace, about that..."

"I hate you. No, no, I don't hate you. I hate that I didn't know." She turned to face me, tears spilling from her eyes. "I didn't know what I was missing. I was fine. Then, I came here and suddenly, my heart feels like it's empty and aches to fill the hole in the middle of it. Part of me wishes that I'd never met you so I'd never have to know about this part of me that desperately needs you."

I swallowed my own emotions down. "Come with me."

She stilled. "What?"

"Come with me." I ignored the warning flags in my brain. "Come with me to Siberia."

"But... You have to take Valentina as a mate. You have to make little Konstantins with her."

"Grace, we can still be together. My life is hardly worth living without you. We could be together."

"Together, as what? I would be your what? Your mistress?" Her tears dried up fast. "You're inviting me to Siberia, to be your mistress? In a palace you share with Valentina? Where your kids will run around? Or will I be kept in some backwoods cabin that your mate won't know about? Will we have our own kids, Kon? Tell me, what will I tell our bastard children when your legitimate kids pass them in town?

"Is there even a town?! You want me to go to Siberia?! Siberia. You want me to leave everything to go to Siberia with you and be your fucking mistress?"

It had been a stupid, spur of the moment idea that slipped out of my mouth before my brain had time to stop it. I didn't blame her for being upset. I had just been trying to grasp at straws. "No, Grace. I don't want that. Any of it. I'm sorry for suggesting it. I just...don't want to leave you."

"Then don't."

"It's not that simple."

"Seems a whole lot simpler than dragging me to Siberia and tucking me away somewhere to be your lifelong side chick."

I bristled. "That's not what I meant."

"Would you introduce me to your friends and family?"

"It's not—"

"That simple?" She snorted and turned away. "It is. It is as simple as you staying if you wanted to. I get it. I'm side chick material. She's wife material."

"Grace, stop."

"No, you stop. Stop acting like I'm more than I am."

I growled, grabbing her shoulders. "More than you are? Grace, to me you're everything. Everything." She pulled out of my grasp. God, I felt like a complete fuckhead.

We walked the rest of the short trip, Grace mumbling angrily to herself.

When we got to the door of her van, she turned. "I think I need to be alone tonight, Kon."

My head was throbbing. My stomach was churning. My heart was aching. I nodded and watched as she entered and clicked the lock in place. I'd go home, sleep for a few hours, and then come back to talk to her. When she was sober. Definitely, when she was sober.

23

GRACE

I barely slept an hour. My head was pounding out a painful rhythm that made my eyes want to cross. It was still dark out when I slipped out and headed to Gray's house. His shower was calling my name.

I passed Alexei on the way up the stairs. He was on guard duty. I nodded to him. "Hey."

"There's the little outlaw." He grinned. "What are you doing out and about so early?"

"Couldn't sleep."

"Kon know you're walking around in the dark all by your lonesome?"

I frowned. "Like he would care. He's about ten minutes from being mated to Atilla the Hun-ess, isn't he?"

Alexei just kept on grinning. "We'll see."

I waved him off, not feeling like my normal happy self, and went inside. I barely got in the door before Gray was in my face, gun drawn. "Put it away."

He sighed. "Jesus, Gracey. What are you doing here?" He cringed away from me. "Smelling like a bad night out at a Mexican cantina."

"I came for your shower. Is that going to be a problem?"

He held up his hands. "Don't bite my head off, little sis. Go ahead and shower. We'll talk after."

"I came for the *shower*. Not conversation. I never want to talk again." I slipped past him and then hesitated. Moving backwards, I wrapped my arms around his waist and sighed. "Maybe we'll talk."

"There she is." He hugged me tight and kissed the top of my head. "G'won, get clean. I'll make some coffee."

I took a long shower, making a pathetic attempt to let the scalding water wash away the memories from the night before. Not even the illegal ones. Just the ones of arguing with Kon. My life was so close to perfect if it wasn't for the one little thing. Only not so little. One huge, ginormous thing, rather.

When I finished and dressed in a pair of leggings and one of Gray's T-shirts, I found him on the couch, two cups of coffee in front of him. I settled next to him and rested my head on his shoulder. "Life is shit."

He laughed. "Oh, yeah?"

"I almost got arrested last night. In some sad attempt to take some kind of control back, I threw a stink bomb through a hotel window." When Gray's face fell open in shock, I chuckled. "Yeah. Kon's future mate was inside the room."

He fell out laughing. "You did not."

"I did."

"You little hellion." He tried to stifle his laughter. "Didn't Dad teach us how to make something a little more dangerous? C'mon, you remember homemade explosives 101, don't you?"

I slapped his arm. "Seriously, Gray?"

"Nope. I try not to be."

I sighed. "I feel like the world is spinning too fast. Everything is just sort of going off the rails. You're some ex-super spy with bad guys after you. I am trying to become a felon while having an illicit affair with an almost mated man."

"Kon's not mating that woman."

"Everyone keeps saying that, but last night, he asked me to come with him to Siberia, to be his *mistress*."

Gray growled. "No, he didn't."

"Yeah, he did."

"I'm going to kill him."

"Sounds good to me." I sighed. "Not. But I wish I really felt that way."

"Whether you feel that way, or not, I may still kill him." He shook his head. "Did he mark you?"

I felt my cheeks burn. "I don't want to talk about it."

"I've already witnessed so many sucker bites and so much beard burn that I'm tempted to gouge my eyes out with a red hot poker. But, I'm talking a *claiming mark*."

"I know what you mean. And I don't want to talk about it."

"He did, didn't he?"

"Gray."

He grunted. "I'm going to ring his neck. That fucker shouldn't have claimed you if he knew he wasn't going to be able to honor you the way you deserve. You're going to be fucking stuck pining away for him for the rest of your life. You two are bound by that mark. It'll drive you both crazy."

I burst into tears and slapped his arm. "Shut up!"

He swore. "I'm sorry, Grace. I... I didn't think."

"I'm just going to go back home."

"Home?"

I got up and wiped my face. "To Freebird. I want to run. I'm tempted to get the hell out of here because it hurts so much, but I'm not going anywhere. I want to set up my life here with my new friends, and you. I'm not going to break because of Kon. He won't be here for much longer, anyway."

He pulled me in for a hug and then ruffled my hair. "Go and sleep it off. Something will work out. It has to."

I left, keeping my face angled away from Alexei so he didn't see me crying. A quick wave without making eye contact, and I set off down the beach. I was heartbroken over a man I barely knew. I'd decided to change my entire way of living in the matter of a week.

And, despite what I'd said to Gray, I wondered if saying goodbye to Kon might, in fact, break me.

Normally, I would've been more alert. I'd have heard the men coming up behind me. I would've known exactly what to do. But, so into my own self-pity and heartache, I might as well have been as helpless as a baby. As one of the men wrapped his arms around me, I opened my mouth to scream just as another hand shoved a rag into my mouth. Immediately, I knew I'd been drugged and my world started to close in on itself.

Anger peppered my hazy thoughts as I lost consciousness. Whoever it was that thought they could fuck with me was going to be hella sorry.

24

KONSTANTIN

As I sat across from Valentina first thing in the morning, I was thinking how much more pleasant it would be to spread honey on my balls and straddle a fire ant mound. I wasn't going through with the mating. No matter what I'd told myself the night before, I couldn't sleep, couldn't think about anything other than the hurt on Grace's face. Anger, too, but it was the pain that I couldn't live with. It came down to a choice between grace and the P.O.L.A.R. team, and in the end, I had to choose Grace.

"I am not going through with any of this." I clasped my hands in front of me and sighed. "Grace is my mate and I claimed her. She wears my claiming mark and I am proud and honored to have her by my side."

"Proud and honored? Proud and fucking honored?" Valentina stood up and started pacing behind her chair. We were in the lobby of her new hotel in Miami. "You claimed a human when you were promised to me?!"

I left a claiming mark on her which I could try to explain away to myself as an accident, a mistake, but that would be a lie. Even then, when I'd done it, although I had yet to admit it, I knew I'd never belong to anyone else. I'd never leave for Siberia, I'd never choose to be with anyone but her.

"No. You think I give a shit about you and your human mate? I am supposed to be queen. ME, dammit! How dare you think our people will accept a human as the alpha queen. Look, I'm willing to forget your indiscretions—all of them. After we're officially mated, you can assume all the dalliances you want, provided you're discrete. I really don't care. But I refuse to lose everything because some human slut couldn't keep her legs together. You will go with me, go through with the mating ceremony, ascend to the throne, or you lose everything."

"I don't want any of it."

She let out an angry scream. "You're not doing this! You're not going to ruin all of my plans for some pathetic human, Konstantin! If you walk away from me, you're never going to be anything. You and your entire little band of misfits will be banished. You'll be stuck on this hellish island for the rest of your miserable lives. Our species will hate you. You'll be a nobody—a nothing."

"The only person I care about being anything to is Grace." I shrugged. "Maybe, you're right. My team will probably hate me for doing this to them, but I have to think that they'd do the same for their mate. I hope you meet your mate one day, Valentina, and you learn what it is I'm choosing over you and why."

"Fuck you, Konstantin! You're going to pay for this!" She picked up a floral arrangement and chucked it at me. "You think that it's just your father you'll face consequences from? Just wait. You'll be lucky if your mate isn't dead by the end of the week."

I growled at her, my bear threatening to come out and rip her to pieces. "If a hair on Grace's head is harmed by you or your people, I'll hunt you down and rip your throat out."

She seemed to believe me. She slumped in her chair and crossed her arms over her chest. I didn't stick around to see what tantrum she'd throw next.

I'd just double crossed my team and it was time to face them and accept whatever anger or wrath they hurled at me. Lord knew I deserved it. I headed to the office before going to Grace. I needed to get it over with. As much as I owed them my loyalty, I owed Grace more.

Serge and Alexei were sitting behind their desks when I walked in. Serge frowned at me. "What are you doing here?"

"I work here." I sniffed the air, scenting Gray. "What's Gray doing here?"

"He might be working here, too." Alexei laughed. "Seems the spook is bored sitting at home. He wants a job."

"Well. Before he joins the team, he might want to know something. You all need to know something. Where are the others?"

Serge shrugged. "It's a slow day. They're on their way. What is it?"

I sat heavily in one of the chairs in front of Serge, just as Gray emerged from the back. Judging by the look on his face, he wasn't glad to see me. I stood back up, preparing for the wolf to charge me, for whatever reason.

"You've got some fucking nerve, you bastard." He bared his teeth at me and rolled his shoulders. "My baby sister is not a fucking mistress."

I winced. "You're right."

"Then why in god's name did you suggest that to her? She came over to my house crying this morning. I should take your head off."

"She was at your house this morning?"

Alexei grunted. "She was crying when she left, too. You really suggested that she be your mistress, man?"

"No! Of course, not. That's not what I meant when I...whatever, listen..." I ground my teeth together and rubbed at my face. "I was wrong. I'm going to find your sister as soon as I'm done here and I'm going to spend the rest of my life making it up to her."

"Here? Or in some hidden room in your palace halfway across the globe?"

I shook my head. "I've abdicated. I just spoke to Valentina and I'll get on the phone with my father soon, although no doubt Valentina's already chewing his ear off."

Serge raised his eyebrows. "What took you so fucking long? I hate to speak ill of a woman, but fuck, I'd rather be locked in a dungeon of torture than mate that awful woman." He shuddered.

"What took me so long was…I'm not walking away without a huge price. A steep one." I sank back into the chair, willing to let Gray attack me if he really wanted to. "A price that we're all going to pay."

"Why did my stomach just sink down to my asshole?" Serge groaned. "Just get it out there."

"IN order to back out, I had to throw P.O.L.A.R.—all of you—under the bus. The team is going to be cut off. And, not just fired from P.O.L.A.R., banished from Siberia—permanently." I swallowed, not untouched by what that meant. "No more Siberia. No visiting. No going back. We're going to lose everything. The main office will probably call any minute with orders to disband the P.O.L.A.R. office here."

Alexei leaned forward. "And you?"

I laughed bitterly. "A lowly peasant, I suppose. A commoner and a prince no more. I'm being stripped of my title and cut off from my family."

"And you're doing all of that for my sister?" Gray sat down next to me and sighed. "And here I was looking forward to kicking your ass. I guess now we gotta make nicey-nicey."

Serge laughed suddenly. "I guess it's fitting that we got sent here because of the first of us finding a mate and now, we're being stranded here because of the last of us finding his mate."

"You don't look as angry as I'd anticipated."

Alexei joined him in laughing. "Brother. We were stuck here before you made this choice. You really think our mates were going to willingly leave here and head off to Siberia? I can't get Heidi away from the beach."

"I never want to see Hannah in those big puffy jackets again, if I'm being honest. I like watching her when she does her tiny-shorts-wiggle." Serge stared into space with a half-grin on his face.

"And there's sex in the water." Alexei also seemed to be re-living his fantasies.

Roman, Dmitry, and Maxim walked in, grinning. Maxim patted

me on the shoulder. "According to the scream queen, you've been demoted to lowly serf. Is it true? I hope to hell it is because, man, I was worried that I was going to be here alone without you assholes. I'm not leaving Parker and this is her home."

Dmitry shrugged. "Plus, I love Kerrigan in a bikini."

Alexei sighed. "And, there's sex in the water."

Maxim groaned. "Are we done here? I was going to do some work, but I'm gonna need a couple hours off. I think I need to find Parker."

I shook my head. "None of this is a big deal to any of you guys?"

Gray nodded. "The part where you stop fucking up and make my sister a happy woman—that's a big deal to me."

Serge rubbed his chin. "Honestly, I was thinking of going in a different direction with P.O.L.A.R., anyway. We were being strangled by the main office, as it was. This just cuts through all the bullshit for me."

I stood up and kept shaking my head. "All this time I was worried that I was going to be throwing you all under the bus if I chose Grace. I should kick all of your asses for not saying anything sooner."

Gray snorted. "Nice try, blaming them. That was all you, dickless."

He wasn't wrong. "I'm going to make it up to her."

The front door flew open and Parker ran in with Heidi and Megan. "She's gone!"

My heart instantly tried to break through my rib cage. "What? Who?"

Parker gestured wildly with her hands. "We went to see Grace and she wasn't there. When we walked towards Gray's house, I caught her scent. With two humans. And chloroform."

"Did you follow her scent trail?"

"To the boat dock. It ends there."

I gripped the desk as my world spun around me. Someone had my mate.

Gray looked as alarmed as I was. He turned to me, his face drained of color. "I hope I'm not wrong about how much Grace has retained from our childhood."

25

GRACE

I woke up slowly, a sour taste at the back of my throat. My stomach lurched and I twisted sideways to avoid throwing up on myself. The slight rocking told me I was on a boat. *Lovely.* I wasn't a huge fan of boats. I was prone to motion sickness and just the idea of it had me ready to toss my cookies.

I tried to sit up, still not sure what was happening, but my hands were locked to my ankles. I tugged at whatever was keeping me in place and forced my breathing to slow, but when the memories began coming back, panic set it. Someone kidnapped me. I fought to regain the memory of how I'd ended up tied up on a boat, but I couldn't.

Panicking wasn't helping anything, so I made myself remain as calm as possible and did my best to take in my surroundings. It was dark, no light coming in from anywhere in the room, except for glowing sliver from a small, narrow window at the very top of the room. Wherever I was, it was dark out. We were on the water and the last thing I remembered was leaving Gray's house. Had I been knocked out all day? Scary thought, but also a blessing. More time for Gray to find me.

Until he did, though, I was going to have to help myself. I started working on the ties on my wrists and ankles. The good thing about our father being a paranoid conspiracy theorist was that he made us train for so many different scenarios. While they'd seemed cruel at the time, especially the ones he put Gray through, I'd come to develop a grudging gratitude every single time I'd found myself in a sticky situation and knew exactly how to handle myself.

The knots were too simple, the work of someone that underestimated a petite, unarmed woman. I was out of them in under a minute. They were wrong about the weapon, too. I unwound the silver beaded bracelet from my wrist—one of my own Etsy creations—and stretched it out in front of me letting the beads fall off. The thin wire would do serious damage in a pinch.

Feeling around the room, I found a pole with a hook on the end of it, something used for dragging in fishing nets. Smiling to myself, I felt my way over to the stairs that led to the upper deck of the boat just as the door above opened and heavy footsteps stomped down toward me.

I backed into the shadows and just as the man got to the bottom few steps, I swung the pole out as hard as I could, taking out his legs. He fell down the few three steps and landed hard on the ground in front of me. Unwilling to take a chance that had incapacitated him, I brought the blunt end of the pole down hard on his head, making sure he wasn't going anywhere for a while.

I searched his body quickly as shouting commenced above. Under him, he had a semi-automatic weapon. These must have been the guys Gray pissed off to be handling weapons like that. I shook my head and yanked the gun free before taking cover behind a couple of boxes on the other side of the room.

"Gregor!" A booming voice echoed through the hold. "What are you doing?"

When Gregor didn't answer, more footsteps came ploughing down the stairs. When bad guy number two noticed his friend on the ground, he shouted and raised his weapon. I aimed and fired off a few shots at his weapon, hitting him in the hands. When he screamed, I fought the urge to throw up again.

"You stupid bitch! I'll kill you!"

"Come any closer and the next round goes into your head, asshole." I really prayed he didn't come closer. I didn't want to shoot him again—especially in the head. I'd shot up plenty of targets, but I'd never actually shot a living, breathing person before. I was already thinking of joining some kind of gun control campaign after having shot him the first time.

"Come out here and face me, bitch." Unless he had a very high pain threshold, I didn't think I got him too badly, probably just grazed him, but he was dripping blood all over the floor.

"Where are we?" I held the gun trained steadily on him. "Who are you and what do you want with me?"

More shouting came from topside, urgent and harried sounding. Gunfire rang out and then a wild, bellowing roar seemed to shake the entire vessel.

"What the fuck was that?"

I didn't look away from my target or allow myself to relax. "That would be my ride off this rowboat."

Another growl sounded closer, the anger and fury evident in it. It was Konstantin. I knew it like I knew my own name, well, better than I knew my own name because sometimes my name...never mind. Konstantin had come for me.

"What the fuck is that?!" Bad guy number two was grasping his useless and bleeding hands to his chest, his face frozen in horror. "What is that sound?!"

"A bear. A big ass, really mean and really angry polar bear, to be exact. And he's coming for me. You boys fucked up bigtime." Everything in me started to settle when the gunfire slowed and then stopped completely, a piercing scream marking the end of the crew above.

"You don't want to be in here when he comes down those stairs. He's going to think you hurt me." I almost felt bad for the asshole.

"Make them stop! I didn't do anything! None of this was my idea! Make them stay away!" His words were swallowed up by a deadly sounding growl that was immediately followed by Gray slamming into him and taking him down. The sounds that followed weren't pleasant, nor were they anything I'd be able to forget anytime soon.

I leaned against the boxes and dropped the weapon. My hands shook as the adrenaline slowly faded, leaving just a sick feeling of nausea and achiness in its wake.

"Gracey!" Gray stood in front of me, naked, blood coating his body. "Are you okay?!"

I covered my eyes and groaned. "I do not want to see that, Gray!"

He laughed but it sounded watery. "Yeah, you're okay."

He led the way up the narrow stairs and I followed him up with my eyes down, not wanting a visual of my brother's naked ass to go along with the frontal one of a few minutes ago that I'd already be scarred from.

As soon as I set foot on the deck of the boat, I was pulled into Kon's big arms and yanked into his naked body. He was covered in blood, too. It even soaked his blonde hair and splattered down his face. He was very much naked and the evidence of his eagerness to see me was pressed into my stomach.

"Fuck, Grace. I thought I'd lost you."

I pushed away from him and stood with my hands on my hips. "Which time? When I was kidnapped, or when you called me your mistress?"

Gray snorted from behind us. "She's not exactly a helpless damsel, is she?"

I shrugged. "Am I supposed to cry and thank you for rescuing me now? I had it all handled when you boys showed up."

Kon scoffed and put his hands on his hips in a pose mocking me. Only, I didn't have a hefty erection completely on display. "Are you serious?"

I nodded. "I'd already taken two of them out. I was on my way up to finish them off when you kids crashed my party."

Gray threw his head back and laughed. "I told you she could handle herself."

Kon grabbed me and easily threw me over his shoulder. Faced

with a very naked ass, I felt subdued for a moment. "I'm taking you home. This is stressing me out."

I sighed. "Is this going to be a common theme?"

"Without a doubt."

Gray grunted. "Hey, by all means, leave me here on cleanup duty. I've got to find myself a mate so I can skip out on the dirty work, too."

26

GRACE

If I thought Konstantin as a man carrying me around was infuriating, I was pushed to a whole other limit when he shifted into his massive polar bear and had me hang on to his fur while he swam us back to shore. On land again, I was soaking wet, freezing, and still so angry with him that I kept contemplating shoving him back in the water and walking home by myself. He still hadn't mentioned Valentina. For all I knew, he'd just come to rescue me before they went off to his kingdom to live unhappily ever after. I didn't know whether I could let my guard down with him.

When he insisted on carrying me back to my trailer, I was so exhausted from the drugging and the adrenaline drop, I let him. He was going to get a piece of my mind, though, so I was just adding his offenses up, making a list of things I was going to get off my chest before he left, while I still had a chance.

He set up the outdoor shower like a pro and put me under it before joining me and taking his time rinsing my hair. When he pulled my shirt over my head and tossed it away, his eyes were hungry as they ran down my bare chest.

"Freebird is too small for two people."

It was the last thing I was expecting him to say, so I was floored into silence.

"I don't fit very well. Especially, in the bed. And we need an indoor shower we can both fit into. Are you opposed to a house?" He peeled my leggings down my legs and helped me out of them. "I just lost my inheritance, and a lot of money, but I have a decent nest egg saved up. Enough to buy a nice house. I've been living in the P.O.L.A.R. house listening to everyone making love to their mates for too long. It's my turn, but I want us to have our own place. On the beach."

I stammered. "What?"

"I do like this outside shower, though. Maybe we'll add one." He peeled my underwear down and then washed the rest of my body. "I don't want to give up seeing your naked, wet body under the moonlight."

I shook my head. "You... You're not leaving?"

"Leaving you? Hell no."

I shoved him so hard that he stumbled into the van door. "And you're just now saying something?!"

He straightened and grinned. "Pardon me, I was busy rescuing you."

"Why?" I stood there, completely exposed, my heart in my throat. "Why aren't you leaving?"

"Because I love you and I won't live without you." He held my gaze. "I'm sorry it took so long. I was trying to maneuver a way out without hurting my team, the guys I care about, and I ended up hurting you. I can't tell you how sorry I am about that. I'm sorry I fucked up."

I put my hand on his chest when he tried to come too close. "You suggested I be your mistress while you made babies with Valentina."

He growled and pulled me into his body. Shutting the water off, he carried me inside and put me down in the middle of the tiny kitchen, my table still broken on the floor. "I was desperate. It was stupid."

"Yeah, it was."

"What do you need from me to be able to forgive me for how stupid I was? I'll do anything. I'm sorry, Grace. You deserved better."

I licked my lips. "I do deserve better."

He frowned and looked away.

"Are you going to be better?" I grinned.

He waggled his brows, his eyes hopeful. "Wanna give me a test run?"

I shrugged and looked back towards my bed. "It's too bad you don't fit in my bed."

Maybe, I was rushing it. I could've spent a while being angry and punishing him, but I would only be punishing myself. I loved him and I wanted him now, tomorrow morning, and for the rest of my life. There was no point in putting it off.

Kon pulled me into his chest. "You're the best thing that's ever happened to me."

I took his hand and pulled him to my bed. "I'm so glad you're not leaving."

He eased me down to the bed and kissed me. I savored every taste, feel, lick, nibble. There was no need to rush or feel like I was doing something wrong. I took his kisses and gave them back, hungry for him, but so content in what he was doing.

When he rolled onto his back, I straddled him, looked down at him possessively. He was mine—all mine. I wanted to mark him the way he'd marked me. So, I did. I leaned down and bit into his left pectoral, right over a tattoo he had there—a polar bear and the letters P-O-L-A-R. I left my own claim on his body.

Kon groaned under me, his eyes glowing violet again. His fingers dug into my hips. "Grace..."

Already ready for him, I lifted my hips and sank down on his shaft. Both of us moaned, the feeling intense. His eyes landed on the mark on my breast and he caressed it.

"I should've marked your neck. I'm going to. I want it to show. Everyone should know that you're mine." He moved his hips. "And I'm yours."

I let my head fall back at the sensation and braced myself on his chest. "Do that again."

He sat up, grabbing my ass, and pumped into me. Our breaths mixed as we kissed. It was broken up only by heated glances at each other, moments lost in each other's gazes.

One of his hands locked into my hair and he pulled it tight, opening my throat to his mouth. He licked a trail up to my ear and then nipped me before pulling my head to the side and raking his teeth across my tender skin.

"I'm going to sink my teeth into your skin, Grace, and I'm going to mark you. Everyone's going to see that you're mine. No one else will ever touch you." His possessiveness heightened the sensation, his breath hot against my ear, his voice barely more than a growl. "You're mine. Forever."

I cried out when he did as he'd promised and sank his teeth in. A wild orgasm stole over me, shaking me. I felt his seed fill me and his tongue lapping at my neck. Clutching at his head, I held onto him as my body shook.

Kon laid back and then rolled us over so he was spooning me, his shaft still buried in me, still hard. His hips gently rocked against me as his tongue stroked over the new mark. "Forever."

I gasped when his hand moved between my thighs and found the sensitive nub hidden there.

He growled against that spot and a fresh wave of need washed over me. "I almost lost you."

I held onto him as he took me again, the sharp, broken edges of my heart melding perfectly back together with his tender murmurings. Kon was mine. I had a mate, and a home, and friends and family. I had everything.

27

KONSTANTIN

"No, you chased me across Siberia like a crazy stalker dude. You kept telling me that I was yours and never stopped to explain what the hell you were talking about." Hannah rolled her eyes and looked down at Serge. "Of course, I did think you were the hottest crazy dude I'd ever met, so there was that."

I wrapped my arms around Grace and breathed in her delicious honey scent. Her hair fell over my face and I smiled into it. We were all having an early dinner at Susie's Bayfront Diner while waiting for Kerrigan's shift to be over so she could join us.

"At least he didn't pretend to be a lost polar bear to learn how to best seduce you." Heidi pretended to glare at Alexei. "I think they're all a bit touched in the noggin, to be honest."

"Hey. Roman didn't do anything nuts. He pulled me out of the water and saved me from a hurricane. I would be fish food right now if not for him." Megan cupped Roman's face and sighed happily. "Either dead or married to a complete loser."

He growled, unhappy with the idea. "You would've left him. You were always way too good for him."

Grace leaned back against me and pressed a kiss to my lips. "They think they got lucky, but I snagged royalty."

Serge snorted. "Royal pain in the ass."

Dmitry shook his head. "I always knew something was up. The way he tiptoed through mud and held his pinky out when he drank tea."

Laughing, I threw a balled up napkin at him. "Shut the fuck up. I've never done any of that."

Kerrigan giggled and removed her apron as she sat on Dmitry's lap. She leaned into Dmitry and whispering something in his ear that had him shifting in his chair. When she saw me watching, she turned bright red and hid her face in her mate's shoulder.

Gray showed up, late as usual. He was soaked in sweat and half undressed. He really was more dog than man. He stretched into his t-shirt, pulling it over his head as he sat with the rest of us. "Sorry, I'm late. I was working on the house."

Grace wiggled on my lap. "How's it coming?!"

He patted her on the head and grinned. "It's coming. I'll be glad when I have something else to do besides work on a house for you and Prince Asshat under you."

I growled. "If I remember correctly, you invited yourself into the work."

"Yeah, yeah." He clapped me on the shoulder as he snatched a cinnamon roll from the basket and sank his teeth into it. "I'm just ready for some real work."

Serge nodded over at me. The look conveyed more than words could have. Being cut off from the main office had caused more of a ripple than we would've liked. The official call had come in only hours after Valentina chewed my father's ear off about dumped and duped and something about a breach of contract. I'd give my father credit for one thing, he hadn't made an idle threat. He'd disbanded P.O.L.A.R. immediately.

Fuck him. We weren't helpless infants cut off from their mother's teat. We'd just take things in a different direction. In fact, our new venture was almost ready.

"Almost there, brother." I nodded at Gray and then kissed Grace's neck. When she shivered, I growled into her ear. "Is it time to go home, yet?"

Grace grinned. "Soon." I sighed happily. The woman had rocked my world and nothing had been the same since I'd met her. I had never been so happy.

"Could you stop making goo-goo eyes at my sister? It's grossing me out." Gray waved his cheeseburger at me. "And, by the way, next time you have someone work on your place, hide your stash of sex toys. I'm not sure if I want to kick your ass or bleach my eyeballs."

I shrugged. "You want me to comment?"

"Fuck no."

Laughing, I nodded. "Didn't think so."

Looking around the table, I felt a deep belonging. Now that my secret was no longer one, I knew for sure that the men around me were my brothers. Even Gray.

Family.

We'd been banished from our homeland, but we were exiled together. At this point, it was hard to even consider it to be punishment since none of us would consider being anywhere but here in Sunkissed Key.

I stood up. "Why am I sitting here, looking at you assholes? I'm taking my mate home."

Serge stood up, too. "My sentiments, exactly."

Gray grumbled. "I hope I'm not this pathetic when I find a mate. *If* I find a mate."

Maxim slapped Gray on the back, hard. "Oh, you're getting a mate, brother. If Parker and her mating service have anything to do with it, you're finding a mate sooner than you think."

I laughed at the look of horror on his face. "Chin up, brother-in-law. The sooner you find a mate, the sooner you can stop snooping through our sex toys and have a stash of your own."

I turned and walked out laughing as Gray's eyes widened and he practically choked on his cheeseburger. Life was good.

. . .

The End.

JOIN OUR GROUP

Please join our Facebook group.
Receive ARCs, notifications of new releases, giveaways and hang with friends.

Click to join Lovestruck Insiders on Facebook.

https://www.facebook.com/groups/PNRreaders/

SPECIAL OFFER

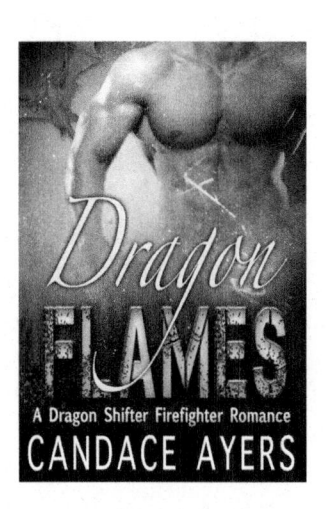

Click for FREE offers.
Plus receive updates, notifications of new releases and awesome reads in your inbox everyday from Lovestruck Romance.

RANCHER BEARS

When the patriarch of the Long family dies, he leaves a will that has each of his five son's scrambling to find a mate. Underneath it all, they find that family is what matters most.

1. Rancher Bear's Baby
2. Rancher Bear's Mail Order Mate
3. Rancher Bear's Surprise Package
4. Rancher Bear's Secret
5. Rancher Bear's Desire
6. Rancher Bears' Merry Christmas

Rancher Bears Complete Box Set

∼

BEARS OF BURDEN

In the southwestern town of Burden, Texas, good ol' bears Hawthorne, Wyatt, Hutch, Sterling, and Sam, and Matt are livin' easy. Beer flows freely, and pretty women are abundant. The last thing the shifters of Burden are thinking about is finding a mate or settling down. But, fate has its own plan...

1. Thorn
2. Wyatt
3. Hutch
4. Sterling
5. Sam
6. Matt

∼

SHIFTERS OF HELL'S CORNER

In the late 1800's, on a homestead in New Mexico, a female shifter named Helen Cartwright, widowed under mysterious circumstances, knew there was power in the feminine bonds of sisterhood. She provided an oasis for those like herself, women who had been dealt the short end of the stick. Like magic, women have flocked to the tiny town of Helen's Corner ever since. Although, nowadays, some call the town by another name, *Hell's Crazy Corner*. (This series is a spin-off of the **Bears of Burden** series.)

1. Wolf Boss
2. Wolf Detective
3. Wolf Soldier
4. Bear Outlaw
5. Wolf Purebred

DRAGONS OF THE BAYOU

Something's lurking in the swamplands of the Deep South. Massive creatures exiled from their home. For each, his only salvation is to find his one true mate.

1. Fire Breathing Beast
2. Fire Breathing Cezar
3. Fire Breathing Blaise
4. Fire Breathing Remy
5. Fire Breathing Armand
6. Fire Breathing Ovide

P.O.L.A.R.

(**P**rivate **O**ps: **L**eague **A**rctic **R**escue) is a specialized, private operations task force—a maritime unit of polar bear shifters. Part of a world-wide, clandestine army comprised of the best of the best shifters, P.O.L.A.R.'s home base is Siberia...until the team pisses somebody off and gets re-assigned to Sunkissed Key, Florida and these arctic shifters suddenly find themselves surrounded by sun, sand, flip-flops and palm trees.

1. Rescue Bear
2. Hero Bear
3. Covert Bear
4. Tactical Bear
5. Royal Bear

∽

CYBERMATES

As bunny shifter, Parker Pettit, struggles to get her new online shifter dating site, Cybermates, off the ground, she's matching up shifters and their mates left and right. (This series is a spin-off of the **P.O.L.A.R.** series.)

1. Cherished Mate
2. Charmed Mate
3. Chased Mate
4. Changed Mate
5. Chosen Mate
6. Craved Mate

∽

KODIAK ISLAND SHIFTERS

On Port Ursa in Kodiak Island Alaska, the Sterling brothers are kind of a big deal.
They own a nationwide chain of outfitter retail stores that they grew from their father's little backwoods camping supply shop.
The only thing missing from the hot bear shifters' lives are mates! But, not for long...

1. Billionaire Bear's Bride (COLTON)
2. The Bear's Flamingo Bride (WYATT)
3. Military Bear's Mate (TUCKER)

Kodiak Island Shifters Complete Box Set

~

SHIFTERS OF DENVER

Nathan: Billionaire Bear- A matchmaker meets her match.
Byron: Heartbreaker Bear- A sexy heartbreaker with eyes for just one woman.
Xavier: Bad Bear - She's a good girl. He's a bad bear.

1. Nathan: Billionaire Bear
2. Byron: Heartbreaker Bear
3. Xavier: Bad Bear

Shifters of Denver Complete Box Set

~

BEARS OF BURDEN on AUDIOBOOK

In the southwestern town of Burden, Texas, good ol' bears Hawthorne, Wyatt, Hutch, Sterling, and Sam, and Matt are livin' easy. Beer flows freely, and pretty women are abundant. The last thing the shifters of Burden are thinking about is finding a mate or settling down. But, fate has its own plan...

1. Thorn
2. Wyatt
3. Hutch
4. Sterling

Printed in Great Britain
by Amazon